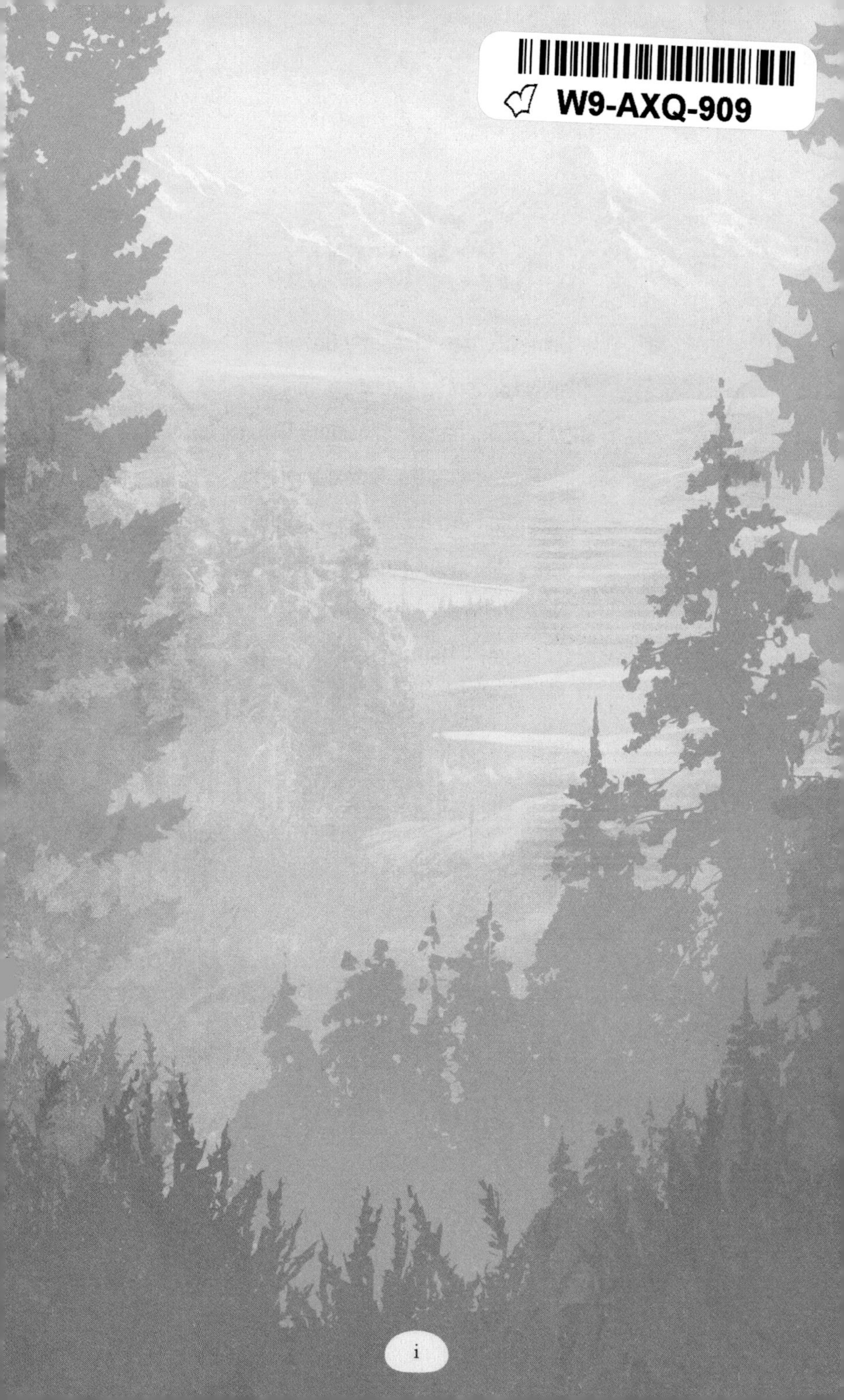

ALSO FROM JOE BOOKS

Disney Frozen Cinestory Comic

Disney Cinderella Cinestory Comic

Disney 101 Dalmatians Cinestory Comic

Disney•Pixar Inside Out Cinestory Comic

Disney Big Hero 6 Cinestory Comic

Disney Princess Comics Treasury

Disney•Pixar Comics Treasury

Disney's Darkwing Duck:
The Definitively Dangerous Edition

Disney · PIXAR

THE GOOD DINOSAUR FUN BOOK

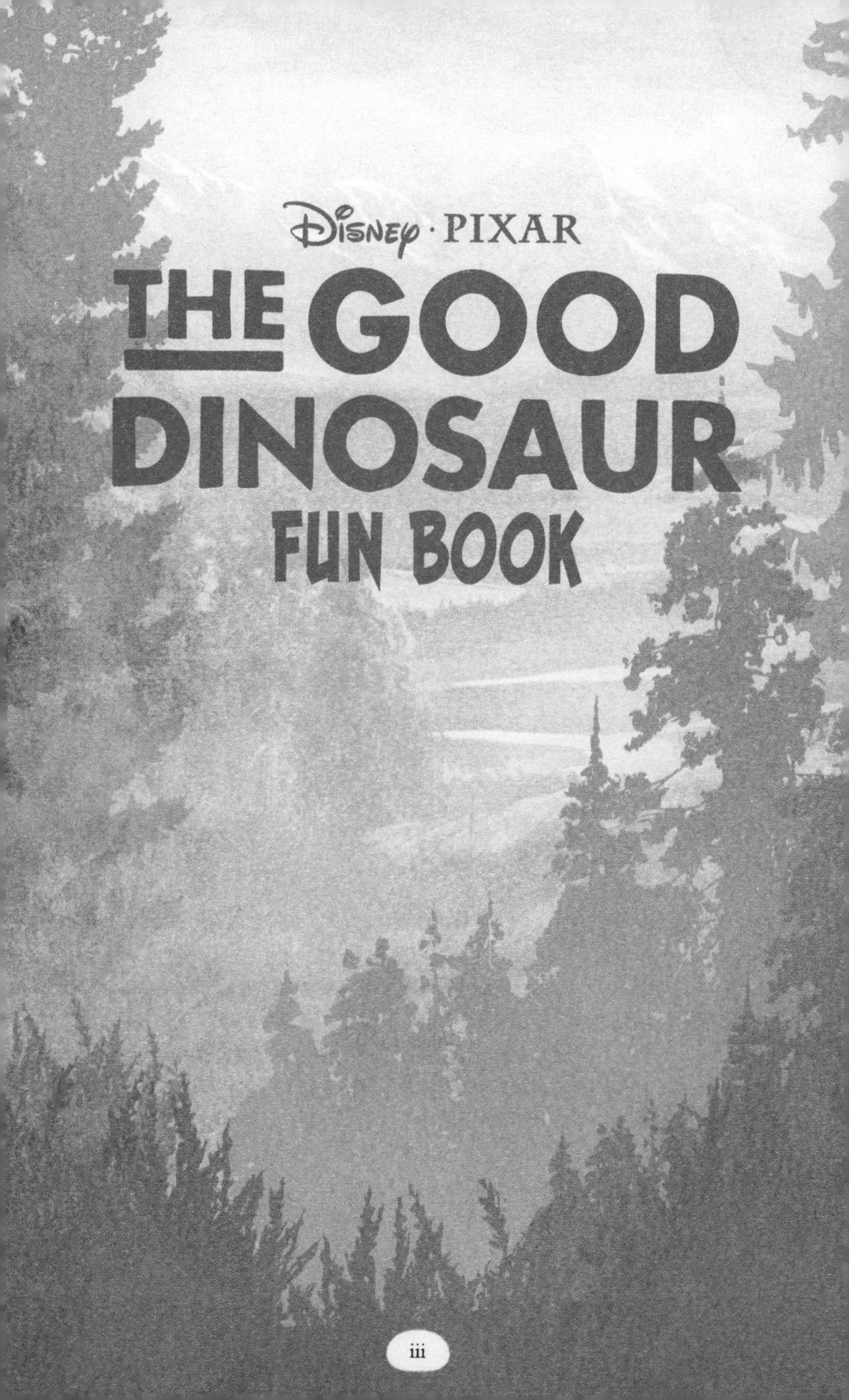

JOE BOOKS INC

Published in the United States by Joe Books
Publisher: Adam Fortier
Associate Publisher: Deanna McFadden
President: Steve Osgoode
COO: Jody Colero
CEO: Jay Firestone

567 Queen St W, Toronto, ON M5V 2B6
www.joebooks.com

Library and Archives Canada Cataloguing in Publication
information is available upon request.

ISBN 978-1-988032-68-9
First Joe Books Edition: November 2015

3 5 7 9 10 8 6 4 2 1

Published in the United States by Joe Books, Inc.

Printed in USA through Avenue4 Communications at Cenveo/Richmond, Virginia

For information regarding the CPSIA on this printed material call
(203) 595-3636 and provide reference # RICH - 613704

DISNEY · PIXAR
THE GOOD DINOSAUR
FUN BOOK

ADAPTATION, DESIGN, LETTERING, LAYOUT AND EDITING:
For Readhead Books: Greg Lockard, Heidi Roux, Salvador Navarro, Ester Salguero, Puste, Ernesto Lovera, Eduardo Alpuente, Alberto Garrido, Aaron Sparrow, and Carolynn Prior.

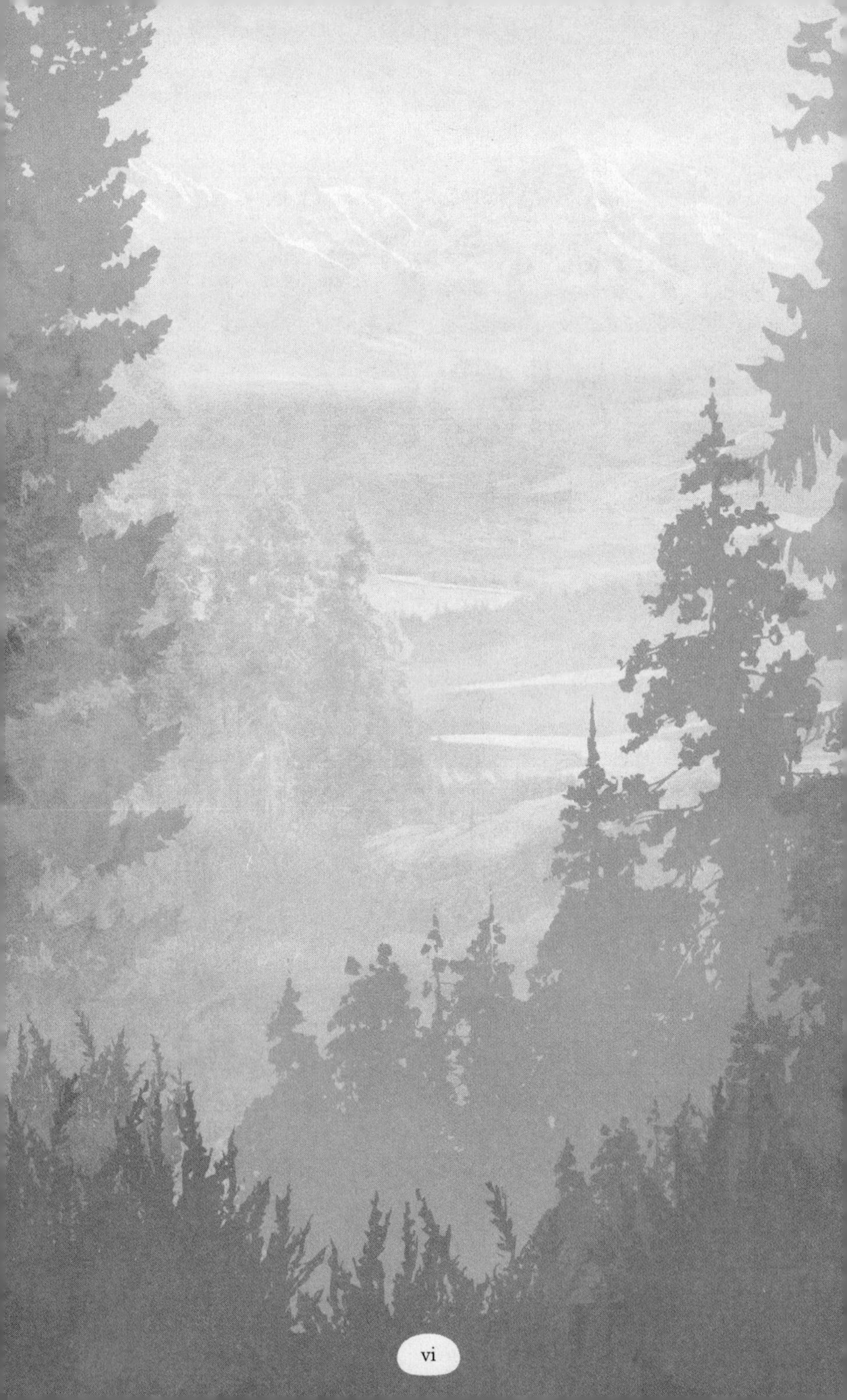

CONTENTS

CONTENTS

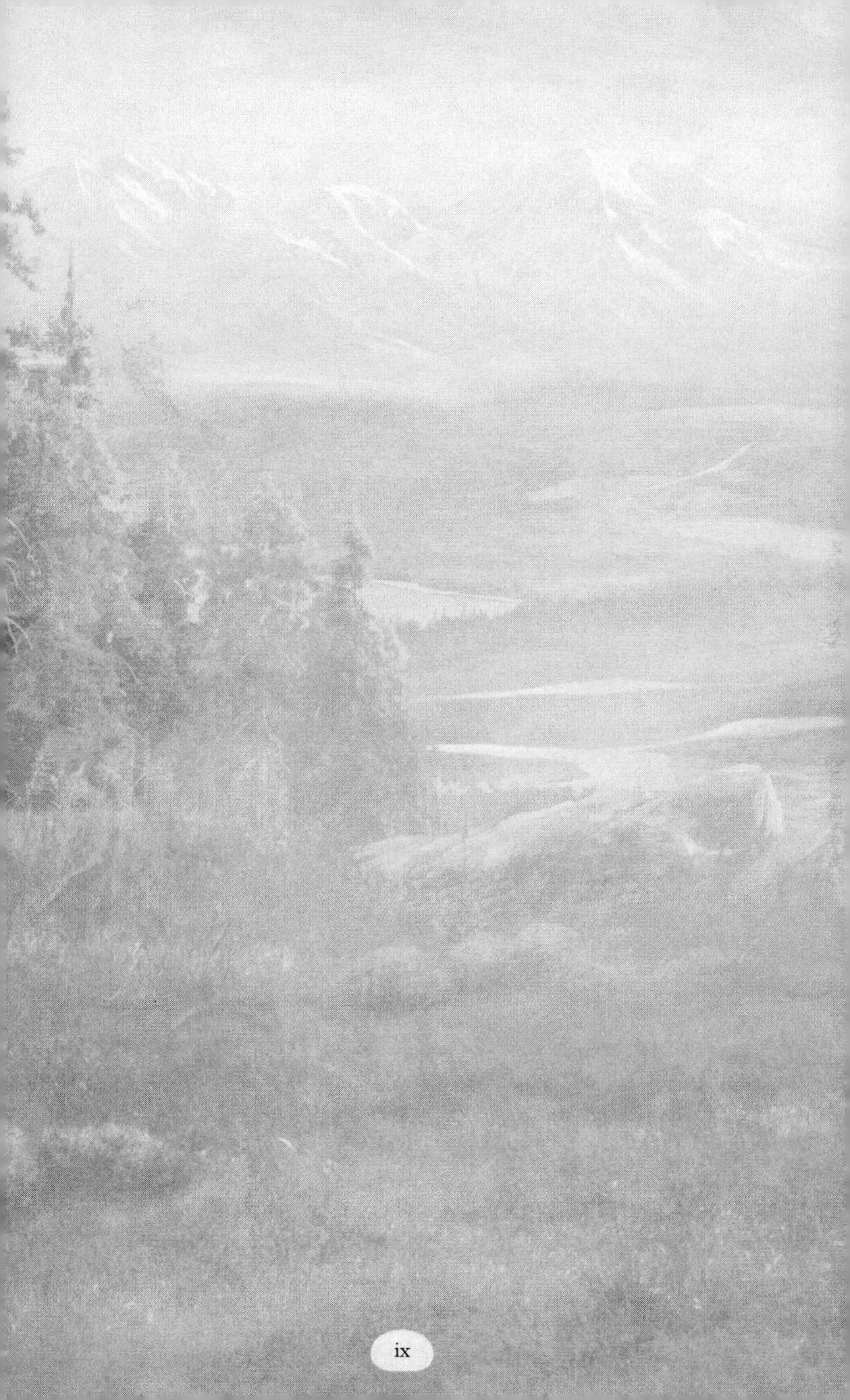

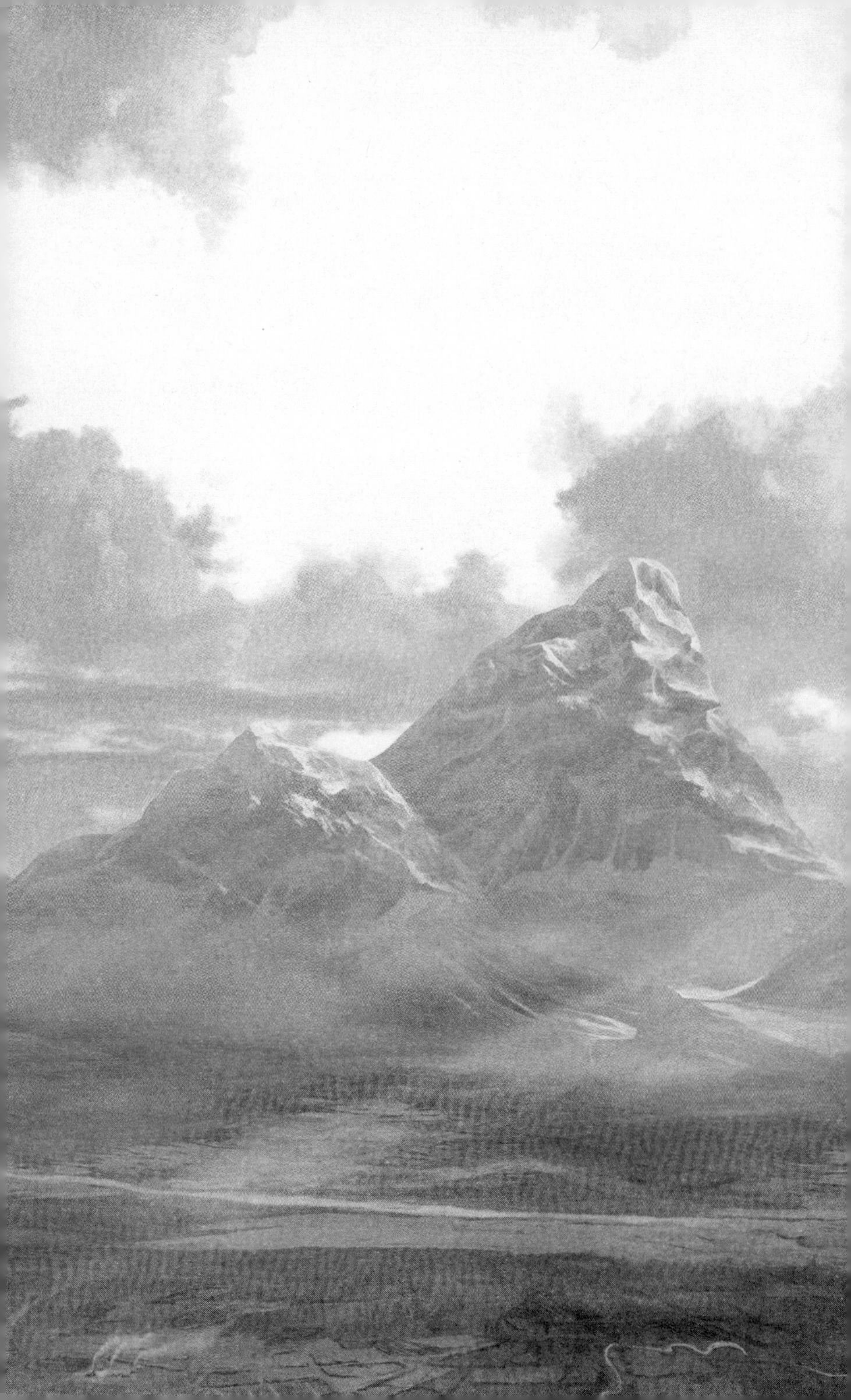

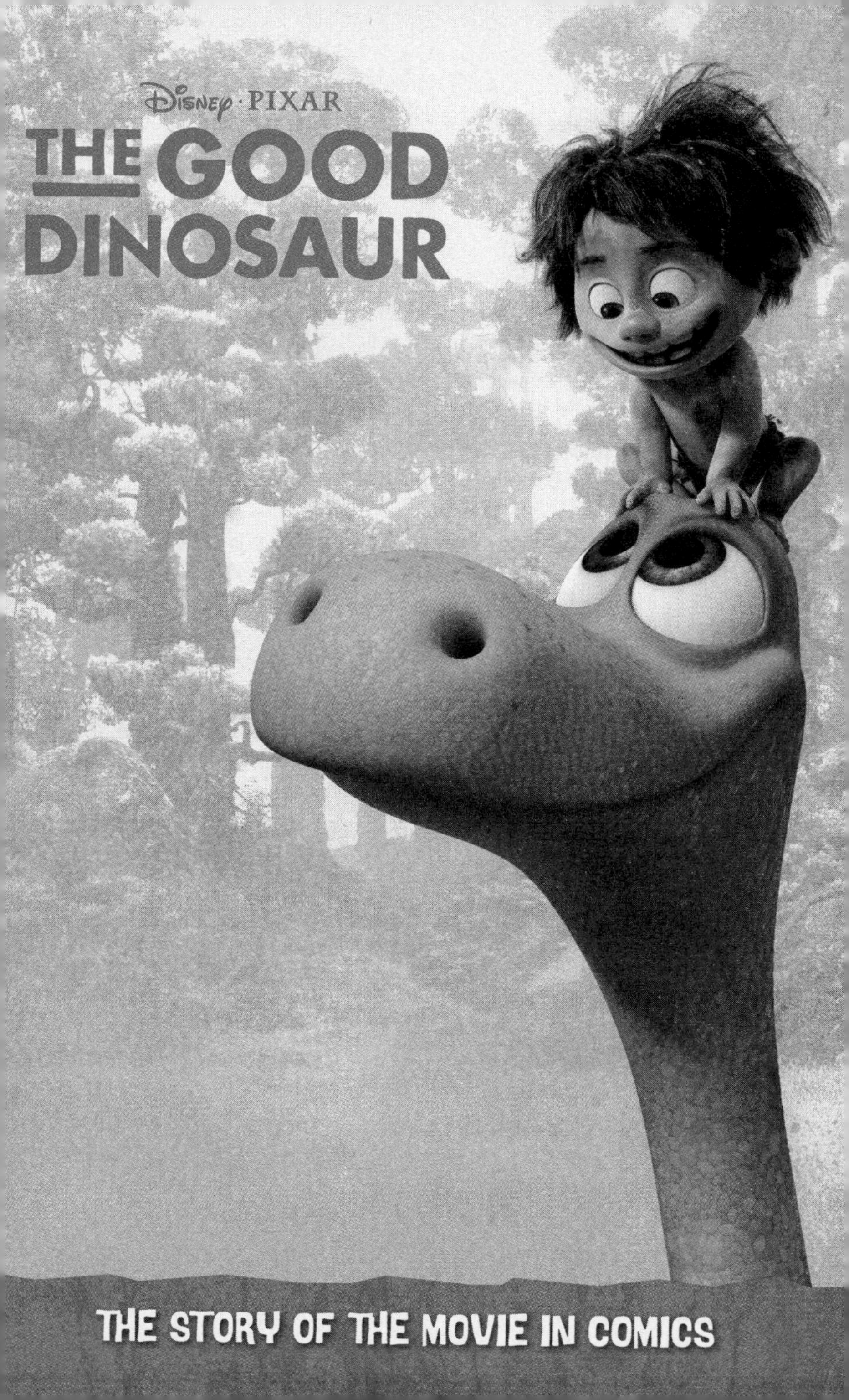
Disney · PIXAR
THE GOOD DINOSAUR
THE STORY OF THE MOVIE IN COMICS

Arlo

Arlo is a 10-year-old Apatosaurus dinosaur. He is shy, nervous and apprehensive. He sees danger everywhere. He wishes he was brave and confident like his father, but he doesn't know how to overcome his fears, even when he finds himself lost in the wilderness, alone and far from home. But there's someone who can help him — the strangest creature Arlo has ever seen: a human boy.

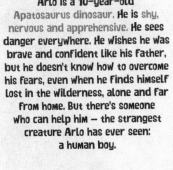

Spot

Spot lives alone in the wilderness. He only speaks in growls and howls, but he can tell a menace from a resource, a friend from a foe. He is wild, tough and fearless and he always knows where to find food thanks to his incredible sense of smell. He can eat berries, bugs and worms, he can swim and find a hiding place fast when he needs it. Spot doesn't like dinosaurs, but he knows Arlo is different from any other.

Poppa/Henry

Henry would do anything to protect his family. He is a bold and brave Apatosaurus and works tirelessly on the farm to provide food before winter comes. Poppa believes Arlo is a lot braver than he thinks.

Buck & Libby

Buck and Libby are Arlo's siblings. Although they were born on the same day as Arlo, Buck and Libby are stronger and more confident than their brother. Buck can rip a tree out of the ground with his teeth, while Libby can plow a mean field all by herself.

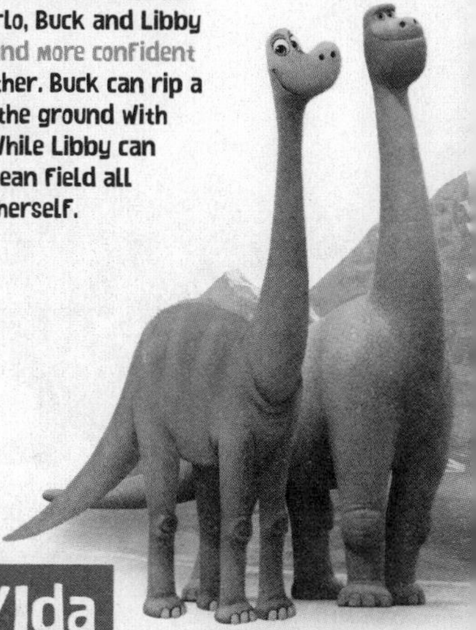

Momma/Ida

Loving, strong and quick-witted, Ida is Henry's wife and the mother of Arlo, Buck and Libby. She helped build the home they all live in. There isn't a day when Ida doesn't work her hardest to keep both her family and their farm thriving.

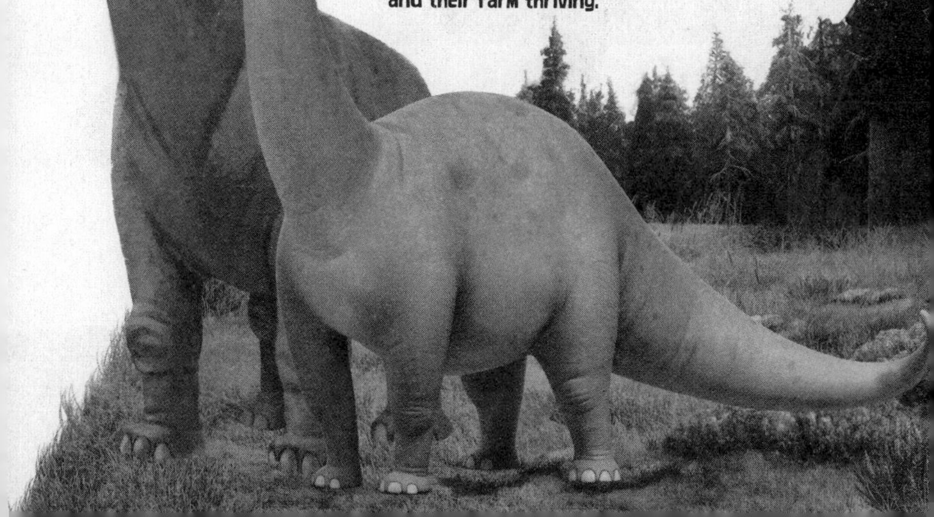

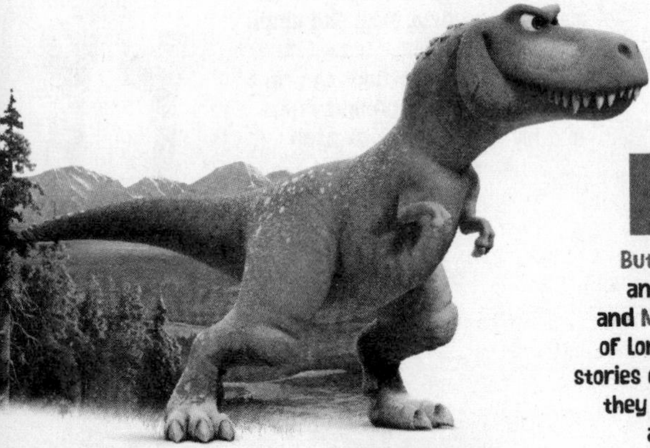

T. rexes

Butch is a veteran rancher and the father of Ramsey and Nash. They all drive a herd of longhorns and love to trade stories over a campfire. Even though they look threatening and like a good fight, they are not bullies at all.

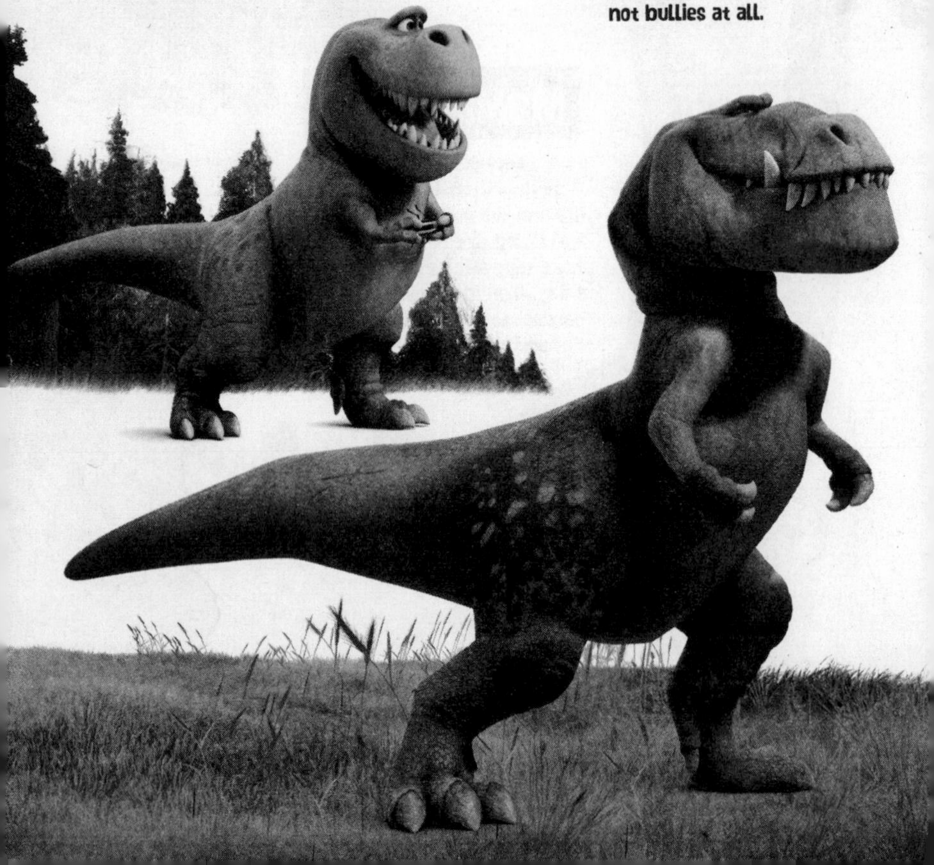

Pterodactyls

These winged dinosaurs are aggressive scavengers, always waiting for a storm to pass and leave some small critter without a shelter. Thunderclap is the leader of the pack.

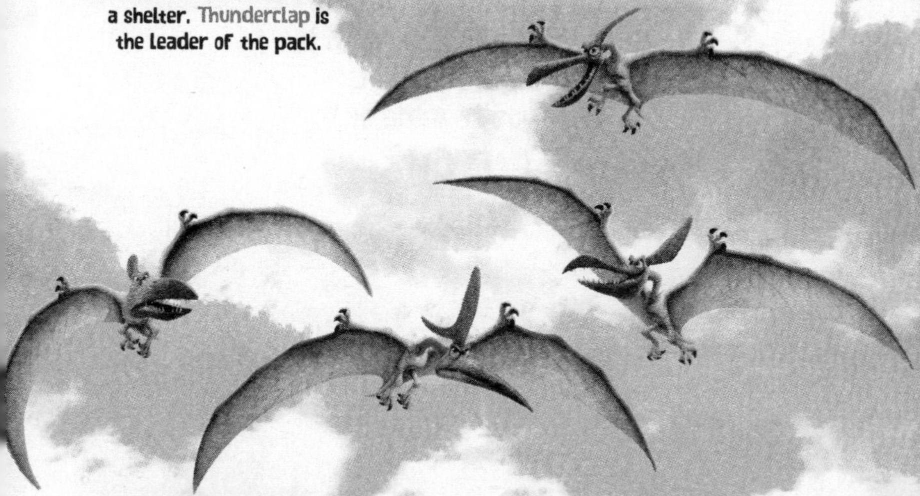

Raptors

Bubbha, Earl, Pervis and Lurleane are thieves. Also known as rustlers, they have no problem stealing from dinosaurs much bigger and stronger than themselves. They are fast, hostile, and fear no dinosaur.

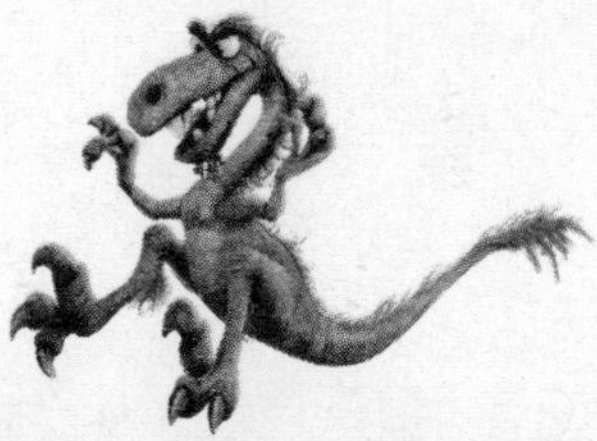

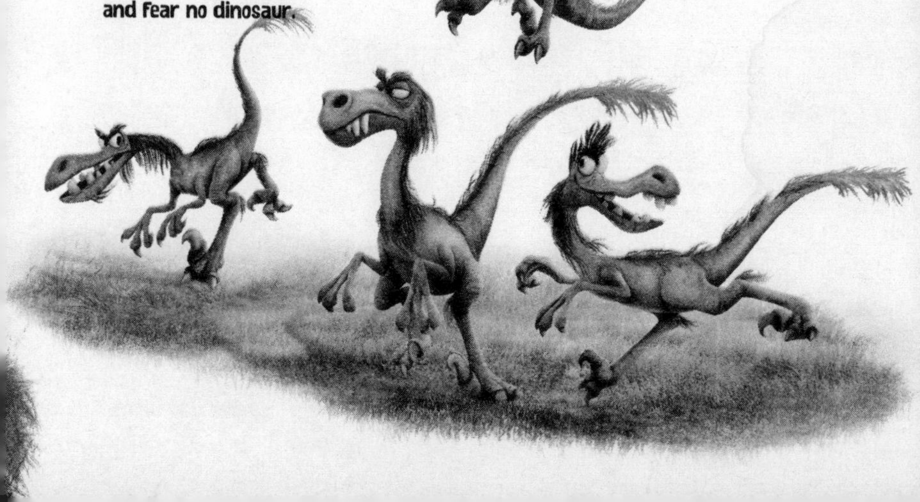

"You can't get rid of fear.
It's like Mother Nature.
You can't beat her or outrun her.
But you can get through it.
You can find out
what you're made of."

BUTCH

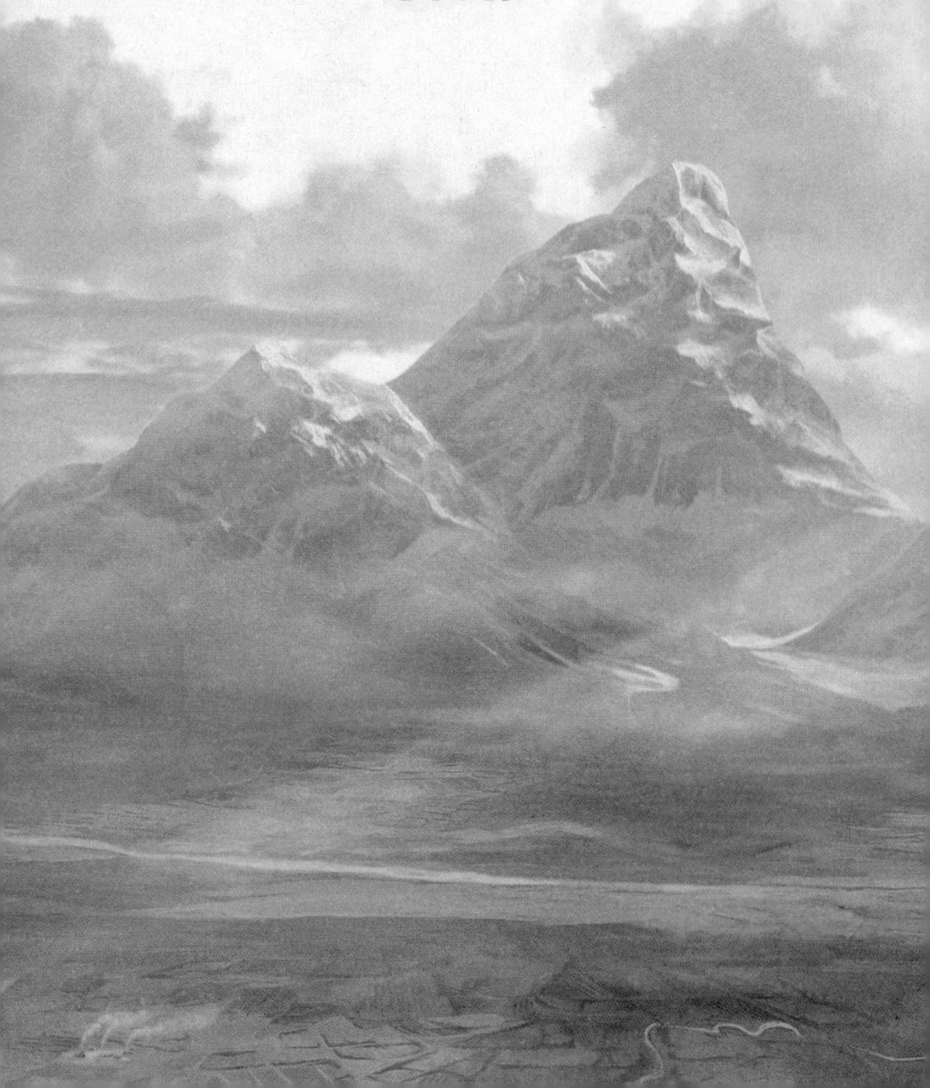

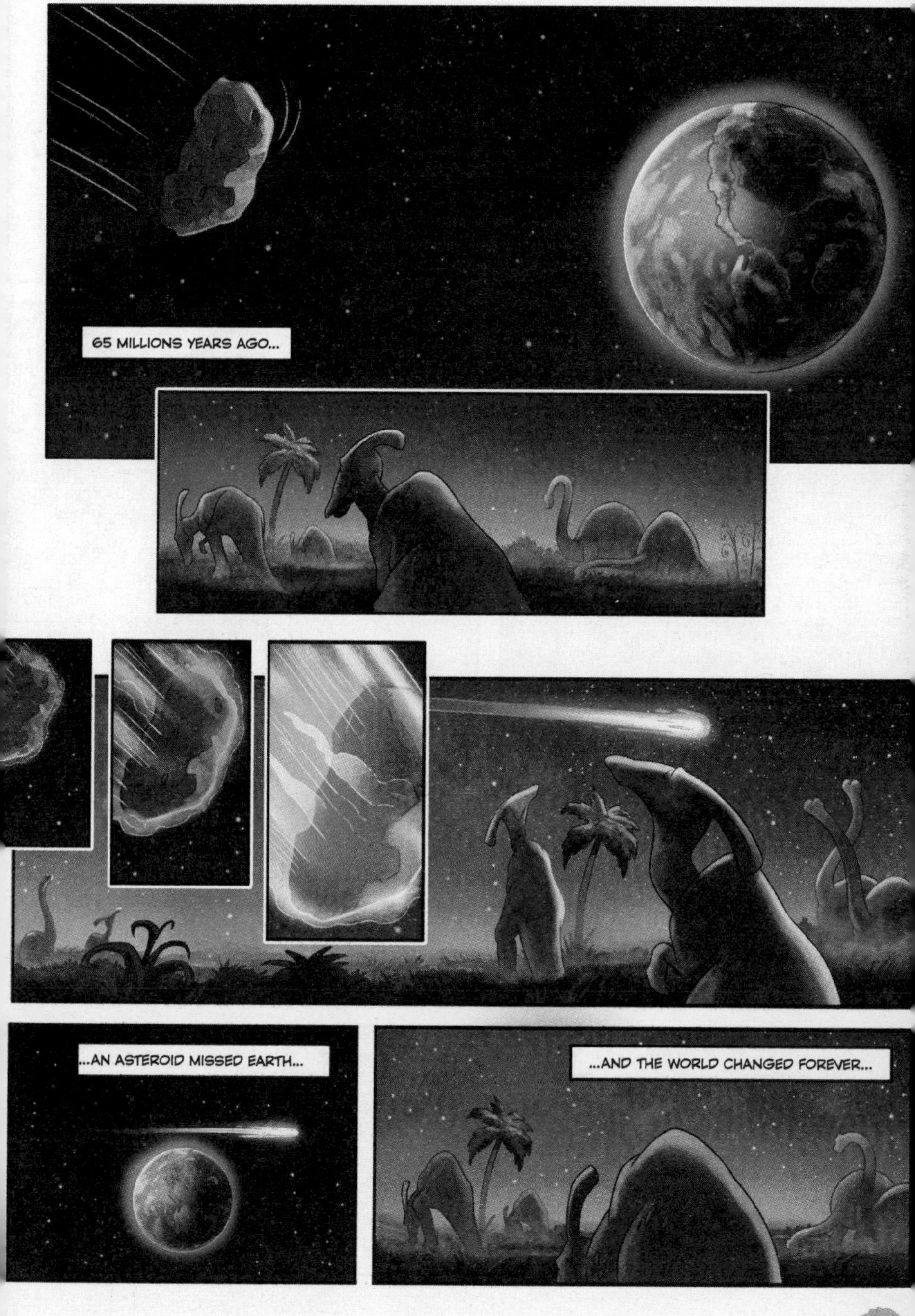
65 MILLIONS YEARS AGO...
...AN ASTEROID MISSED EARTH...
...AND THE WORLD CHANGED FOREVER...

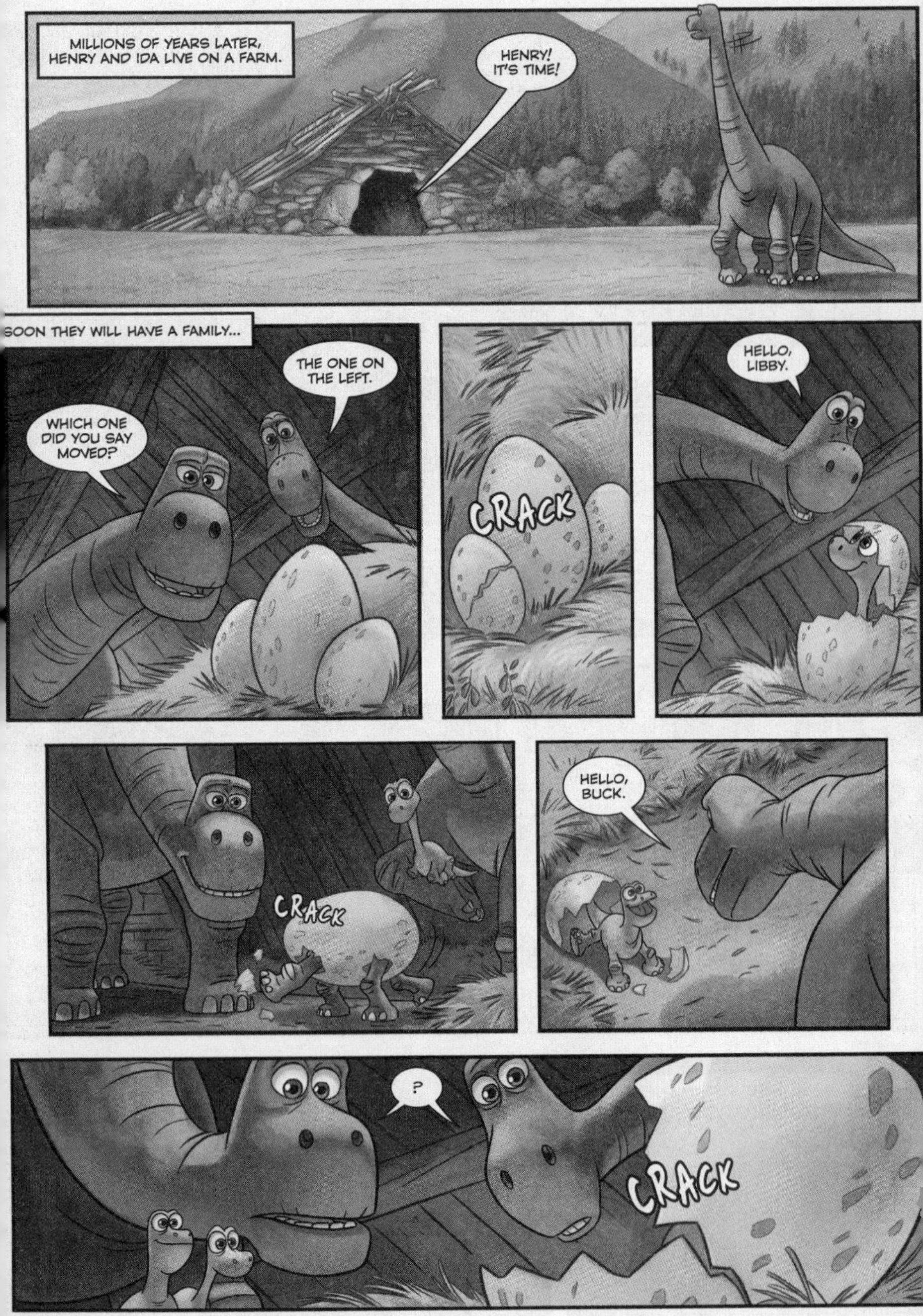
MILLIONS OF YEARS LATER, HENRY AND IDA LIVE ON A FARM.
HENRY! IT'S TIME!
SOON THEY WILL HAVE A FAMILY...
WHICH ONE DID YOU SAY MOVED?
THE ONE ON THE LEFT.
CRACK
HELLO, LIBBY.
CRACK
HELLO, BUCK.
?
CRACK

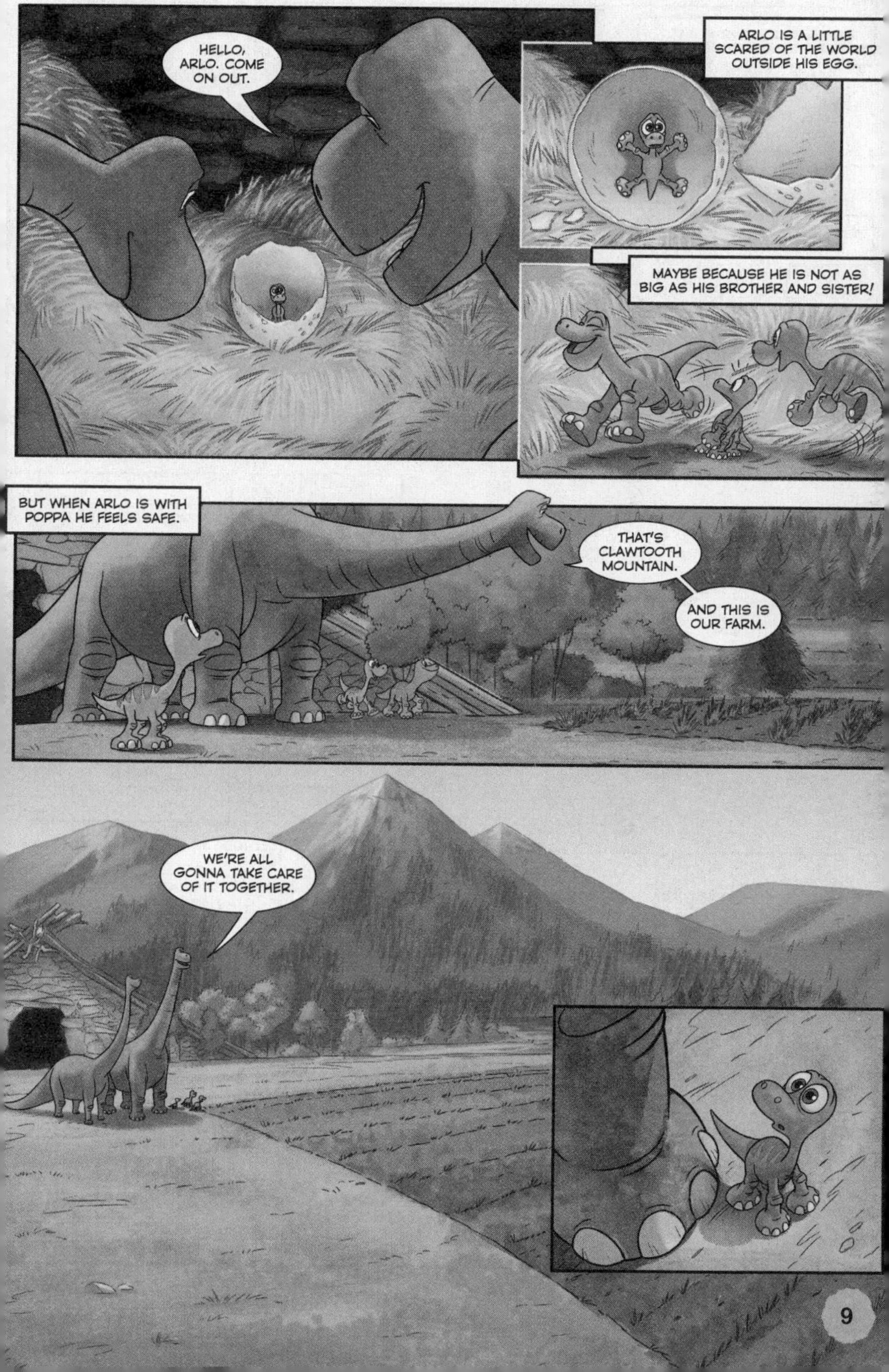
HELLO, ARLO. COME ON OUT.
ARLO IS A LITTLE SCARED OF THE WORLD OUTSIDE HIS EGG.
MAYBE BECAUSE HE IS NOT AS BIG AS HIS BROTHER AND SISTER!
BUT WHEN ARLO IS WITH POPPA HE FEELS SAFE.
THAT'S CLAWTOOTH MOUNTAIN.
AND THIS IS OUR FARM.
WE'RE ALL GONNA TAKE CARE OF IT TOGETHER.

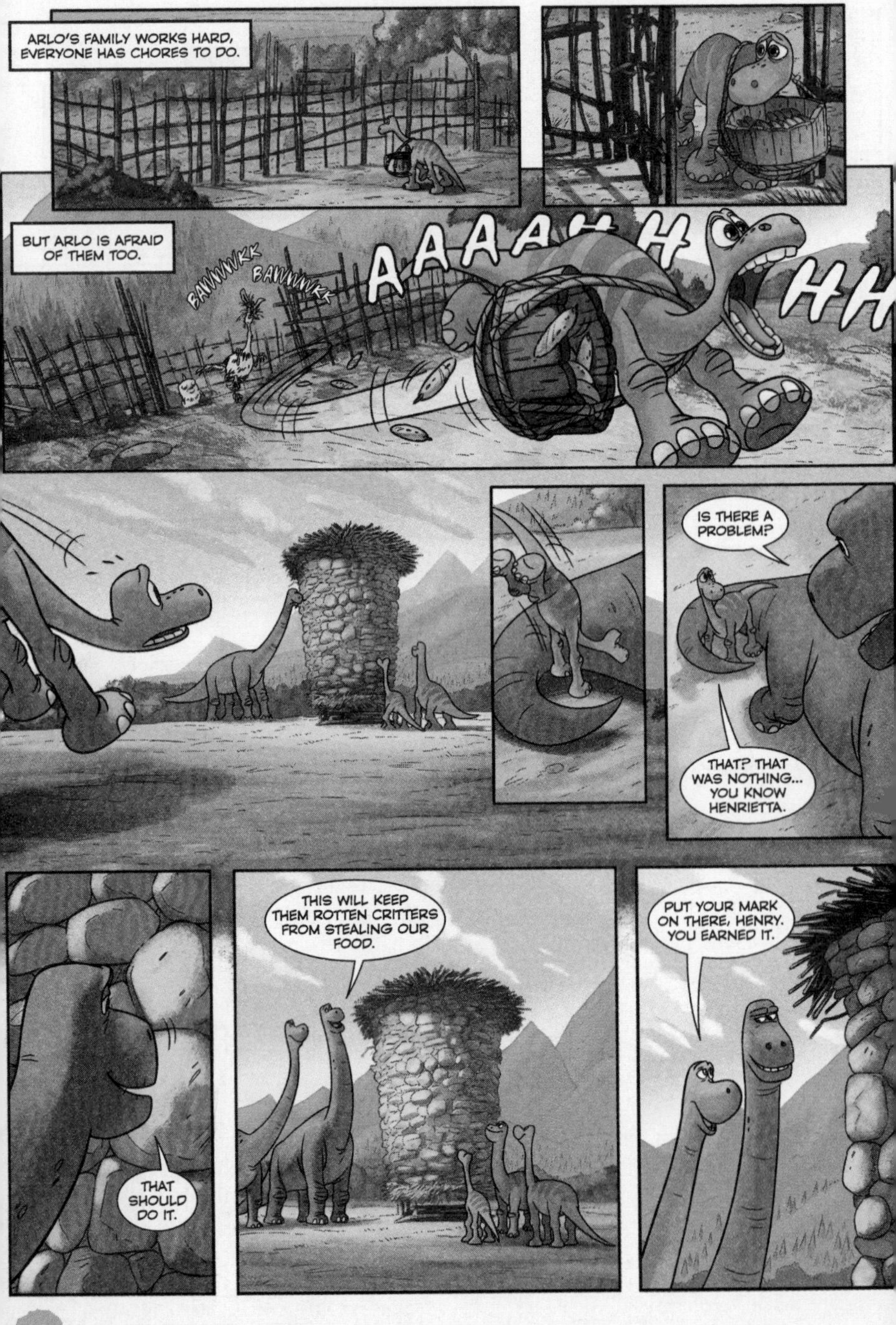
ARLO'S FAMILY WORKS HARD, EVERYONE HAS CHORES TO DO.
BUT ARLO IS AFRAID OF THEM TOO.
BAWWWWKK
BAWWWWKK
AAAAAHHHH
IS THERE A PROBLEM?
THAT? THAT WAS NOTHING... YOU KNOW HENRIETTA.
THAT SHOULD DO IT.
THIS WILL KEEP THEM ROTTEN CRITTERS FROM STEALING OUR FOOD.
PUT YOUR MARK ON THERE, HENRY. YOU EARNED IT.

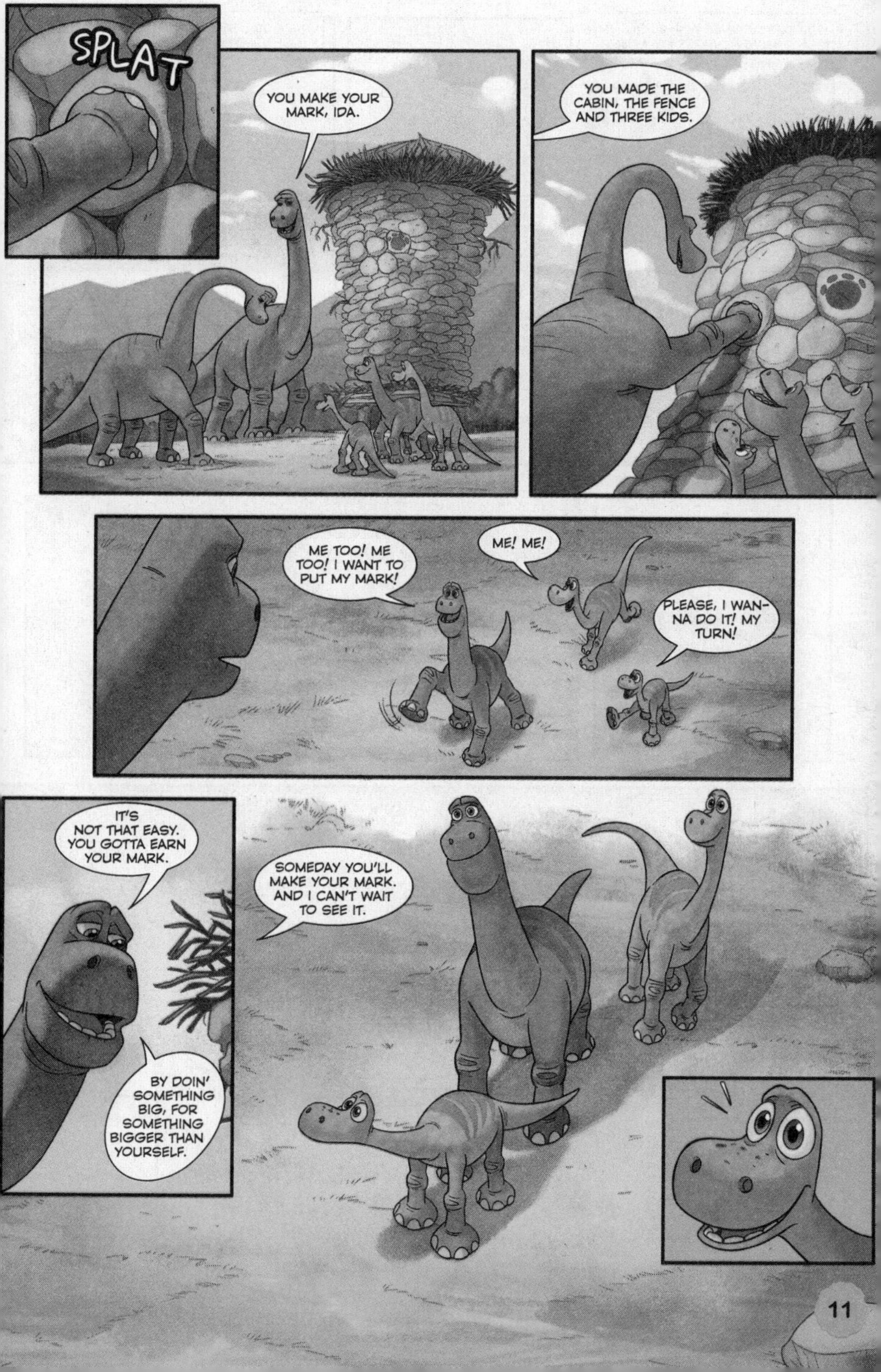
SPLAT
YOU MAKE YOUR MARK, IDA.
YOU MADE THE CABIN, THE FENCE AND THREE KIDS.
ME TOO! ME TOO! I WANT TO PUT MY MARK!
ME! ME!
PLEASE, I WAN-NA DO IT! MY TURN!
IT'S NOT THAT EASY. YOU GOTTA EARN YOUR MARK.
BY DOIN' SOMETHING BIG, FOR SOMETHING BIGGER THAN YOURSELF.
SOMEDAY YOU'LL MAKE YOUR MARK. AND I CAN'T WAIT TO SEE IT.

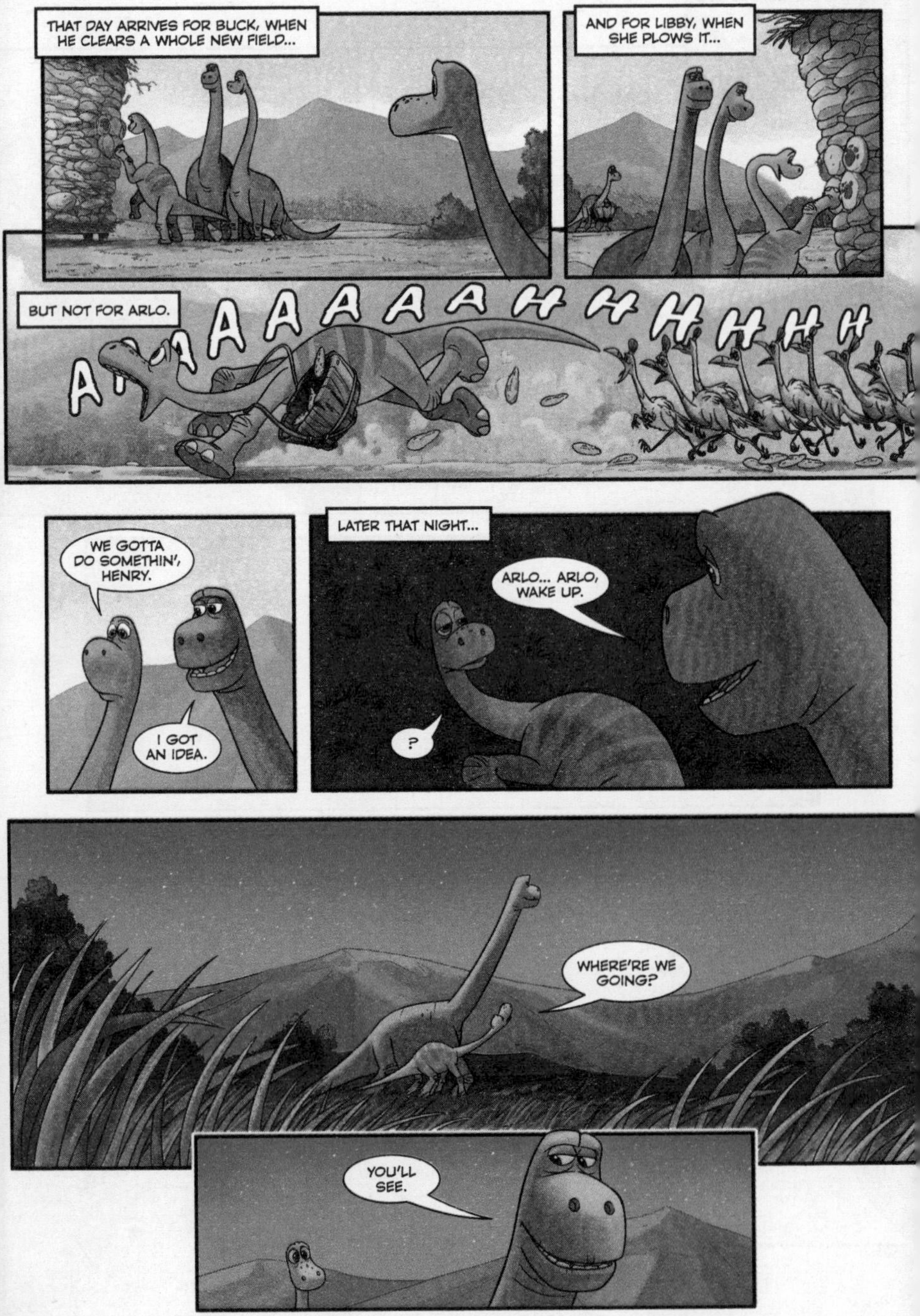
THAT DAY ARRIVES FOR BUCK, WHEN HE CLEARS A WHOLE NEW FIELD...
AND FOR LIBBY, WHEN SHE PLOWS IT...
BUT NOT FOR ARLO.
AAAAAAAAAHHHHHHHHH
WE GOTTA DO SOMETHIN', HENRY.
I GOT AN IDEA.
LATER THAT NIGHT...
ARLO... ARLO, WAKE UP.
?
WHERE'RE WE GOING?
YOU'LL SEE.

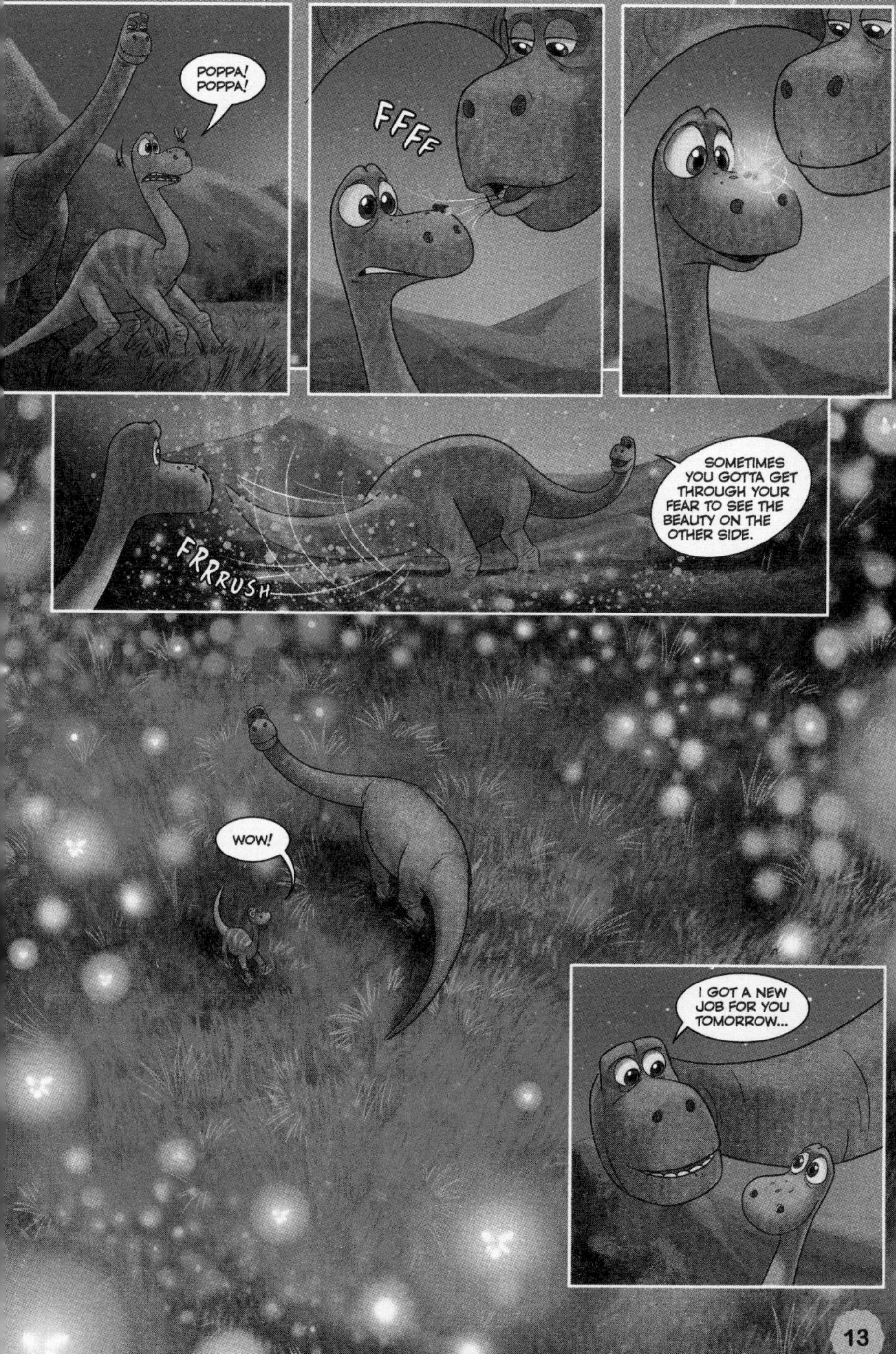
POPPA! POPPA!
FFFF
SOMETIMES YOU GOTTA GET THROUGH YOUR FEAR TO SEE THE BEAUTY ON THE OTHER SIDE.
FRRRUSH
WOW!
I GOT A NEW JOB FOR YOU TOMORROW...

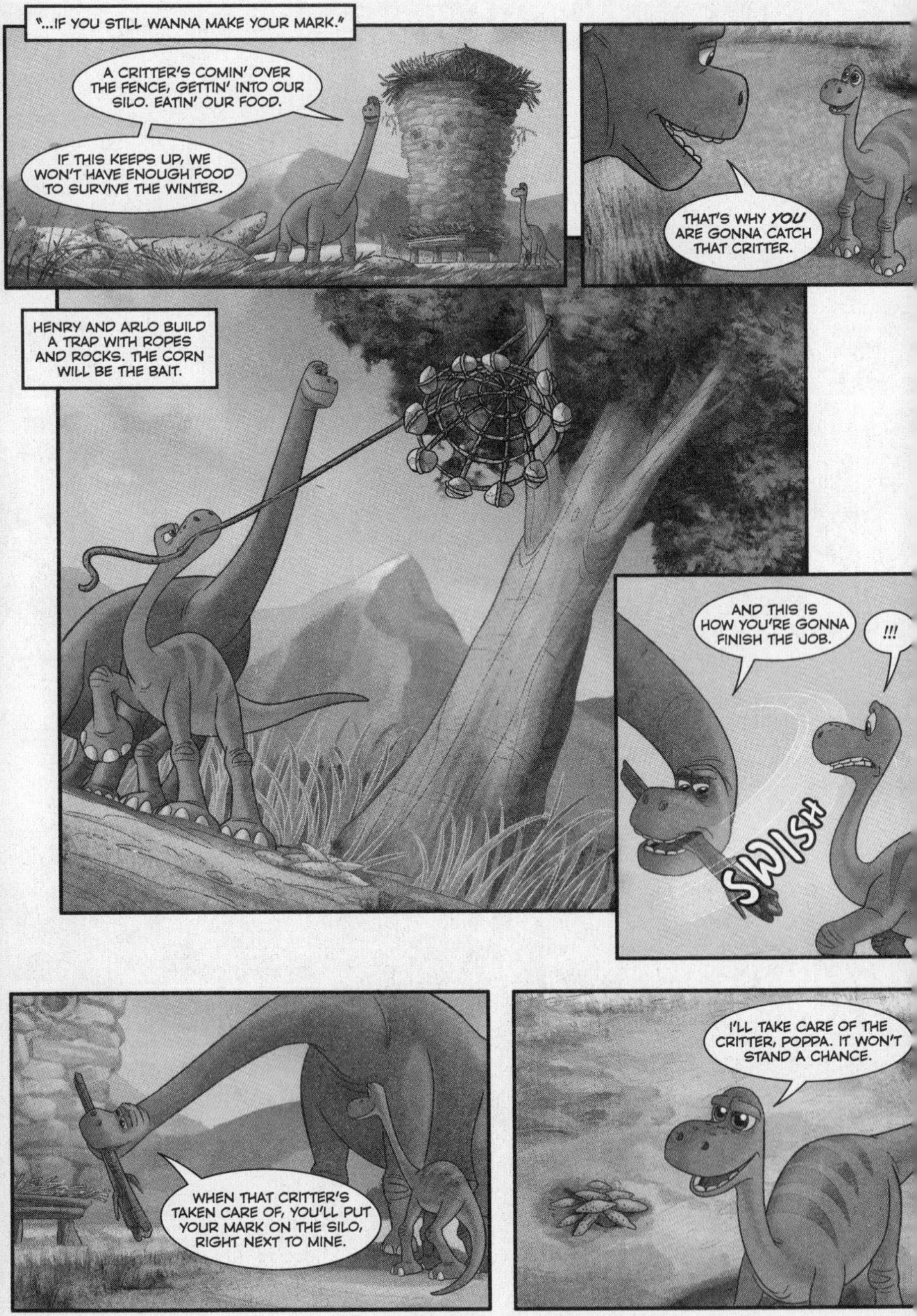
"...IF YOU STILL WANNA MAKE YOUR MARK."
A CRITTER'S COMIN' OVER THE FENCE, GETTIN' INTO OUR SILO. EATIN' OUR FOOD.
IF THIS KEEPS UP, WE WON'T HAVE ENOUGH FOOD TO SURVIVE THE WINTER.
THAT'S WHY YOU ARE GONNA CATCH THAT CRITTER.
HENRY AND ARLO BUILD A TRAP WITH ROPES AND ROCKS. THE CORN WILL BE THE BAIT.
AND THIS IS HOW YOU'RE GONNA FINISH THE JOB.
!!!
SWISH
WHEN THAT CRITTER'S TAKEN CARE OF, YOU'LL PUT YOUR MARK ON THE SILO, RIGHT NEXT TO MINE.
I'LL TAKE CARE OF THE CRITTER, POPPA. IT WON'T STAND A CHANCE.

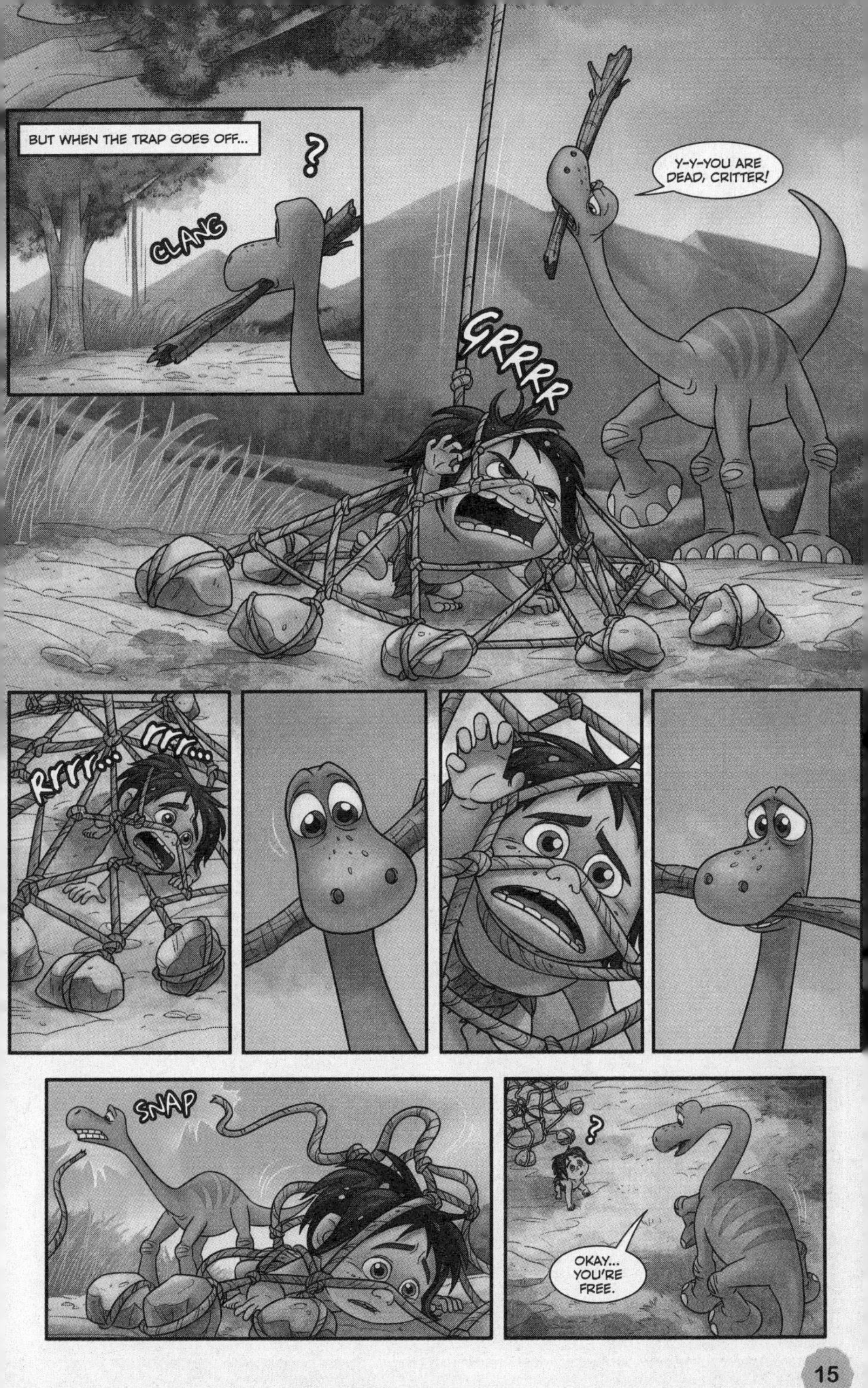
BUT WHEN THE TRAP GOES OFF...
?
CLANG
Y-Y-YOU ARE DEAD, CRITTER!
GRRRR
Rrrr... rrrr...
SNAP
?
OKAY... YOU'RE FREE.

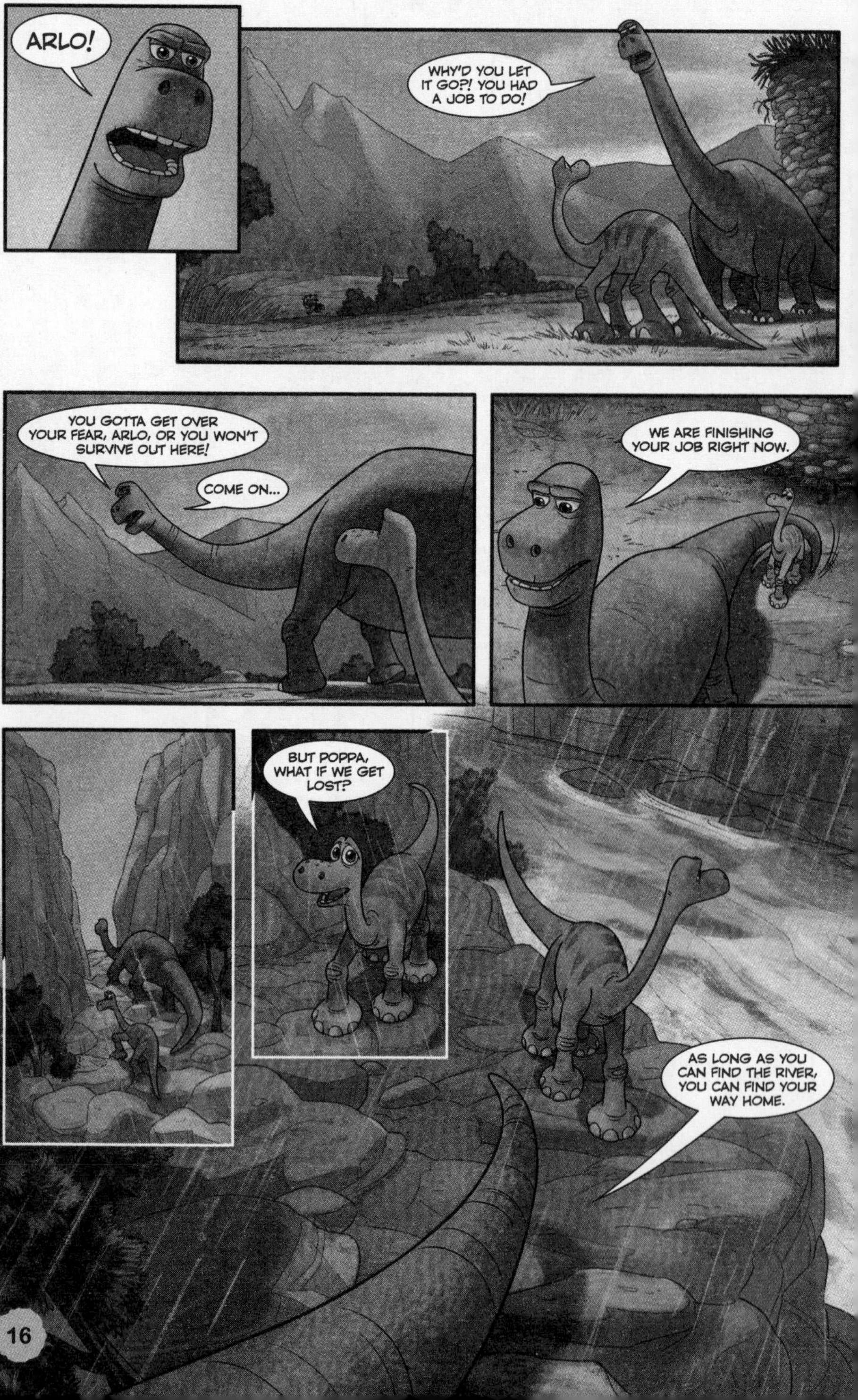
ARLO!
WHY'D YOU LET IT GO?! YOU HAD A JOB TO DO!
YOU GOTTA GET OVER YOUR FEAR, ARLO, OR YOU WON'T SURVIVE OUT HERE!
COME ON...
WE ARE FINISHING YOUR JOB RIGHT NOW.
BUT POPPA, WHAT IF WE GET LOST?
AS LONG AS YOU CAN FIND THE RIVER, YOU CAN FIND YOUR WAY HOME.

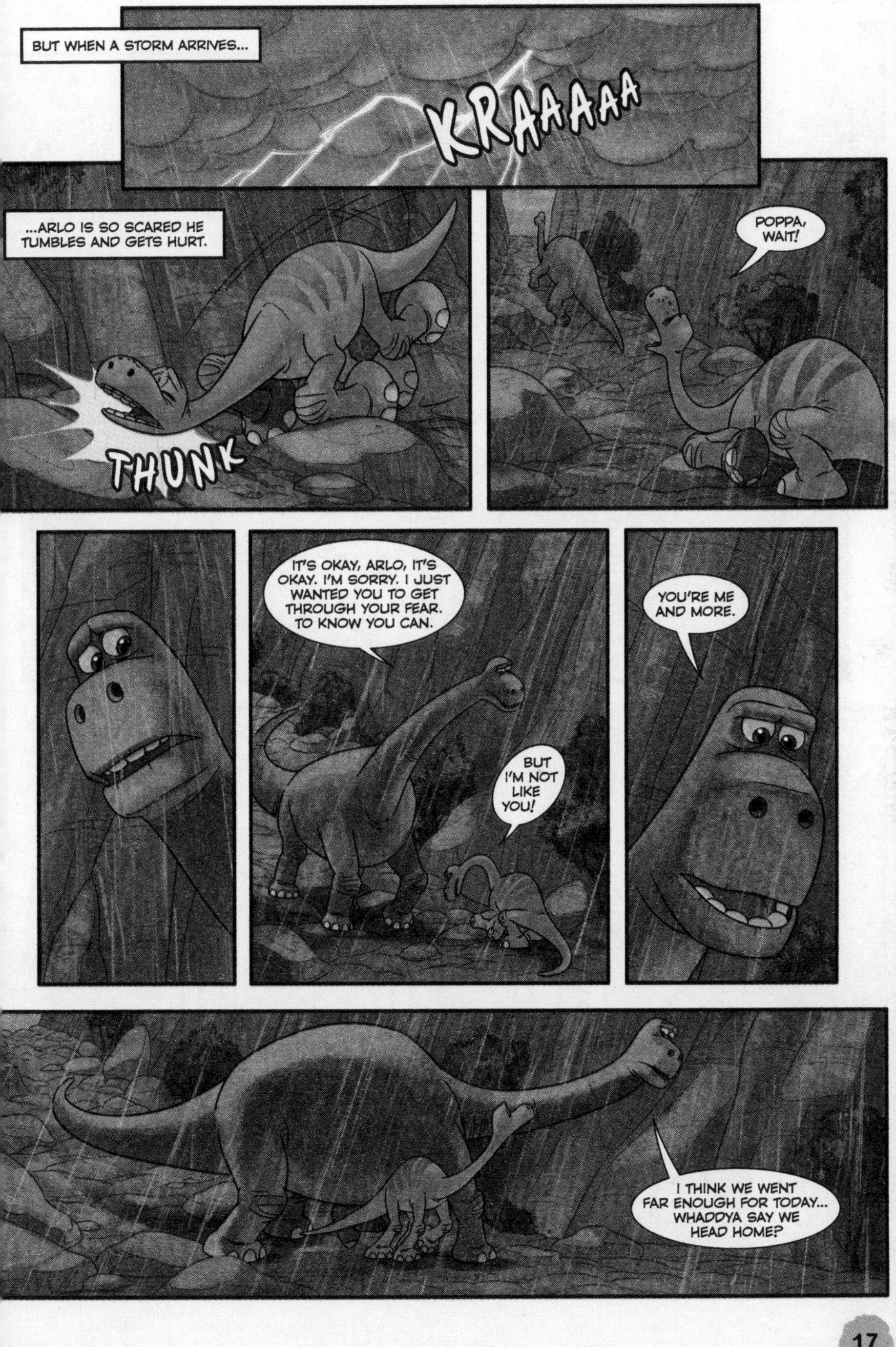
BUT WHEN A STORM ARRIVES...
KRAAAAA
...ARLO IS SO SCARED HE TUMBLES AND GETS HURT.
THUNK
POPPA, WAIT!
IT'S OKAY, ARLO, IT'S OKAY. I'M SORRY. I JUST WANTED YOU TO GET THROUGH YOUR FEAR. TO KNOW YOU CAN.
BUT I'M NOT LIKE YOU!
YOU'RE ME AND MORE.
I THINK WE WENT FAR ENOUGH FOR TODAY... WHADDYA SAY WE HEAD HOME?

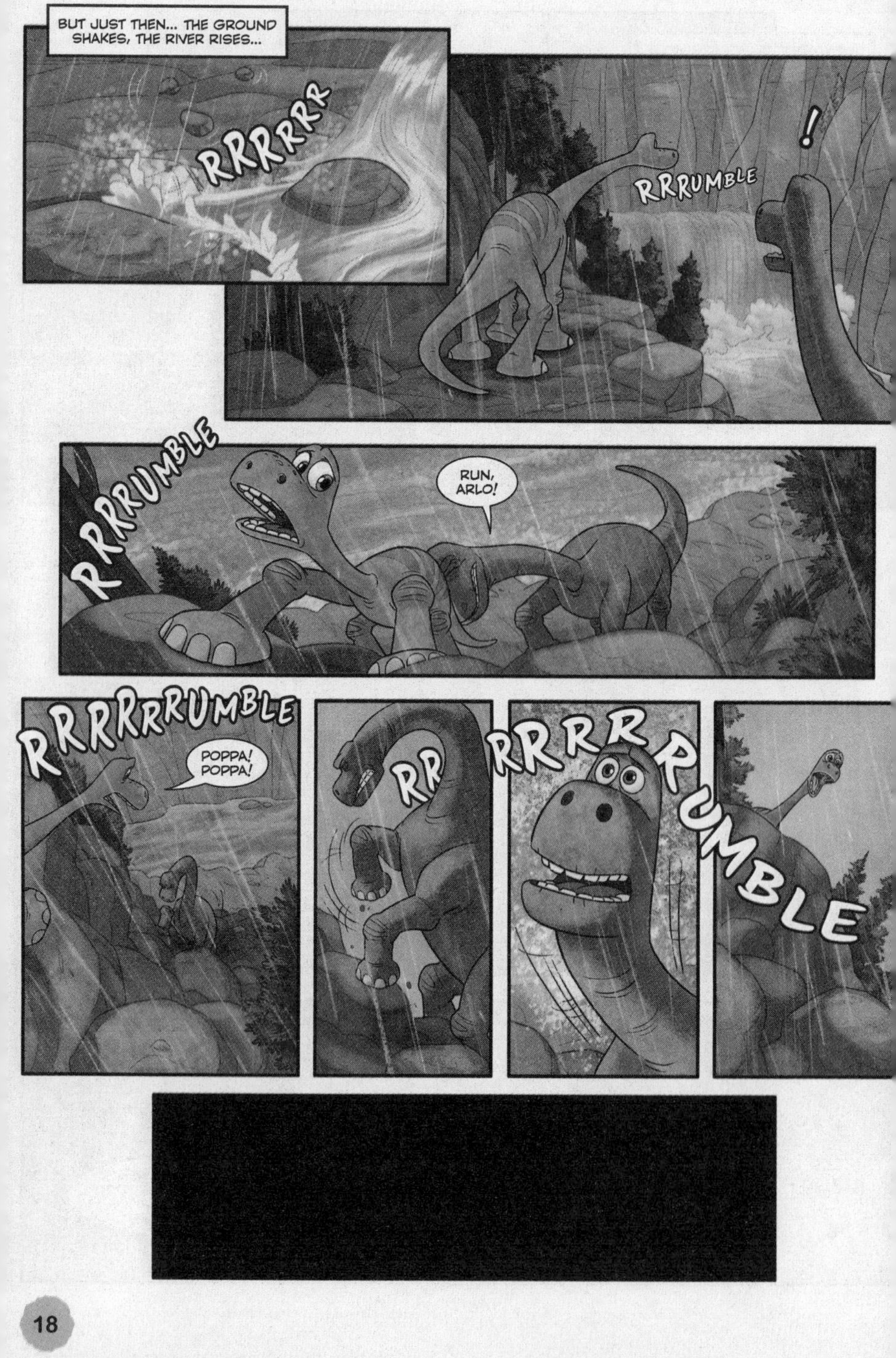
BUT JUST THEN... THE GROUND SHAKES, THE RIVER RISES...
RRRRRR
RRRUMBLE
!
RRRRUMBLE
RUN, ARLO!
RRRRRRUMBLE
POPPA! POPPA!
RR
RRRRRRUMBLE

[redacted]

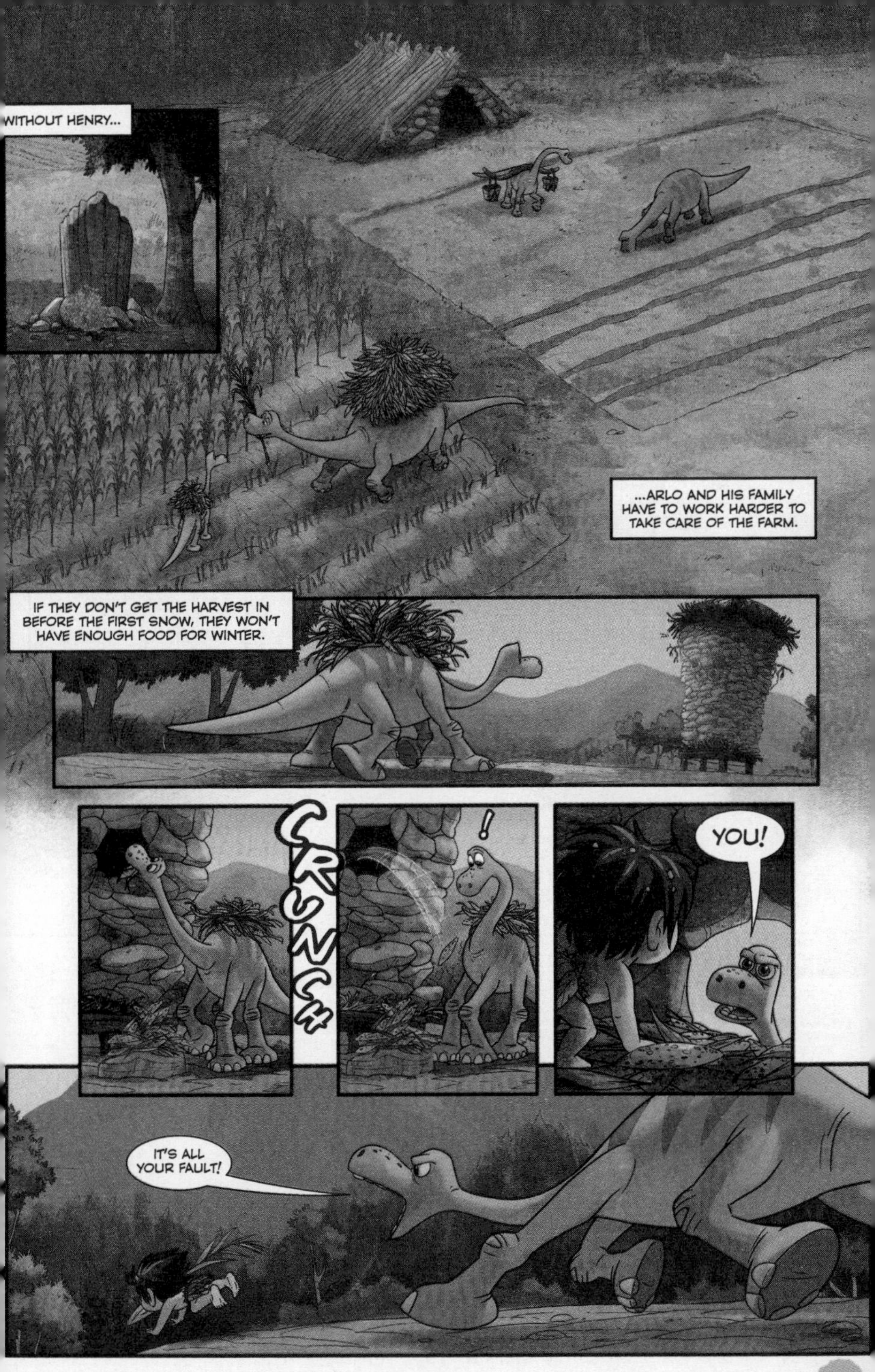
WITHOUT HENRY...
...ARLO AND HIS FAMILY HAVE TO WORK HARDER TO TAKE CARE OF THE FARM.
IF THEY DON'T GET THE HARVEST IN BEFORE THE FIRST SNOW, THEY WON'T HAVE ENOUGH FOOD FOR WINTER.
CRUNCH
!
YOU!
IT'S ALL YOUR FAULT!

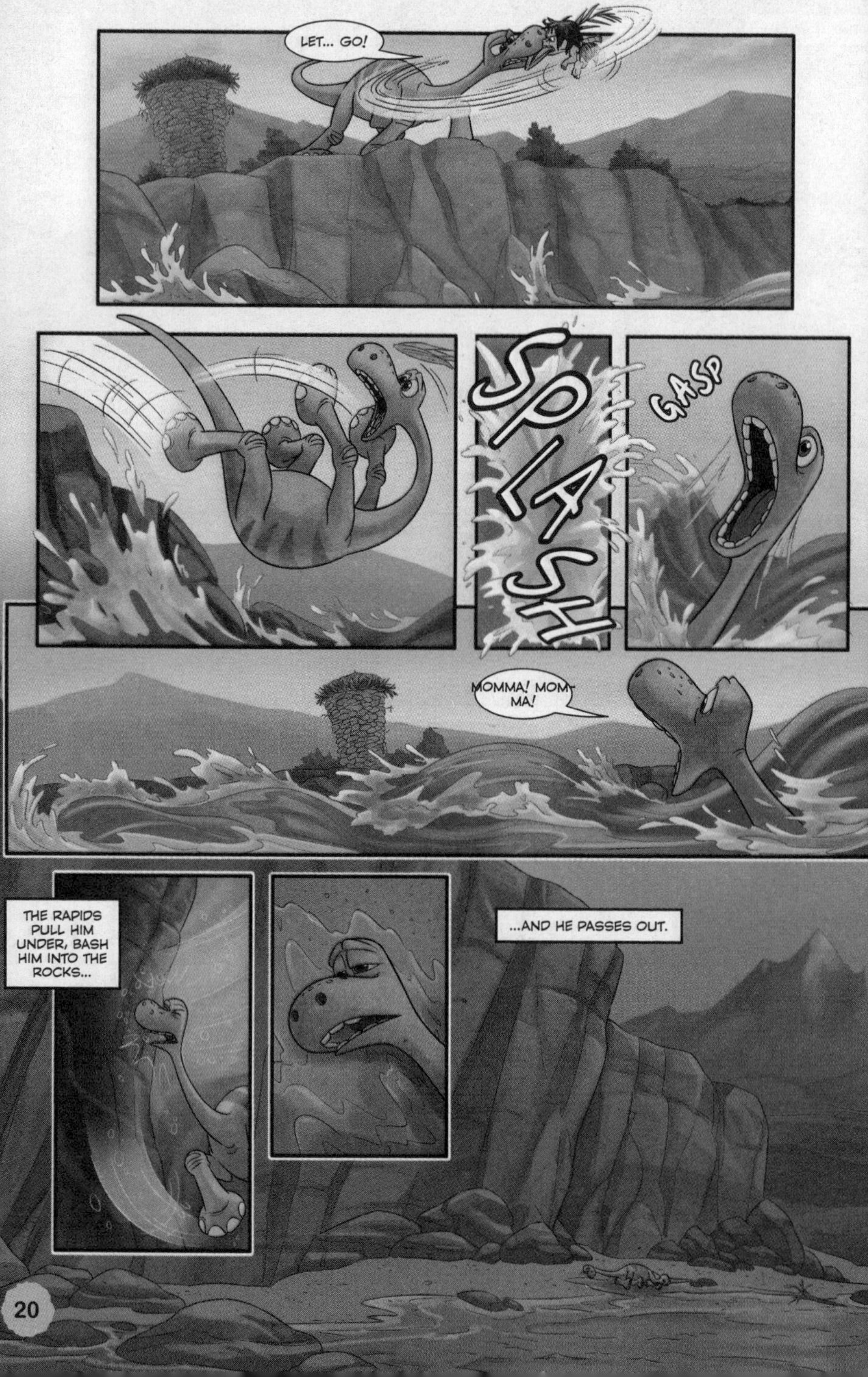
LET... GO!
SPLASH
GASP
MOMMA! MOMMA!
THE RAPIDS PULL HIM UNDER, BASH HIM INTO THE ROCKS...
...AND HE PASSES OUT.

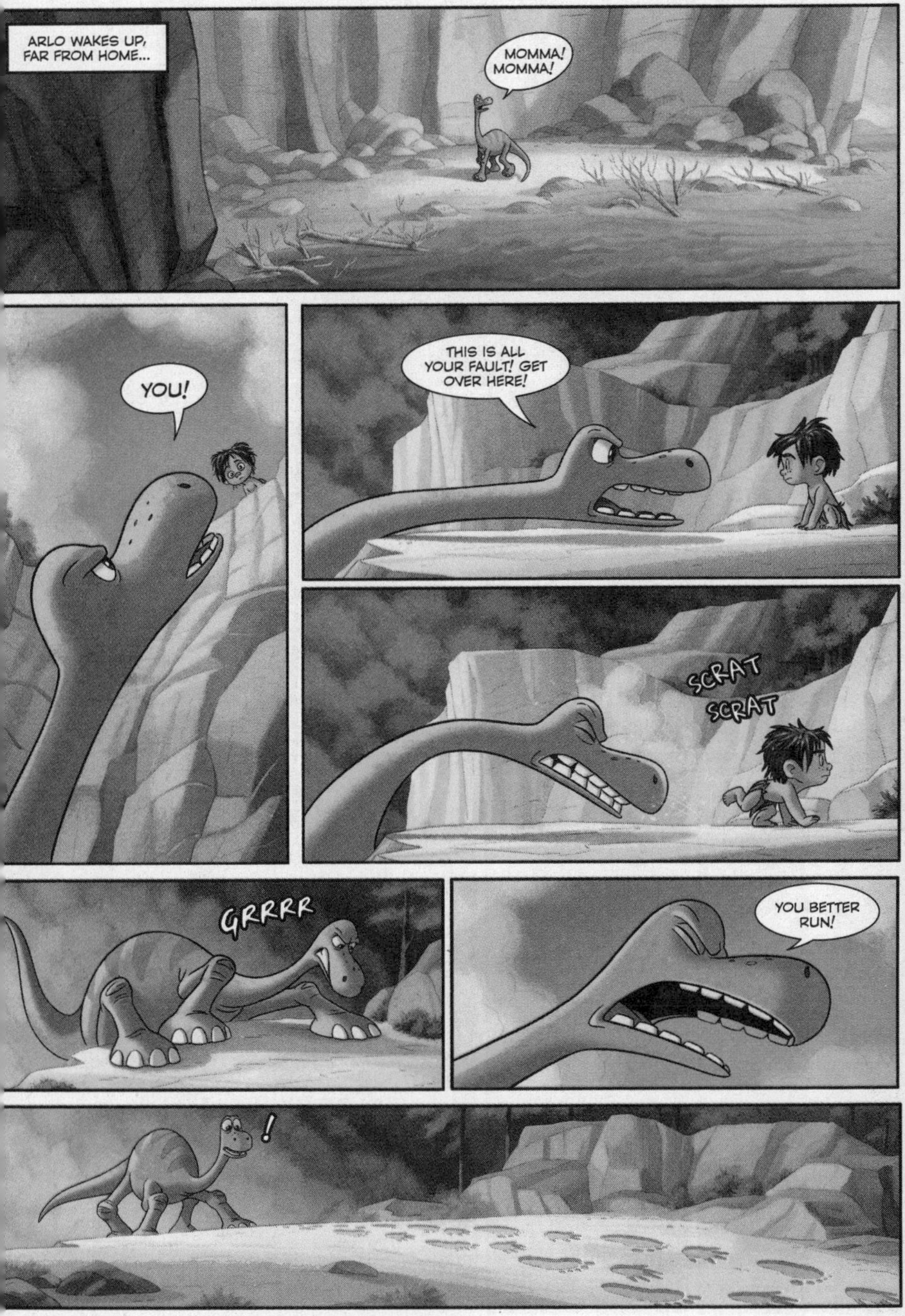

ARLO WAKES UP, FAR FROM HOME...
MOMMA! MOMMA!
YOU!
THIS IS ALL YOUR FAULT! GET OVER HERE!
SCRAT
SCRAT
GRRRR
YOU BETTER RUN!
!

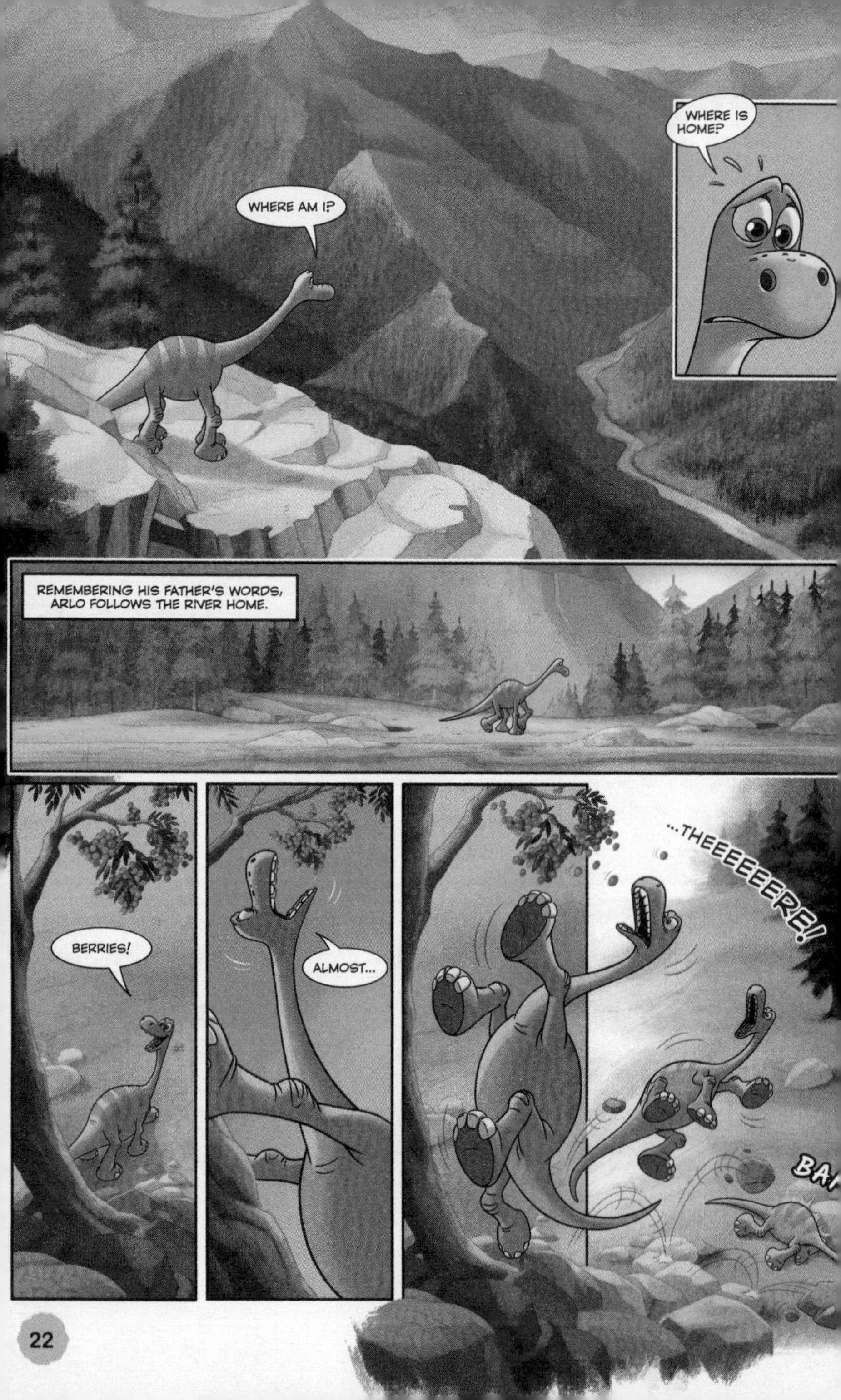
WHERE AM I?
WHERE IS HOME?
REMEMBERING HIS FATHER'S WORDS, ARLO FOLLOWS THE RIVER HOME.
BERRIES!
ALMOST...
...THEEEEEEERE!
BA

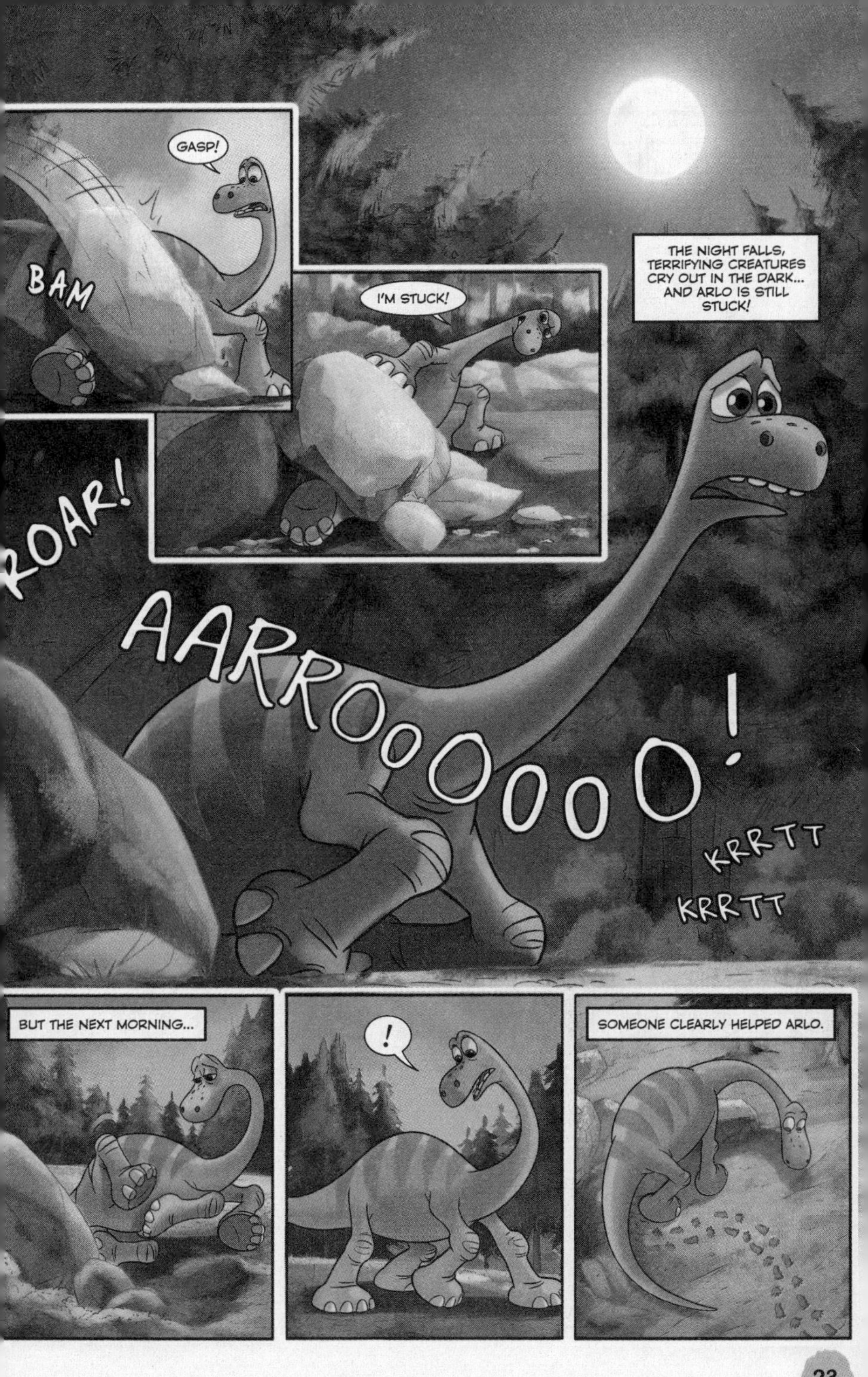
GASP!
BAM
I'M STUCK!
ROAR!
THE NIGHT FALLS, TERRIFYING CREATURES CRY OUT IN THE DARK... AND ARLO IS STILL STUCK!
AARROOOOOOO!
KRRTT
KRRTT
BUT THE NEXT MORNING...
!
SOMEONE CLEARLY HELPED ARLO.

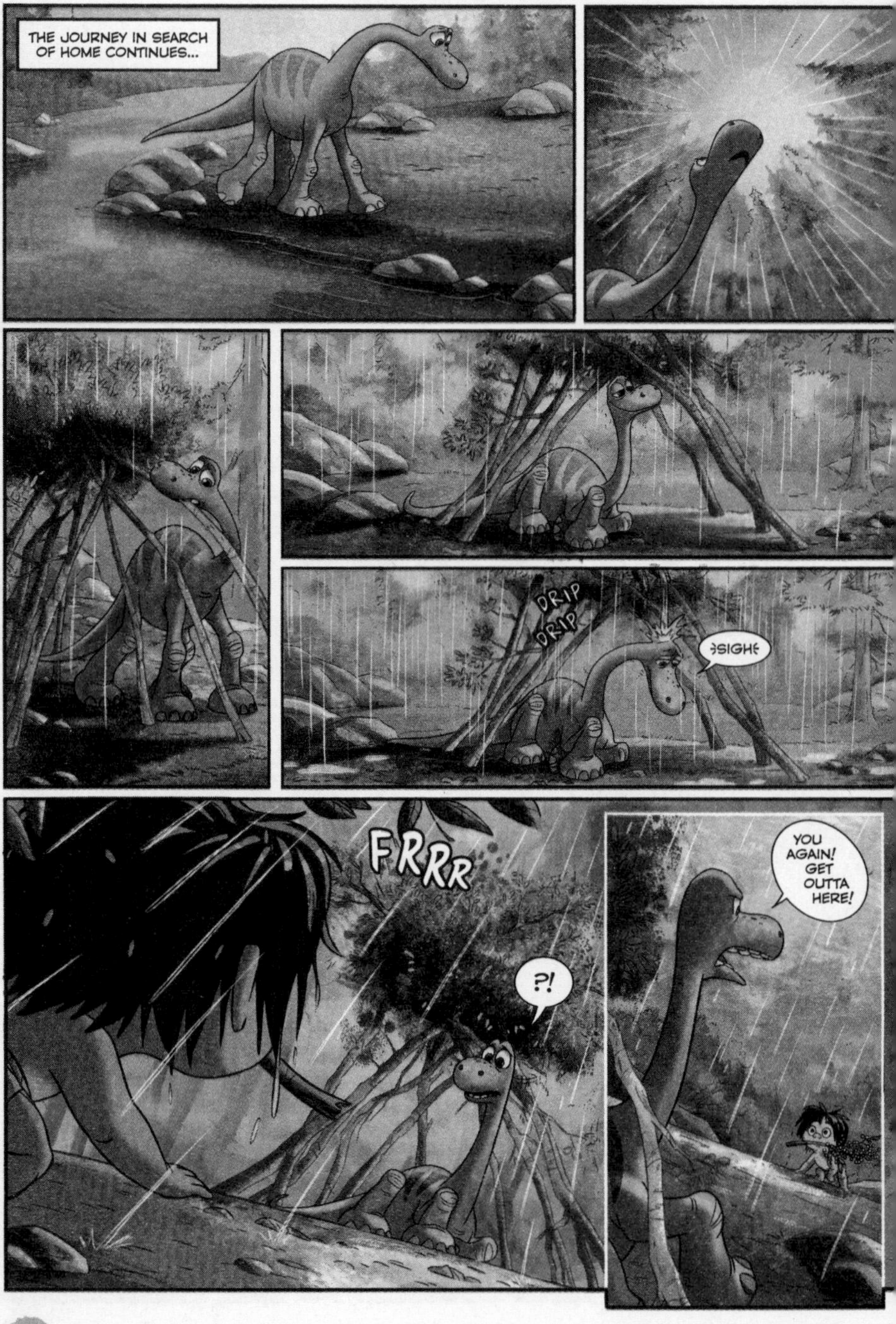
THE JOURNEY IN SEARCH OF HOME CONTINUES...
DRIP
DRIP
SIGH
FRRR
?!
YOU AGAIN! GET OUTTA HERE!

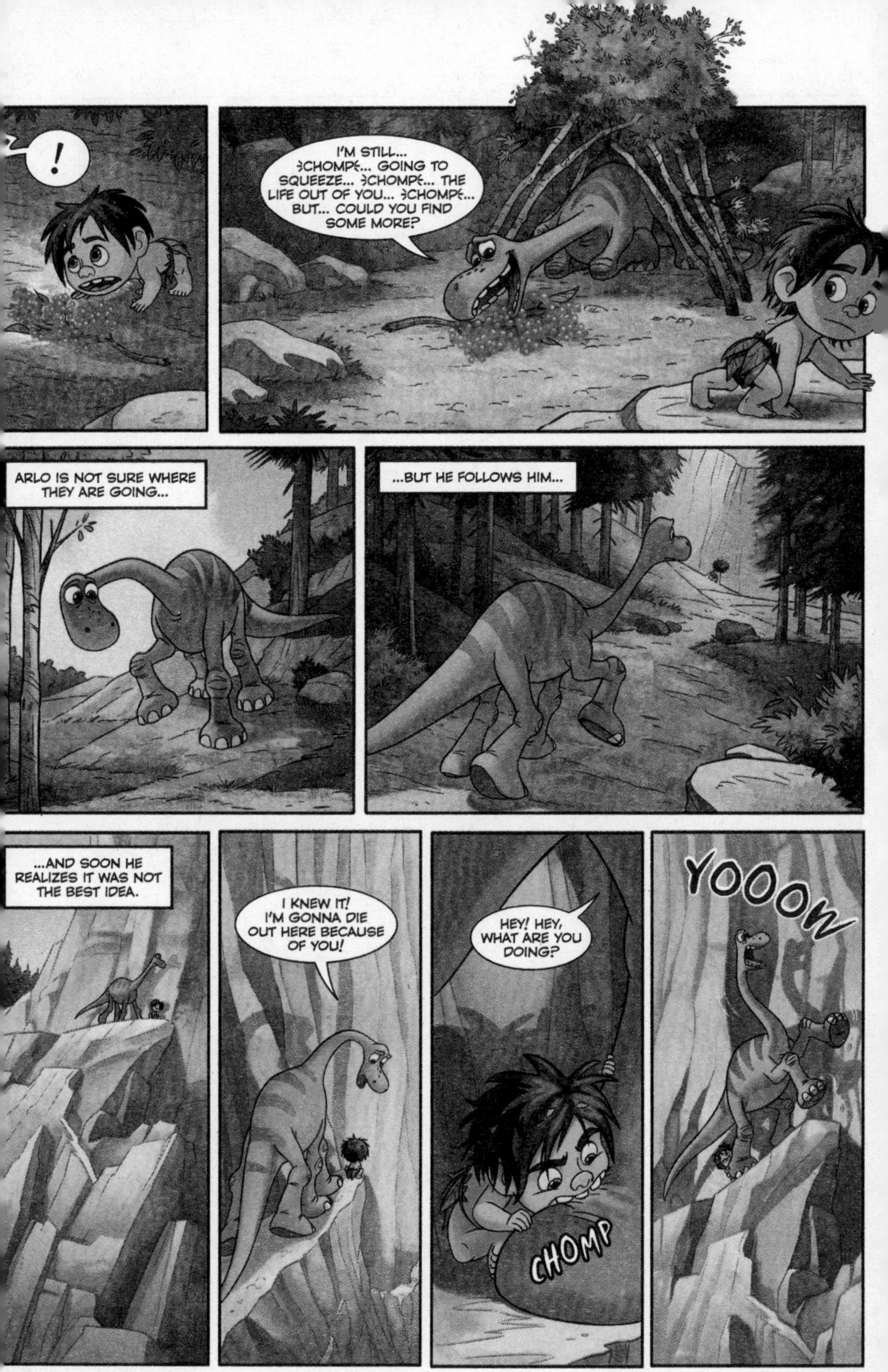
!
I'M STILL... ƎCHOMPƐ... GOING TO SQUEEZE... ƎCHOMPƐ... THE LIFE OUT OF YOU... ƎCHOMPƐ... BUT... COULD YOU FIND SOME MORE?
ARLO IS NOT SURE WHERE THEY ARE GOING...
...BUT HE FOLLOWS HIM...
...AND SOON HE REALIZES IT WAS NOT THE BEST IDEA.
I KNEW IT! I'M GONNA DIE OUT HERE BECAUSE OF YOU!
HEY! HEY, WHAT ARE YOU DOING?
CHOMP
YOOOW

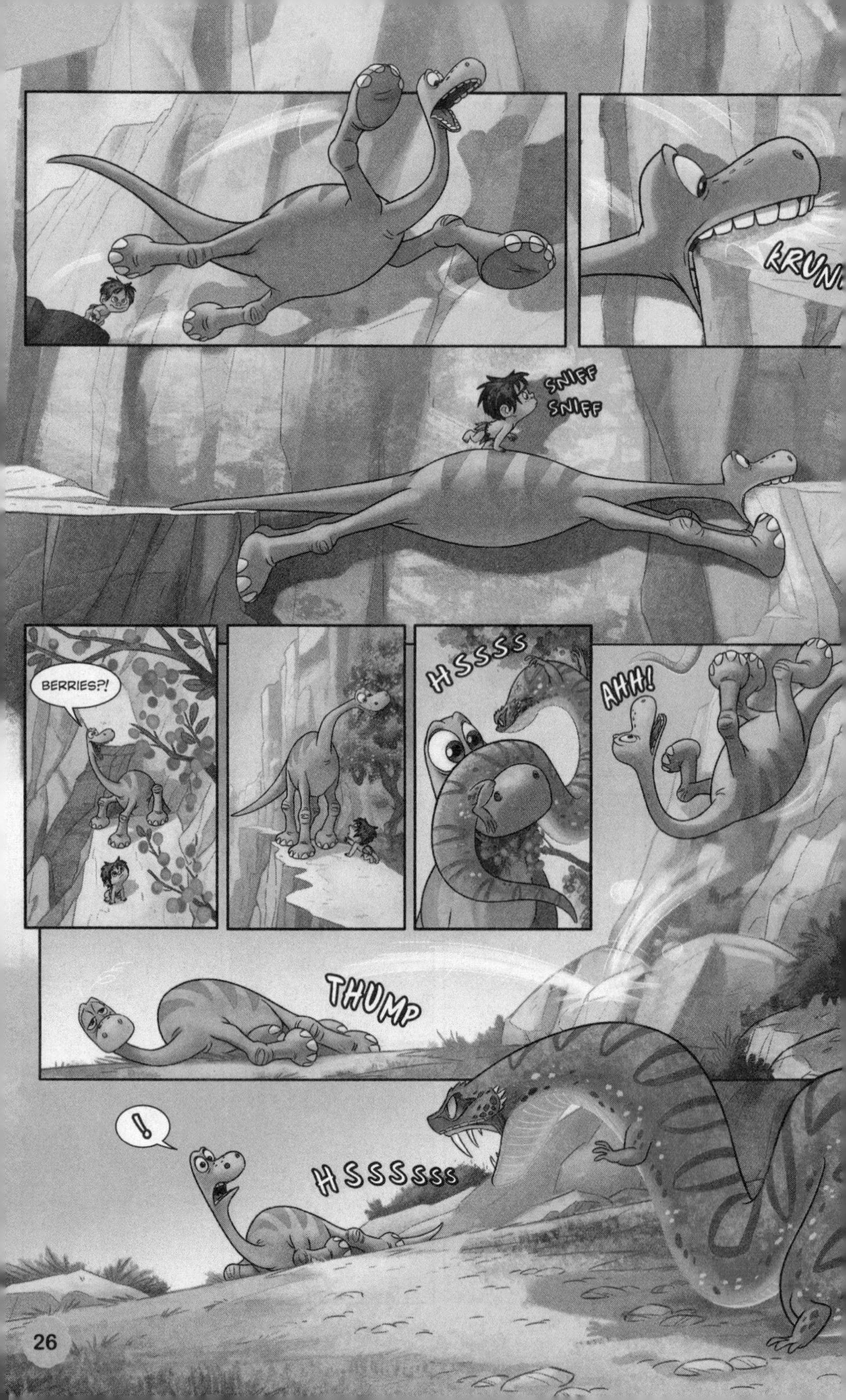
KRUN
SNIFF
SNIFF
BERRIES?!
HSSSS
AHH!
THUMP
!
HSSSSSS

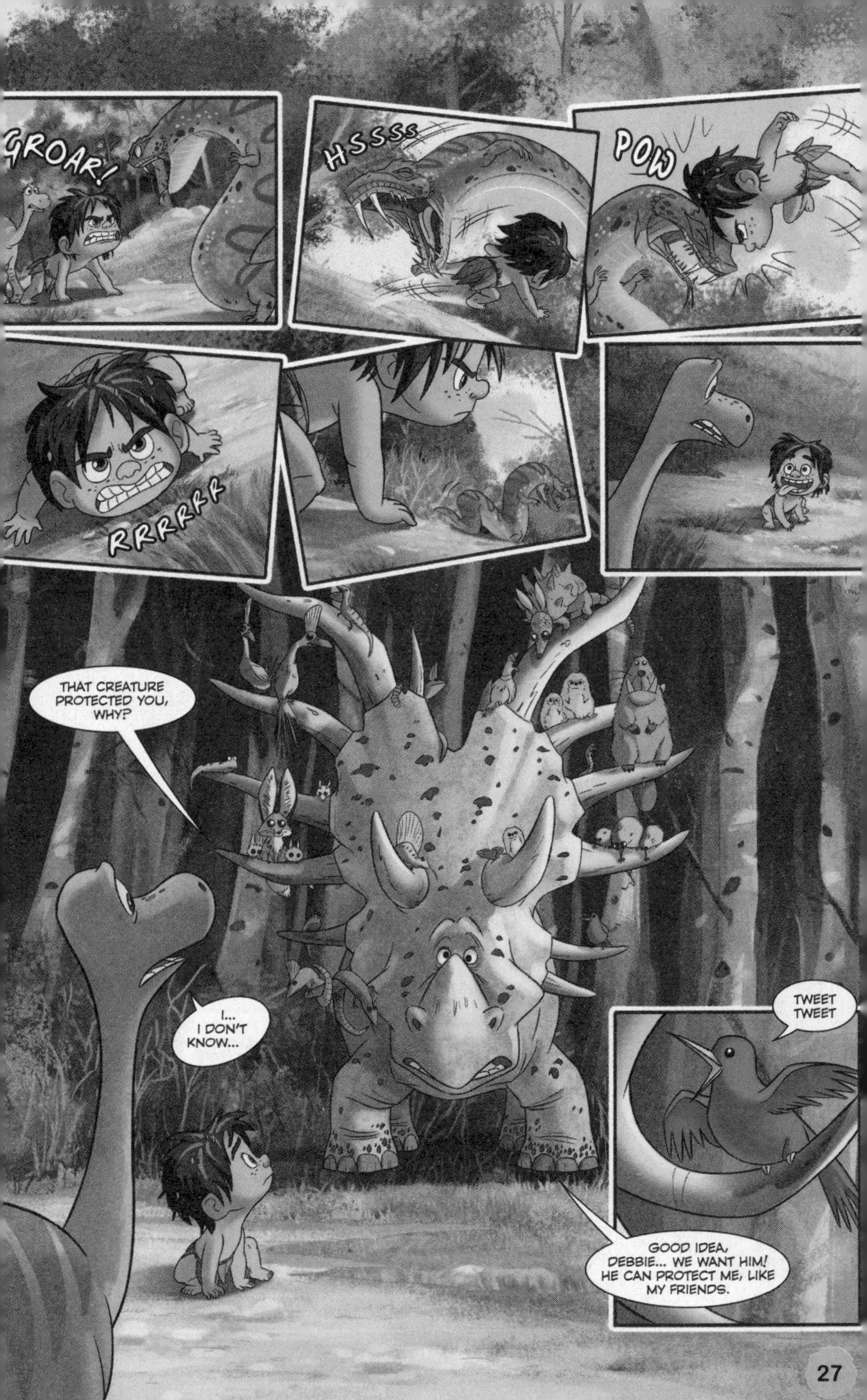
GROAR!
HSSSSS
POW
RRRRRR
THAT CREATURE PROTECTED YOU, WHY?
I... I DON'T KNOW...
TWEET TWEET
GOOD IDEA, DEBBIE... WE WANT HIM! HE CAN PROTECT ME, LIKE MY FRIENDS.

WAIT, HE... HE'S WITH ME!

IF HE'S WITH YOU, WHAT IS HIS NAME?

I... I DON'T KNOW...

I NAME HIM, I KEEP HIM.

ARLO AND THE STRANGE STYRACOSAURUS IMMEDIATELY START CALLING OUT NAMES.

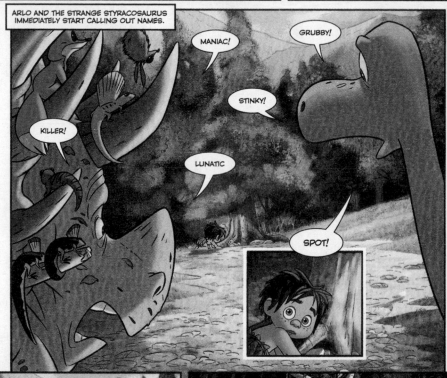

MANIAC!

GRUBBY!

STINKY!

KILLER!

LUNATIC

SPOT!

SPOT! COME HERE, SPOT!

HE'S NAMED. YOU CLEARLY ARE CONNECTED.

THAT CREATURE WILL KEEP YOU SAFE. DON'T EVER LOSE HIM.

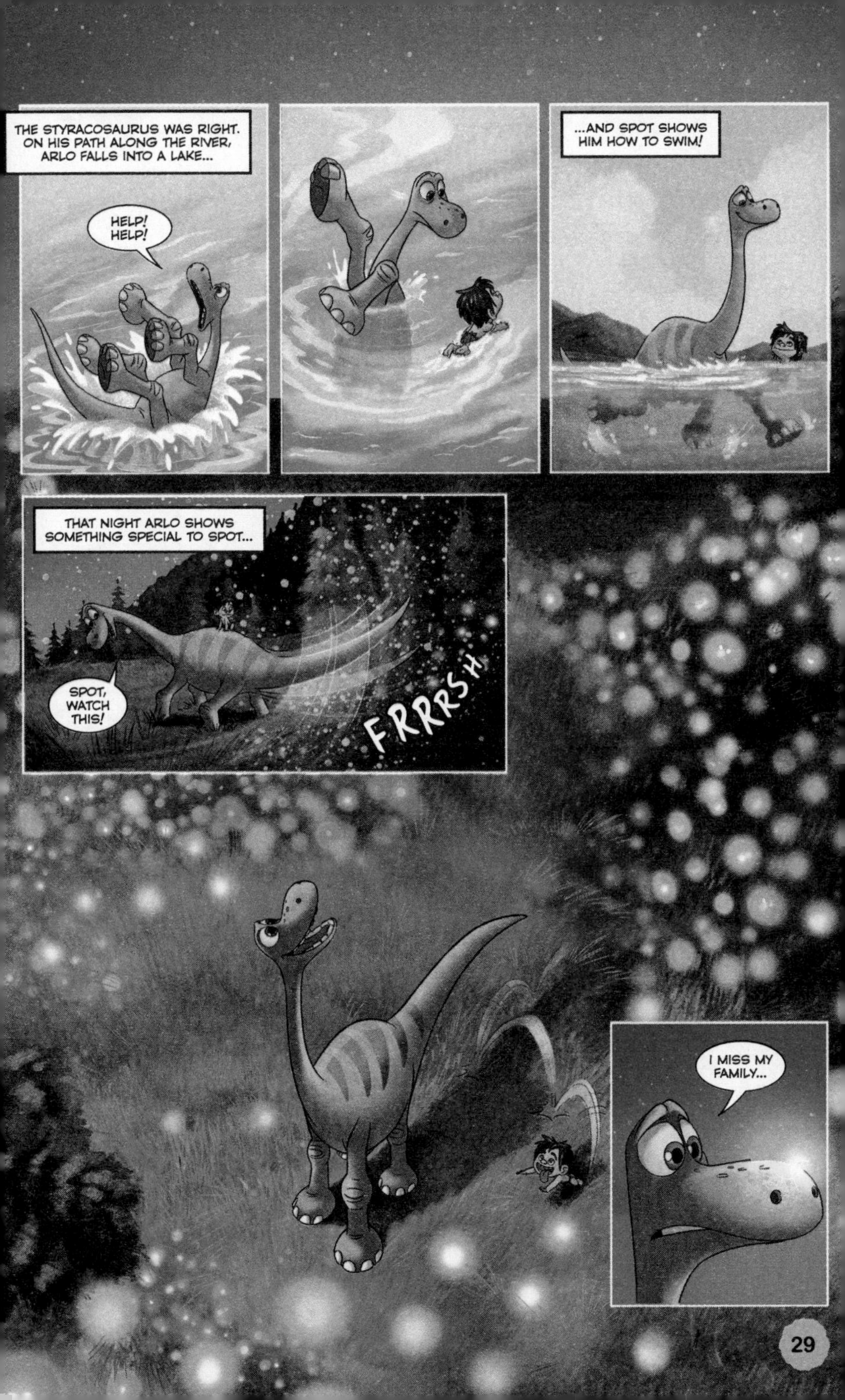
THE STYRACOSAURUS WAS RIGHT. ON HIS PATH ALONG THE RIVER, ARLO FALLS INTO A LAKE...
HELP! HELP!
...AND SPOT SHOWS HIM HOW TO SWIM!
THAT NIGHT ARLO SHOWS SOMETHING SPECIAL TO SPOT...
SPOT, WATCH THIS!
FRRRSH
I MISS MY FAMILY...

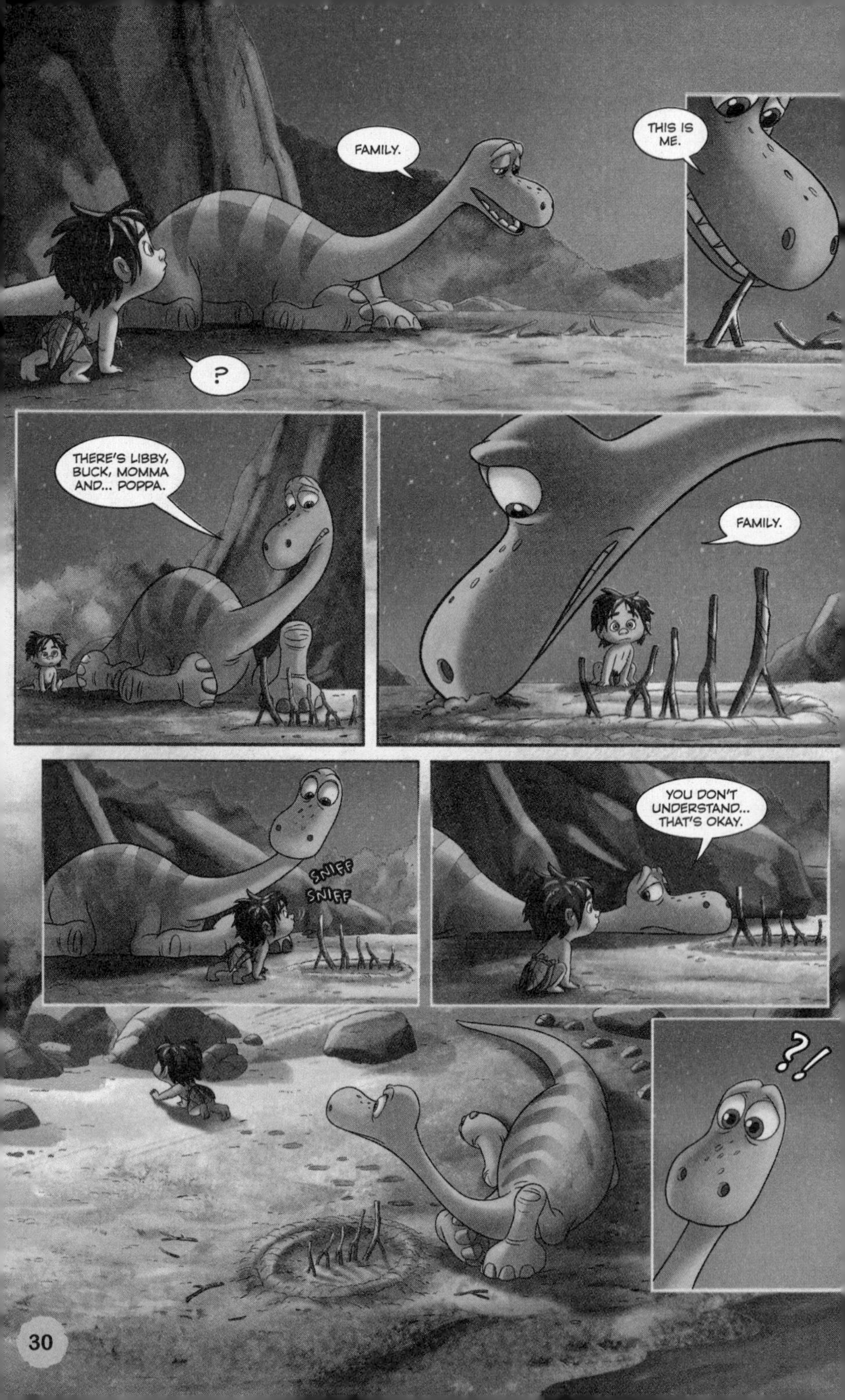
FAMILY.
?
THIS IS ME.
THERE'S LIBBY, BUCK, MOMMA AND... POPPA.
FAMILY.
SNIFF
SNIFF
YOU DON'T UNDERSTAND... THAT'S OKAY.
?!

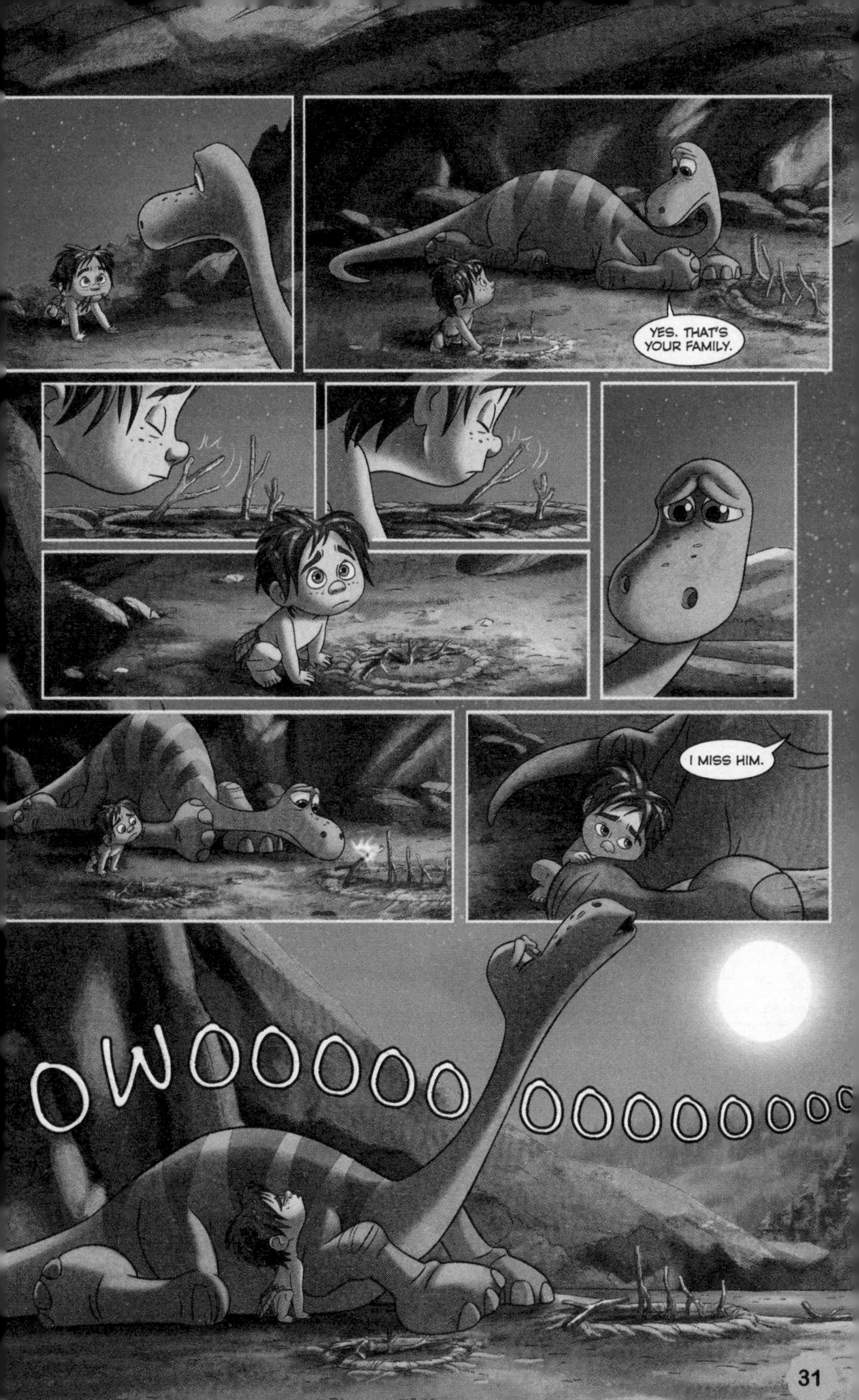
YES. THAT'S YOUR FAMILY.
I MISS HIM.
OWOOOOOOOOOOOOOO

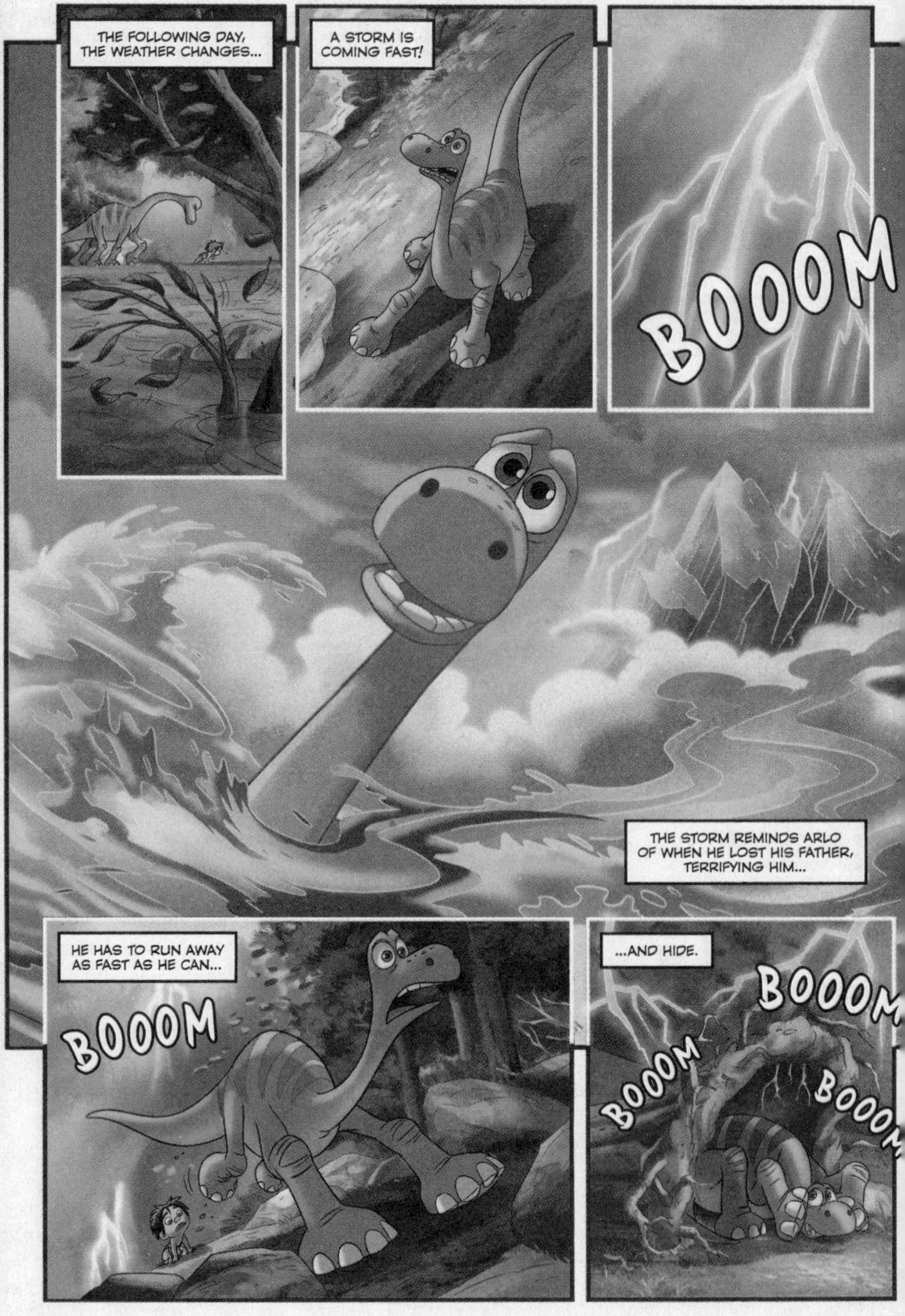
THE FOLLOWING DAY, THE WEATHER CHANGES...
A STORM IS COMING FAST!
BOOOM
THE STORM REMINDS ARLO OF WHEN HE LOST HIS FATHER, TERRIFYING HIM...
HE HAS TO RUN AWAY AS FAST AS HE CAN...
BOOOM
...AND HIDE.
BOOOM
BOOOM
BOOOM

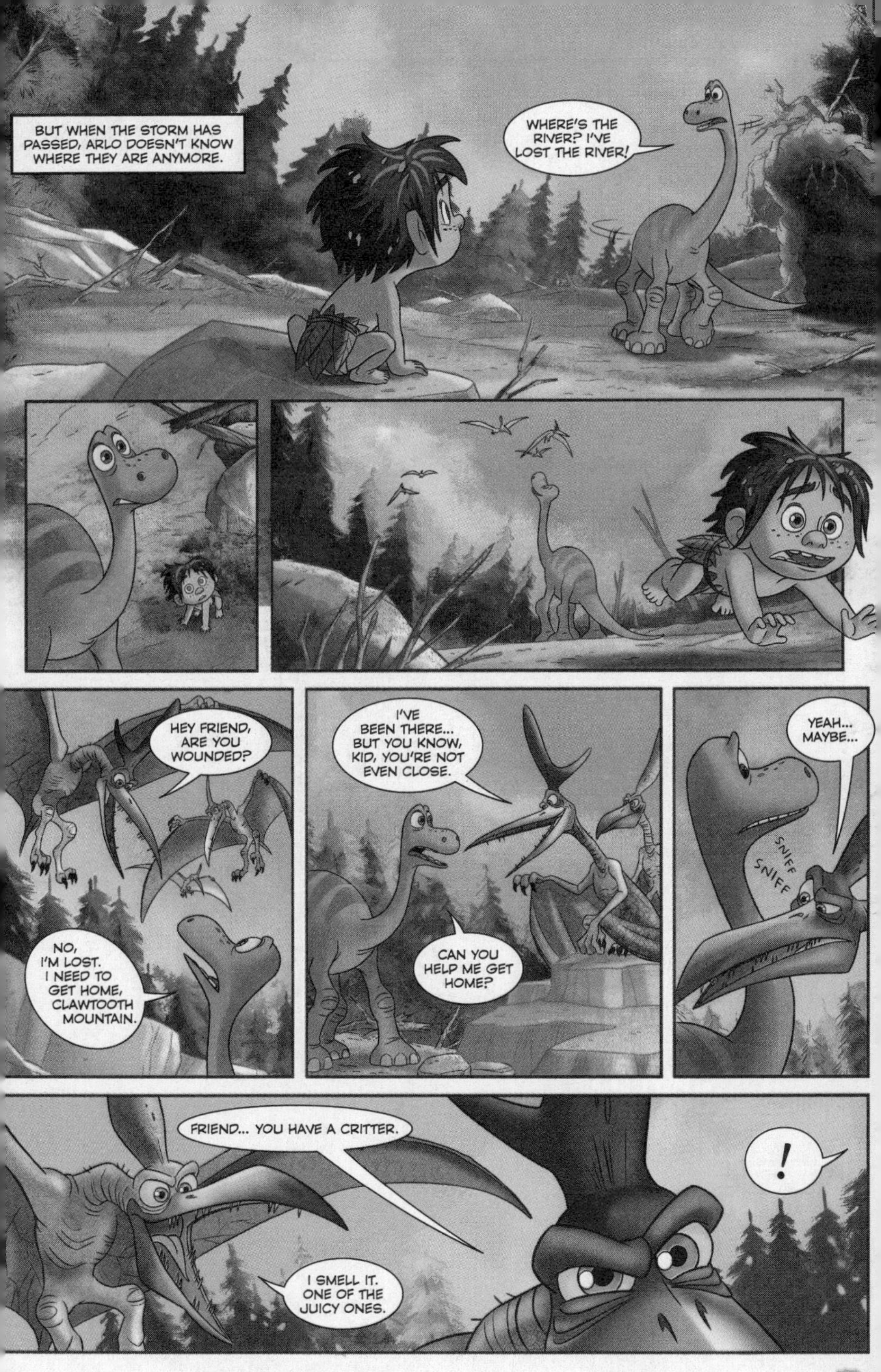
BUT WHEN THE STORM HAS PASSED, ARLO DOESN'T KNOW WHERE THEY ARE ANYMORE.
WHERE'S THE RIVER? I'VE LOST THE RIVER!
HEY FRIEND, ARE YOU WOUNDED?
NO, I'M LOST. I NEED TO GET HOME, CLAWTOOTH MOUNTAIN.
I'VE BEEN THERE... BUT YOU KNOW, KID, YOU'RE NOT EVEN CLOSE.
CAN YOU HELP ME GET HOME?
YEAH... MAYBE...
SNIFF
SNIFF
FRIEND... YOU HAVE A CRITTER.
!
I SMELL IT. ONE OF THE JUICY ONES.

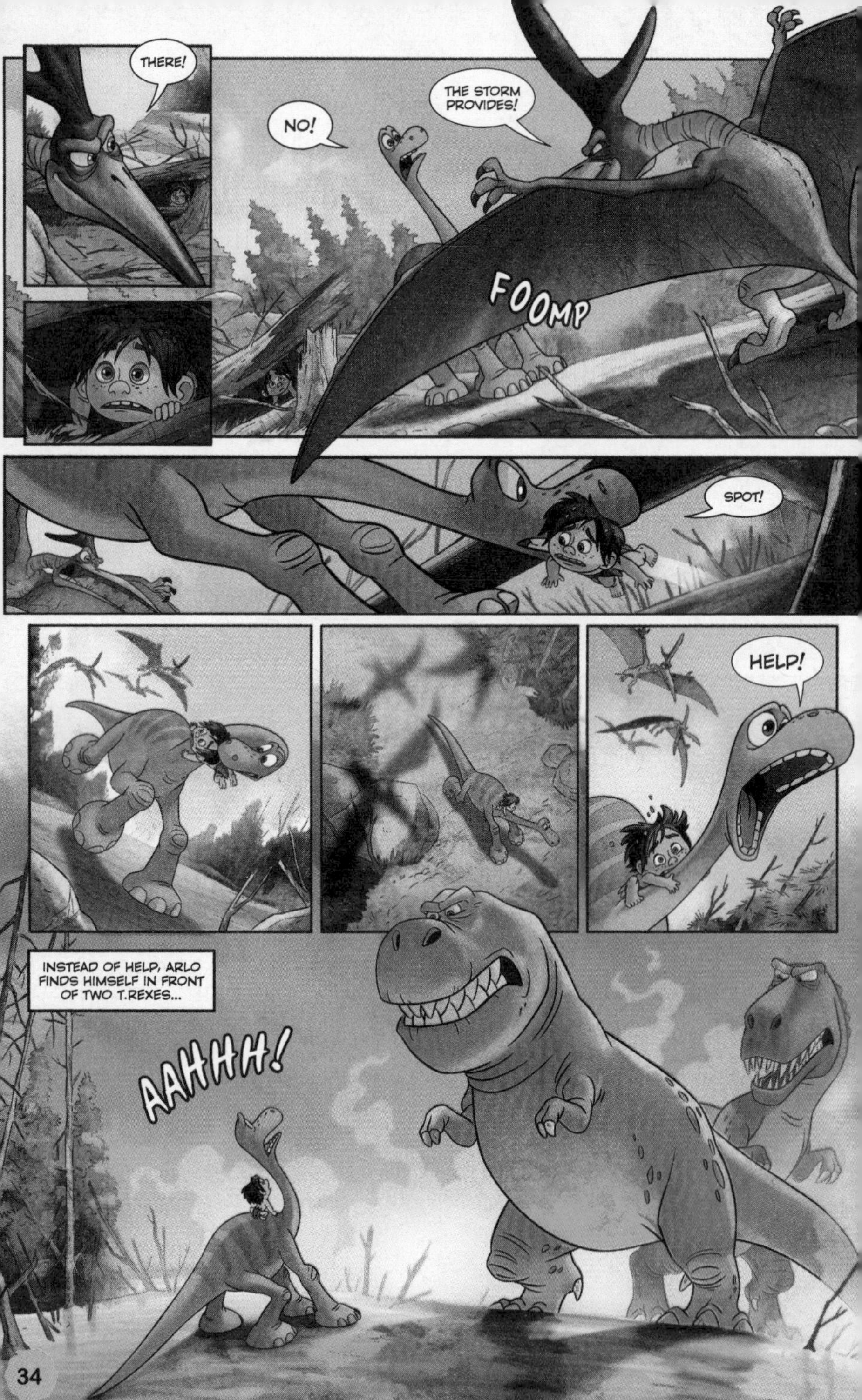
THERE!
NO!
THE STORM PROVIDES!
FOOMP
SPOT!
HELP!
INSTEAD OF HELP, ARLO FINDS HIMSELF IN FRONT OF TWO T.REXES...
AAHHH!

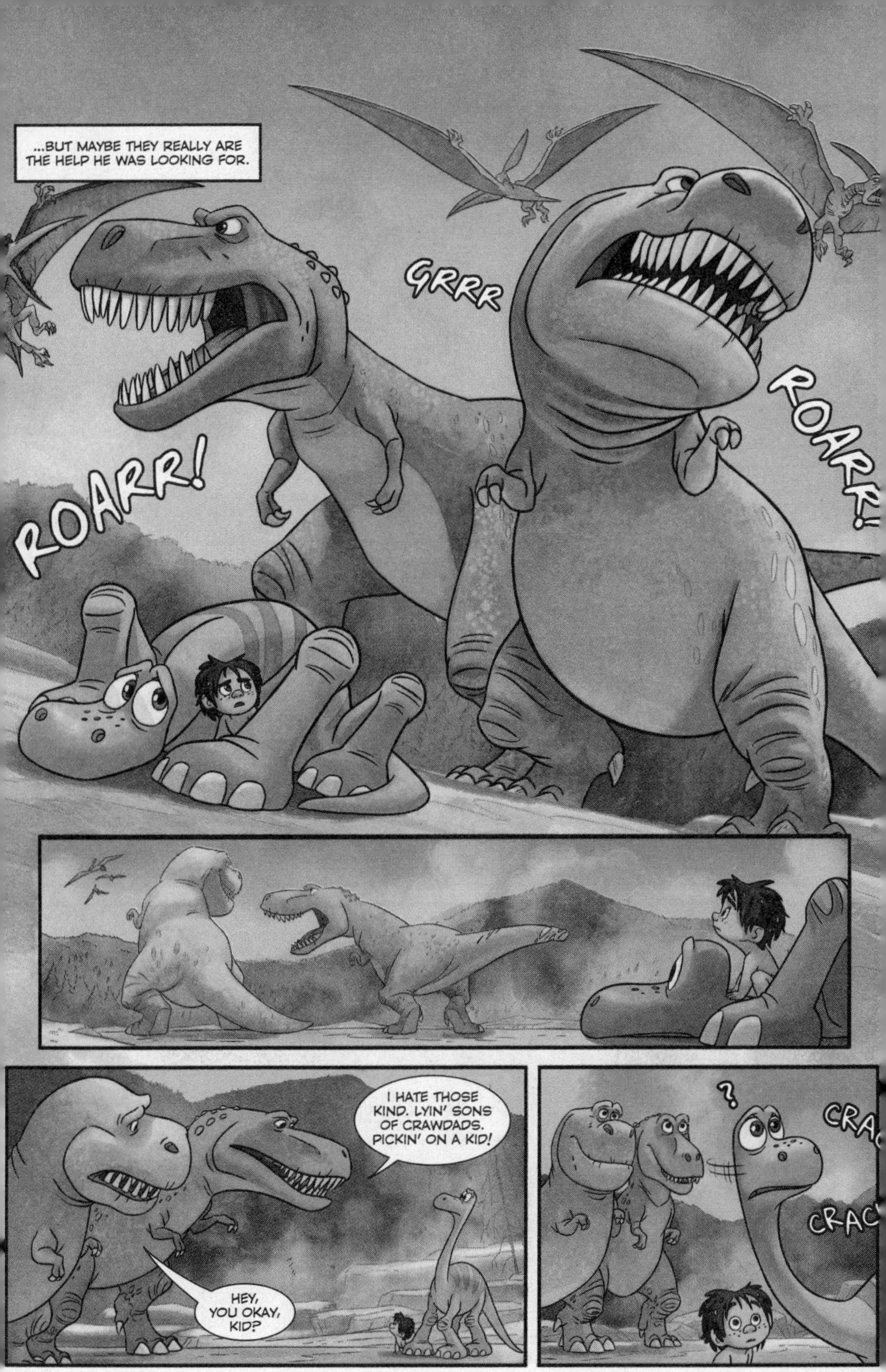
...BUT MAYBE THEY REALLY ARE THE HELP HE WAS LOOKING FOR.
GRRR
ROARR!
ROARR!
I HATE THOSE KIND. LYIN' SONS OF CRAWDADS. PICKIN' ON A KID!
HEY, YOU OKAY, KID?
?
CRAC
CRAC

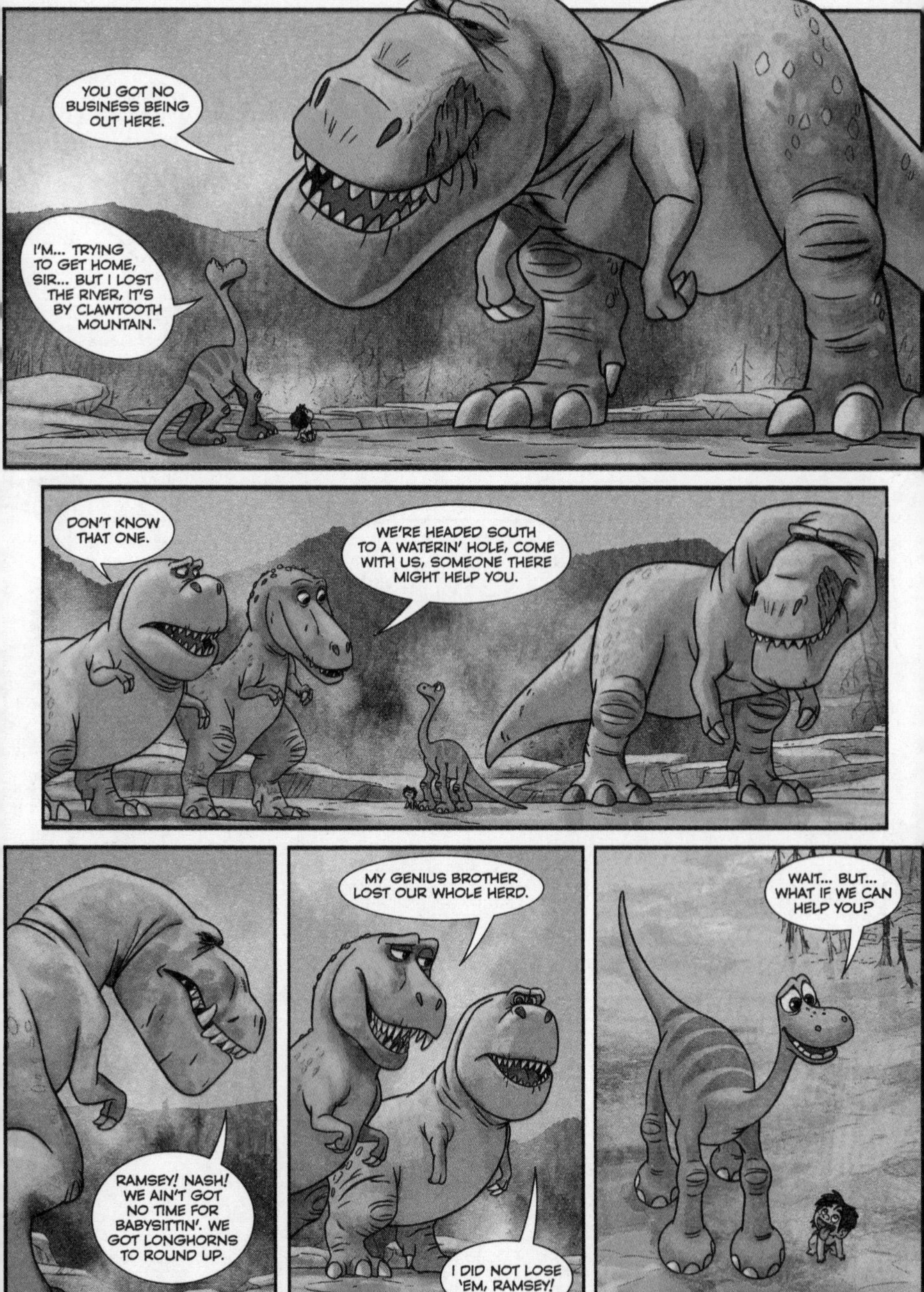
YOU GOT NO BUSINESS BEING OUT HERE.
I'M... TRYING TO GET HOME, SIR... BUT I LOST THE RIVER, IT'S BY CLAWTOOTH MOUNTAIN.
DON'T KNOW THAT ONE.
WE'RE HEADED SOUTH TO A WATERIN' HOLE, COME WITH US, SOMEONE THERE MIGHT HELP YOU.
RAMSEY! NASH! WE AIN'T GOT NO TIME FOR BABYSITTIN'. WE GOT LONGHORNS TO ROUND UP.
MY GENIUS BROTHER LOST OUR WHOLE HERD.
I DID NOT LOSE 'EM, RAMSEY!
WAIT... BUT... WHAT IF WE CAN HELP YOU?

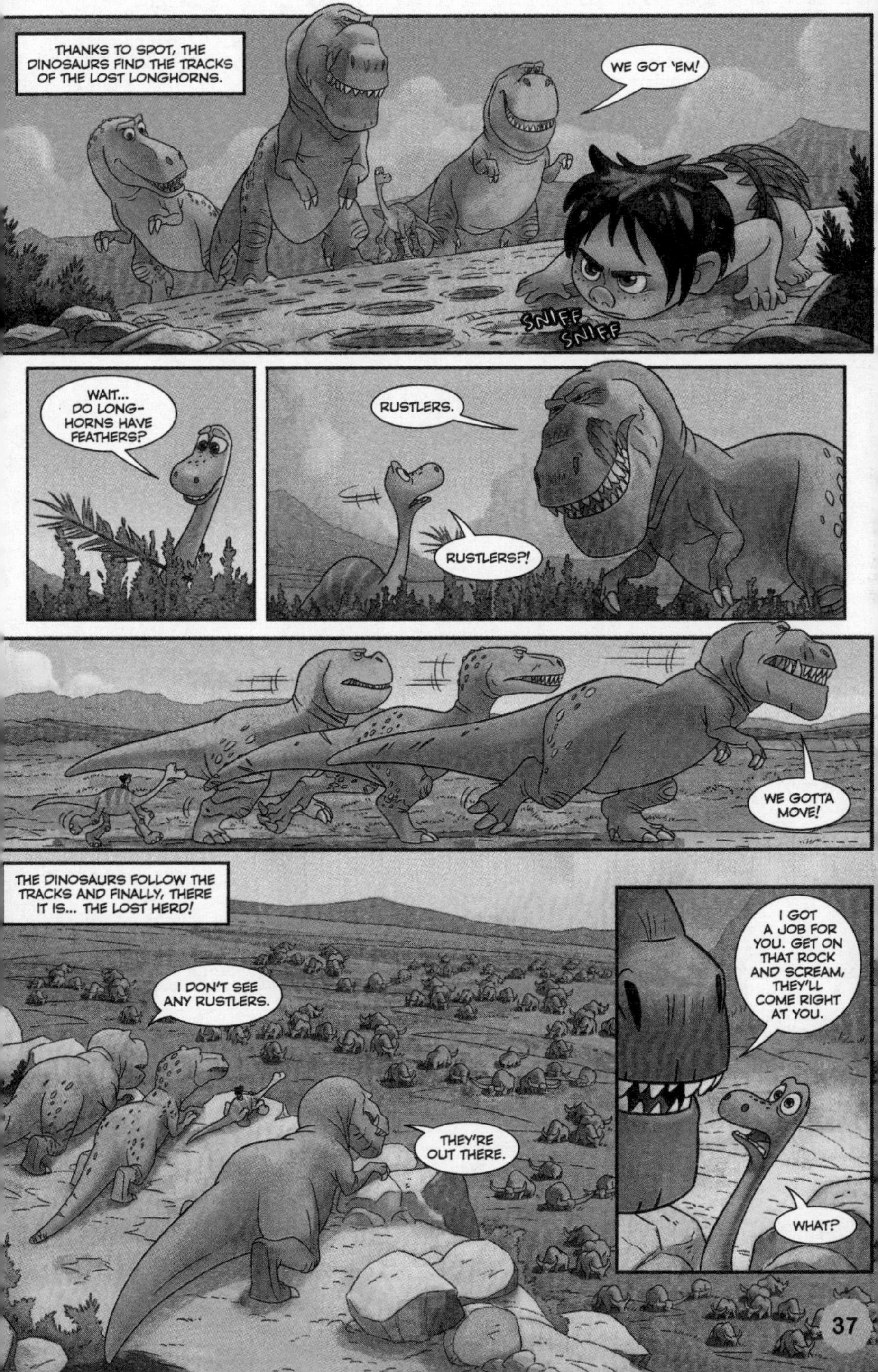
THANKS TO SPOT, THE DINOSAURS FIND THE TRACKS OF THE LOST LONGHORNS.
WE GOT 'EM!
SNIFF SNIFF
WAIT... DO LONG-HORNS HAVE FEATHERS?
RUSTLERS.
RUSTLERS?!
WE GOTTA MOVE!
THE DINOSAURS FOLLOW THE TRACKS AND FINALLY, THERE IT IS... THE LOST HERD!
I DON'T SEE ANY RUSTLERS.
THEY'RE OUT THERE.
I GOT A JOB FOR YOU. GET ON THAT ROCK AND SCREAM, THEY'LL COME RIGHT AT YOU.
WHAT?

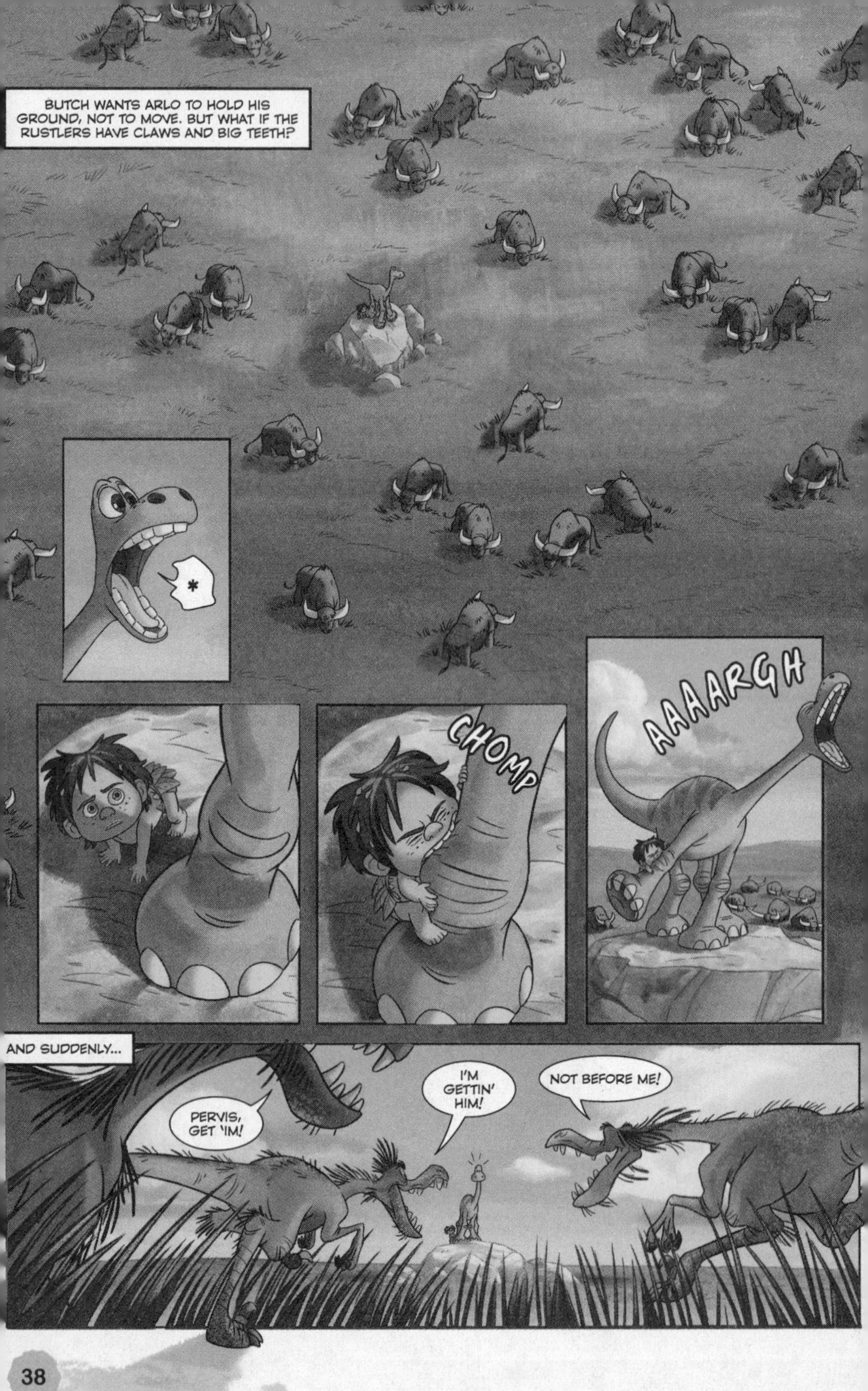
BUTCH WANTS ARLO TO HOLD HIS GROUND, NOT TO MOVE. BUT WHAT IF THE RUSTLERS HAVE CLAWS AND BIG TEETH?
*
CHOMP
AAAARGH
AND SUDDENLY...
PERVIS, GET 'IM!
I'M GETTIN' HIM!
NOT BEFORE ME!

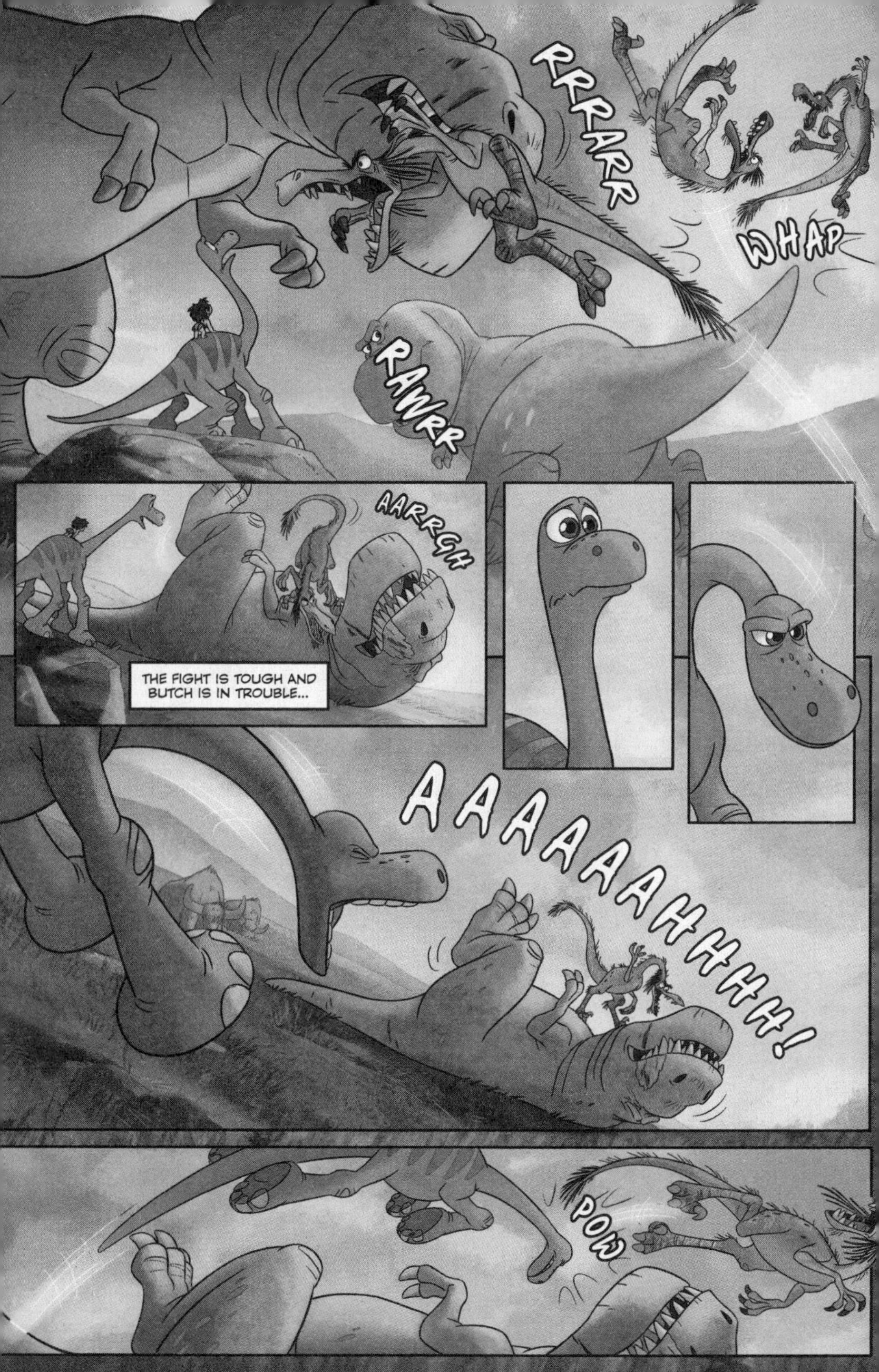
RRRARR
WHAP
RAWRR
AARRGH
THE FIGHT IS TOUGH AND BUTCH IS IN TROUBLE...
AAAAAAHHHHH!
POW

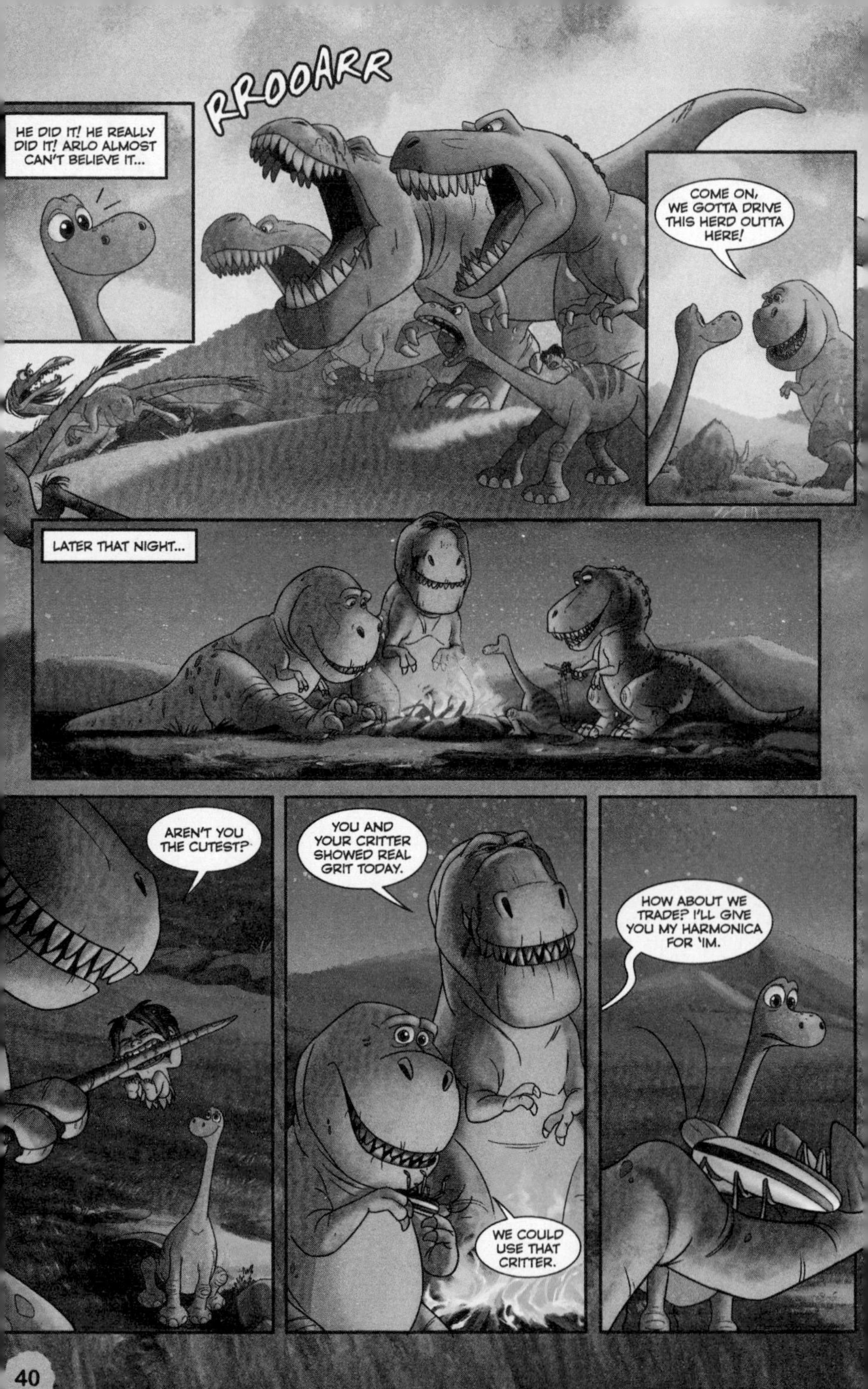

RROOARR
HE DID IT! HE REALLY DID IT! ARLO ALMOST CAN'T BELIEVE IT...
COME ON, WE GOTTA DRIVE THIS HERD OUTTA HERE!
LATER THAT NIGHT...
AREN'T YOU THE CUTEST?
YOU AND YOUR CRITTER SHOWED REAL GRIT TODAY.
WE COULD USE THAT CRITTER.
HOW ABOUT WE TRADE? I'LL GIVE YOU MY HARMONICA FOR 'IM.

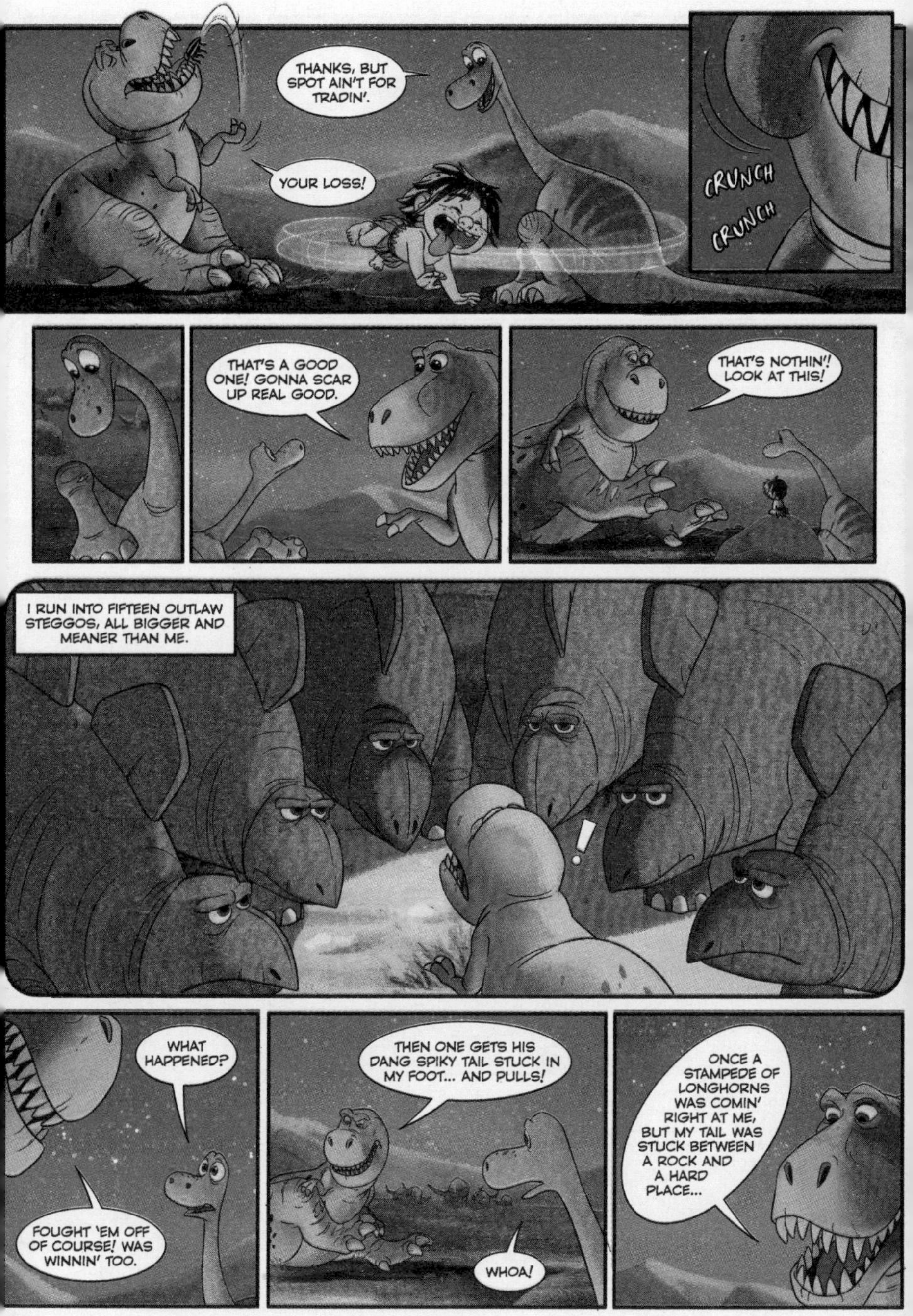
THANKS, BUT SPOT AIN'T FOR TRADIN'.
YOUR LOSS!
CRUNCH
CRUNCH
THAT'S A GOOD ONE! GONNA SCAR UP REAL GOOD.
THAT'S NOTHIN'! LOOK AT THIS!
I RUN INTO FIFTEEN OUTLAW STEGGOS, ALL BIGGER AND MEANER THAN ME.
!
WHAT HAPPENED?
FOUGHT 'EM OFF OF COURSE! WAS WINNIN' TOO.
THEN ONE GETS HIS DANG SPIKY TAIL STUCK IN MY FOOT... AND PULLS!
WHOA!
ONCE A STAMPEDE OF LONGHORNS WAS COMIN' RIGHT AT ME, BUT MY TAIL WAS STUCK BETWEEN A ROCK AND A HARD PLACE...

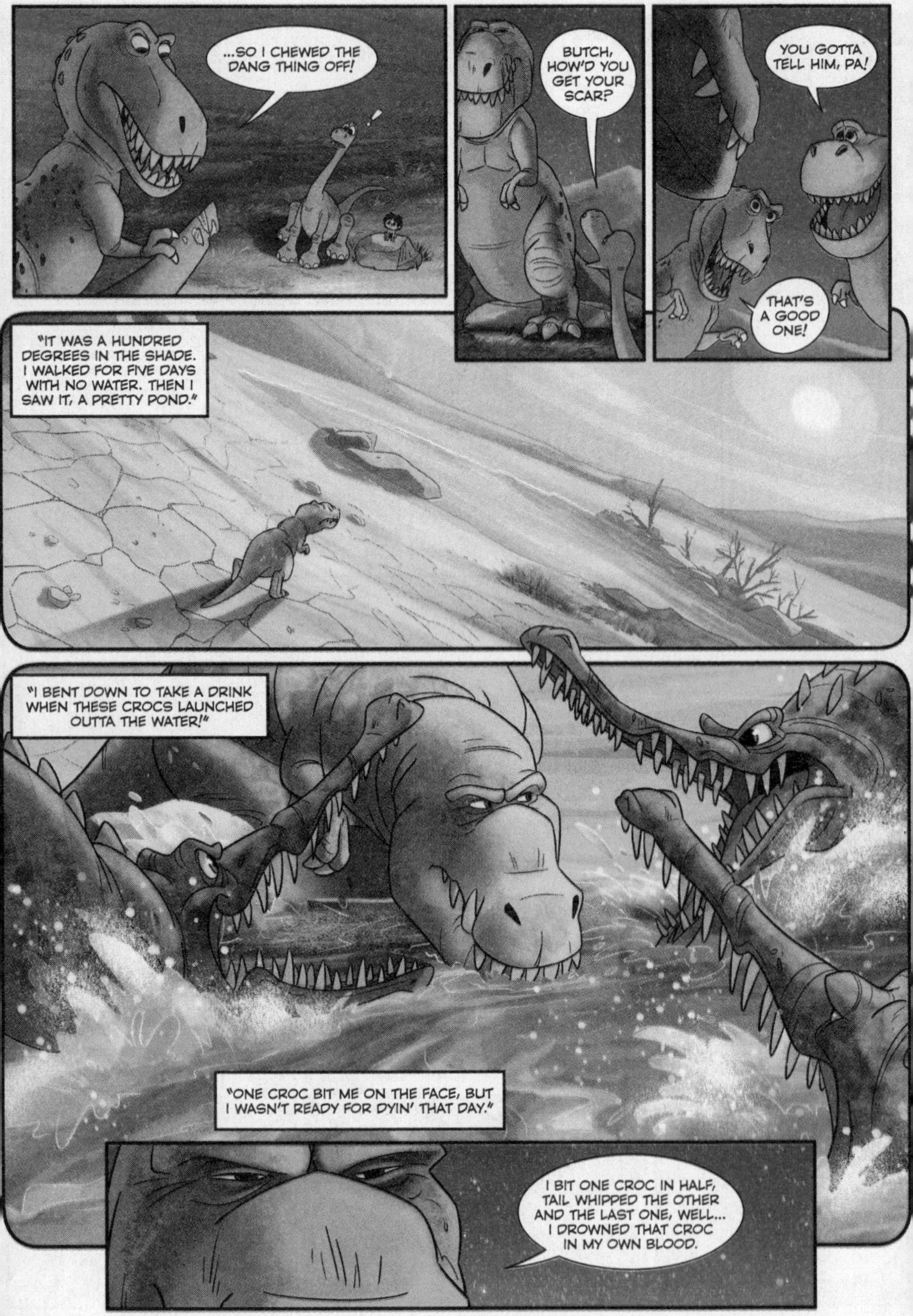

...SO I CHEWED THE DANG THING OFF!
BUTCH, HOW'D YOU GET YOUR SCAR?
YOU GOTTA TELL HIM, PA!
THAT'S A GOOD ONE!
"IT WAS A HUNDRED DEGREES IN THE SHADE. I WALKED FOR FIVE DAYS WITH NO WATER. THEN I SAW IT, A PRETTY POND."
"I BENT DOWN TO TAKE A DRINK WHEN THESE CROCS LAUNCHED OUTTA THE WATER!"
"ONE CROC BIT ME ON THE FACE, BUT I WASN'T READY FOR DYIN' THAT DAY."
I BIT ONE CROC IN HALF, TAIL WHIPPED THE OTHER AND THE LAST ONE, WELL... I DROWNED THAT CROC IN MY OWN BLOOD.

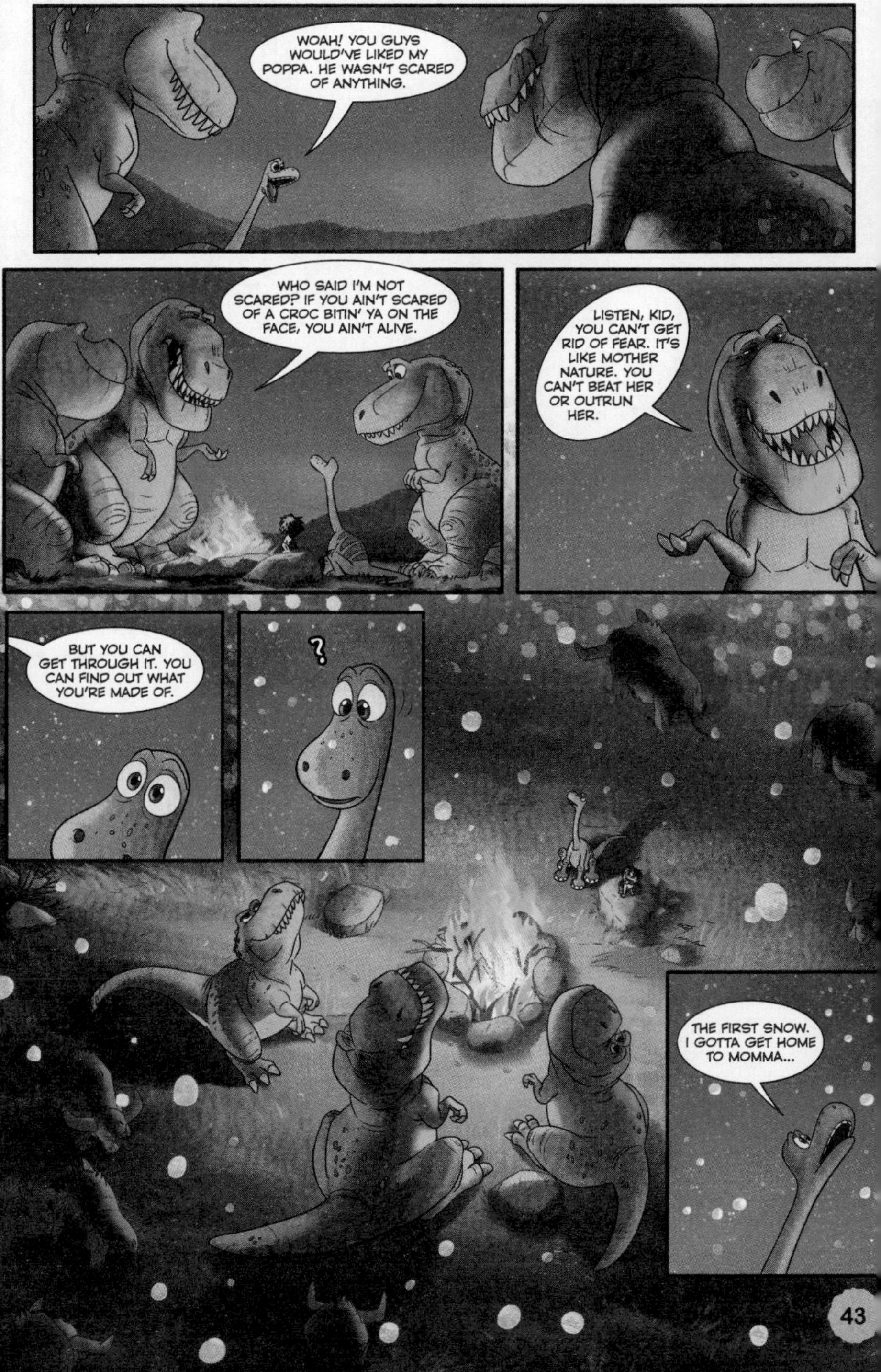
WOAH! YOU GUYS WOULD'VE LIKED MY POPPA. HE WASN'T SCARED OF ANYTHING.
WHO SAID I'M NOT SCARED? IF YOU AIN'T SCARED OF A CROC BITIN' YA ON THE FACE, YOU AIN'T ALIVE.
LISTEN, KID, YOU CAN'T GET RID OF FEAR. IT'S LIKE MOTHER NATURE. YOU CAN'T BEAT HER OR OUTRUN HER.
BUT YOU CAN GET THROUGH IT. YOU CAN FIND OUT WHAT YOU'RE MADE OF.
?
THE FIRST SNOW. I GOTTA GET HOME TO MOMMA...

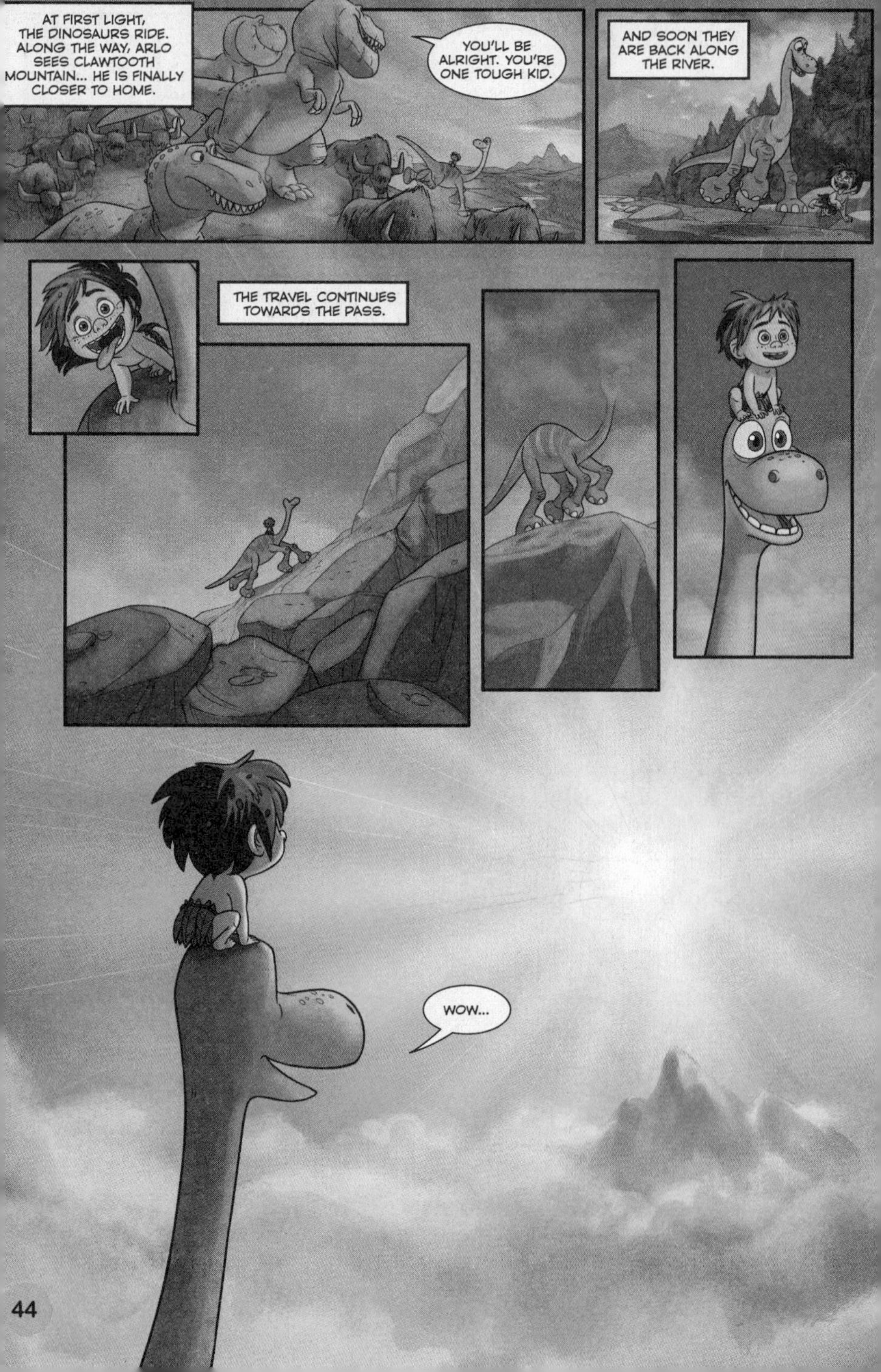
AT FIRST LIGHT, THE DINOSAURS RIDE. ALONG THE WAY, ARLO SEES CLAWTOOTH MOUNTAIN... HE IS FINALLY CLOSER TO HOME.
YOU'LL BE ALRIGHT. YOU'RE ONE TOUGH KID.
AND SOON THEY ARE BACK ALONG THE RIVER.
THE TRAVEL CONTINUES TOWARDS THE PASS.
WOW...

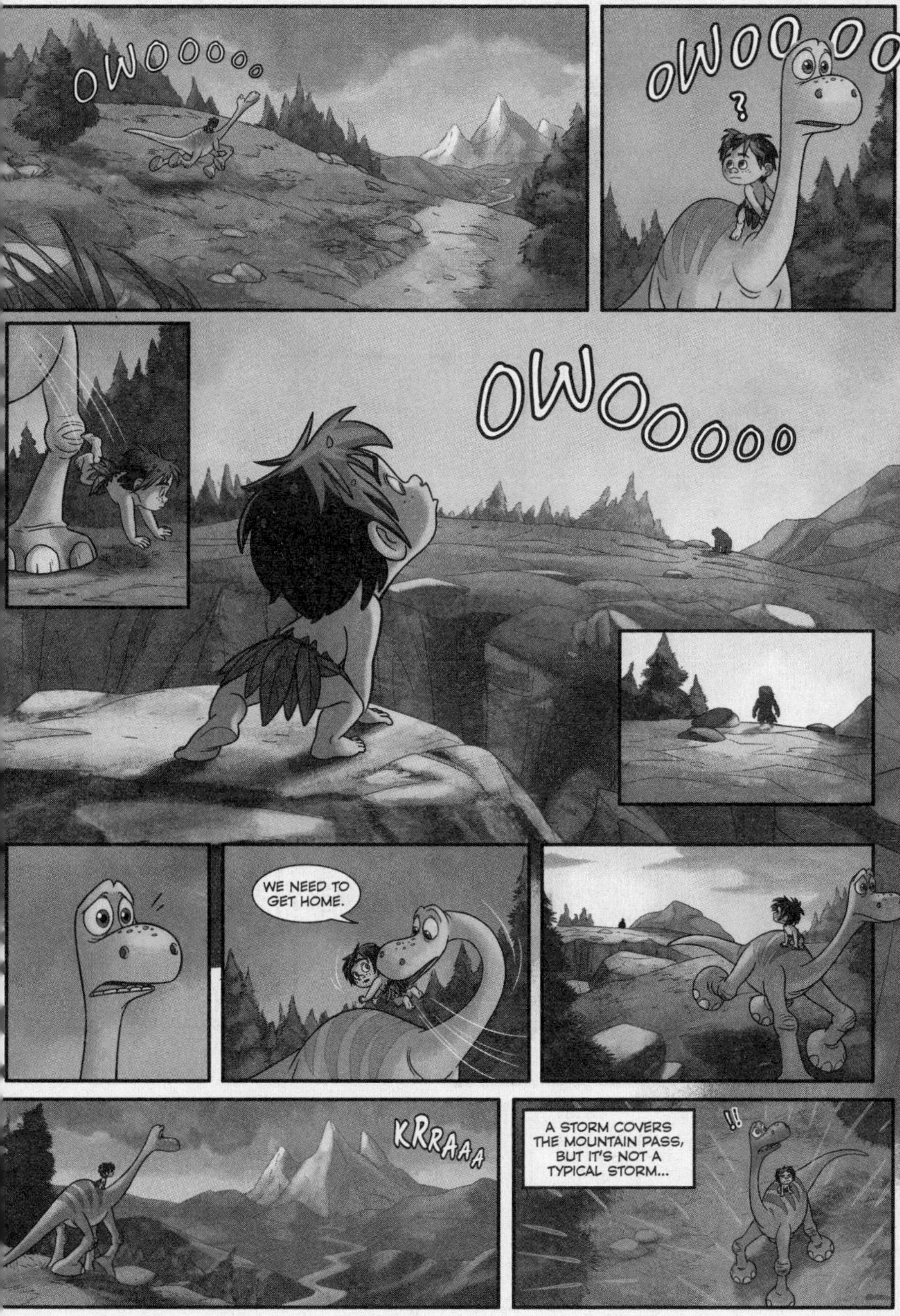
OWOOOOO
OWOO OO
?
OWOOOOOO
WE NEED TO GET HOME.
KRRAAA
A STORM COVERS THE MOUNTAIN PASS, BUT IT'S NOT A TYPICAL STORM...
!!

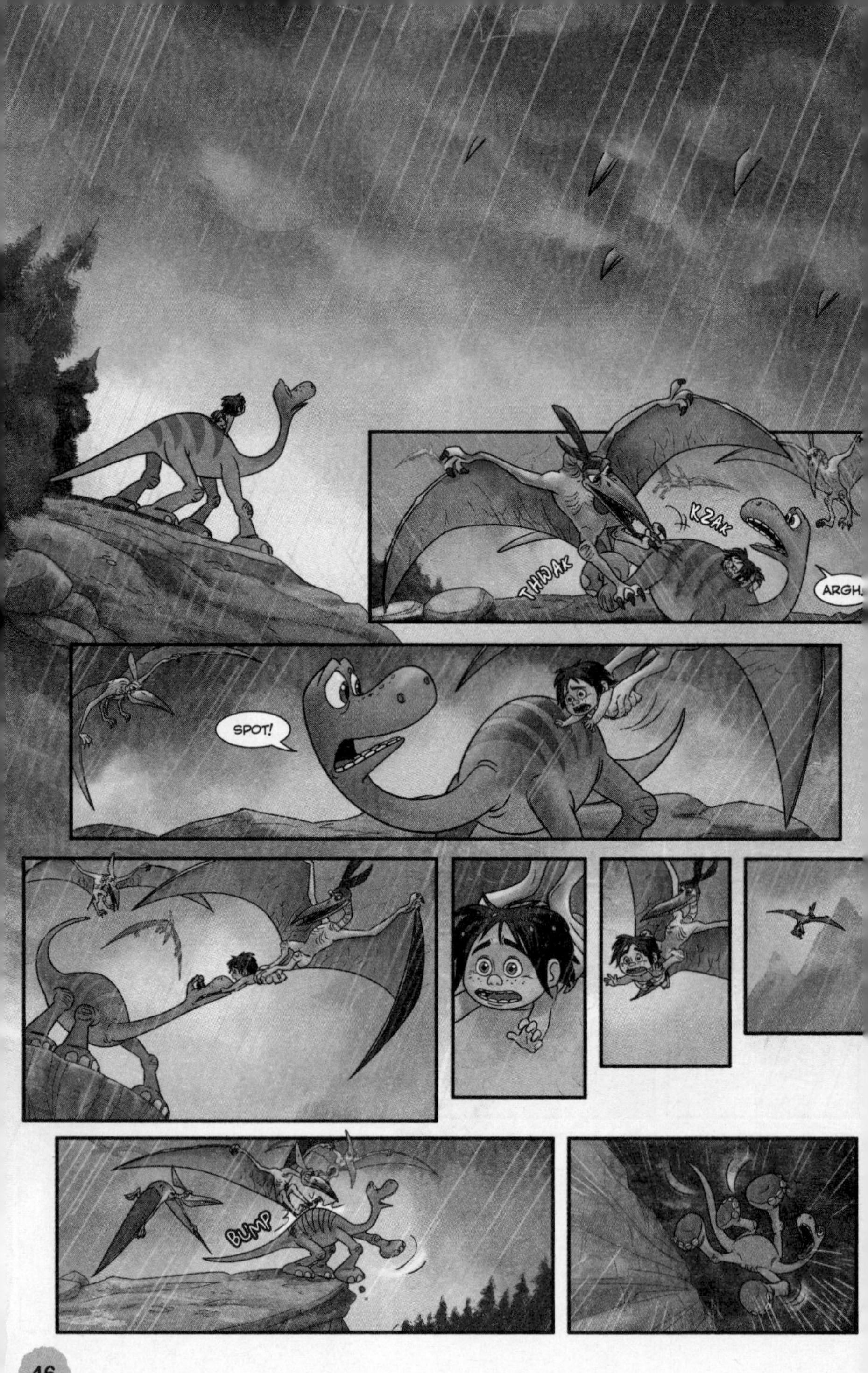
THWAK
KZAK
ARGH
SPOT!
BUMP

FRRUSH

SPOT!

BUT SPOT IS GONE. THE PTERODACTYL TOOK HIM AWAY...

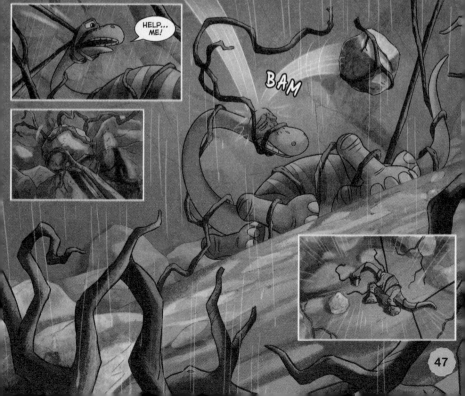

HELP... ME!

BAM

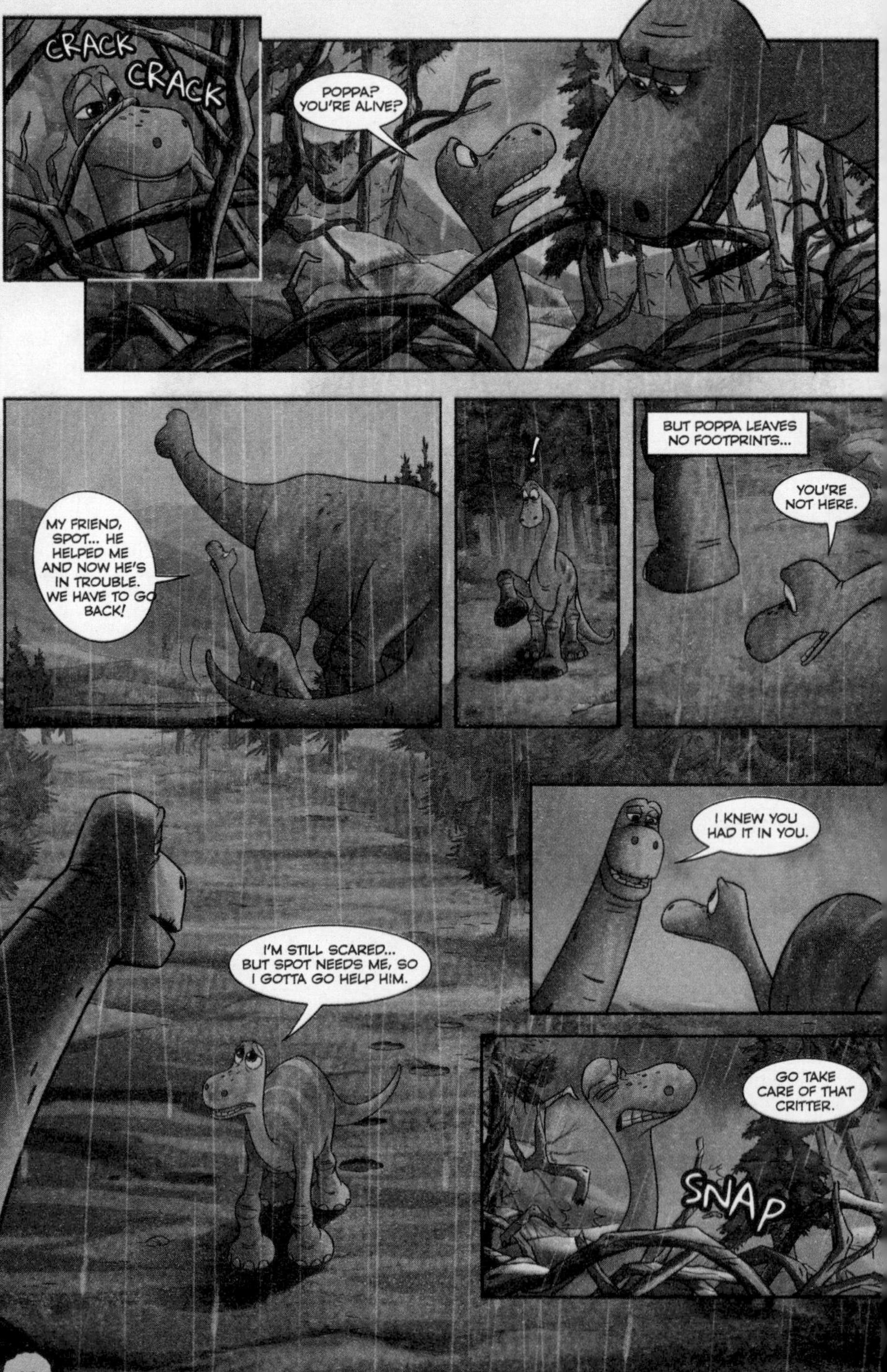
CRACK
CRACK
POPPA? YOU'RE ALIVE?
MY FRIEND, SPOT... HE HELPED ME AND NOW HE'S IN TROUBLE. WE HAVE TO GO BACK!
!
BUT POPPA LEAVES NO FOOTPRINTS...
YOU'RE NOT HERE.
I'M STILL SCARED... BUT SPOT NEEDS ME, SO I GOTTA GO HELP HIM.
I KNEW YOU HAD IT IN YOU.
GO TAKE CARE OF THAT CRITTER.
SNAP

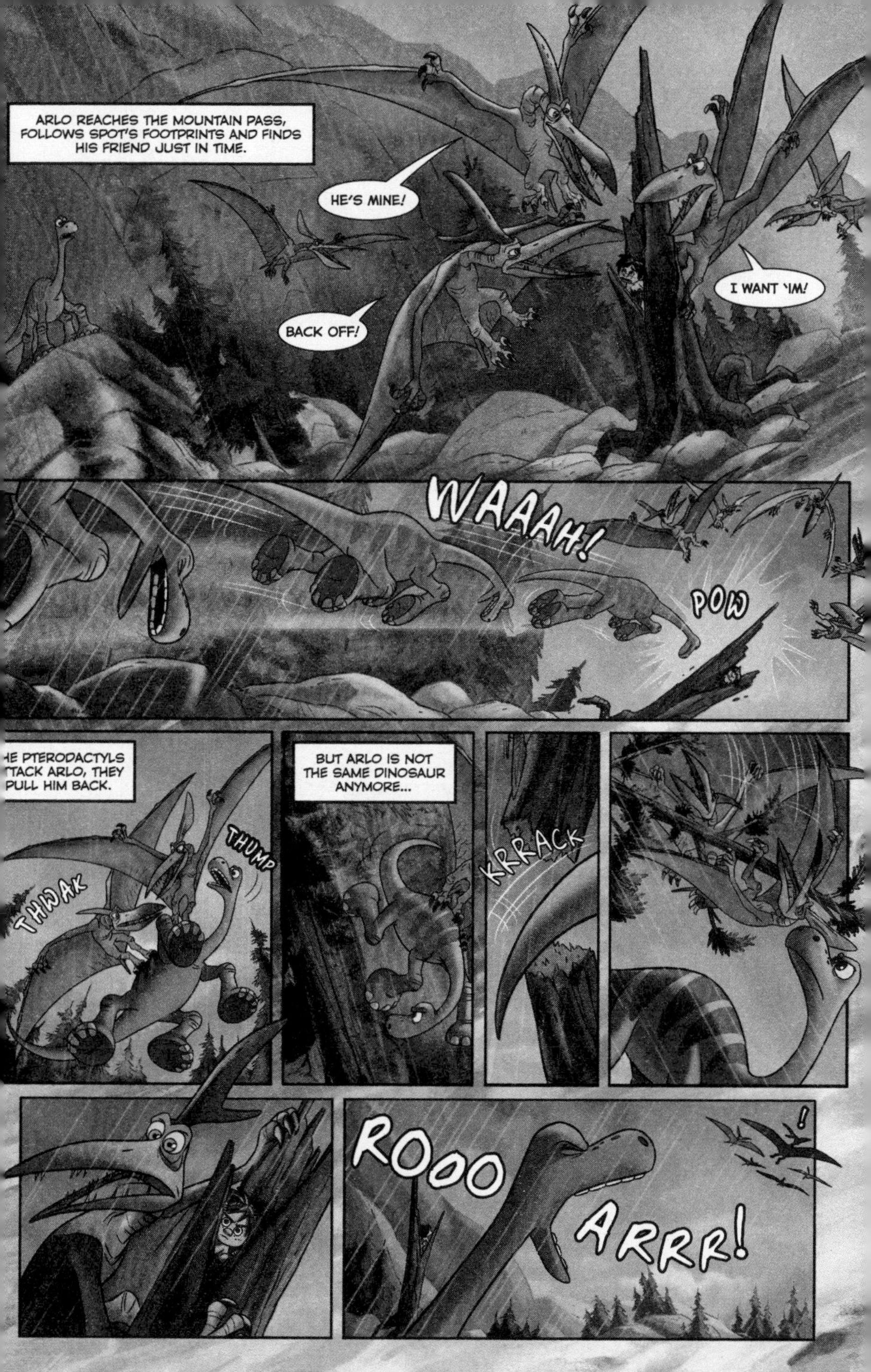
ARLO REACHES THE MOUNTAIN PASS, FOLLOWS SPOT'S FOOTPRINTS AND FINDS HIS FRIEND JUST IN TIME.
HE'S MINE!
I WANT 'IM!
BACK OFF!
WAAAAH!
POW
HE PTERODACTYLS TTACK ARLO, THEY PULL HIM BACK.
THUMP
THWAK
BUT ARLO IS NOT THE SAME DINOSAUR ANYMORE...
KRRACK
!
ROOO ARRR!

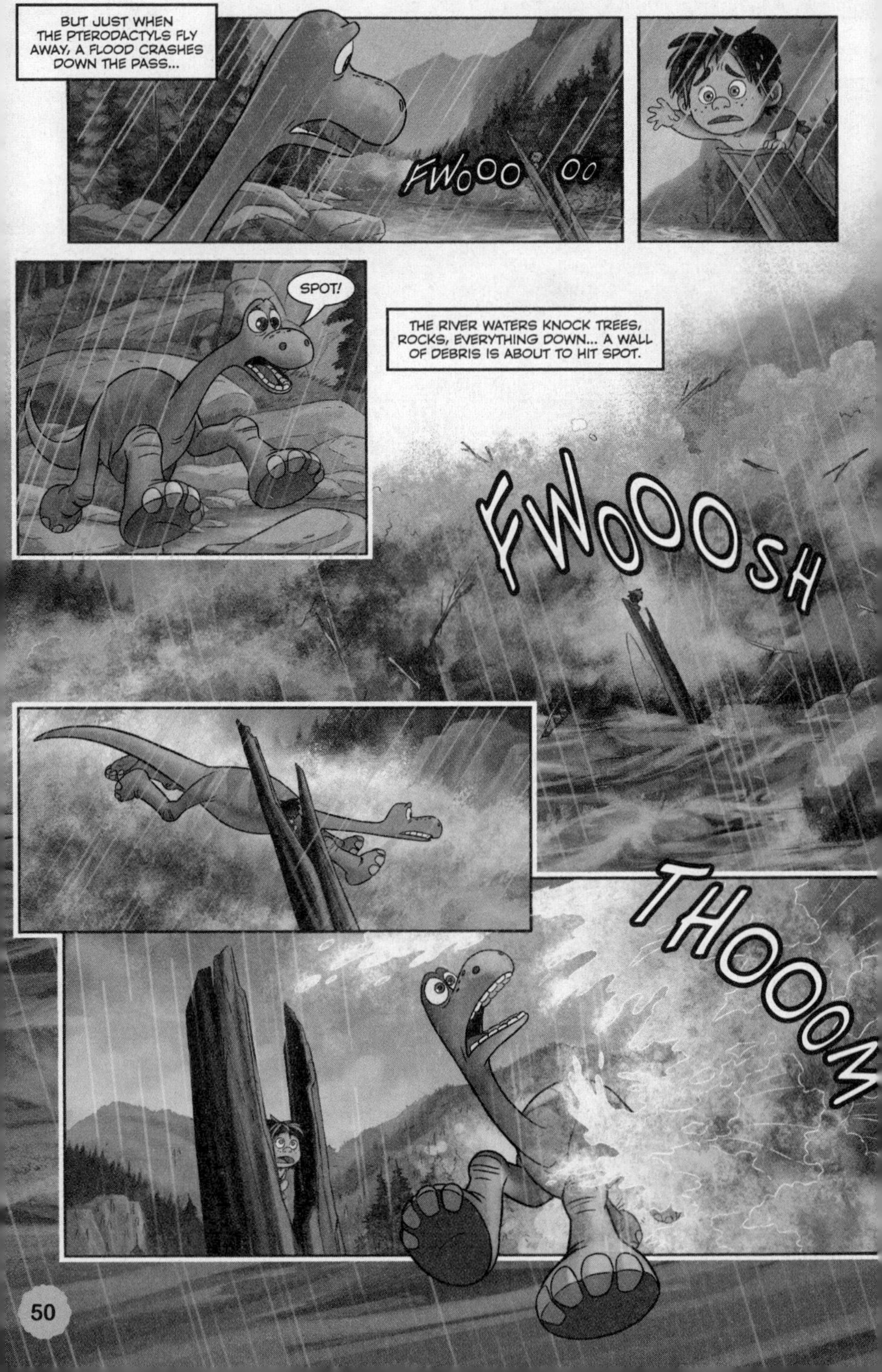
BUT JUST WHEN THE PTERODACTYLS FLY AWAY, A FLOOD CRASHES DOWN THE PASS...
FWOOO OO
SPOT!
THE RIVER WATERS KNOCK TREES, ROCKS, EVERYTHING DOWN... A WALL OF DEBRIS IS ABOUT TO HIT SPOT.
FWOOOSH
THOOOM

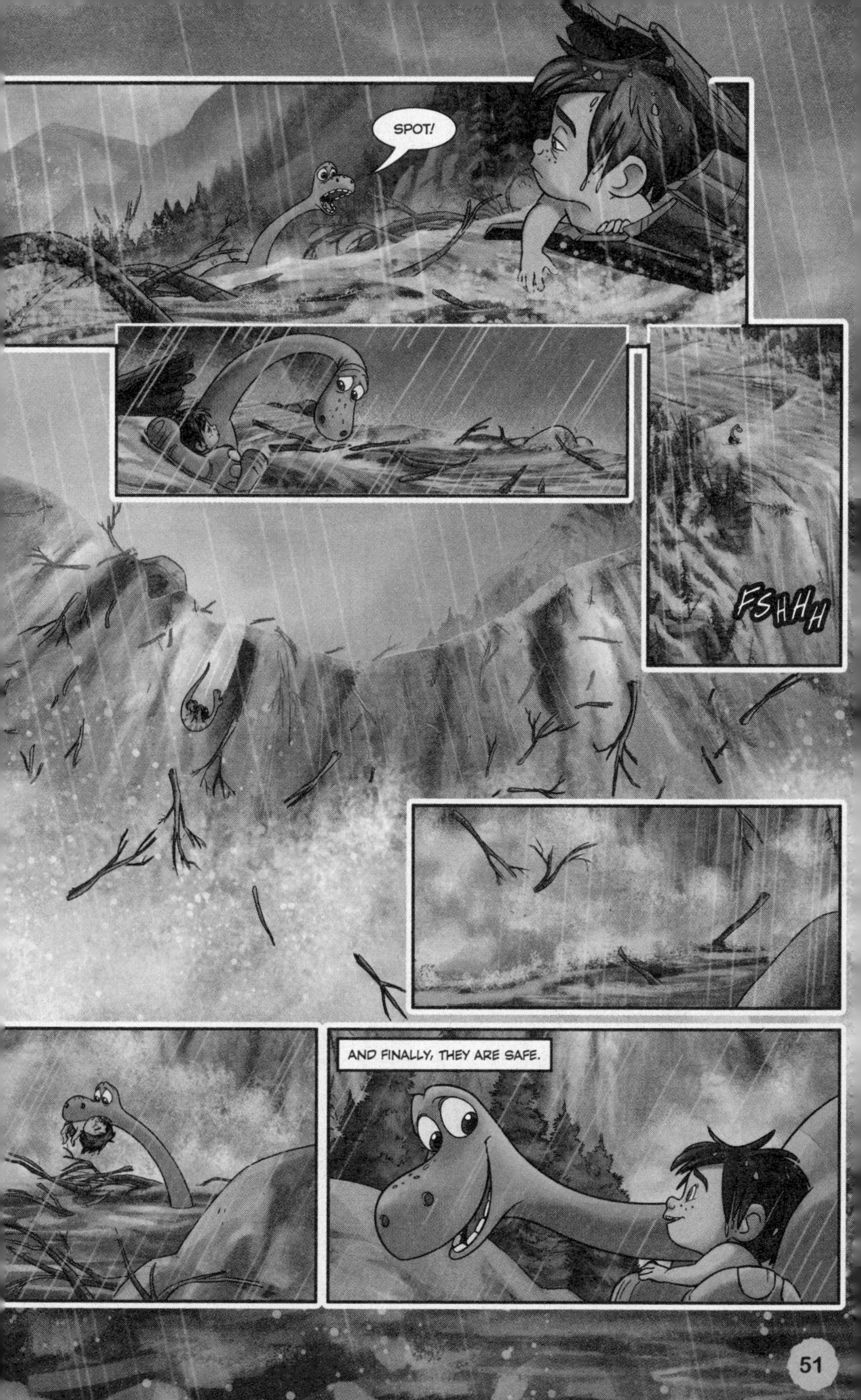
SPOT!
FSHHH
AND FINALLY, THEY ARE SAFE.

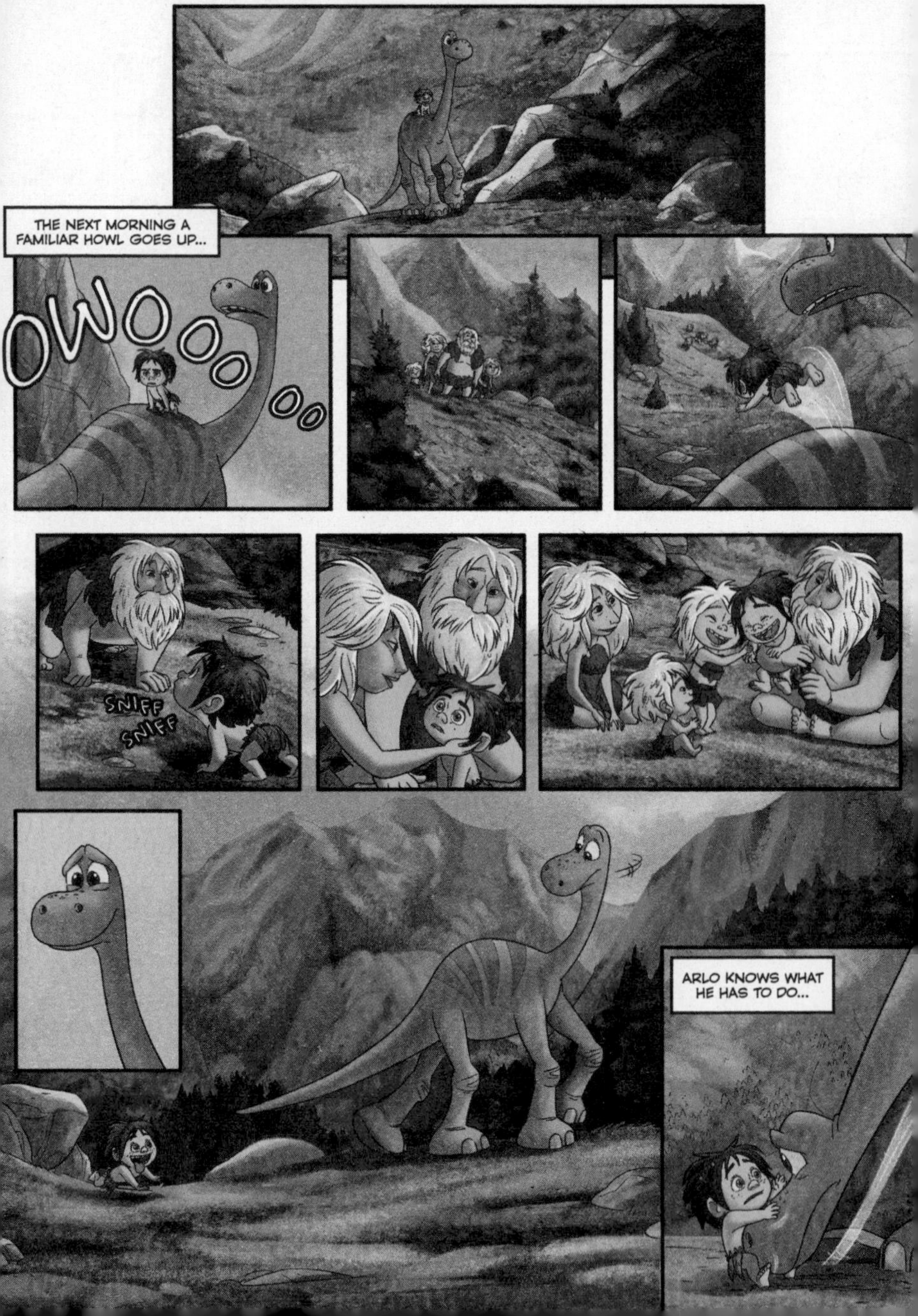
THE NEXT MORNING A FAMILIAR HOWL GOES UP...
OWOOOOOO
SNIFF SNIFF
ARLO KNOWS WHAT HE HAS TO DO...

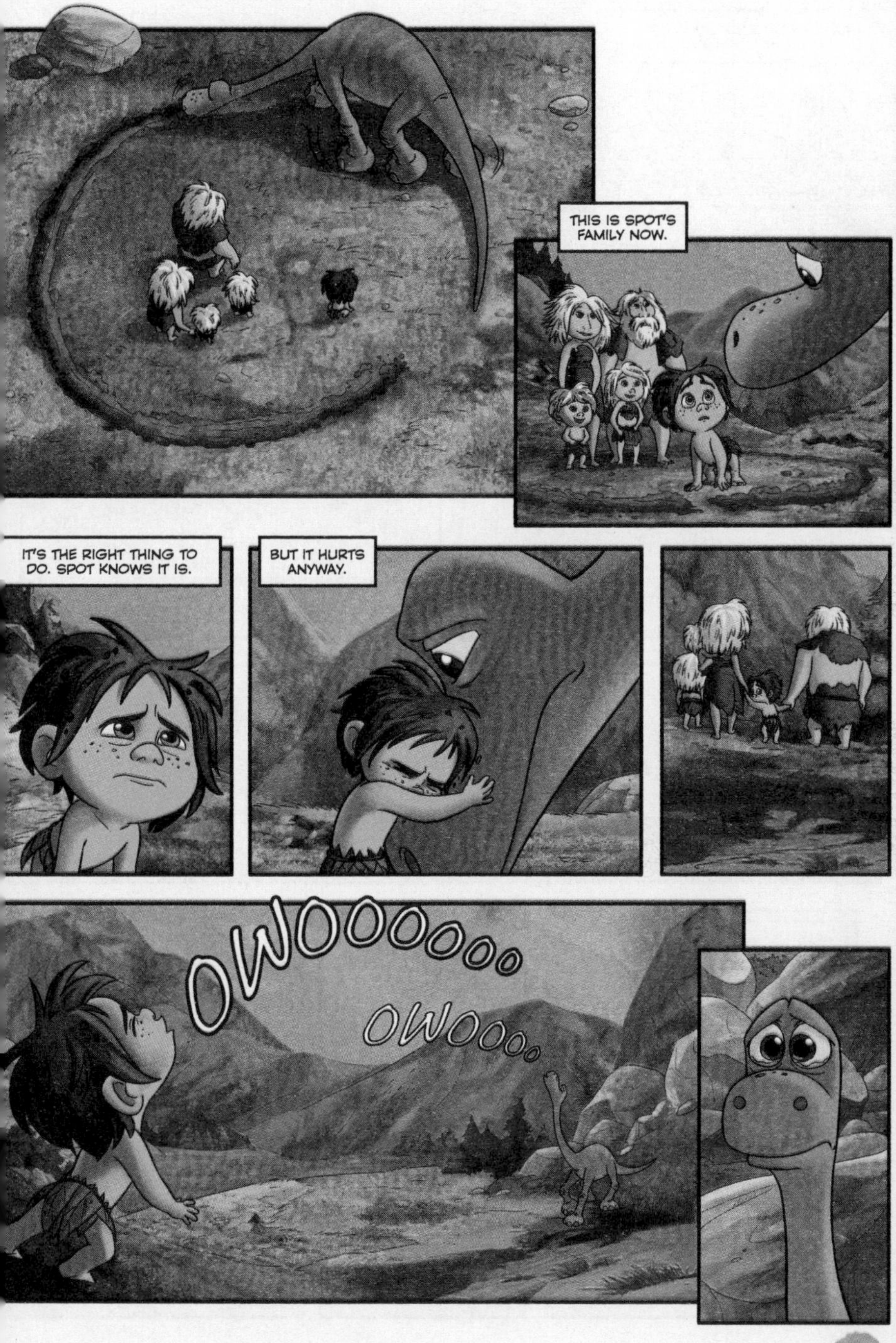
THIS IS SPOT'S FAMILY NOW.
IT'S THE RIGHT THING TO DO. SPOT KNOWS IT IS.
BUT IT HURTS ANYWAY.
OWOOOOOO
OWOOOO

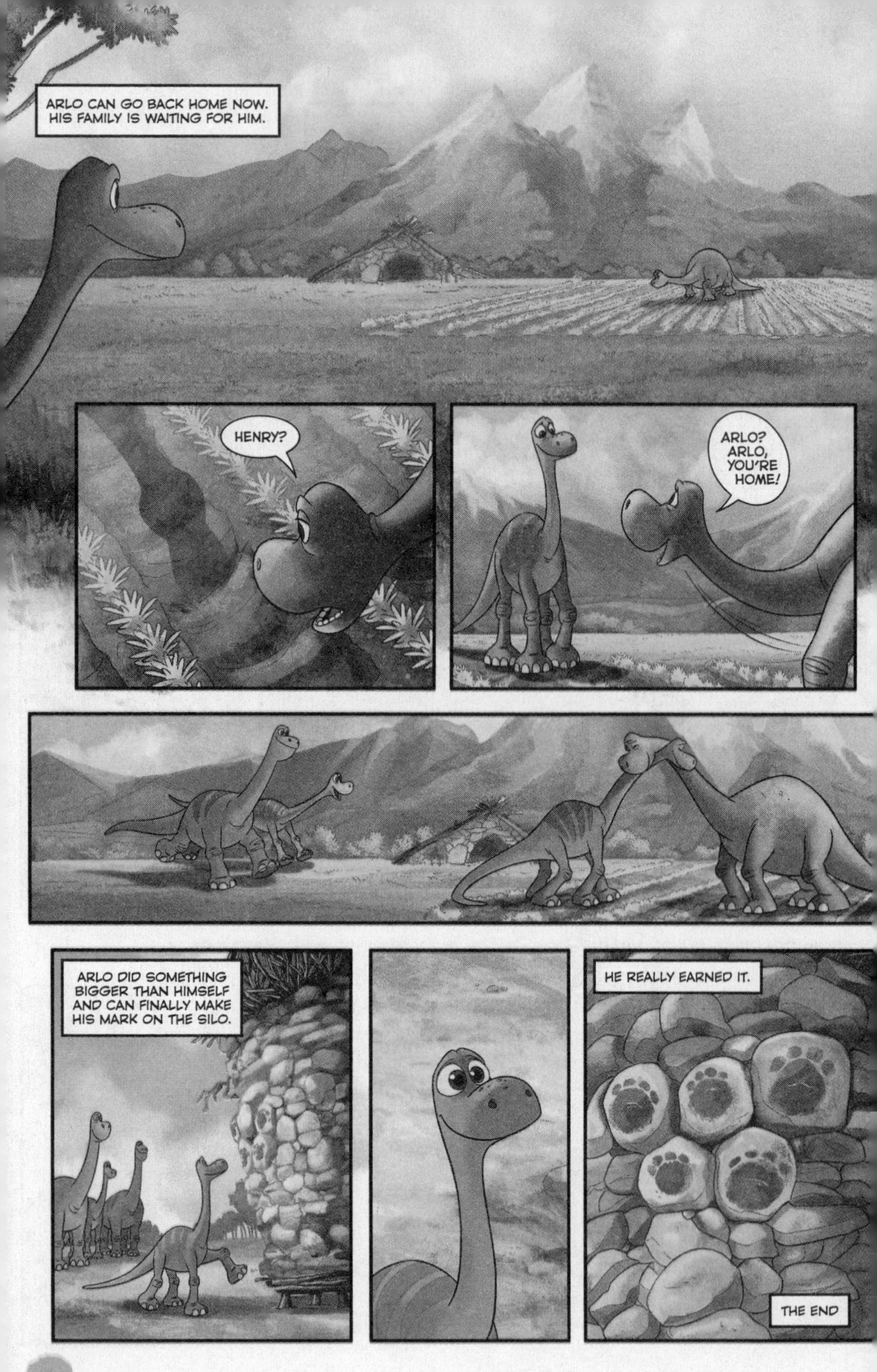
ARLO CAN GO BACK HOME NOW. HIS FAMILY IS WAITING FOR HIM.
HENRY?
ARLO? ARLO, YOU'RE HOME!
ARLO DID SOMETHING BIGGER THAN HIMSELF AND CAN FINALLY MAKE HIS MARK ON THE SILO.
HE REALLY EARNED IT.
THE END

Disney · PIXAR

THE GOOD DINOSAUR

the Graphic Novel

Manuscript Adaptation
Alessandro Ferrari
Layout
Denise Shimabukuro
Cleanup
Andrea Greppi, Veronica di Lorenzo
Paint
Angela Capolupo, Gregor Krysinski, Livio Cacciatore, Ludmila Steblyanko, Andrea Cagol
Editorial Pages
co-d S.r.l. - Milano
Pre-Press
Edizioni BD S.R.L.
Special Thanks To
Kelsey Mann, Matt Nolte, Margo Zimmerman, Melissa Bernabei, Kelly Bonbright, Elena Maria Naggi, Amy Novesky, Carlo Resca, Shiho Tilley, Scott Tilley, Laura Uyeda

DISNEY PUBLISHING WORLDWIDE
Global Magazines, Comics and PartWorks
Publisher
Gianfranco Cordara
Editorial Director
Bianca Coletti
Editorial Team
Guido Frazzini (Director, Comics), Stefano Ambrosio (Executive Editor, New IP), Carlotta Quattrocolo (Executive Editor, Franchise), Camilla Vedove (Senior Manager, Editorial Development), Behnoosh Khalili (Senior Editor), Julie Dorris (Senior Editor)
Design
Enrico Soave (Senior Designer)
Art
Ken Shue (VP, Global Art), Roberto Santillo (Creative Director), Marco Ghiglione (Creative Manager), Stefano Attardi (Computer Art Designer)
Portfolio Management
Olivia Ciancarelli (Director)
Business & Marketing
Mariantonietta Galla (Marketing Manager), Virpi Korhonen (Editorial Manager), Kristen Ginter (Publishing Coordinator)

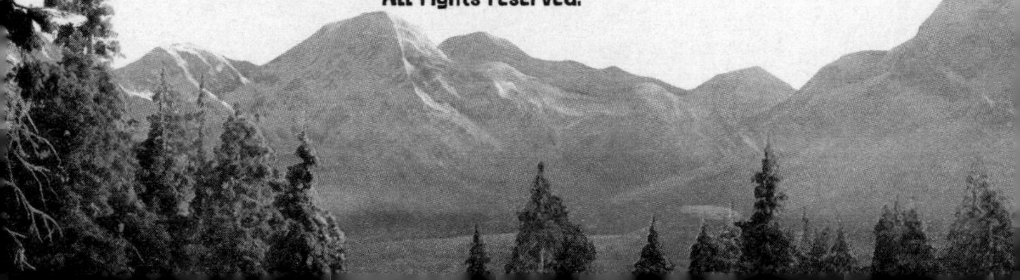

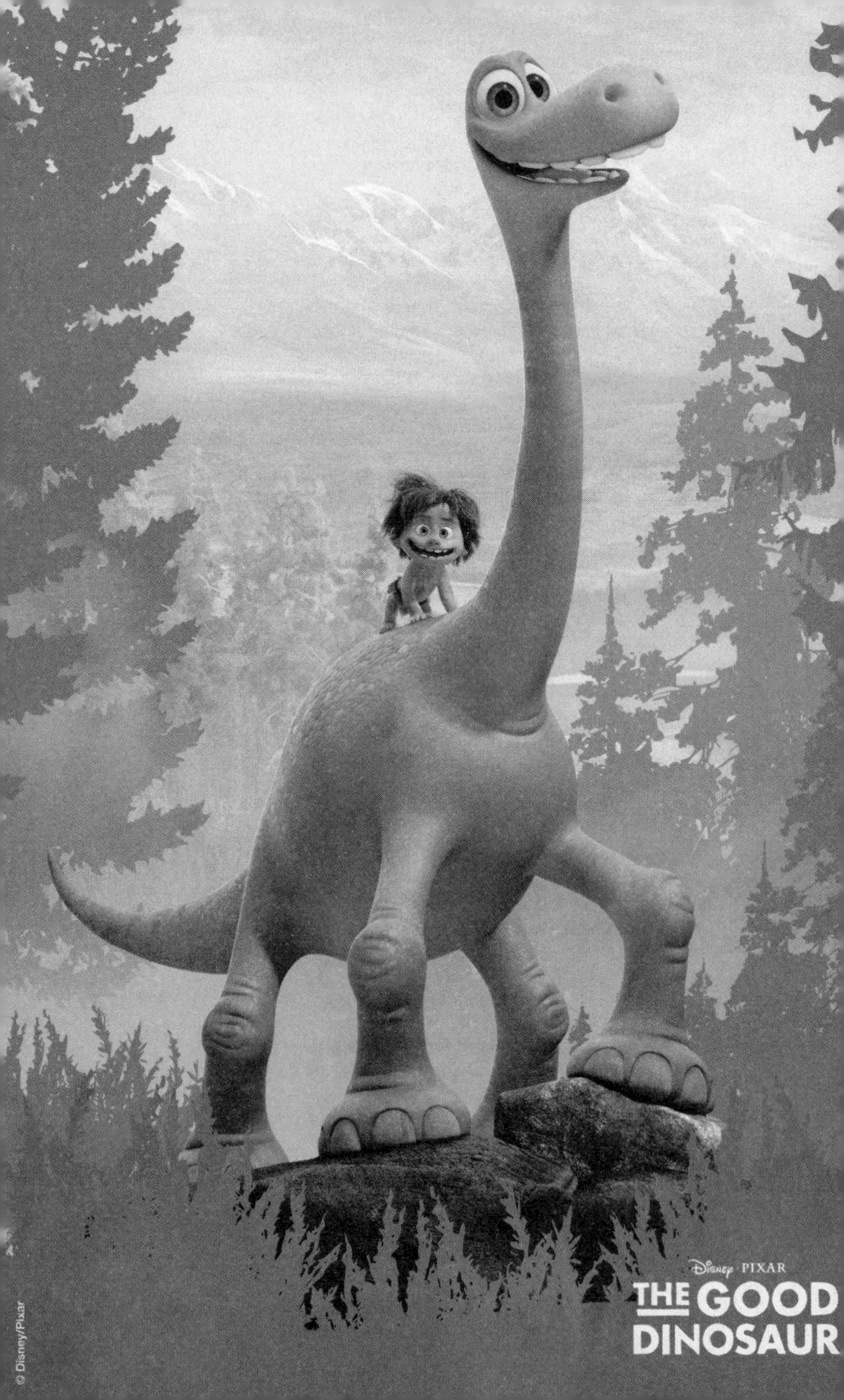
Disney · PIXAR
THE GOOD DINOSAUR
© Disney/Pixar

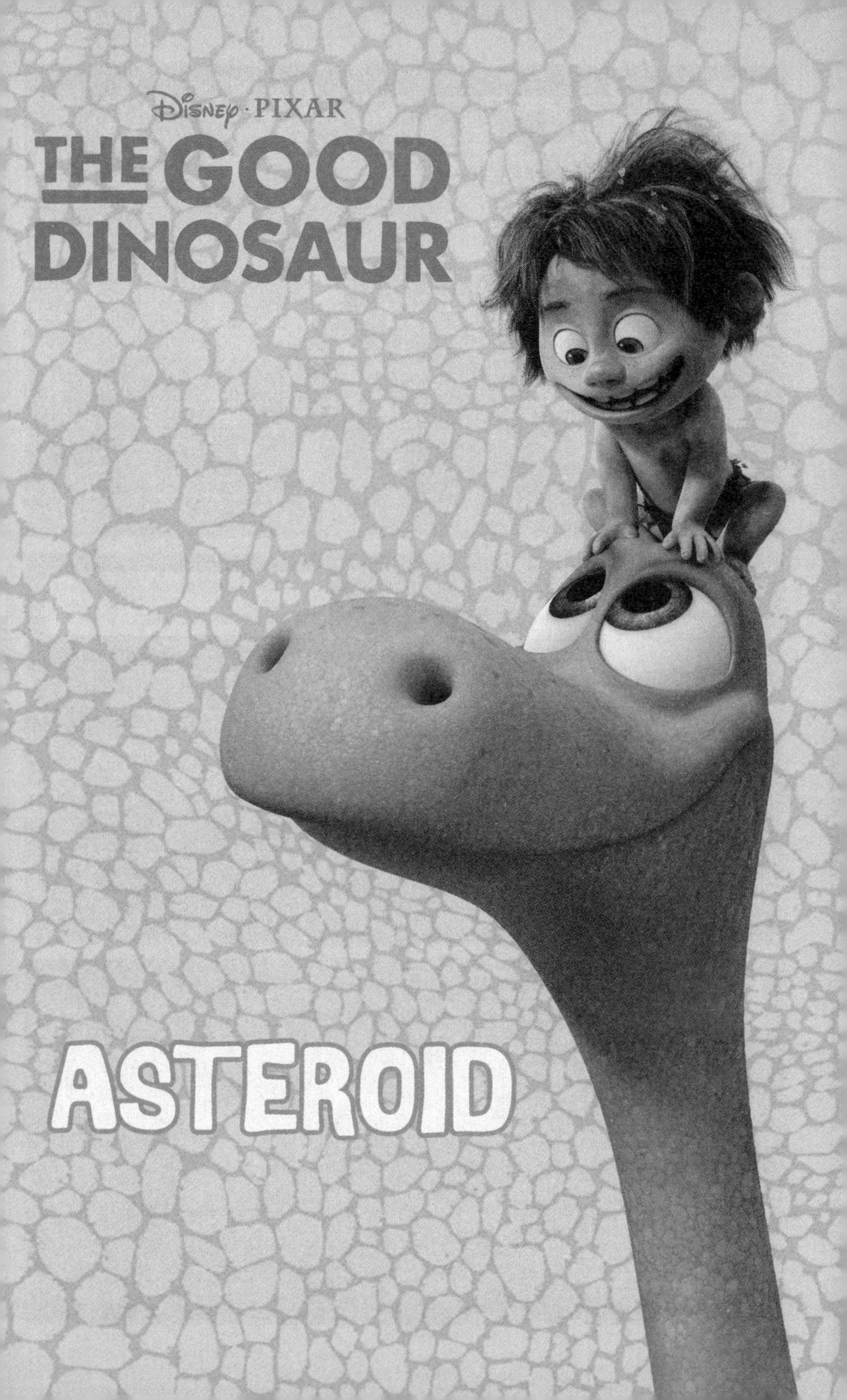
Disney · PIXAR
THE GOOD DINOSAUR
ASTEROID

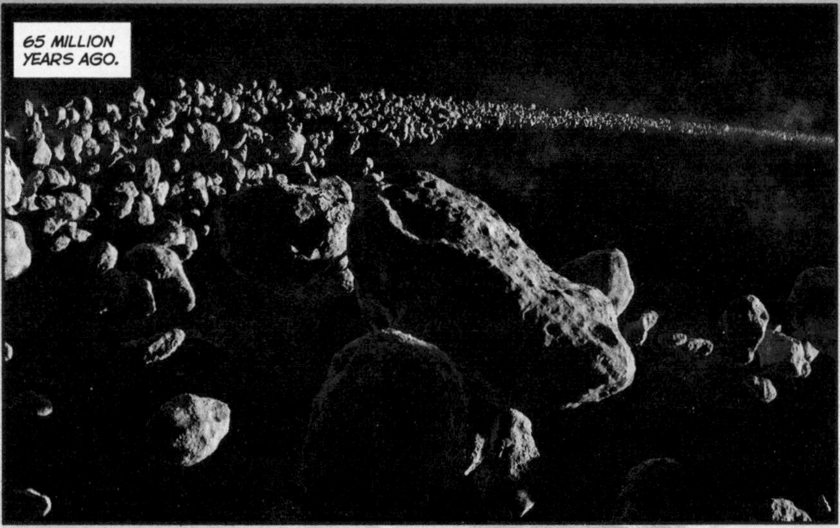
65 MILLION YEARS AGO.

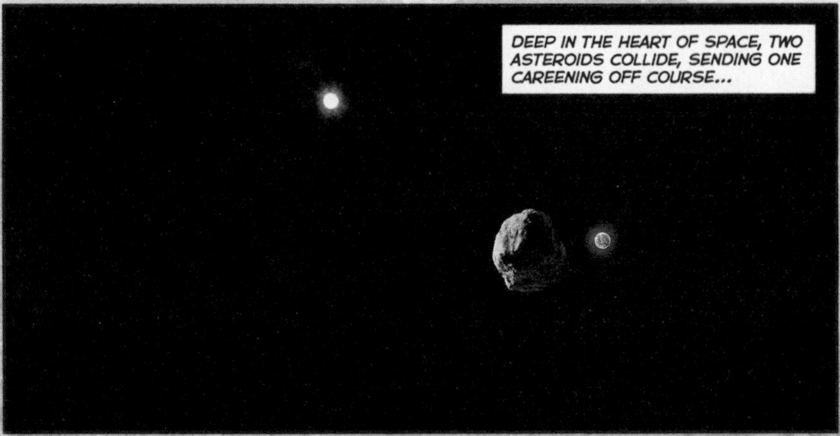
DEEP IN THE HEART OF SPACE, TWO ASTEROIDS COLLIDE, SENDING ONE CAREENING OFF COURSE...

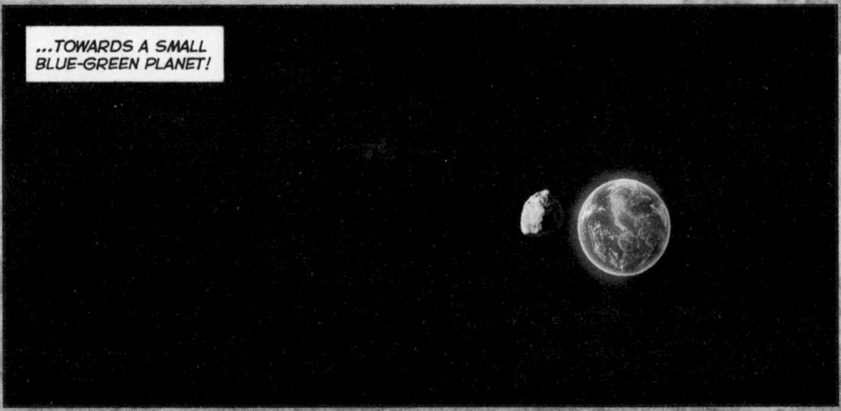
...TOWARDS A SMALL BLUE-GREEN PLANET!

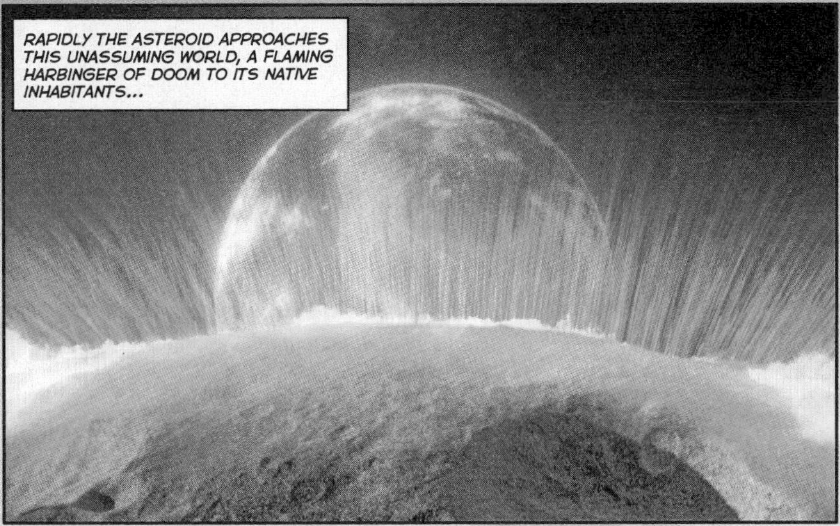
RAPIDLY THE ASTEROID APPROACHES THIS UNASSUMING WORLD, A FLAMING HARBINGER OF DOOM TO ITS NATIVE INHABITANTS...

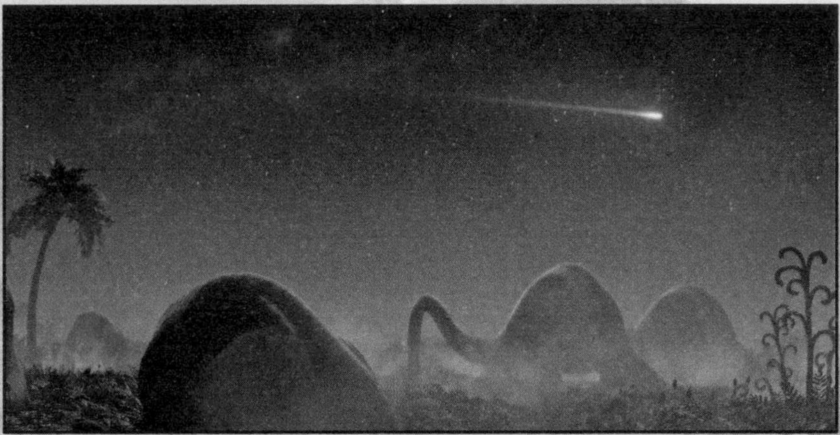

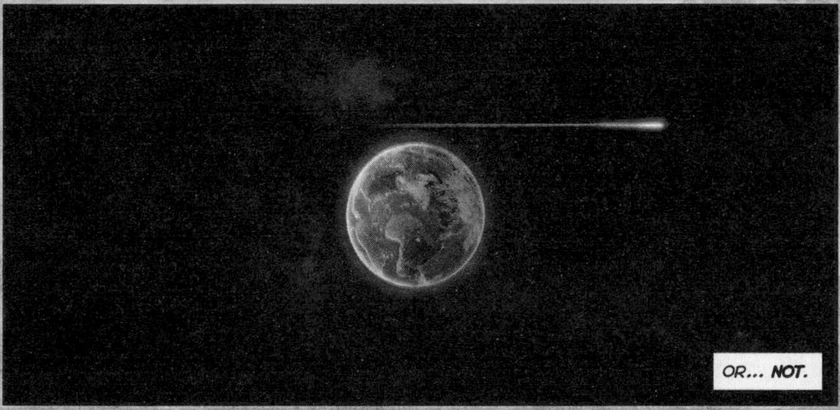
OR... NOT.

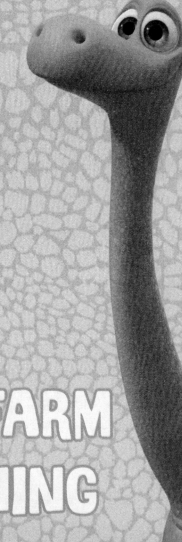

Disney · PIXAR
THE GOOD DINOSAUR

THE FARM
OPENING

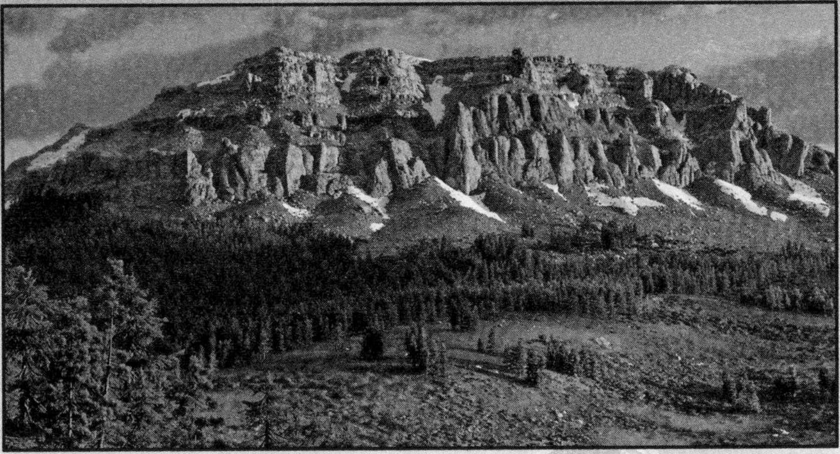

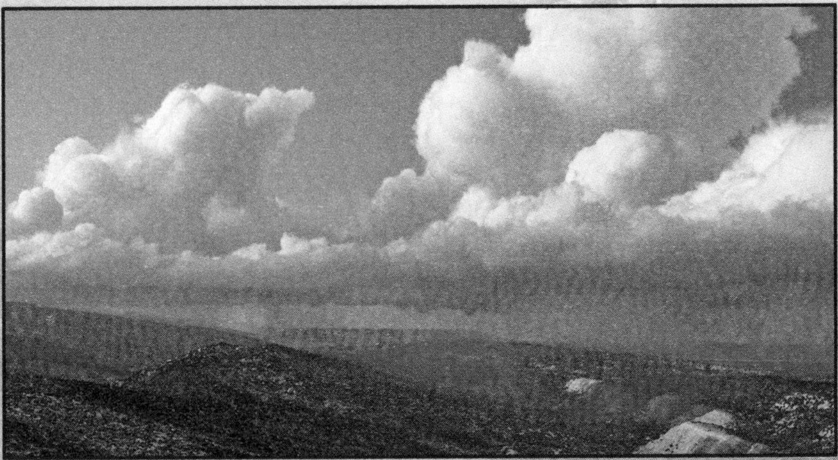

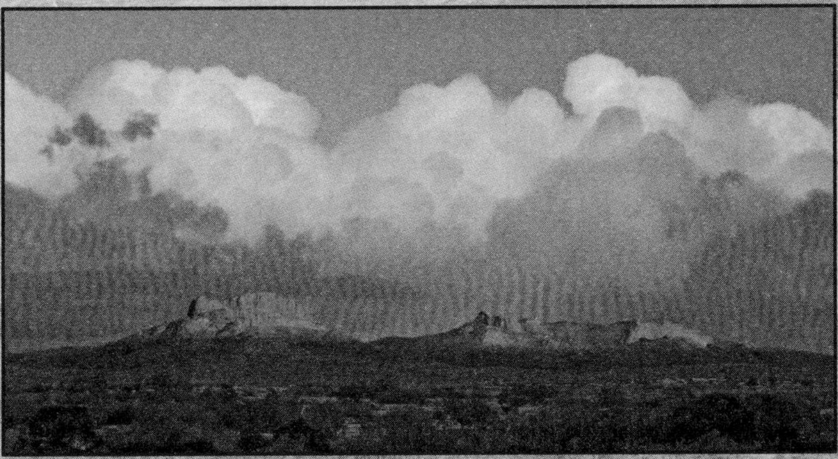

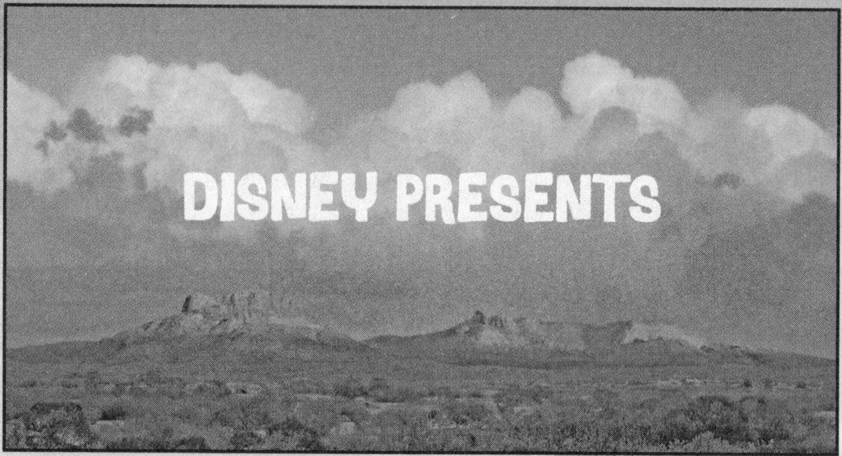
DISNEY PRESENTS

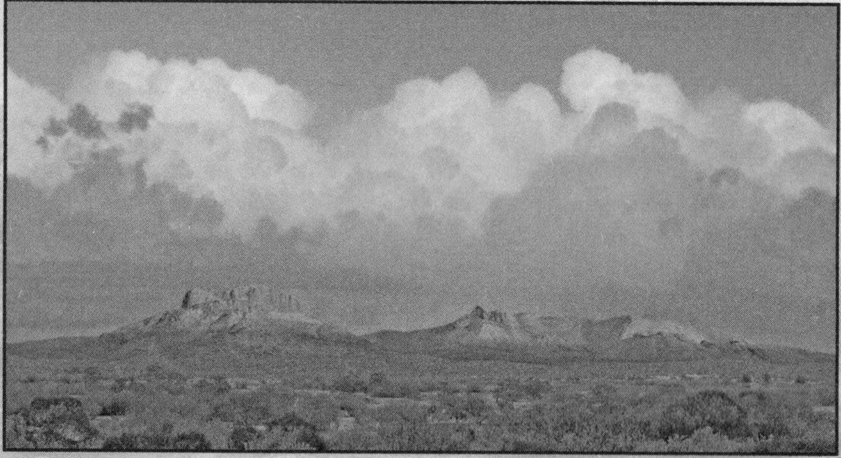

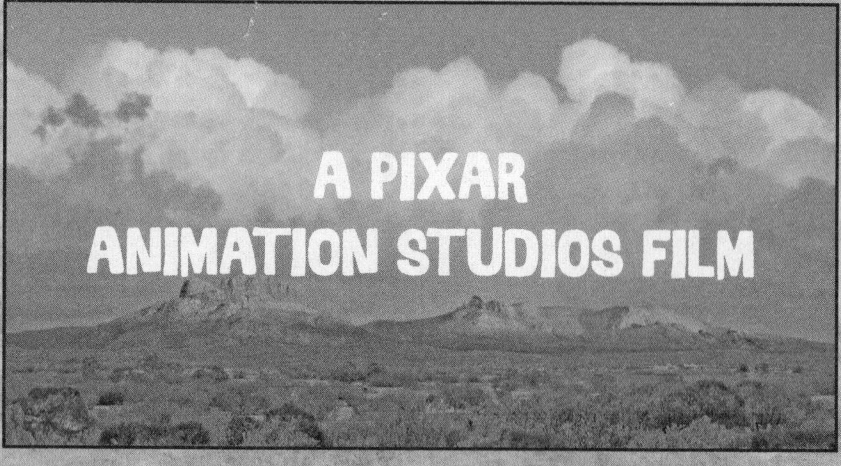
A PIXAR
ANIMATION STUDIOS FILM

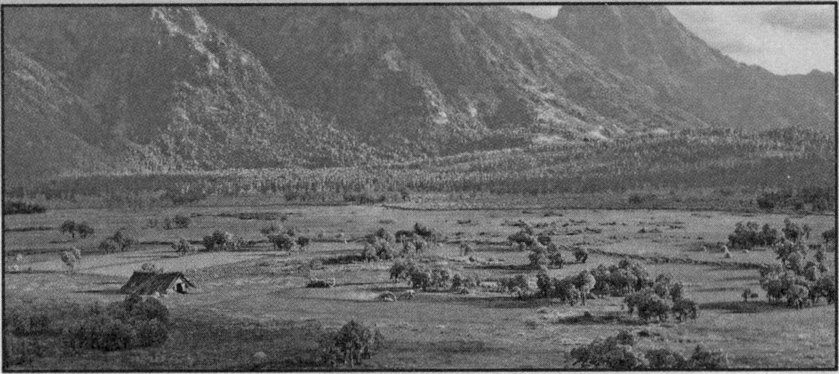

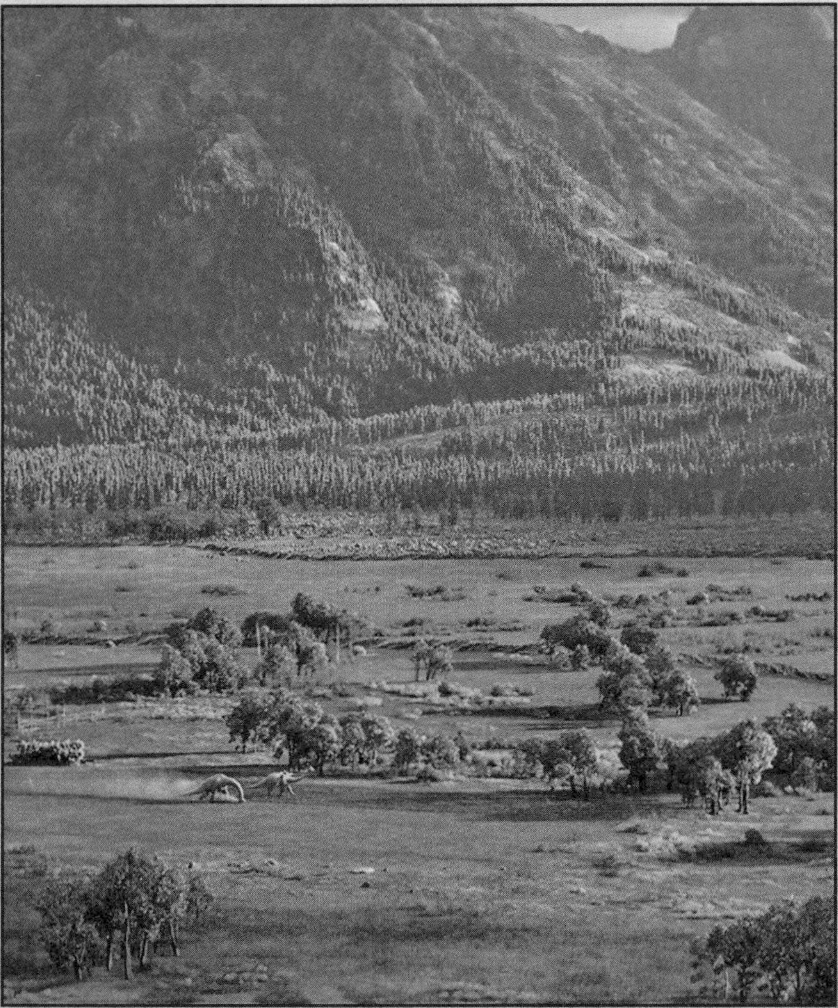

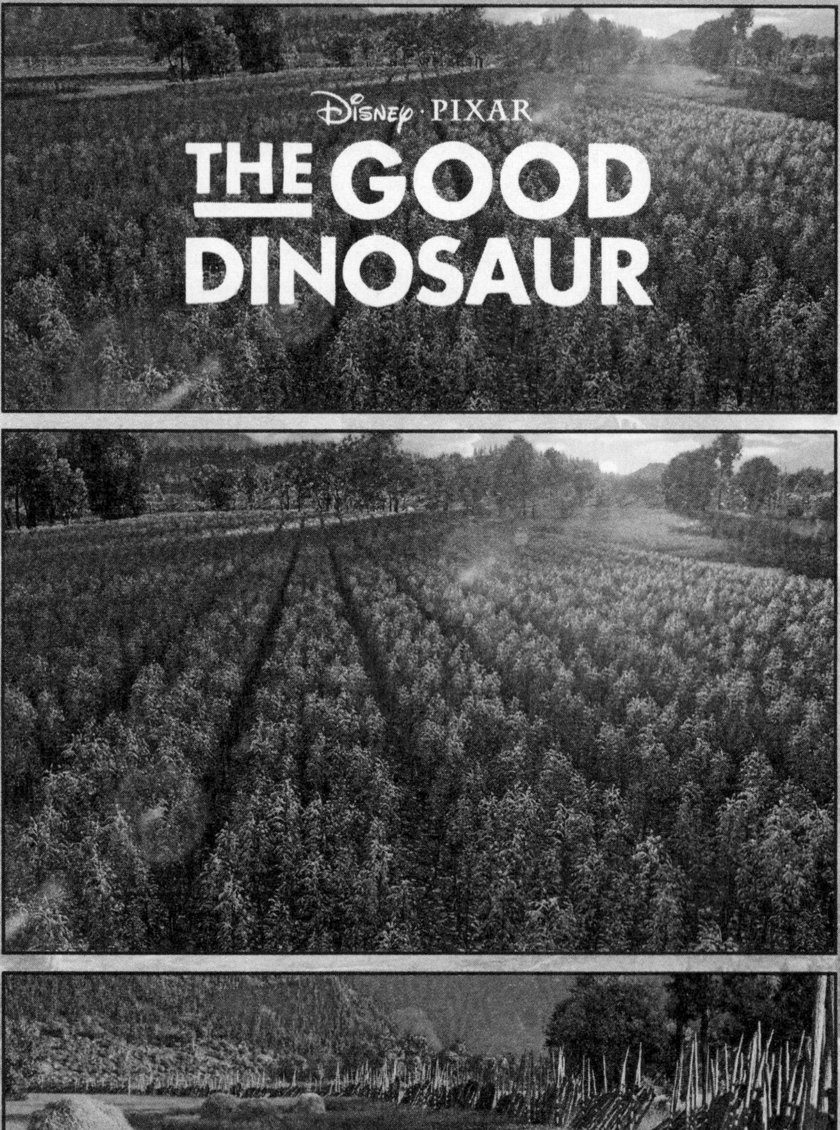
Disney · PIXAR
THE GOOD DINOSAUR

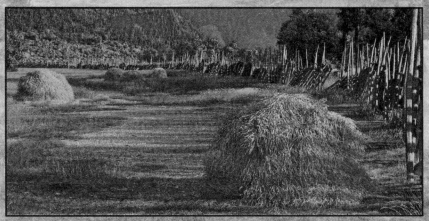

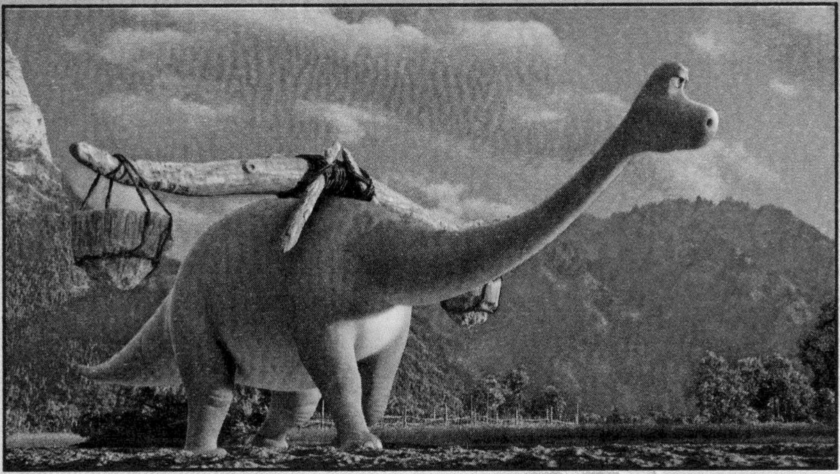

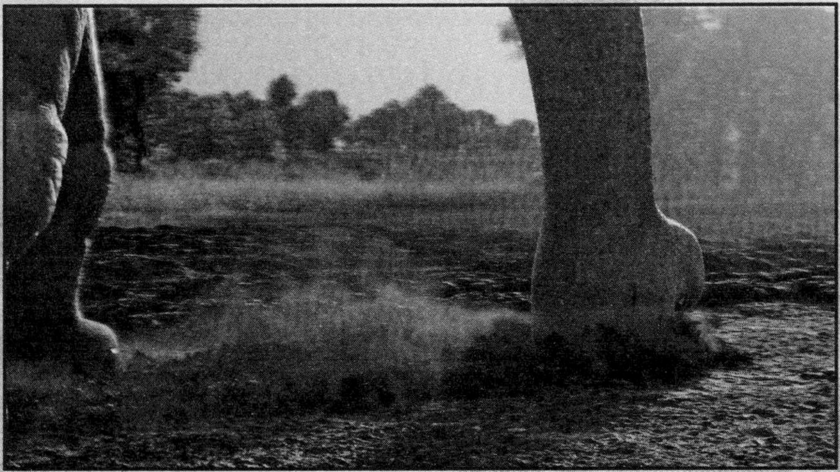

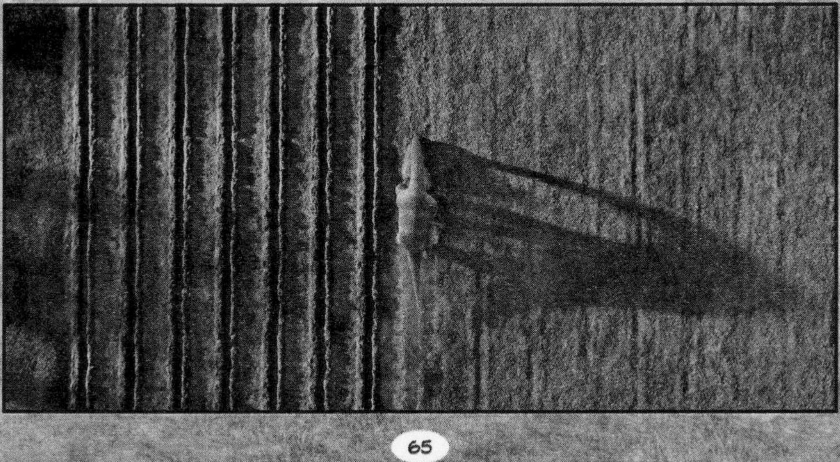

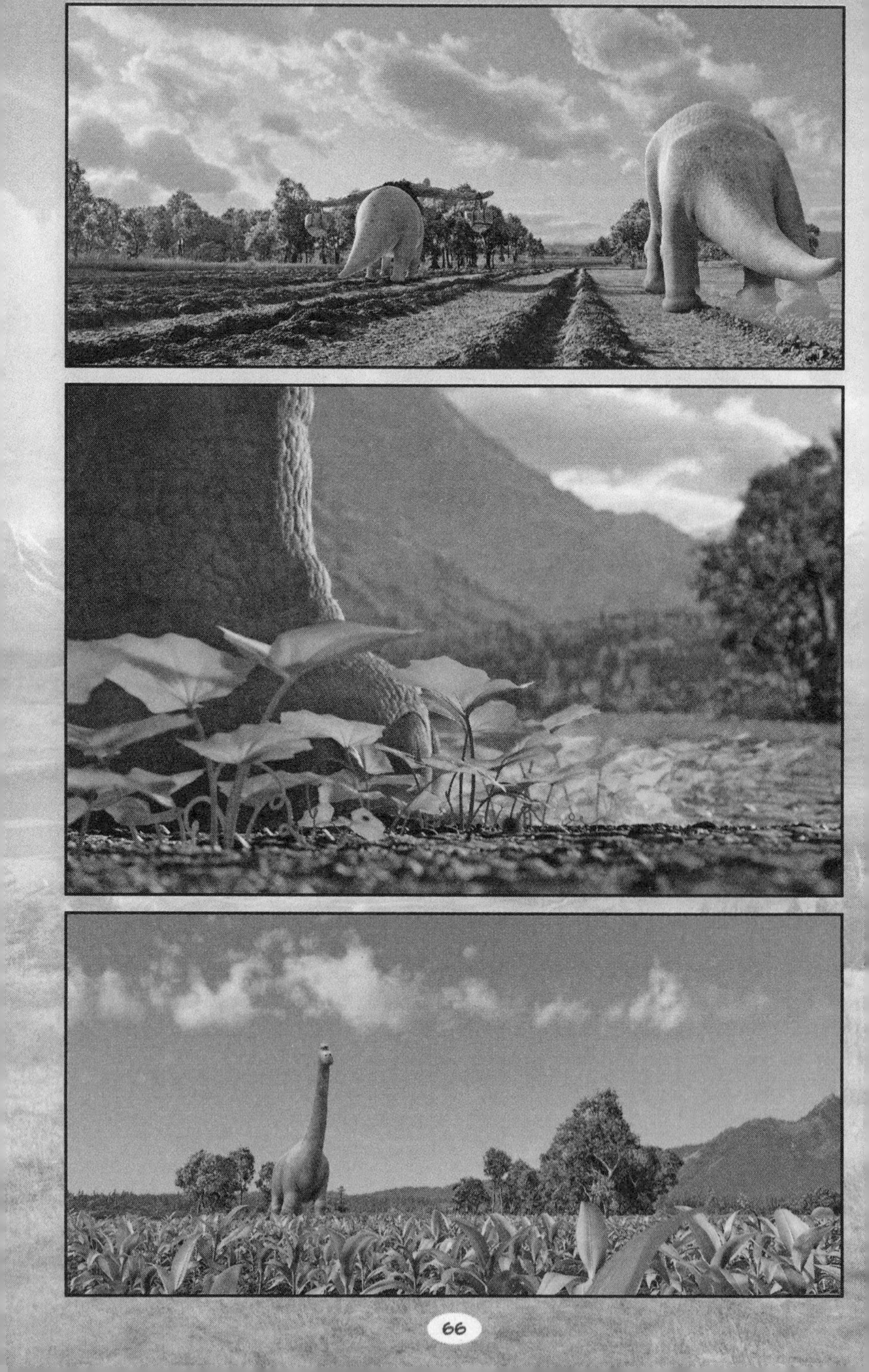

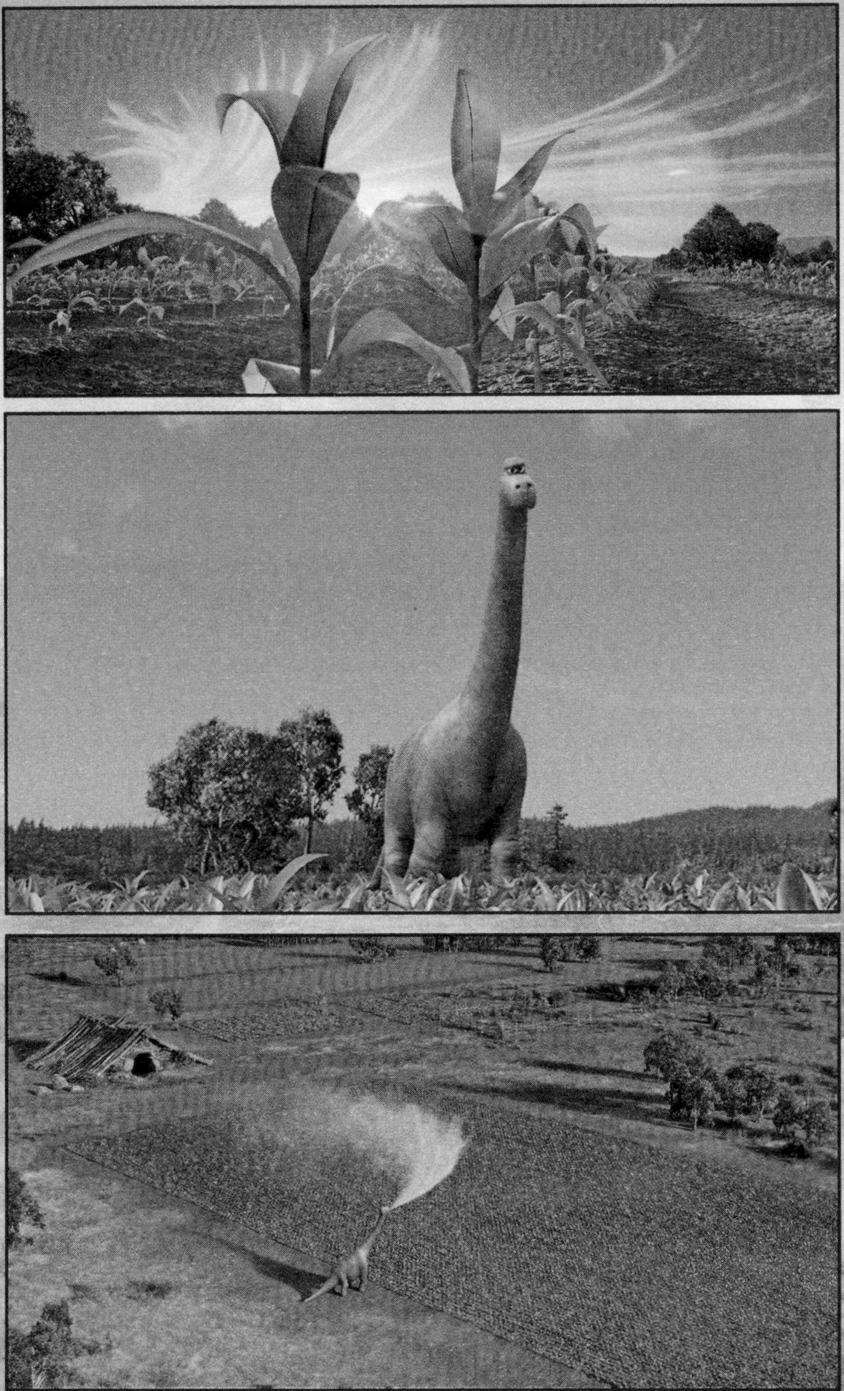

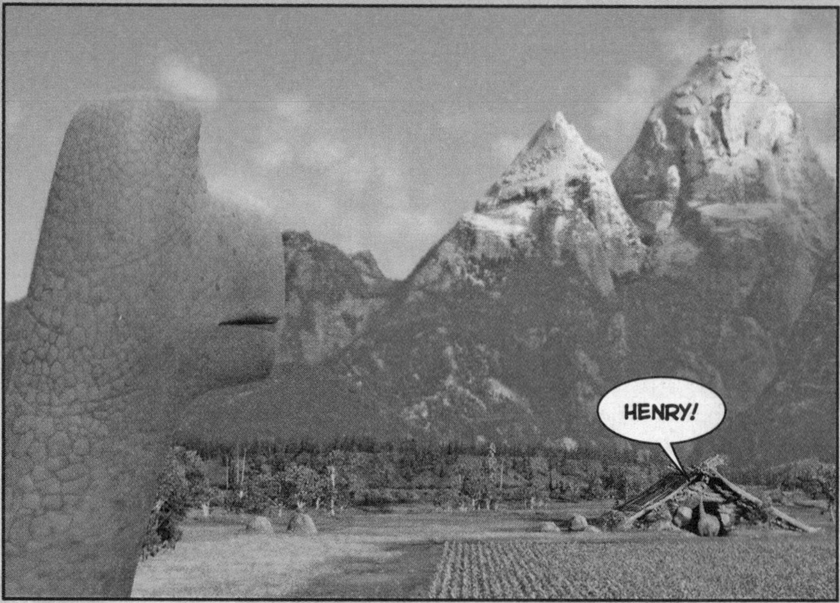
HENRY!

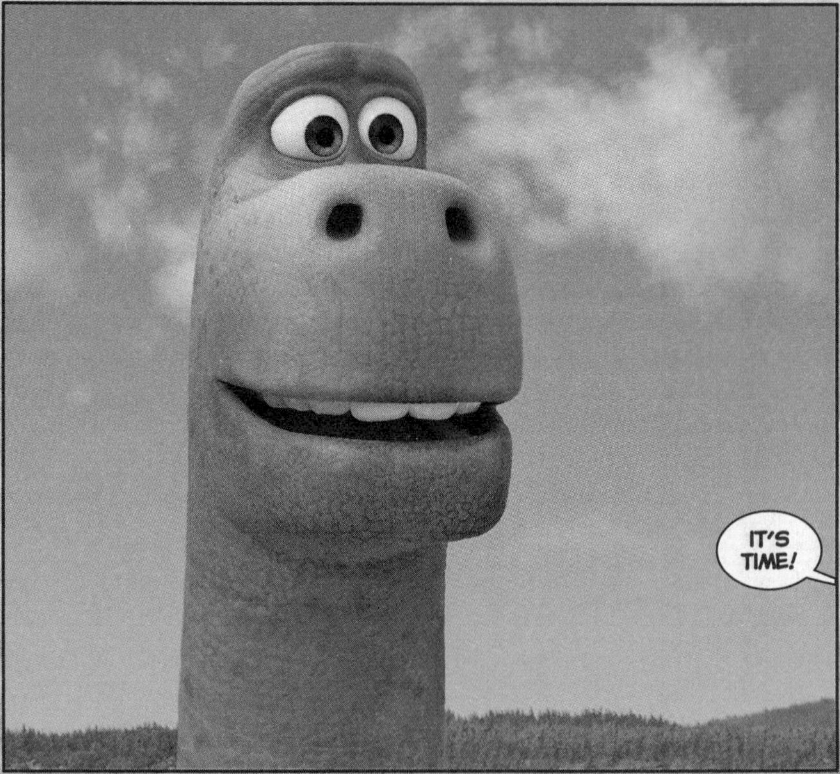
IT'S
TIME!

DISNEP · PIXAR

THE GOOD DINOSAUR

ARLO IS BORN

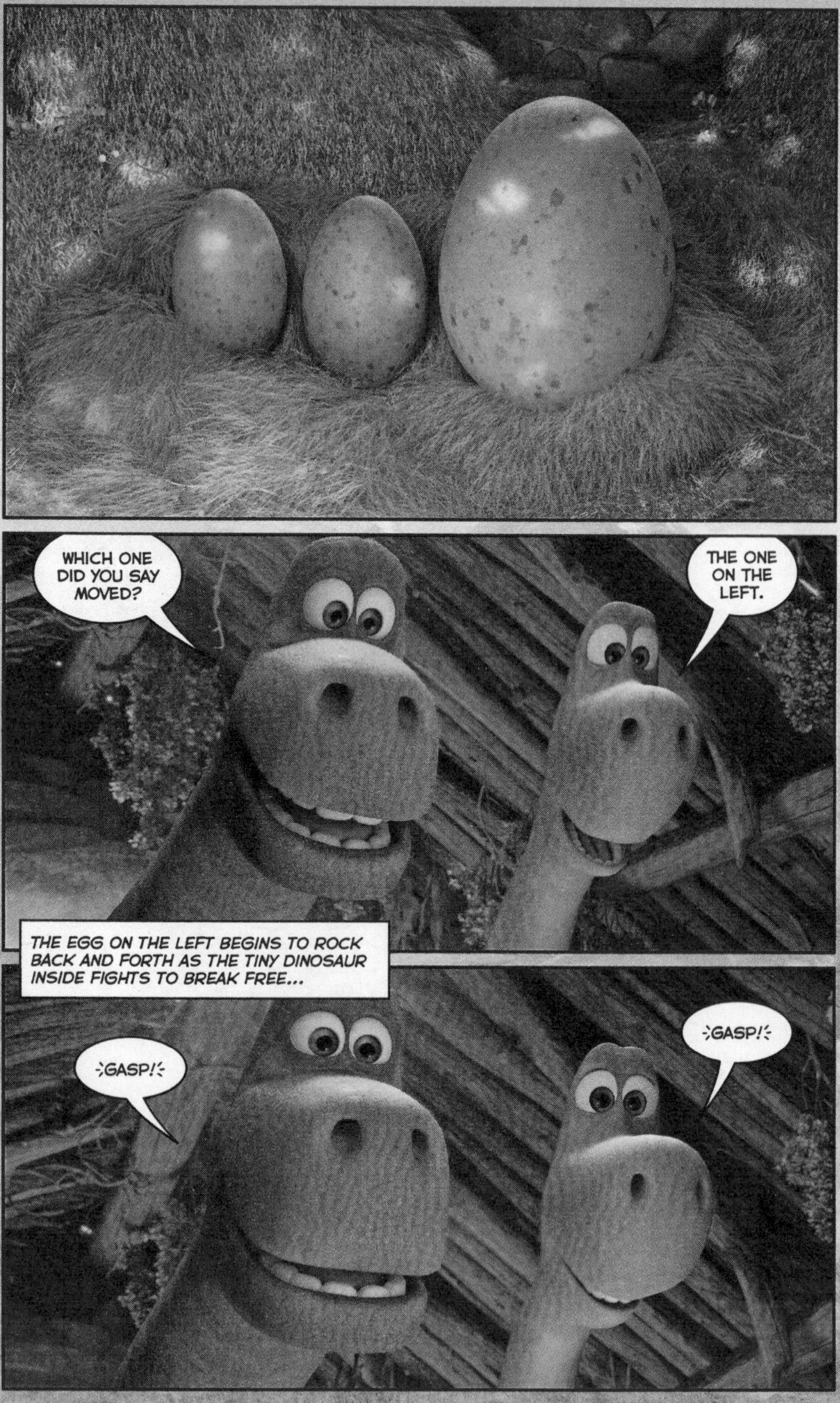
WHICH ONE DID YOU SAY MOVED?
THE ONE ON THE LEFT.
THE EGG ON THE LEFT BEGINS TO ROCK BACK AND FORTH AS THE TINY DINOSAUR INSIDE FIGHTS TO BREAK FREE...
GASP!
GASP!

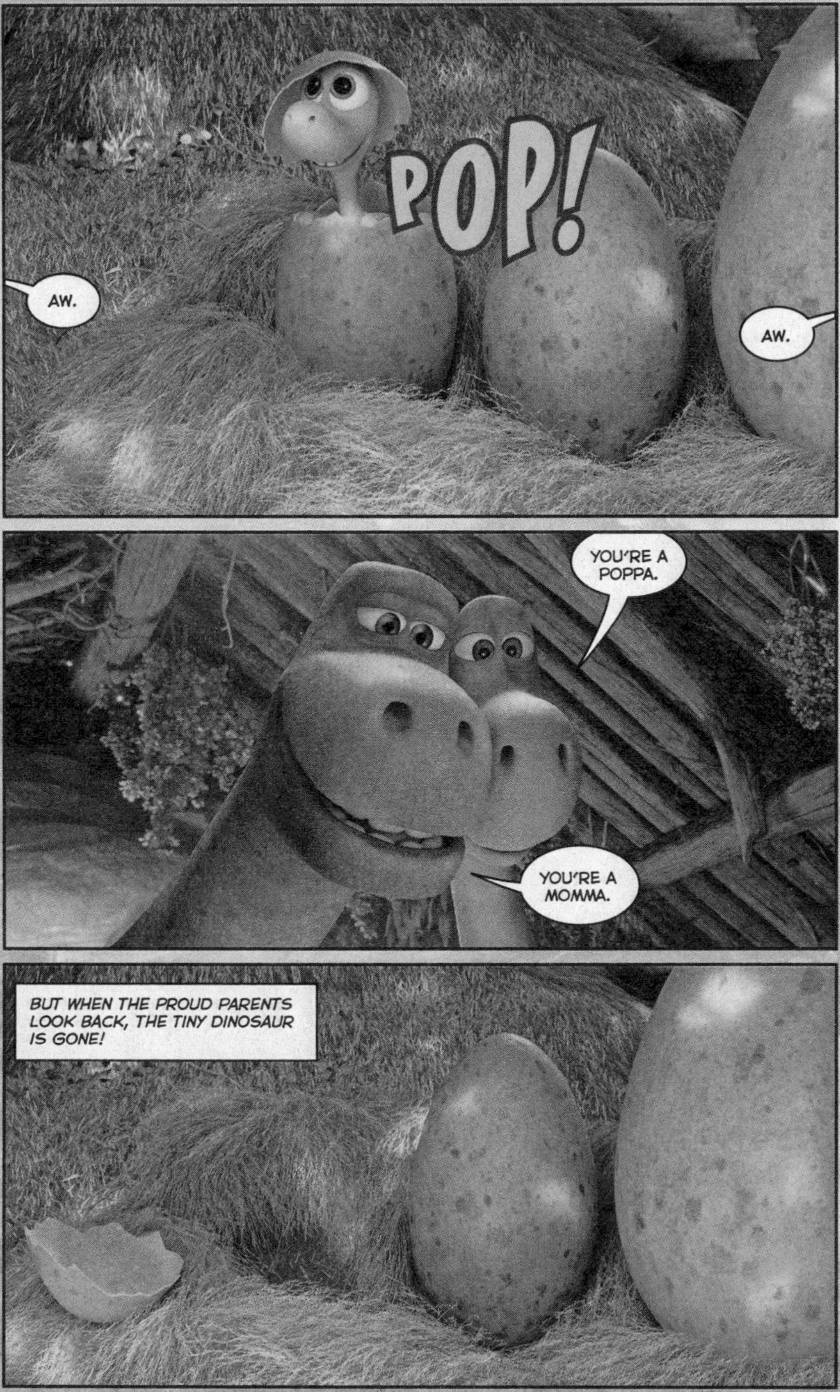
POP!
AW.
AW.
YOU'RE A POPPA.
YOU'RE A MOMMA.
BUT WHEN THE PROUD PARENTS LOOK BACK, THE TINY DINOSAUR IS GONE!

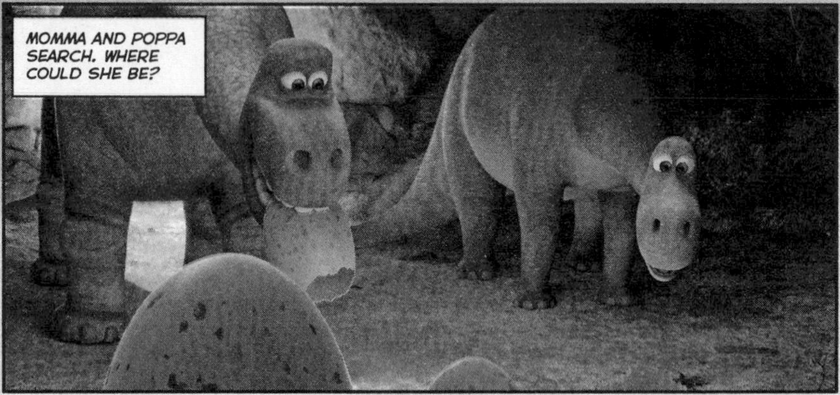
MOMMA AND POPPA SEARCH. WHERE COULD SHE BE?

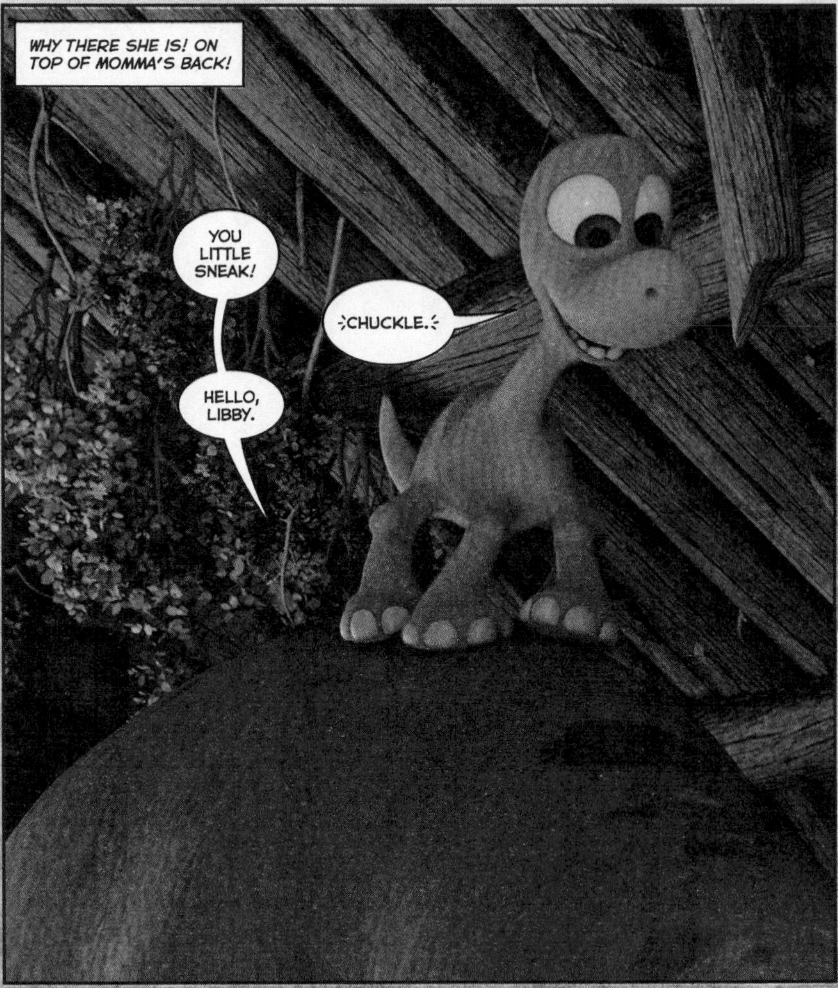
WHY THERE SHE IS! ON TOP OF MOMMA'S BACK!
YOU LITTLE SNEAK!
HELLO, LIBBY.
CHUCKLE.

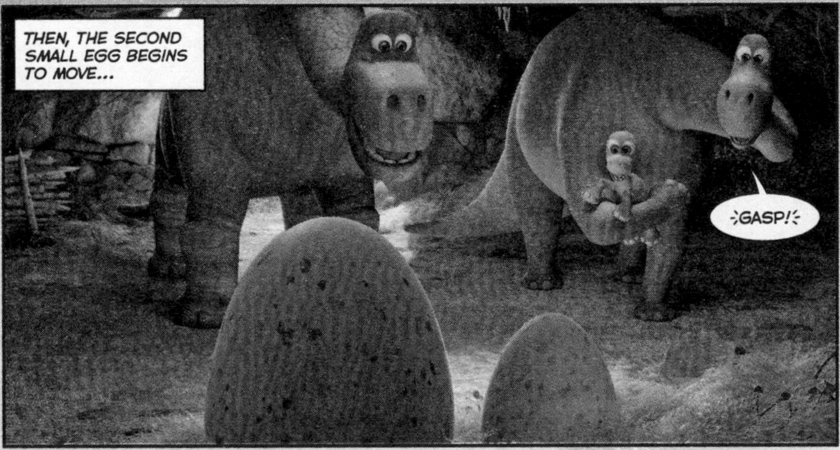
THEN, THE SECOND SMALL EGG BEGINS TO MOVE...
GASP!

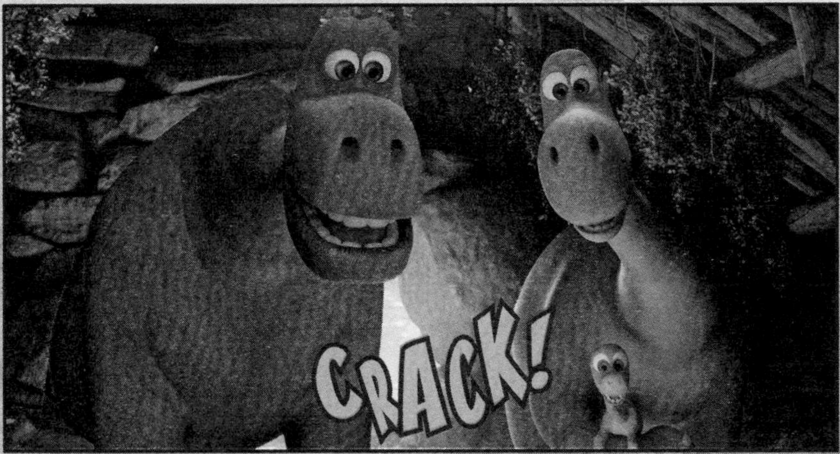
CRACK!

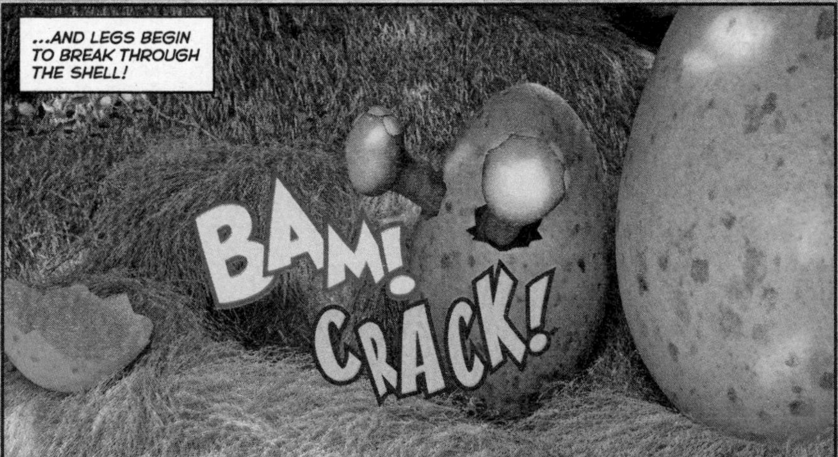
...AND LEGS BEGIN TO BREAK THROUGH THE SHELL!
BAM!
CRACK!

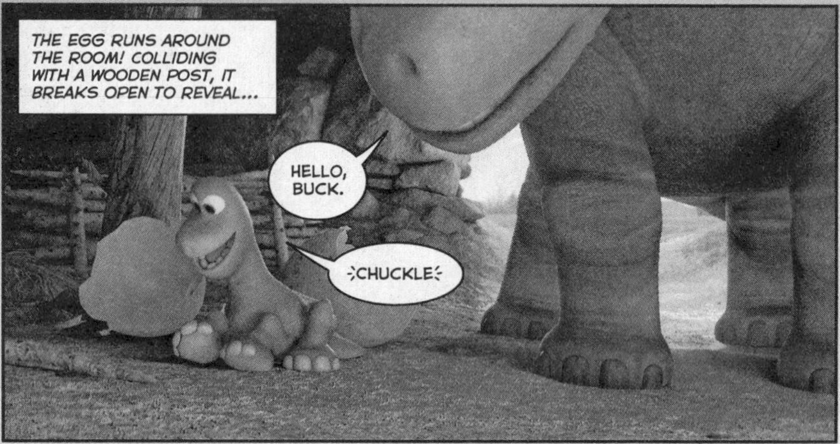
THE EGG RUNS AROUND THE ROOM! COLLIDING WITH A WOODEN POST, IT BREAKS OPEN TO REVEAL...
HELLO, BUCK.
CHUCKLE

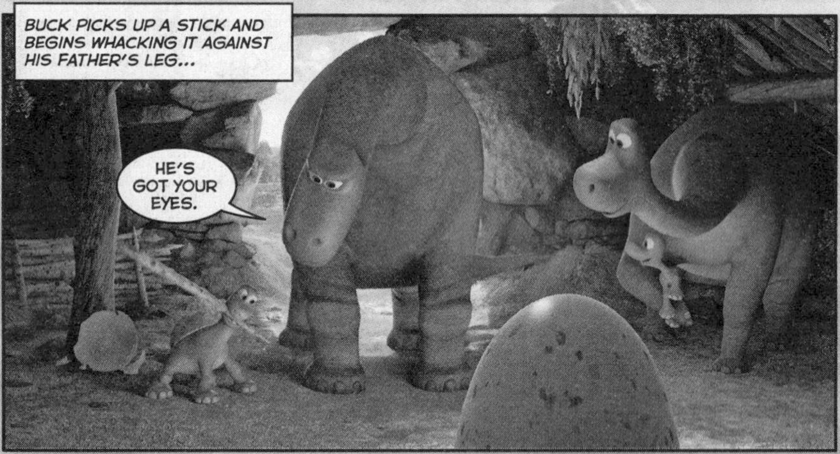
BUCK PICKS UP A STICK AND BEGINS WHACKING IT AGAINST HIS FATHER'S LEG...
HE'S GOT YOUR EYES.

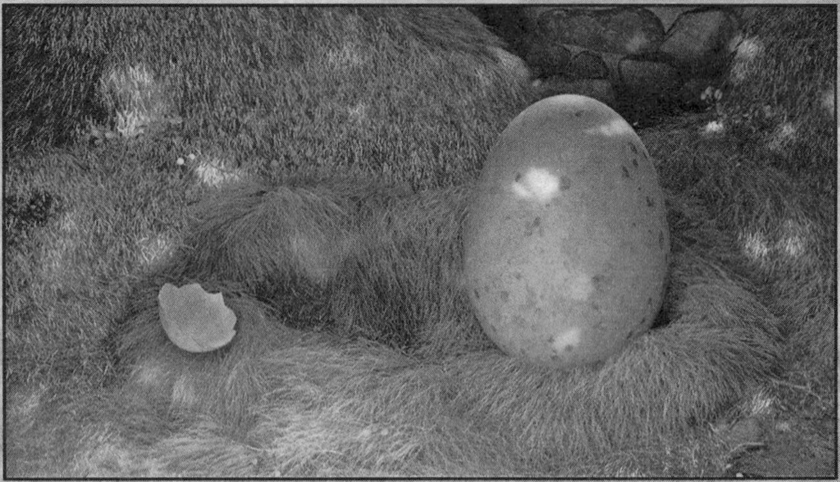

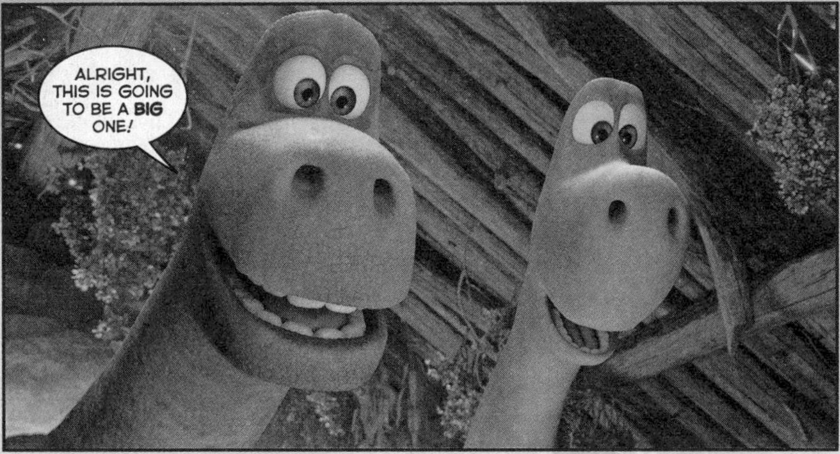
ALRIGHT, THIS IS GOING TO BE A BIG ONE!

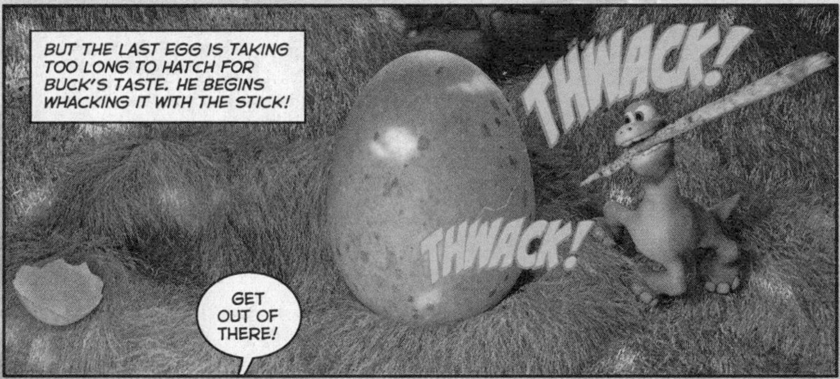
BUT THE LAST EGG IS TAKING TOO LONG TO HATCH FOR BUCK'S TASTE. HE BEGINS WHACKING IT WITH THE STICK!
THWACK!
THWACK!
GET OUT OF THERE!

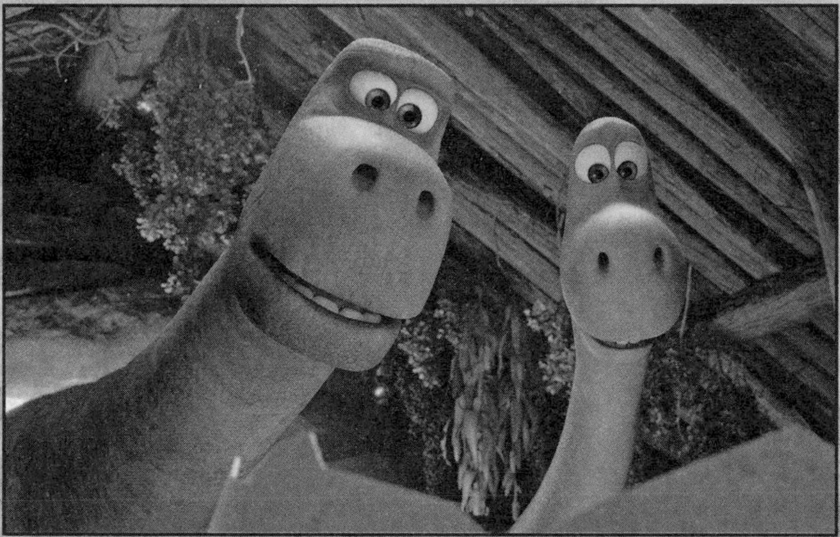

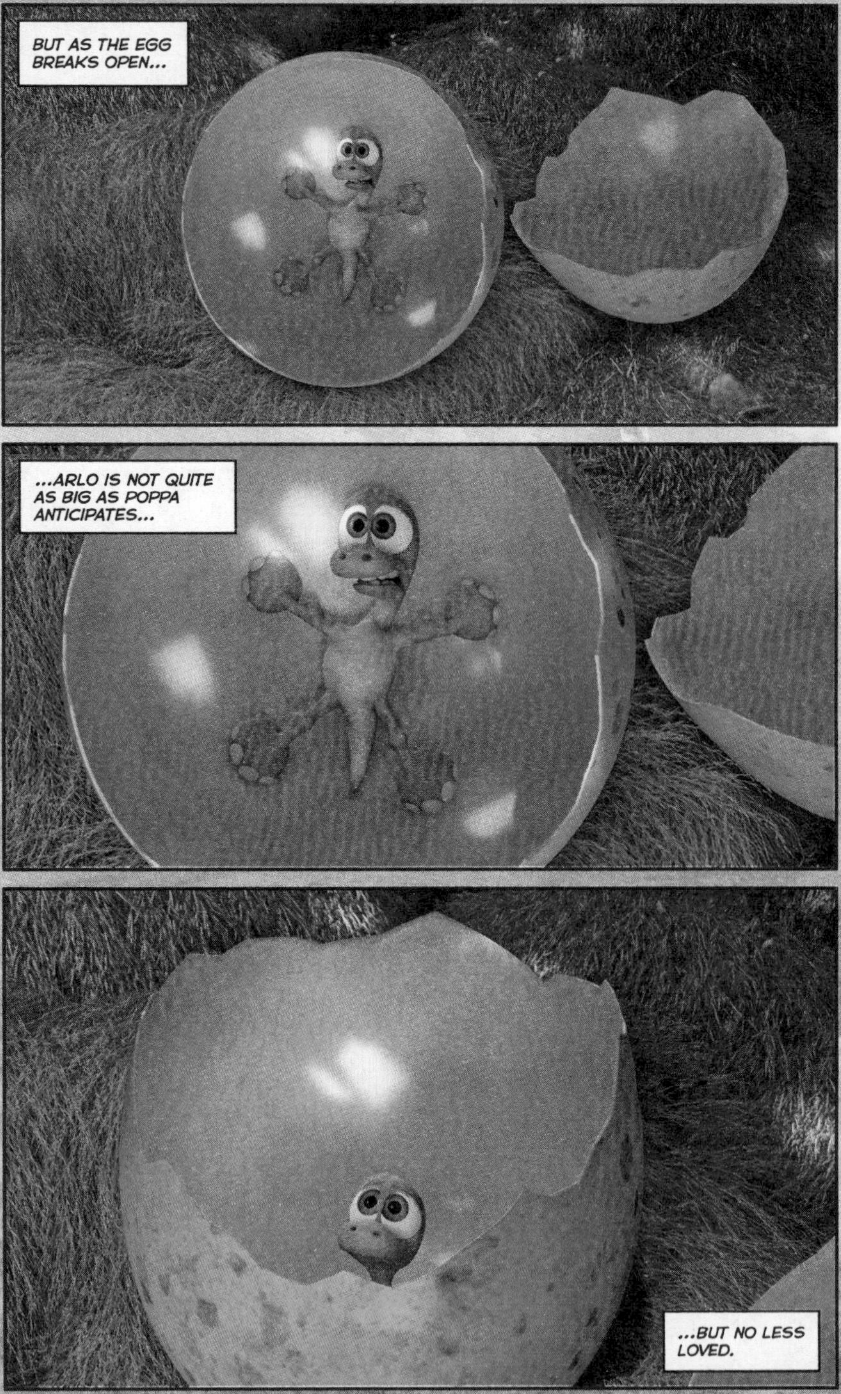
BUT AS THE EGG BREAKS OPEN...
...ARLO IS NOT QUITE AS BIG AS POPPA ANTICIPATES...
...BUT NO LESS LOVED.

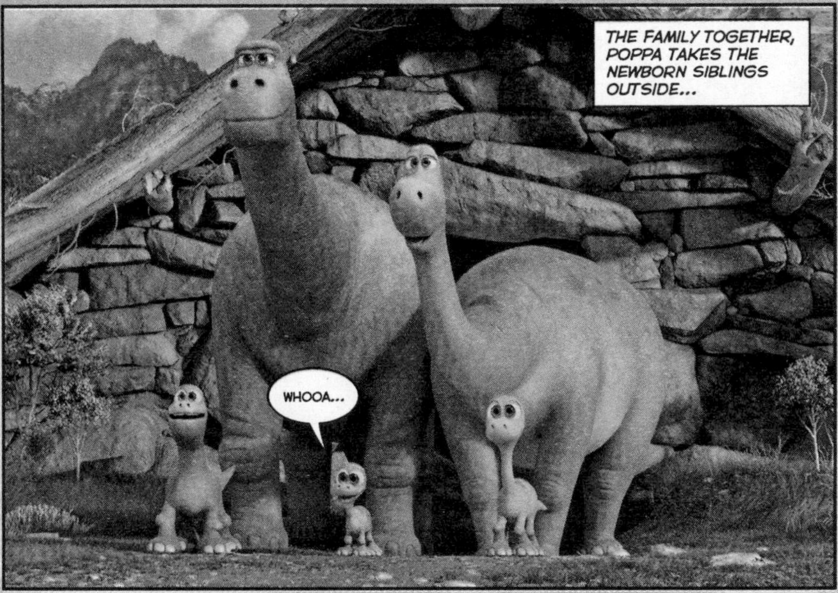
THE FAMILY TOGETHER, POPPA TAKES THE NEWBORN SIBLINGS OUTSIDE...
WHOOA...

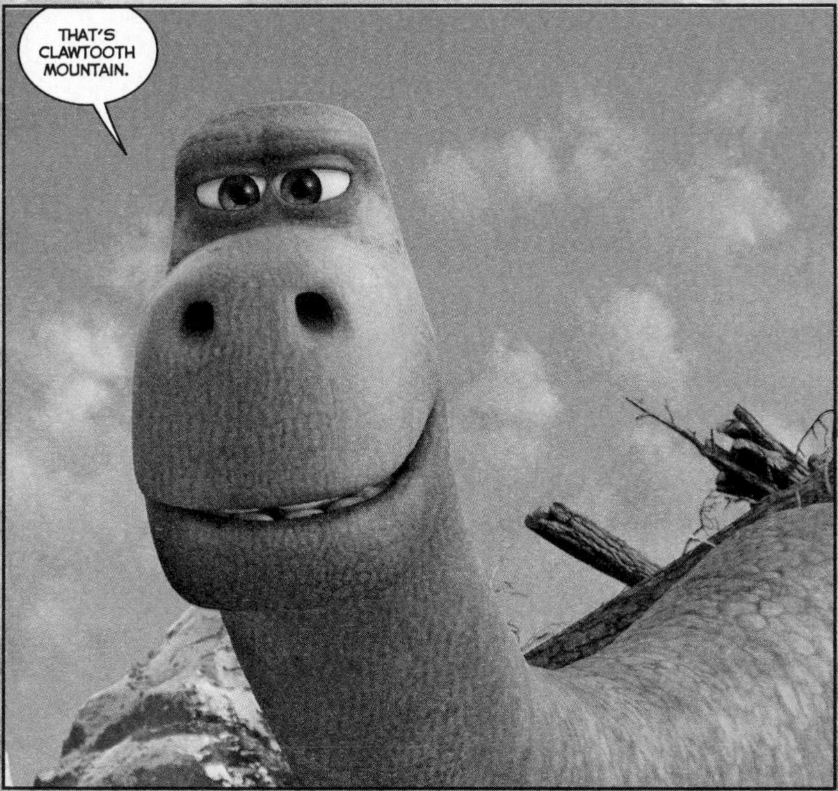
THAT'S CLAWTOOTH MOUNTAIN.

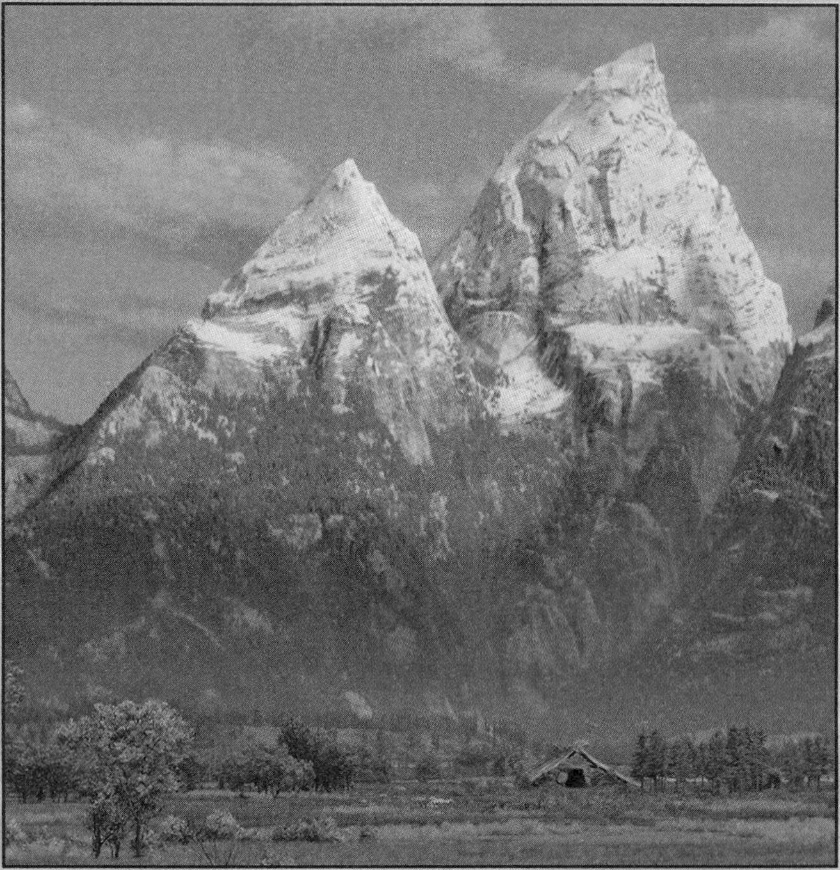

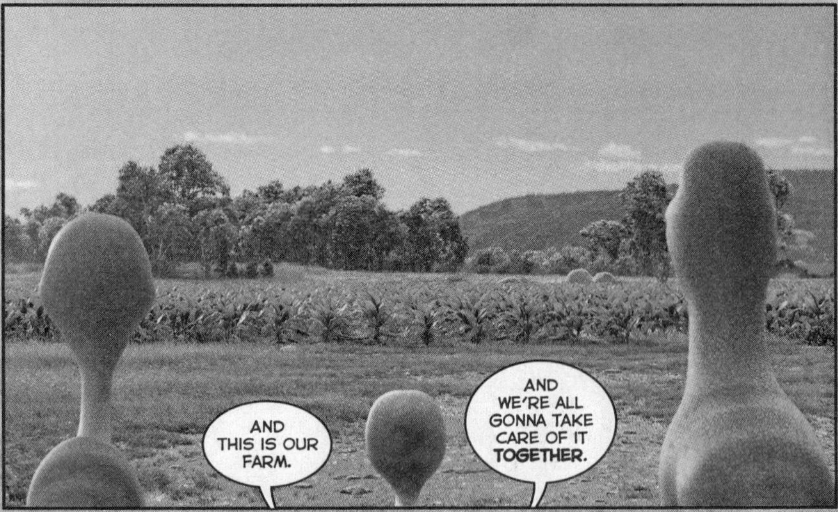
AND THIS IS OUR FARM.
AND WE'RE ALL GONNA TAKE CARE OF IT TOGETHER.

Disney·PIXAR

THE GOOD DINOSAUR

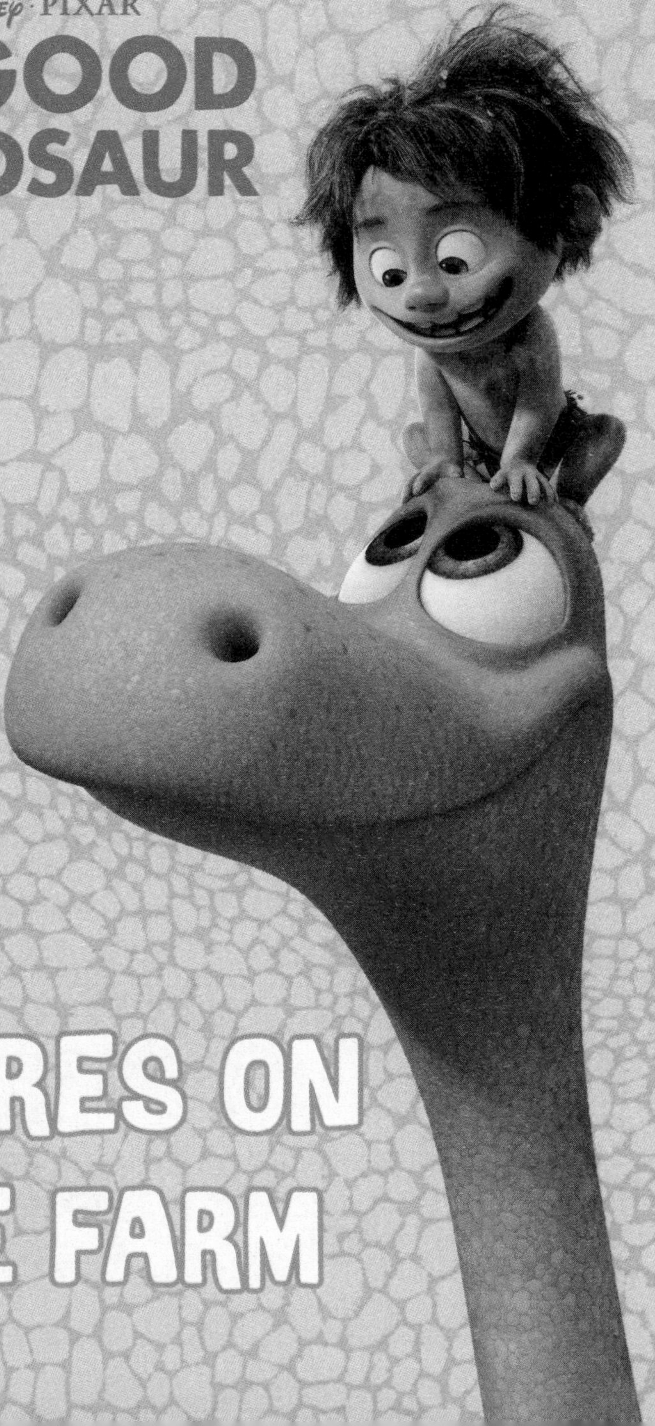

CHORES ON THE FARM

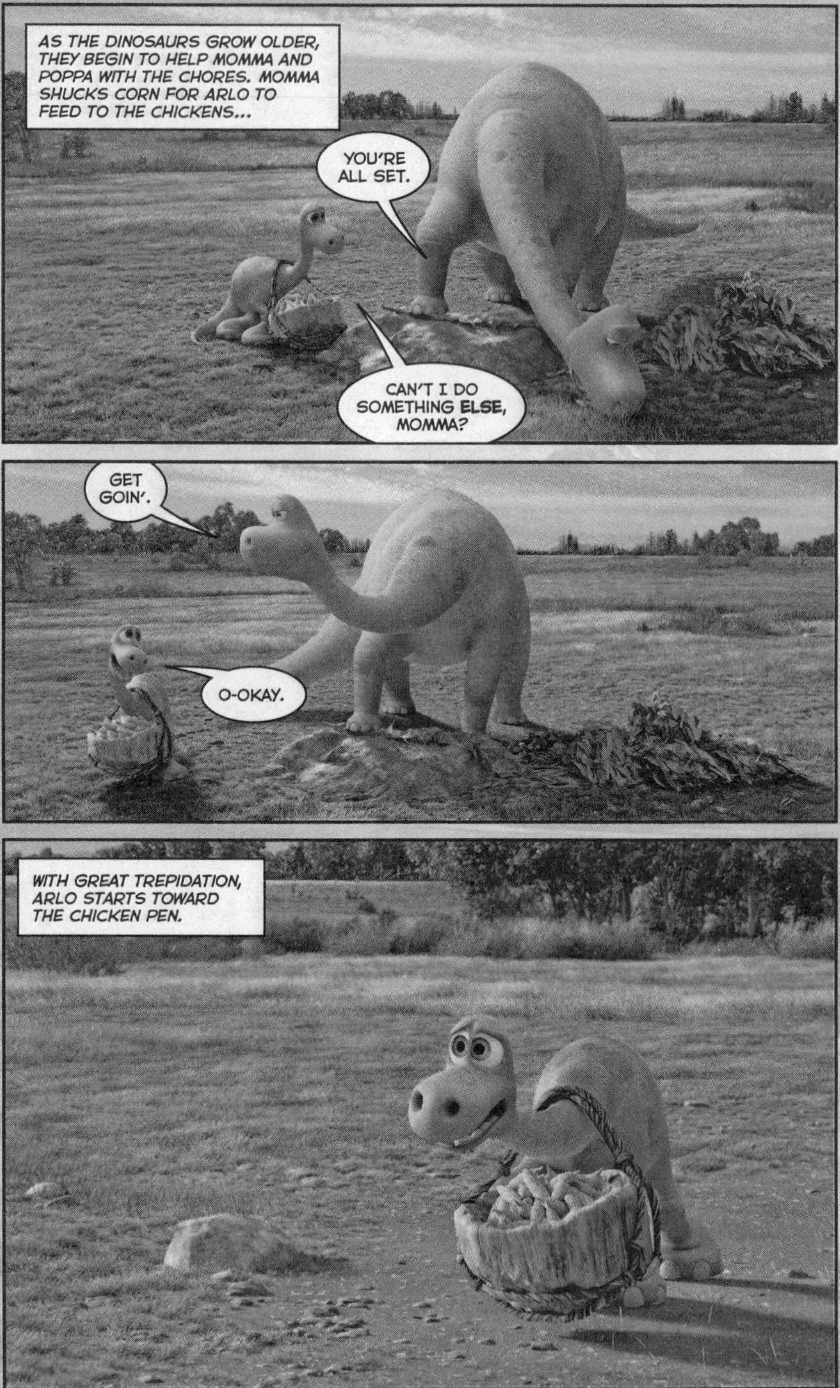
AS THE DINOSAURS GROW OLDER, THEY BEGIN TO HELP MOMMA AND POPPA WITH THE CHORES. MOMMA SHUCKS CORN FOR ARLO TO FEED TO THE CHICKENS...
YOU'RE ALL SET.
CAN'T I DO SOMETHING **ELSE**, MOMMA?
GET GOIN'.
O-OKAY.
WITH GREAT TREPIDATION, ARLO STARTS TOWARD THE CHICKEN PEN.

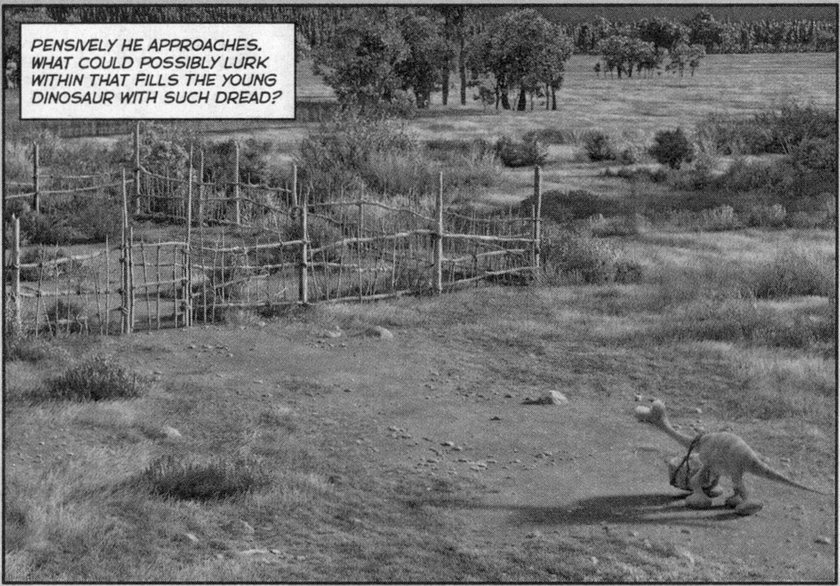
PENSIVELY HE APPROACHES. WHAT COULD POSSIBLY LURK WITHIN THAT FILLS THE YOUNG DINOSAUR WITH SUCH DREAD?

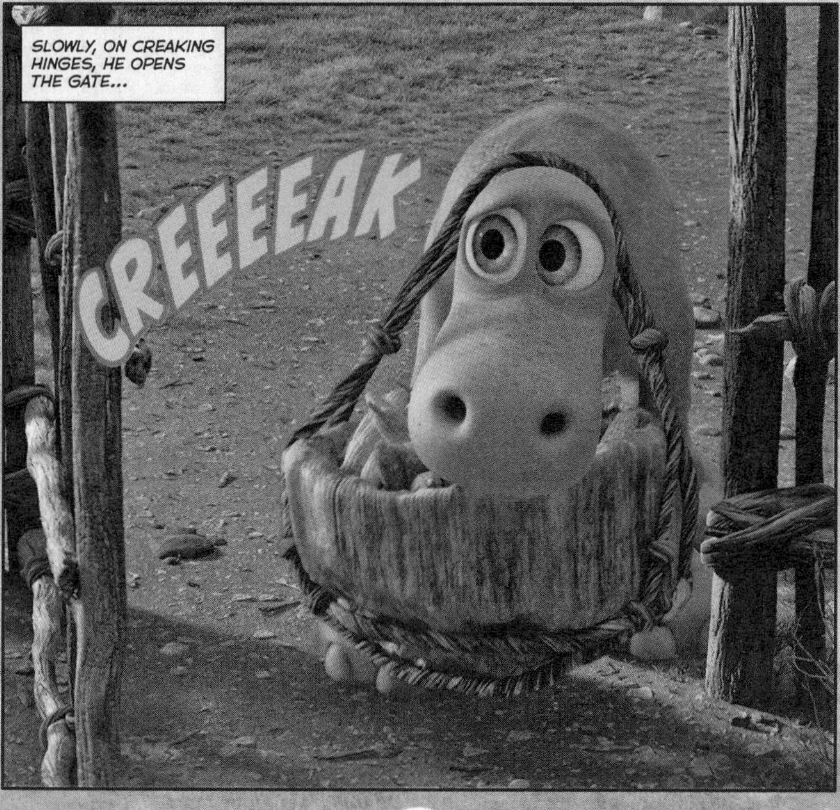
SLOWLY, ON CREAKING HINGES, HE OPENS THE GATE...
CREEEEAK

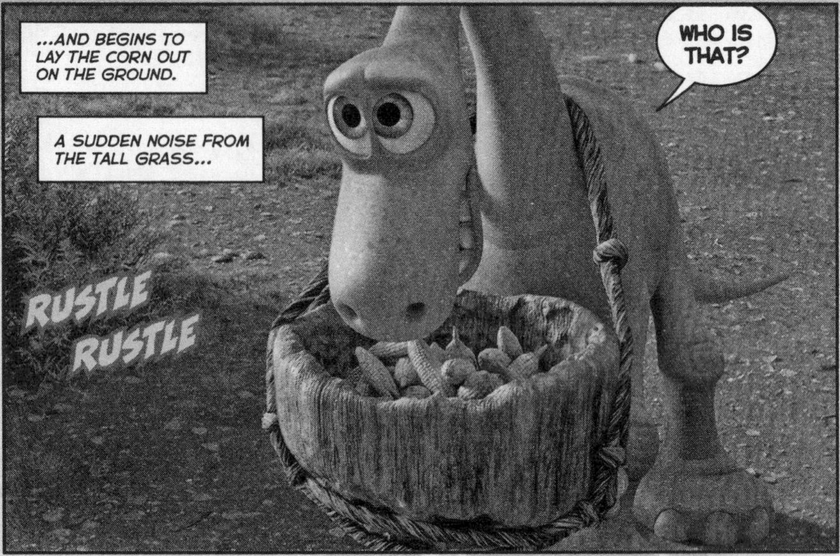
...AND BEGINS TO LAY THE CORN OUT ON THE GROUND.
A SUDDEN NOISE FROM THE TALL GRASS...
WHO IS THAT?
RUSTLE RUSTLE

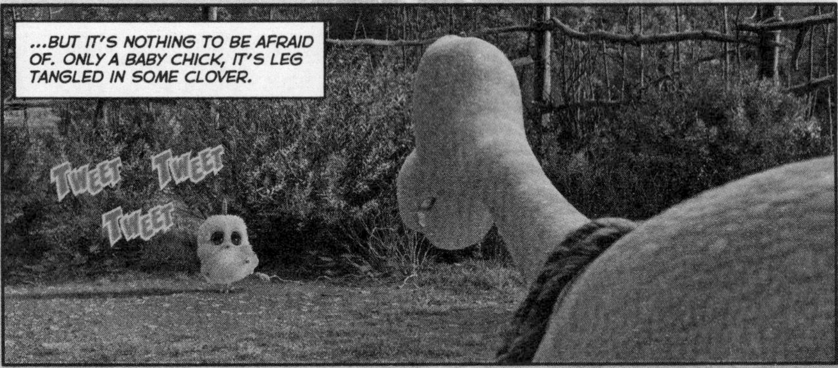
...BUT IT'S NOTHING TO BE AFRAID OF. ONLY A BABY CHICK, IT'S LEG TANGLED IN SOME CLOVER.
TWEET TWEET TWEET

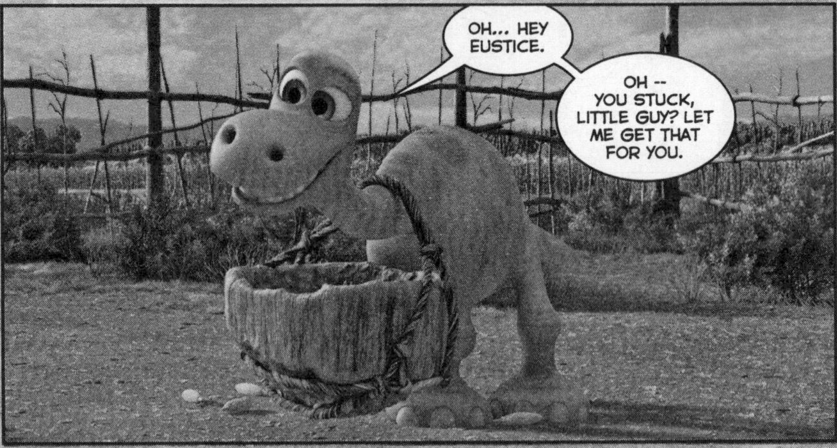
OH... HEY EUSTICE.
OH -- YOU STUCK, LITTLE GUY? LET ME GET THAT FOR YOU.

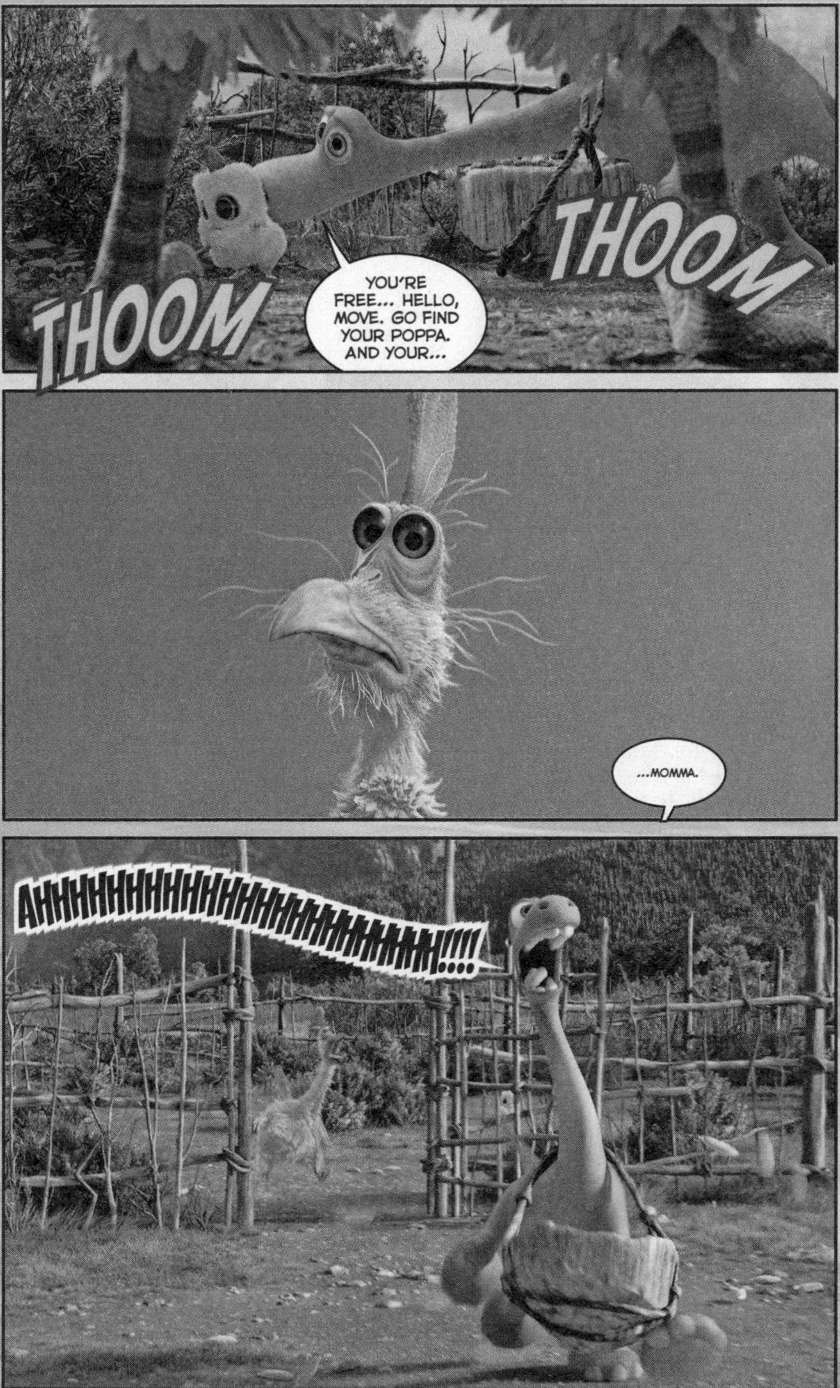
THOOM
YOU'RE FREE... HELLO, MOVE. GO FIND YOUR POPPA. AND YOUR...
THOOM
...MOMMA.
AHHHHHHHHHHHHHHHHHHHHHHHHHHHHHHHH!!!!

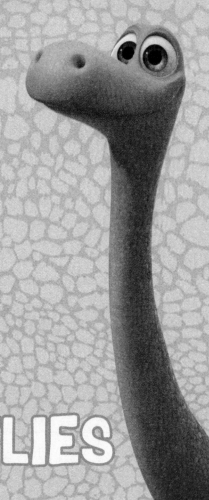

DISNEP · PIXAR

THE GOOD DINOSAUR

FIREFLIES

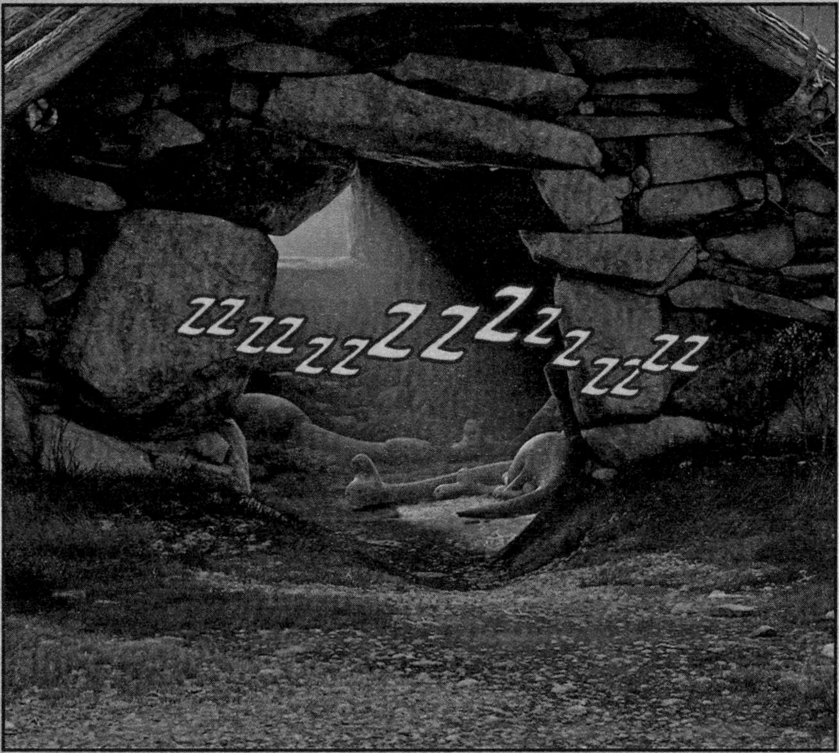
ZZZZZZZZZZZZZZZZZZZ

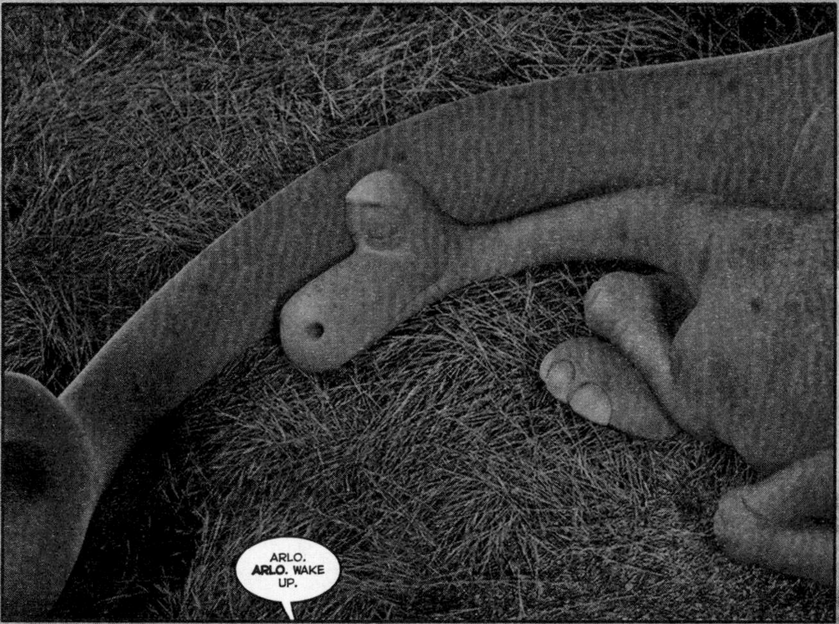
ARLO. ARLO. WAKE UP.

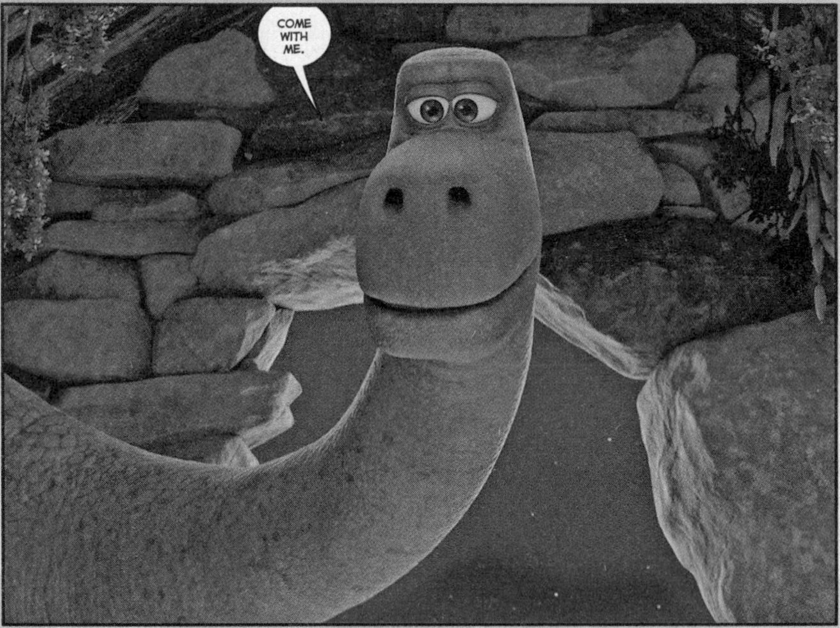
COME WITH ME.

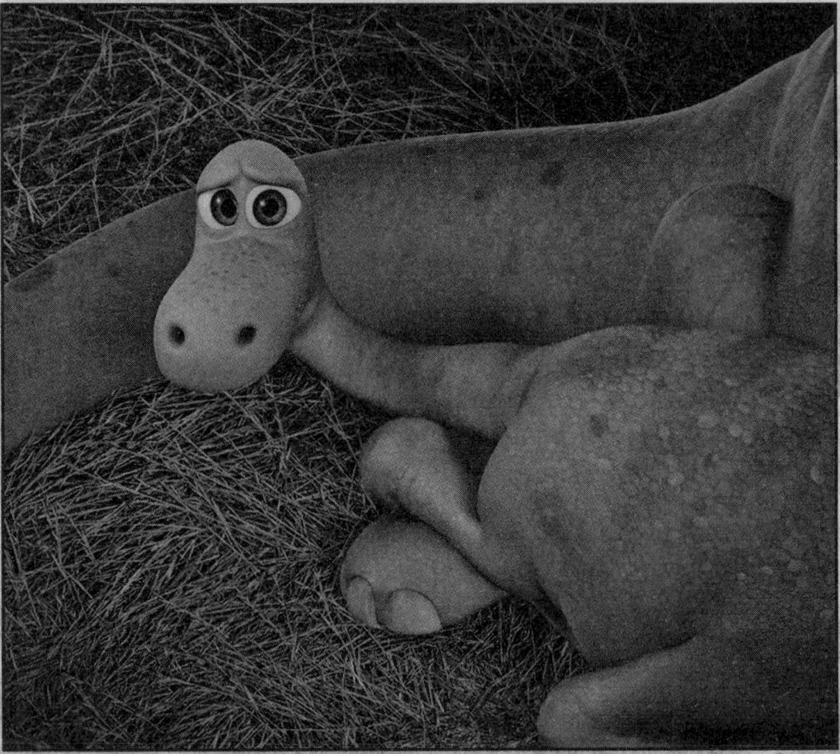

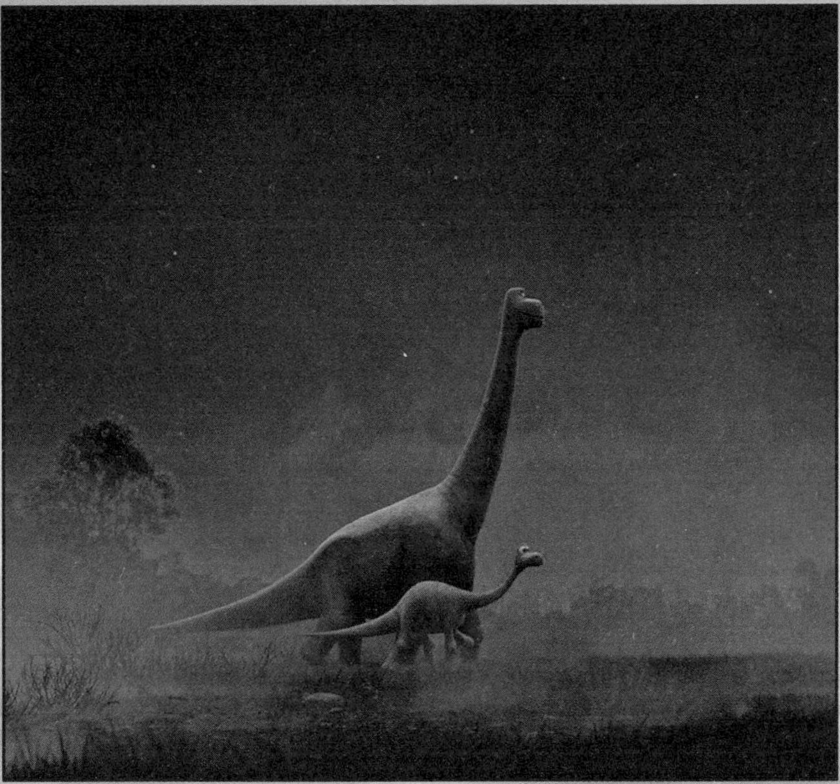

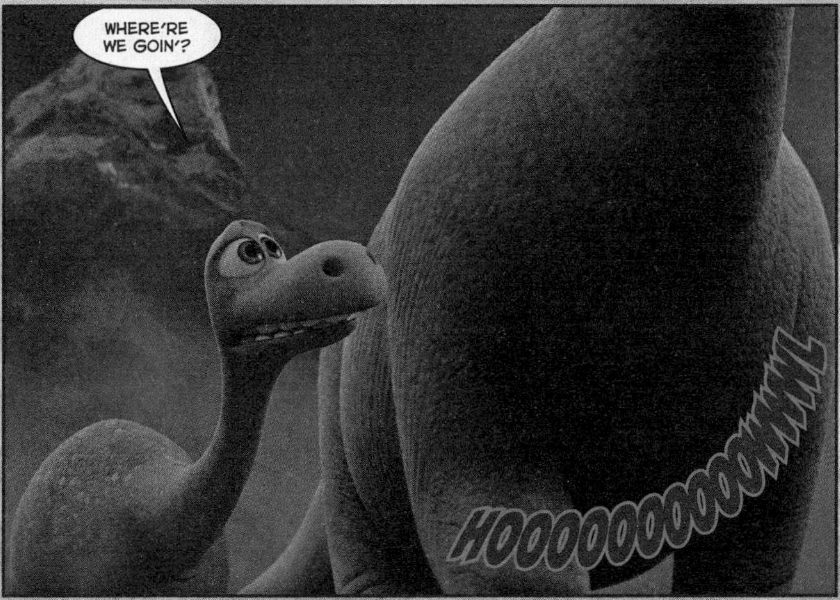
WHERE'RE WE GOIN'?
HOOOOOOOOOOWWL

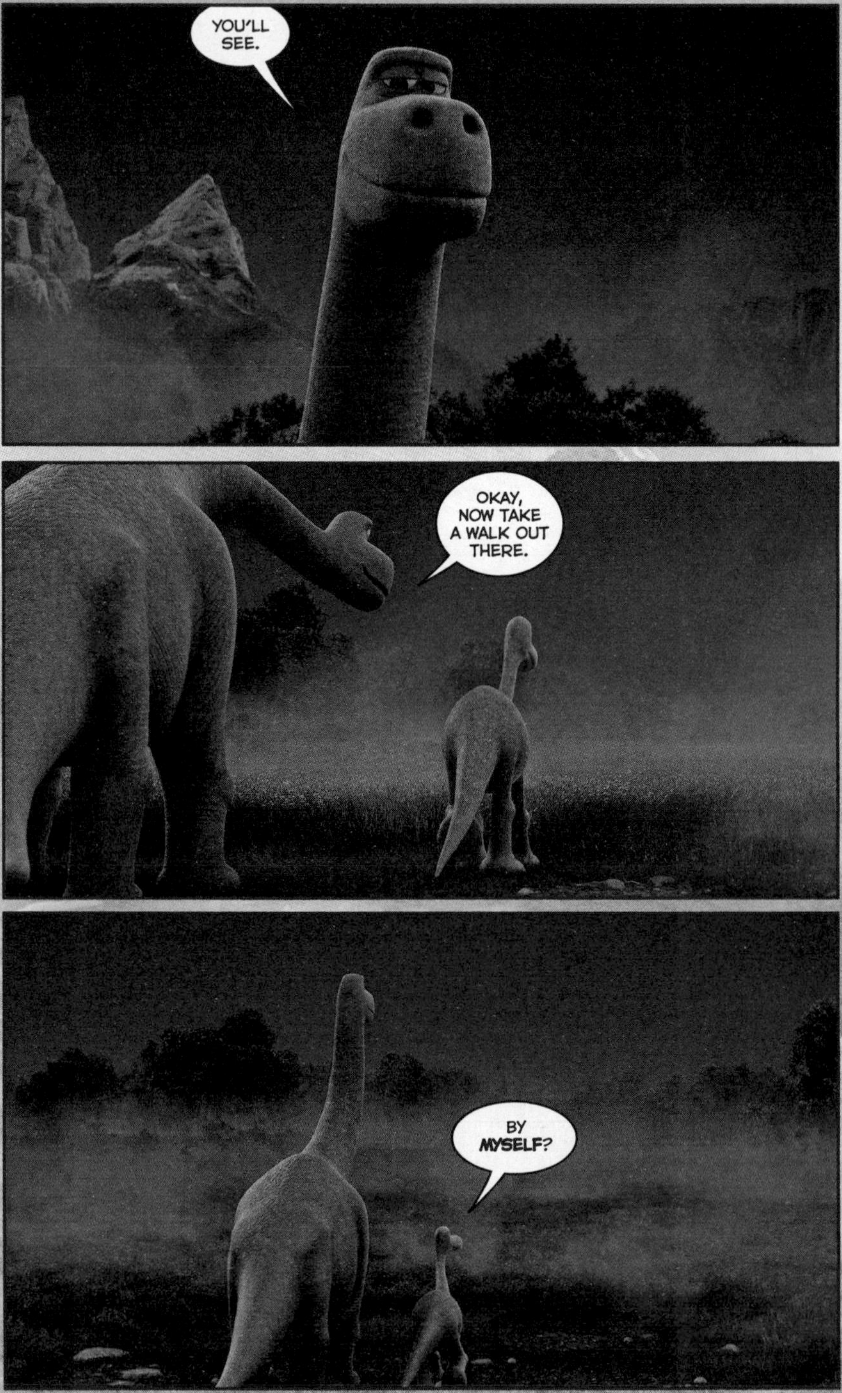

YOU'LL SEE.
OKAY, NOW TAKE A WALK OUT THERE.
BY MYSELF?

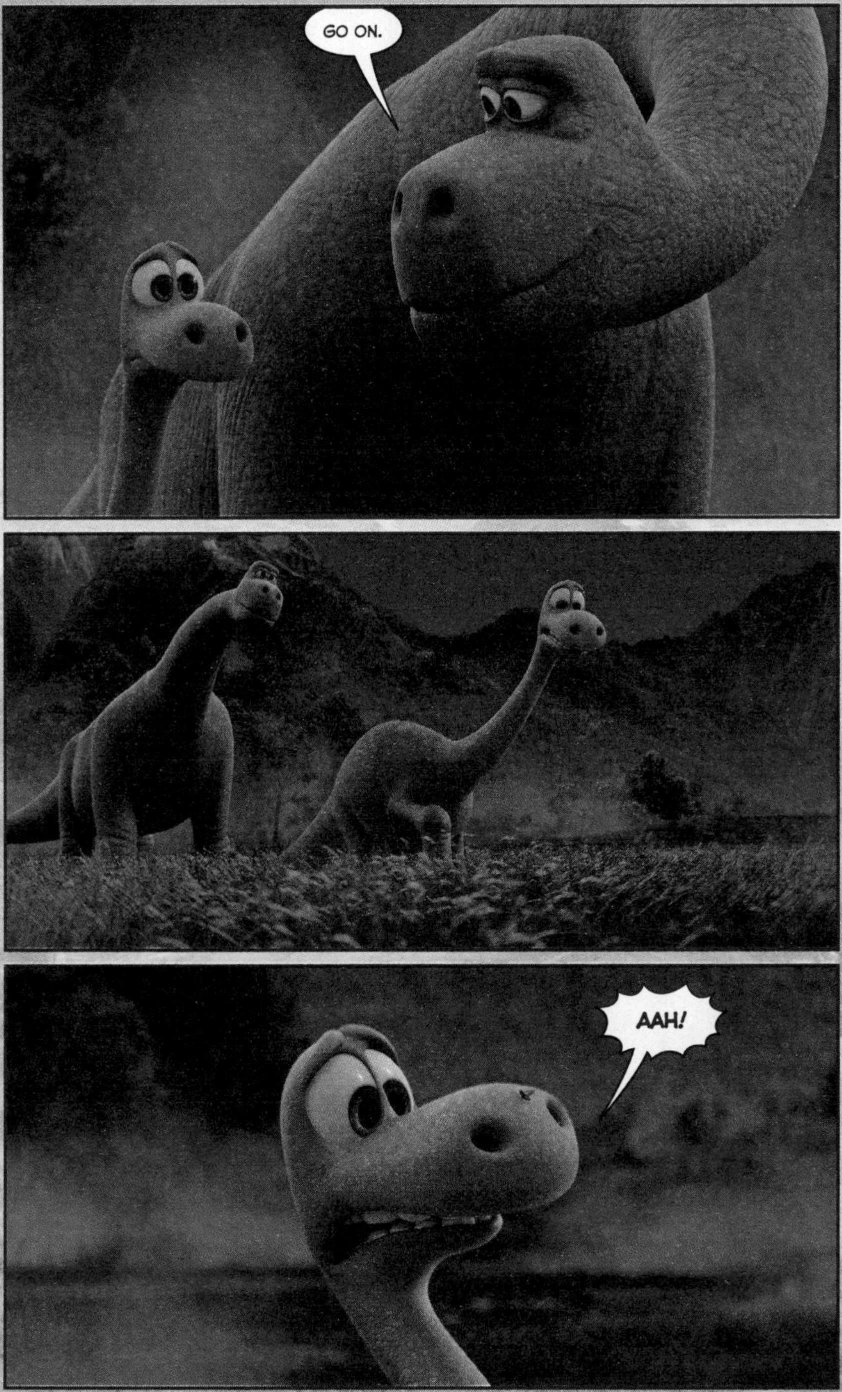
GO ON.
AAH!

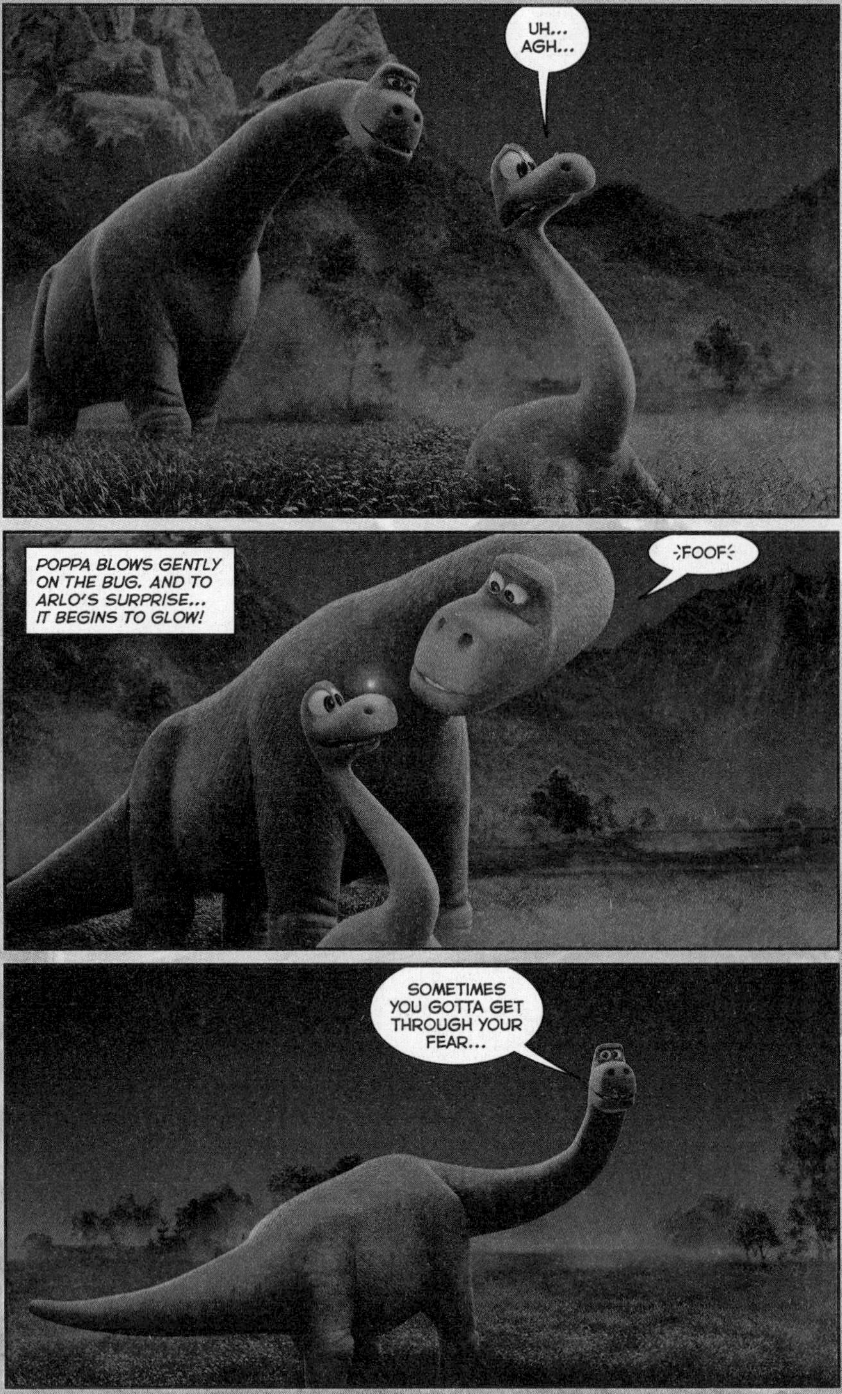
UH... AGH...
POPPA BLOWS GENTLY ON THE BUG. AND TO ARLO'S SURPRISE... IT BEGINS TO GLOW!
FOOF
SOMETIMES YOU GOTTA GET THROUGH YOUR FEAR...

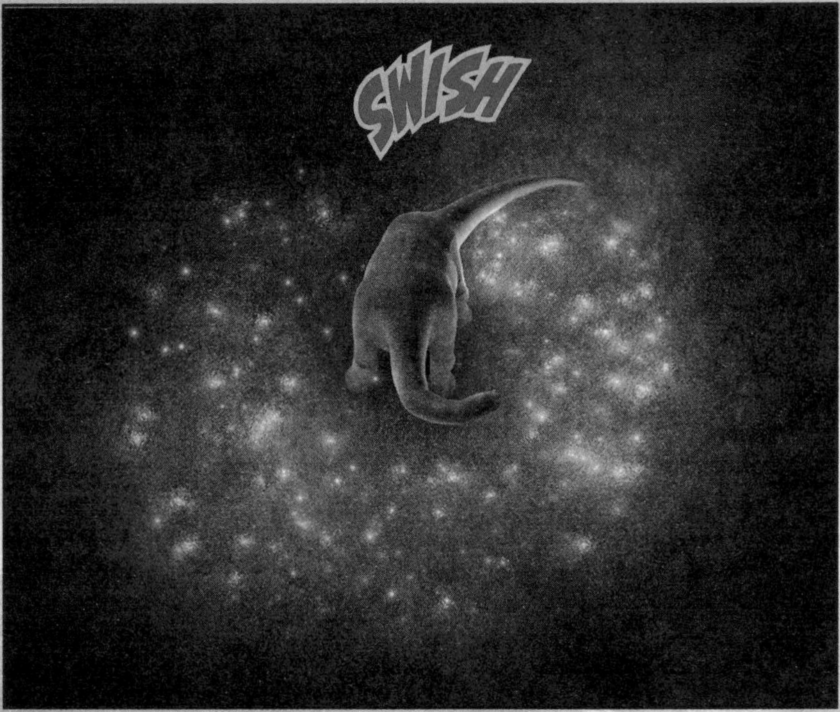
SWISH

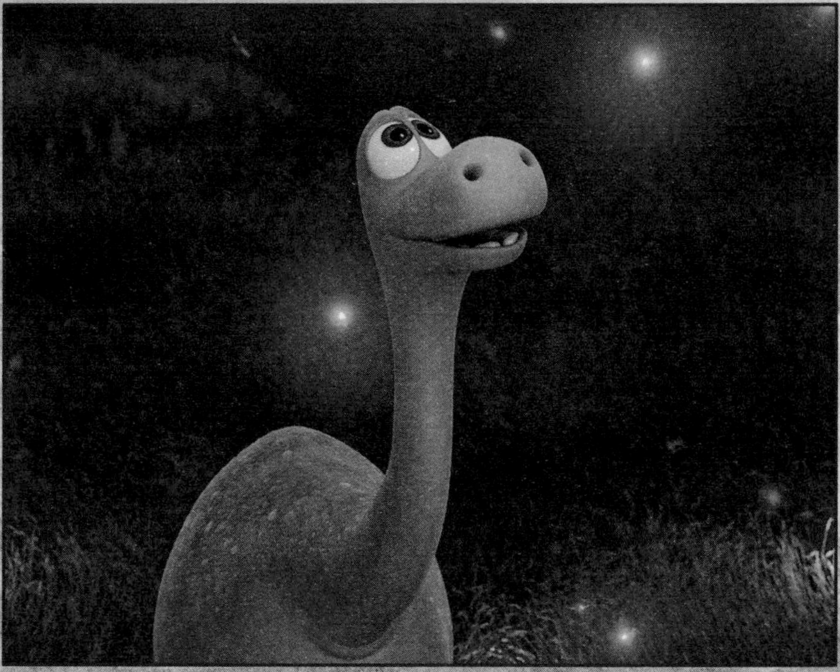

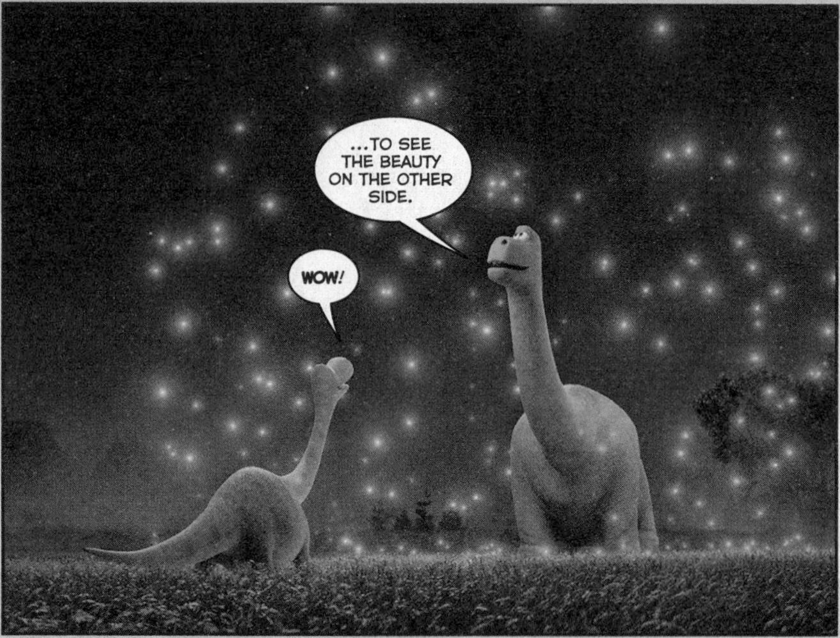
...TO SEE THE BEAUTY ON THE OTHER SIDE.
WOW!

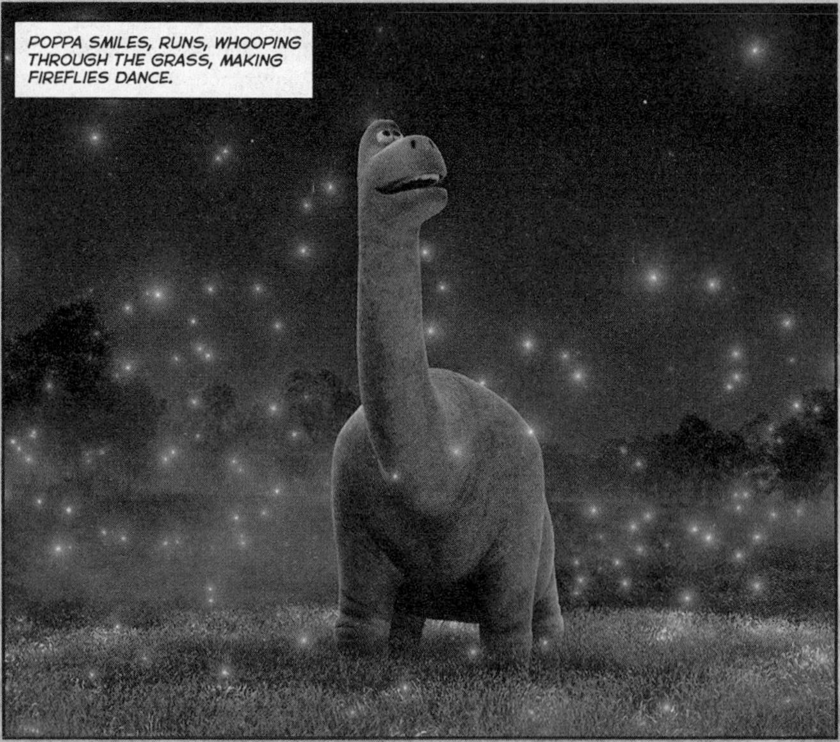
POPPA SMILES, RUNS, WHOOPING THROUGH THE GRASS, MAKING FIREFLIES DANCE.

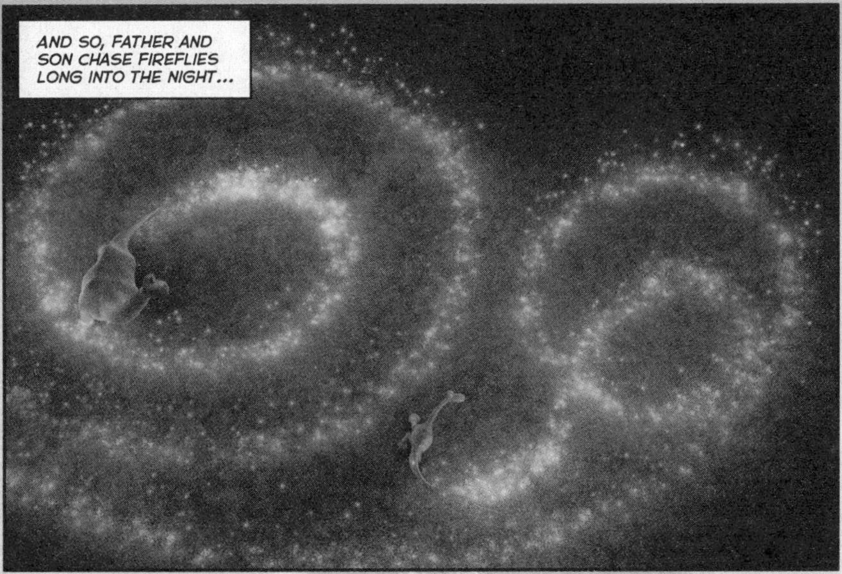
AND SO, FATHER AND SON CHASE FIREFLIES LONG INTO THE NIGHT...

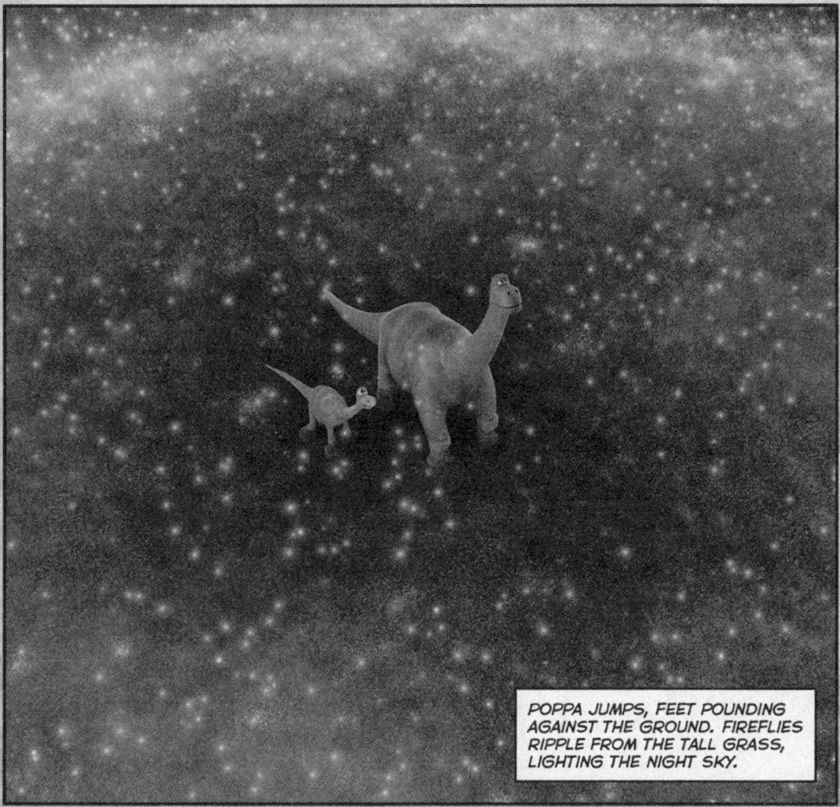
POPPA JUMPS, FEET POUNDING AGAINST THE GROUND. FIREFLIES RIPPLE FROM THE TALL GRASS, LIGHTING THE NIGHT SKY.

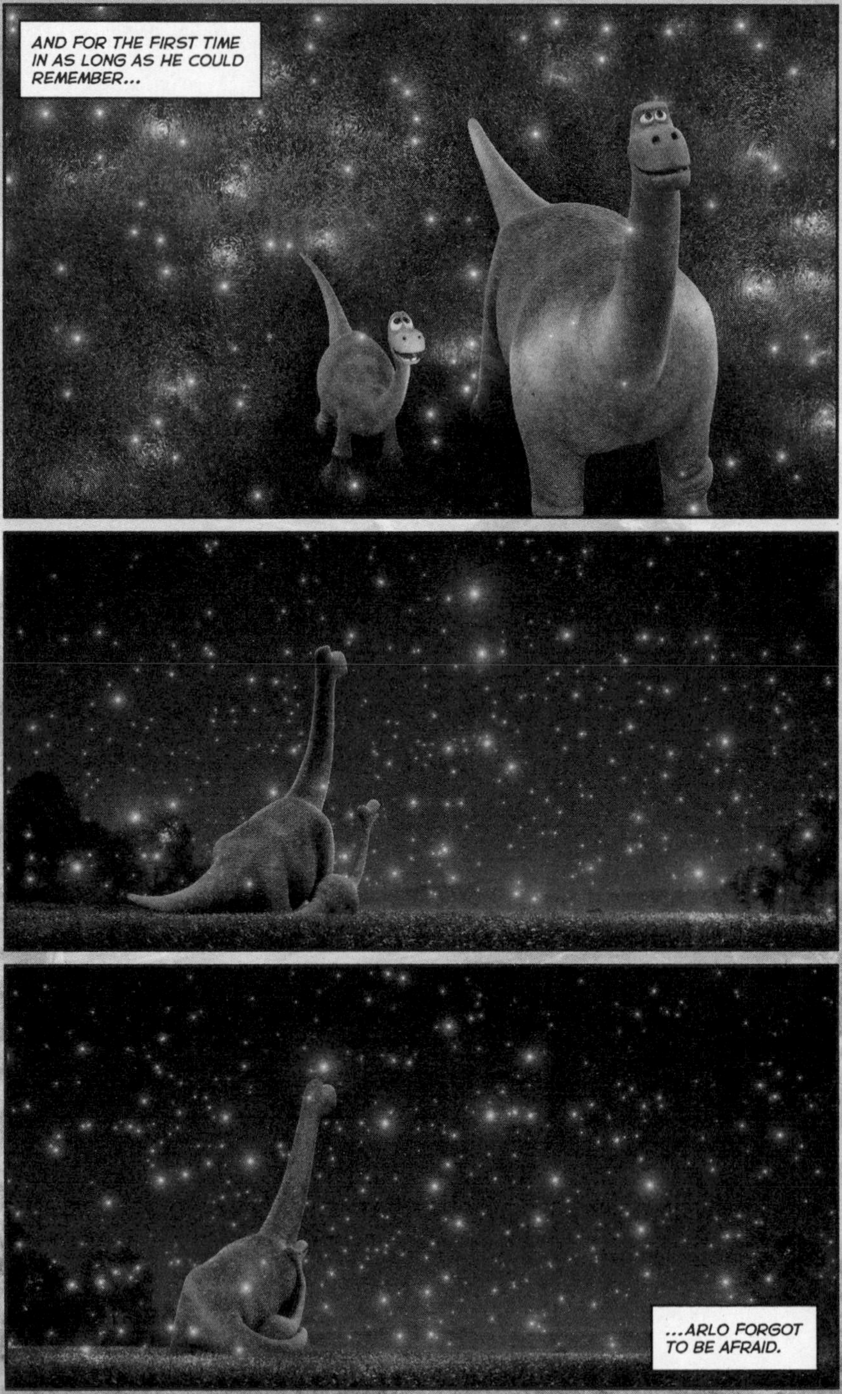
AND FOR THE FIRST TIME IN AS LONG AS HE COULD REMEMBER...
...ARLO FORGOT TO BE AFRAID.

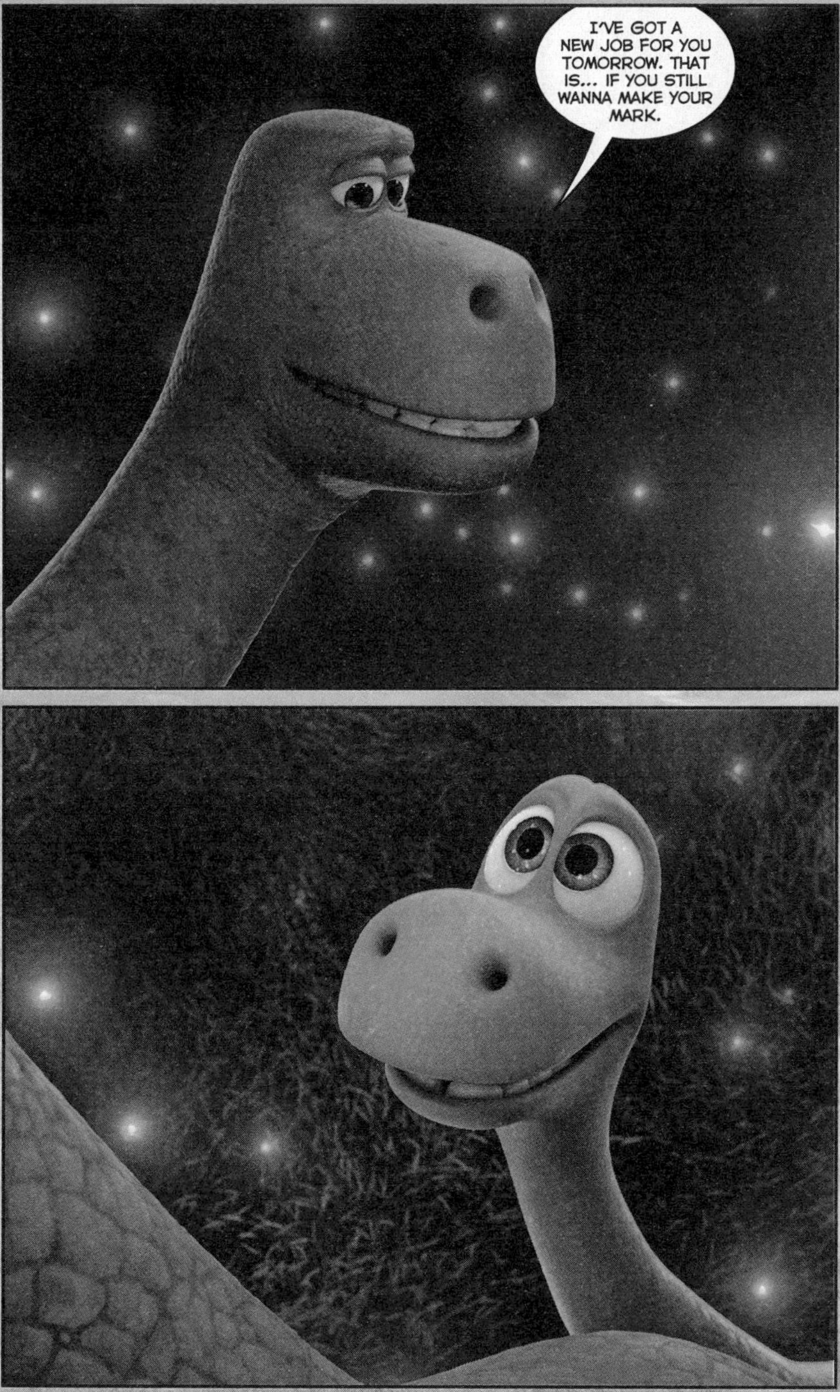
I'VE GOT A NEW JOB FOR YOU TOMORROW. THAT IS... IF YOU STILL WANNA MAKE YOUR MARK.

THE GOOD DINOSAUR

Disney · PIXAR

SHAMAN

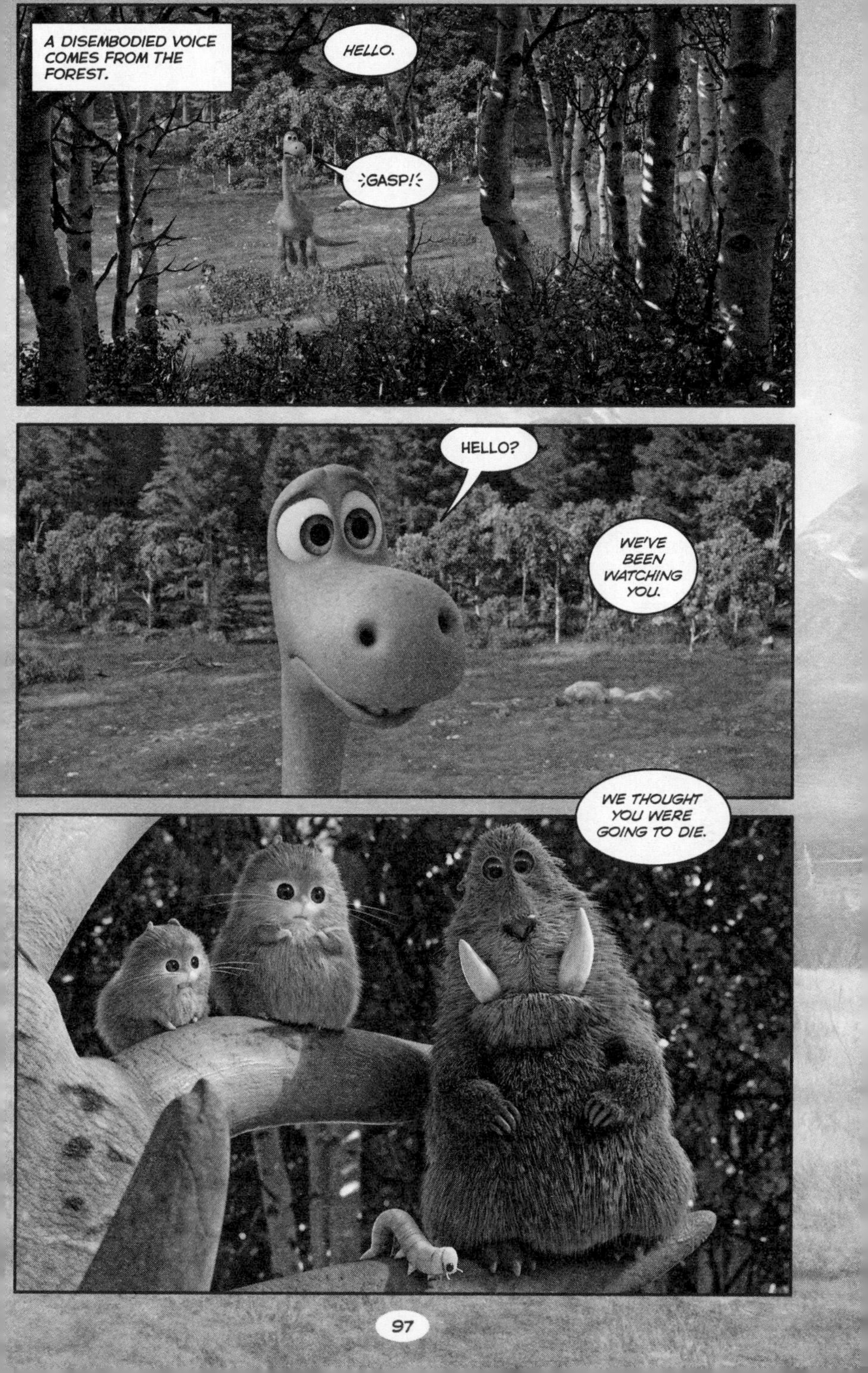
A DISEMBODIED VOICE COMES FROM THE FOREST.
HELLO.
GASP!
HELLO?
WE'VE BEEN WATCHING YOU.
WE THOUGHT YOU WERE GOING TO DIE.

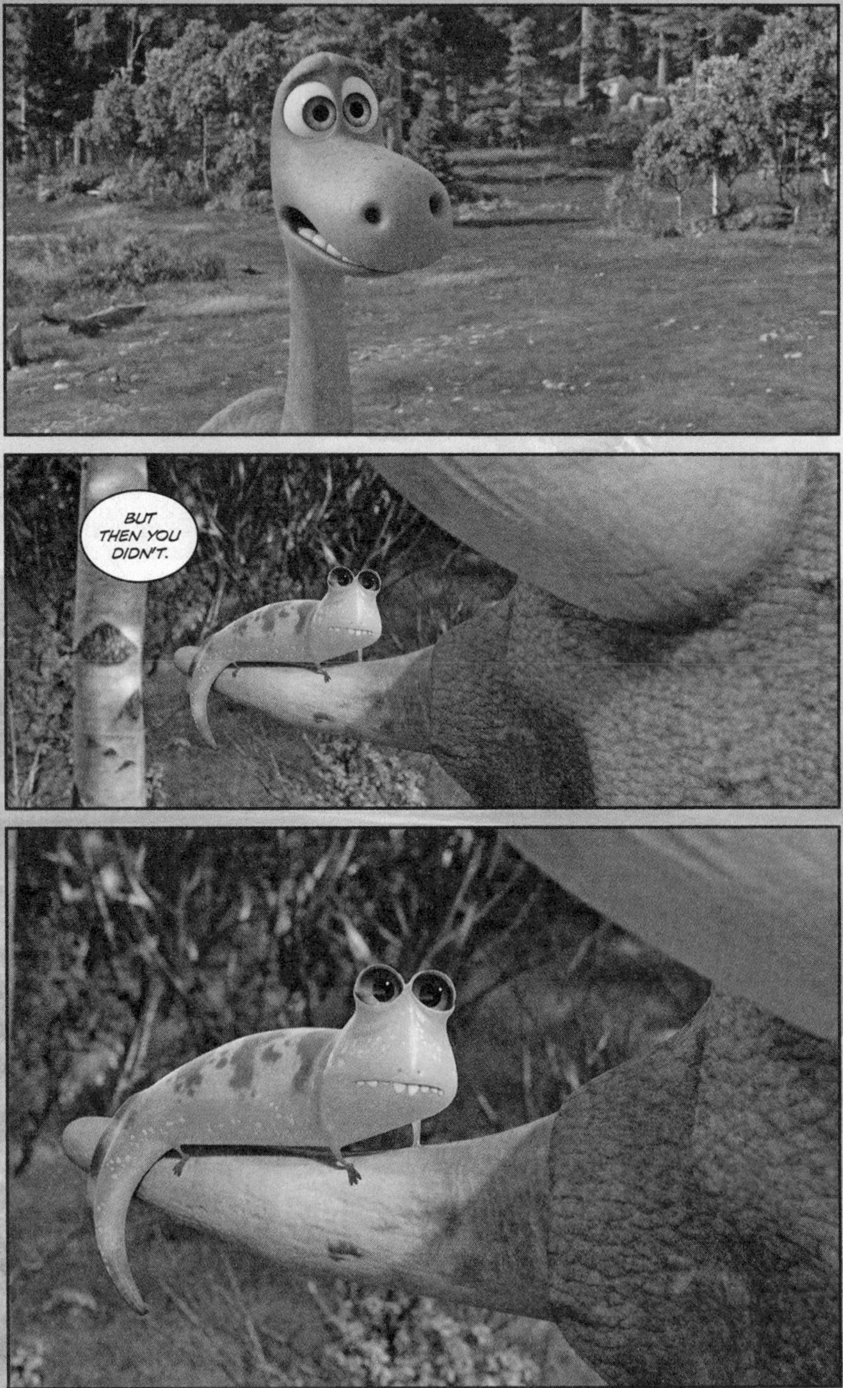
BUT THEN YOU DIDN'T.

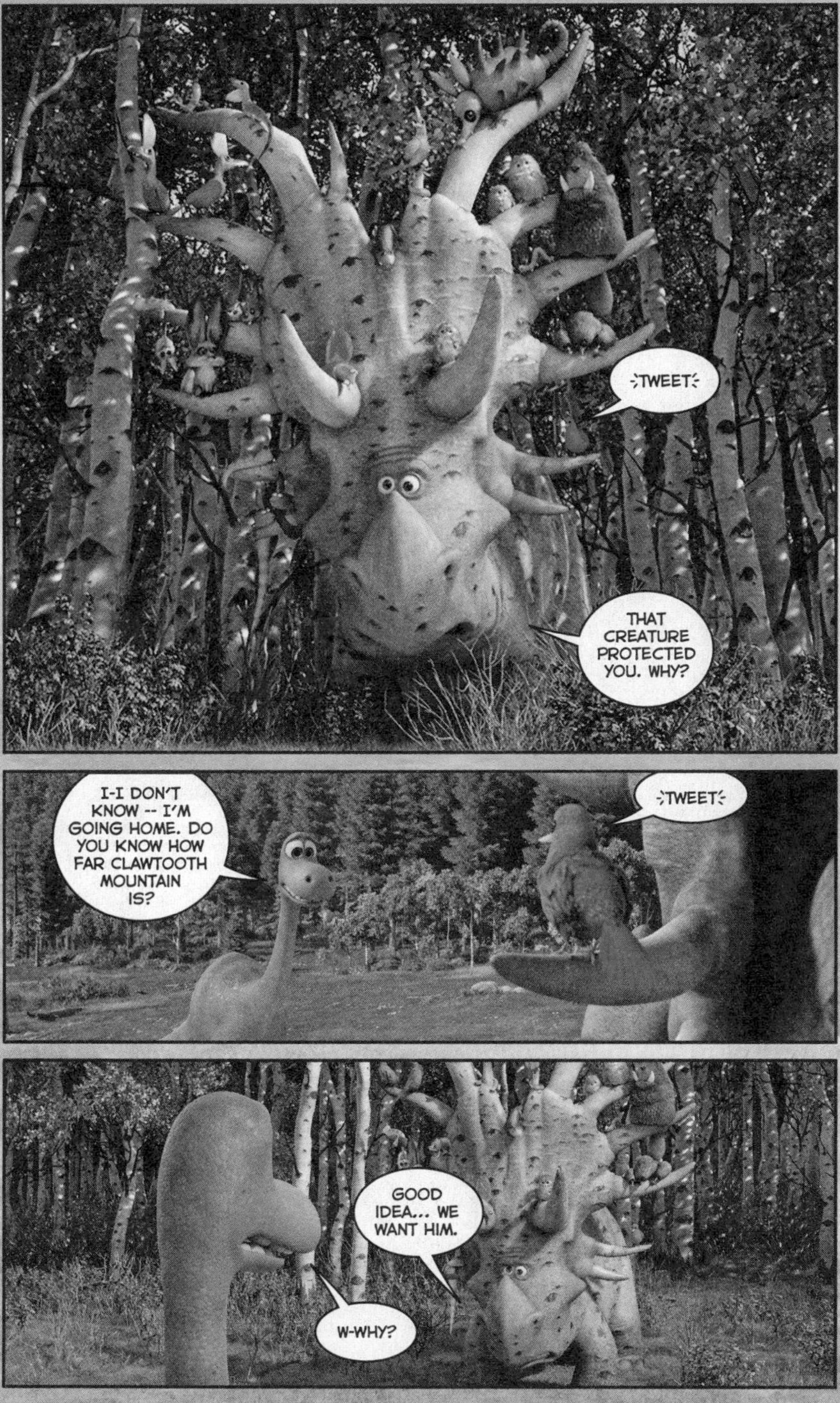
TWEET
THAT CREATURE PROTECTED YOU. WHY?
I-I DON'T KNOW -- I'M GOING HOME. DO YOU KNOW HOW FAR CLAWTOOTH MOUNTAIN IS?
TWEET
GOOD IDEA... WE WANT HIM.
W-WHY?

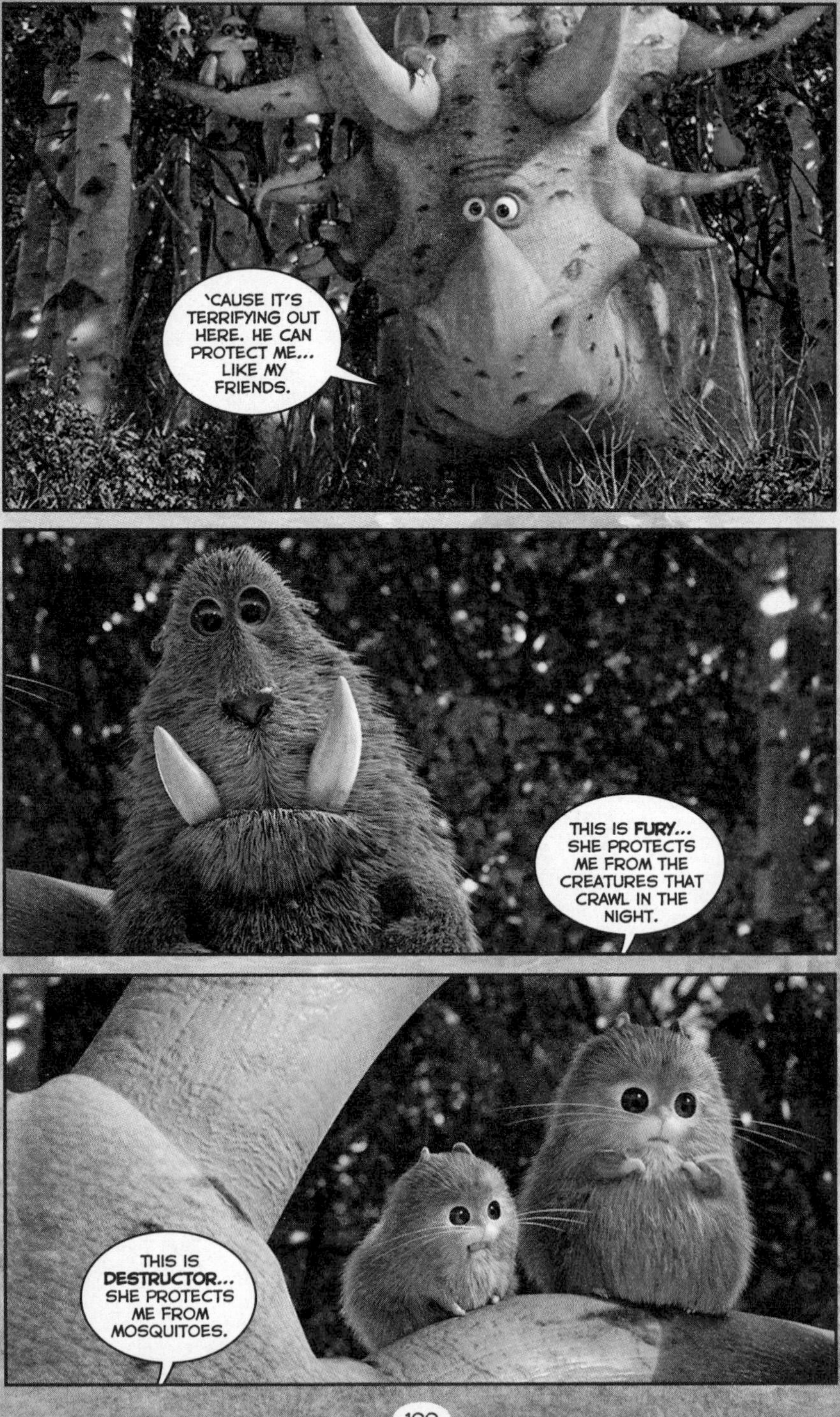
'CAUSE IT'S TERRIFYING OUT HERE. HE CAN PROTECT ME... LIKE MY FRIENDS.
THIS IS **FURY**... SHE PROTECTS ME FROM THE CREATURES THAT CRAWL IN THE NIGHT.
THIS IS **DESTRUCTOR**... SHE PROTECTS ME FROM MOSQUITOES.

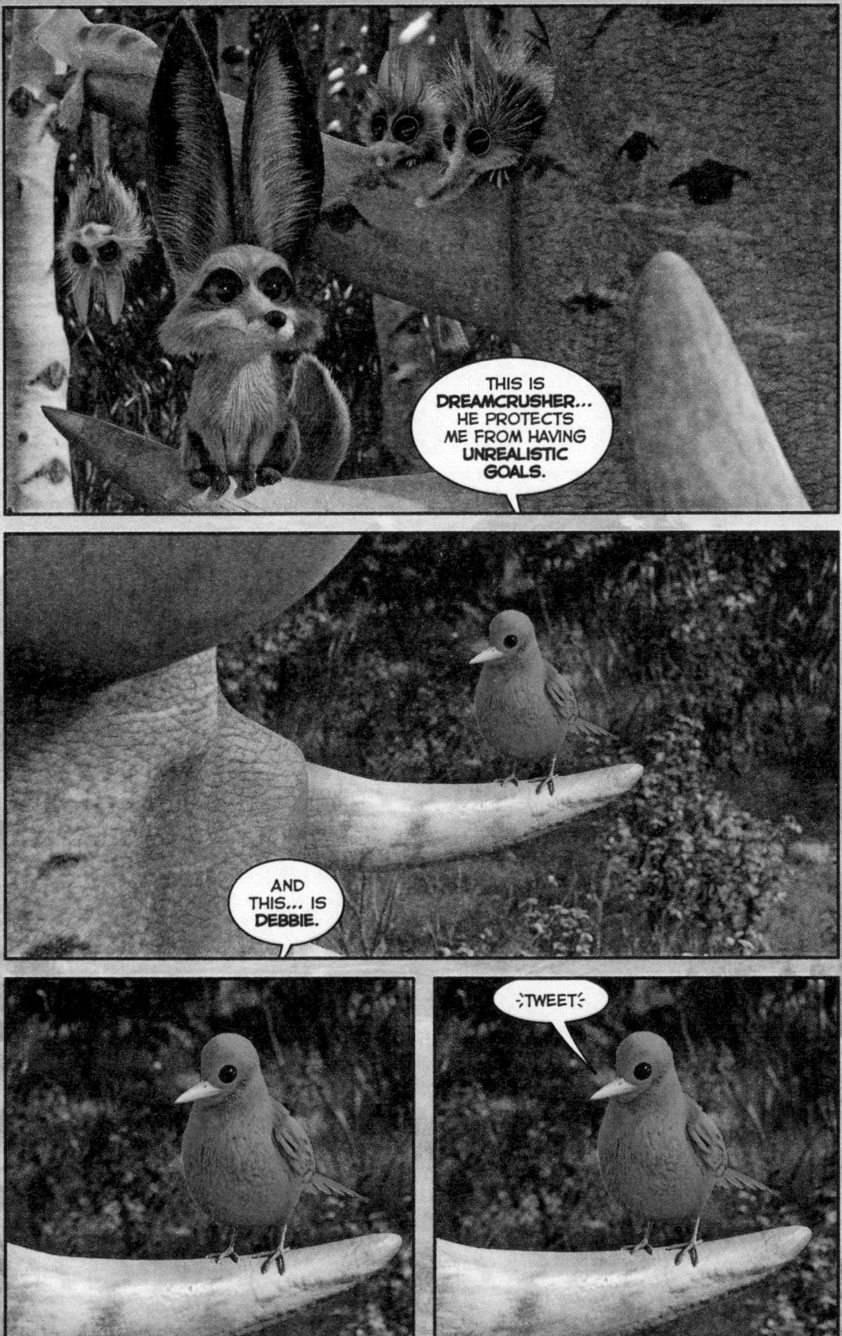
THIS IS DREAMCRUSHER... HE PROTECTS ME FROM HAVING UNREALISTIC GOALS.
AND THIS... IS DEBBIE.
TWEET

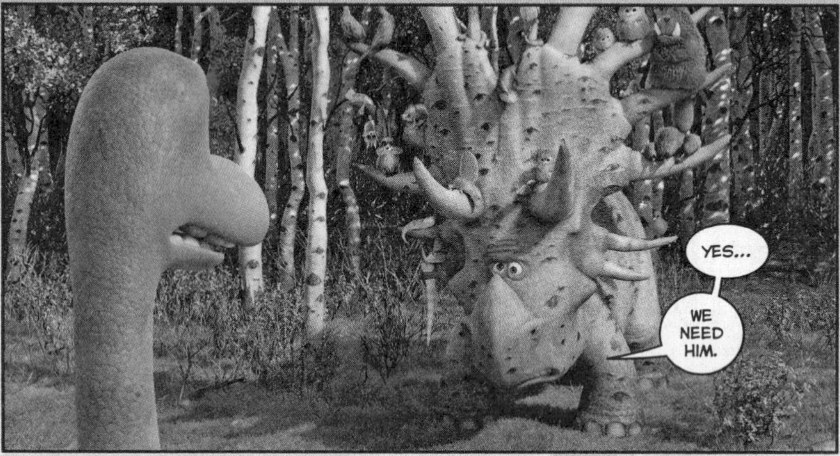
YES...
WE NEED HIM.

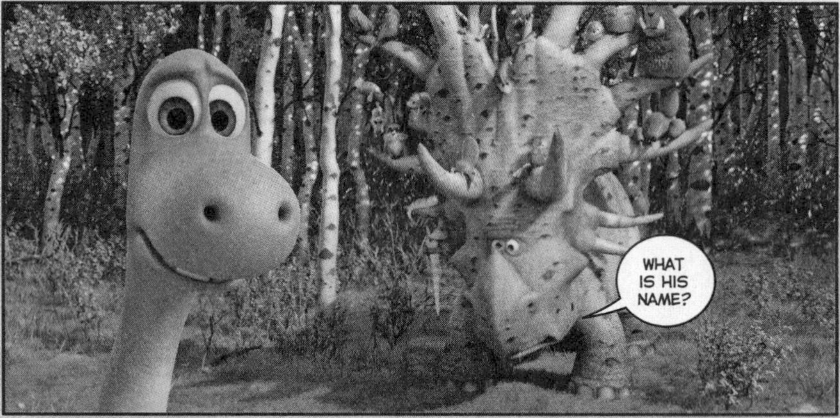
WHAT IS HIS NAME?

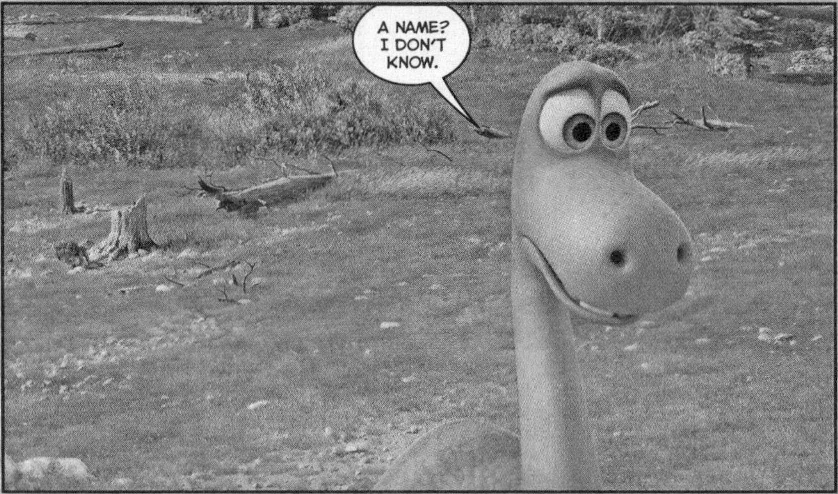
A NAME? I DON'T KNOW.

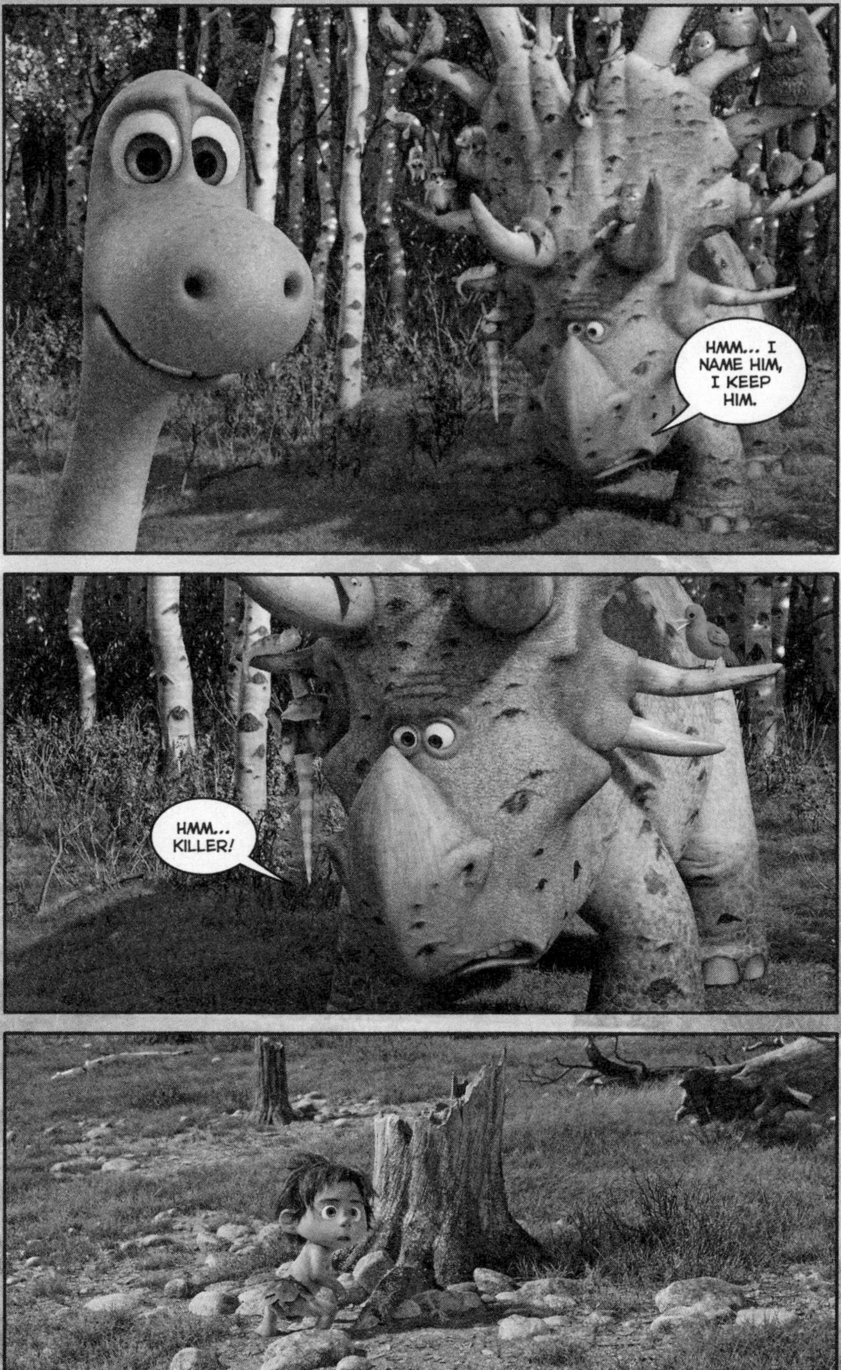
HMM... I NAME HIM, I KEEP HIM.
HMM... KILLER!

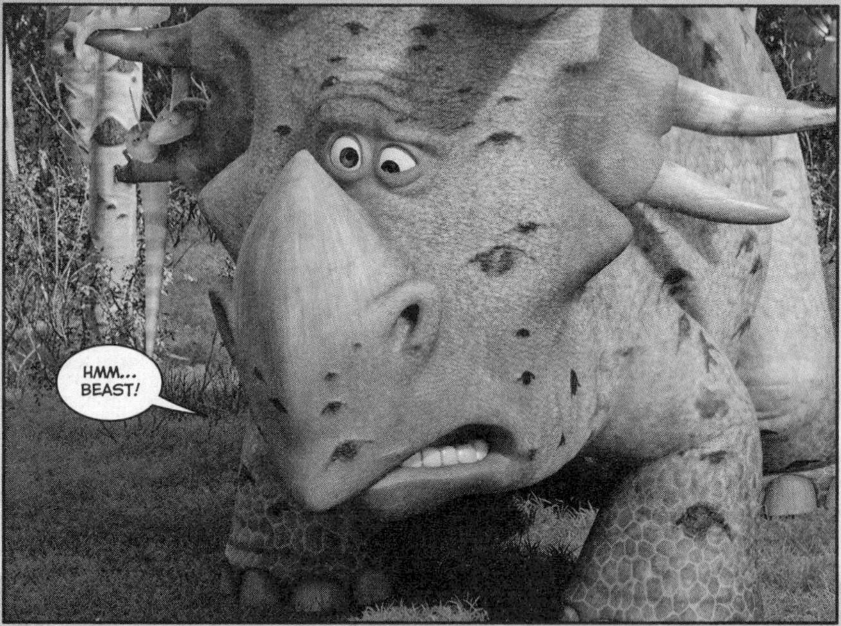
HMM...
BEAST!

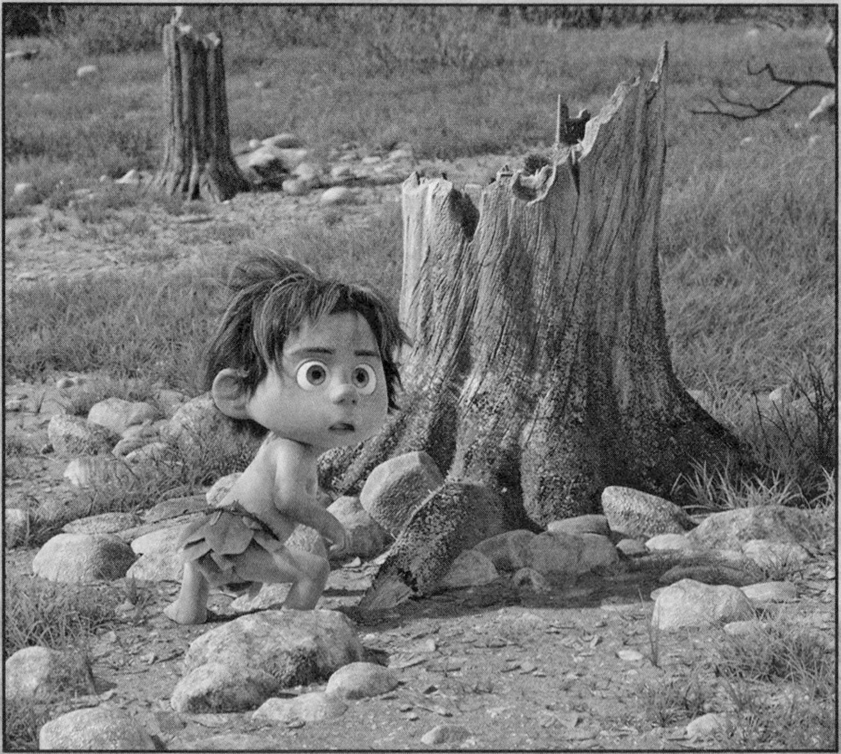

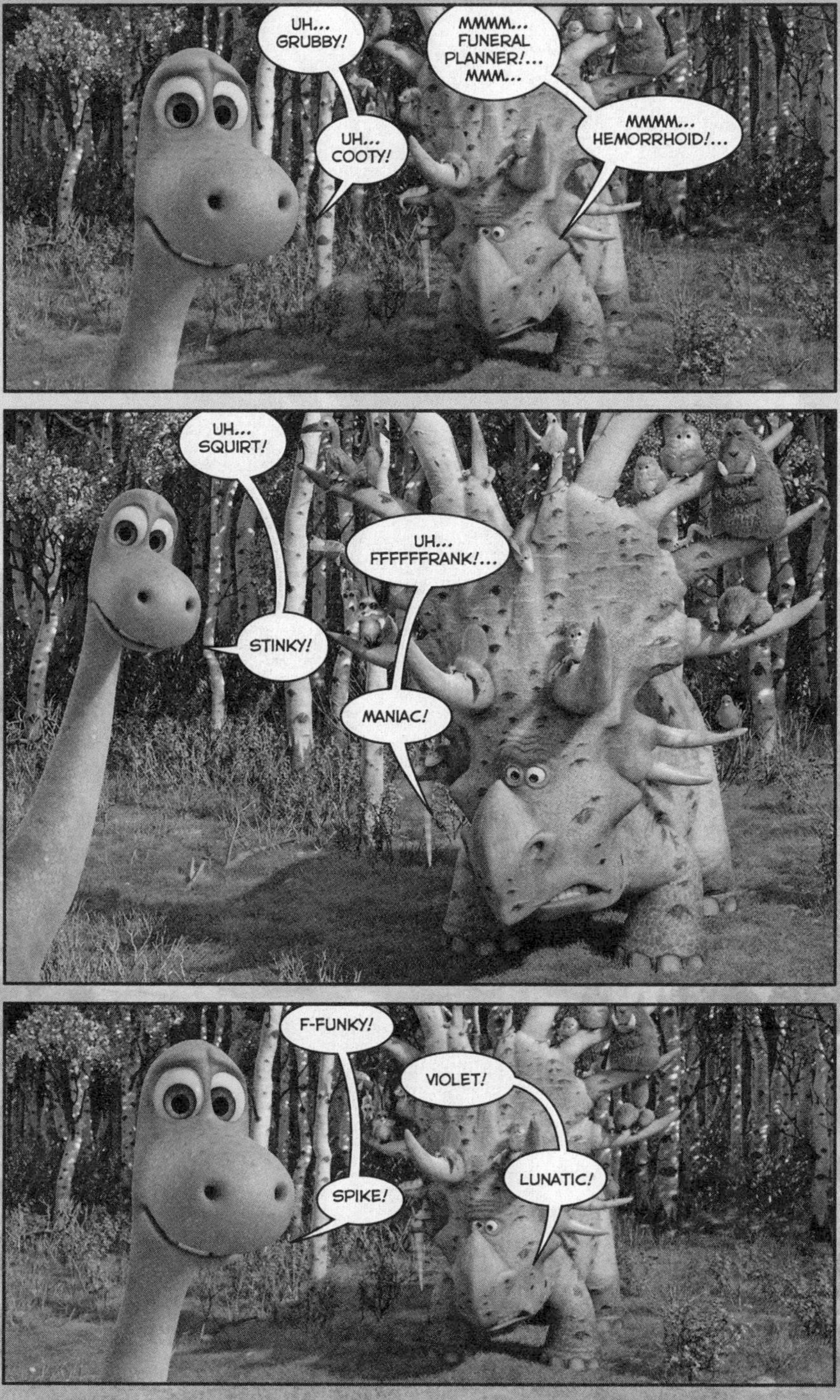
UH... GRUBBY!
MMMM... FUNERAL PLANNER!... MMM...
UH... COOTY!
MMMM... HEMORRHOID!...
UH... SQUIRT!
UH... FFFFFFRANK!...
STINKY!
MANIAC!
F-FUNKY!
VIOLET!
SPIKE!
LUNATIC!

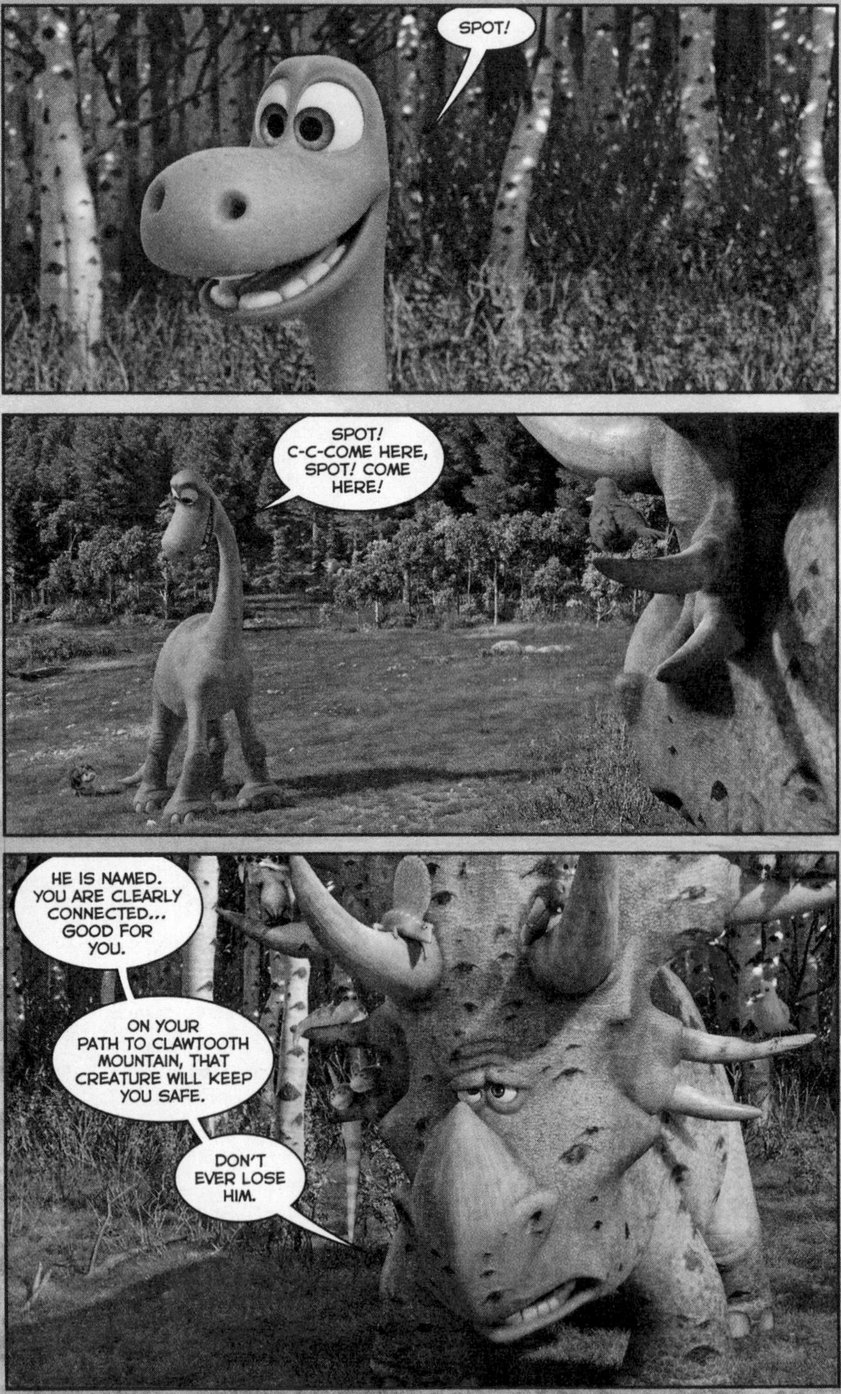
SPOT!
SPOT! C-C-COME HERE, SPOT! COME HERE!
HE IS NAMED. YOU ARE CLEARLY CONNECTED... GOOD FOR YOU.
ON YOUR PATH TO CLAWTOOTH MOUNTAIN, THAT CREATURE WILL KEEP YOU SAFE.
DON'T EVER LOSE HIM.

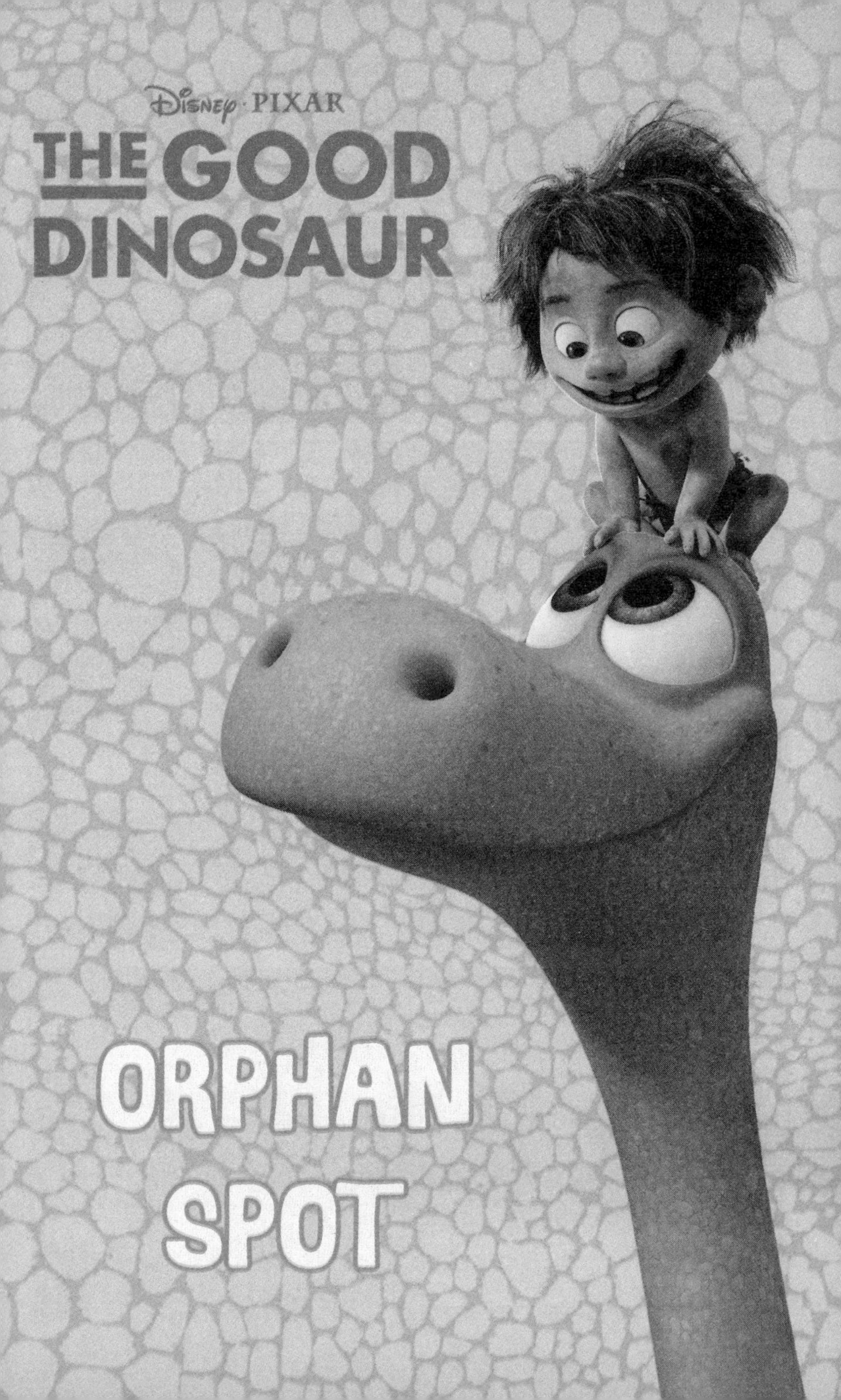
Disney·PIXAR
THE GOOD DINOSAUR
ORPHAN
SPOT

SPOT, WATCH THIS!

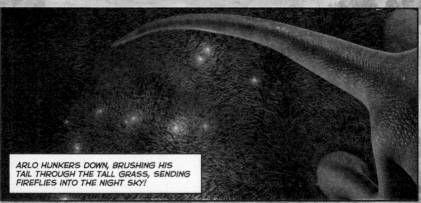

ARLO HUNKERS DOWN, BRUSHING HIS TAIL THROUGH THE TALL GRASS, SENDING FIREFLIES INTO THE NIGHT SKY!

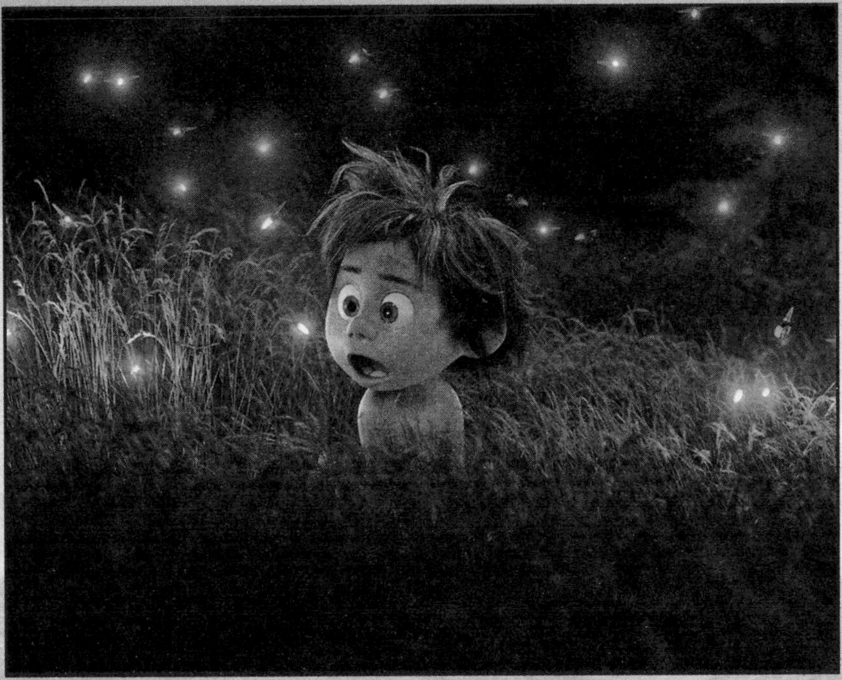

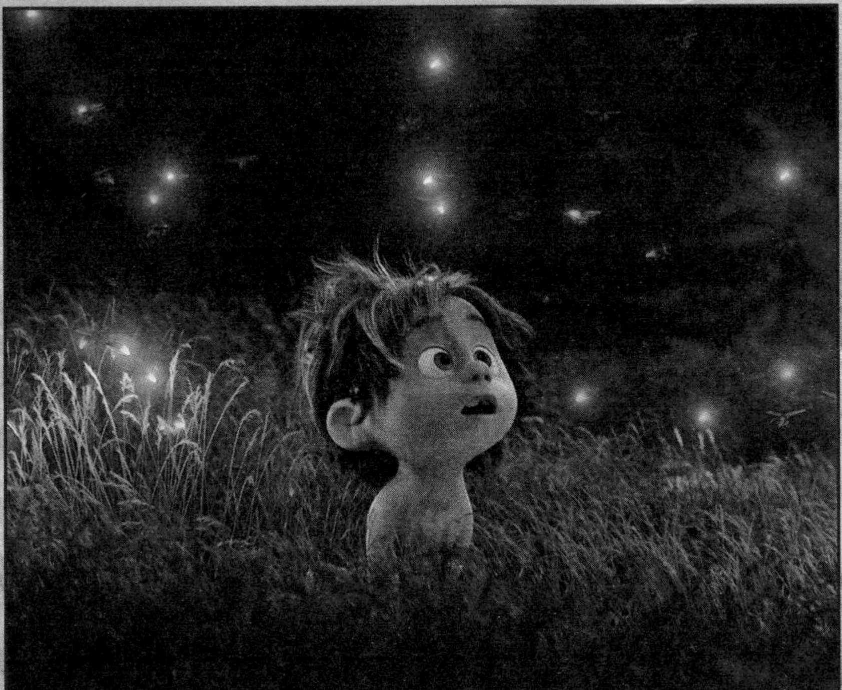

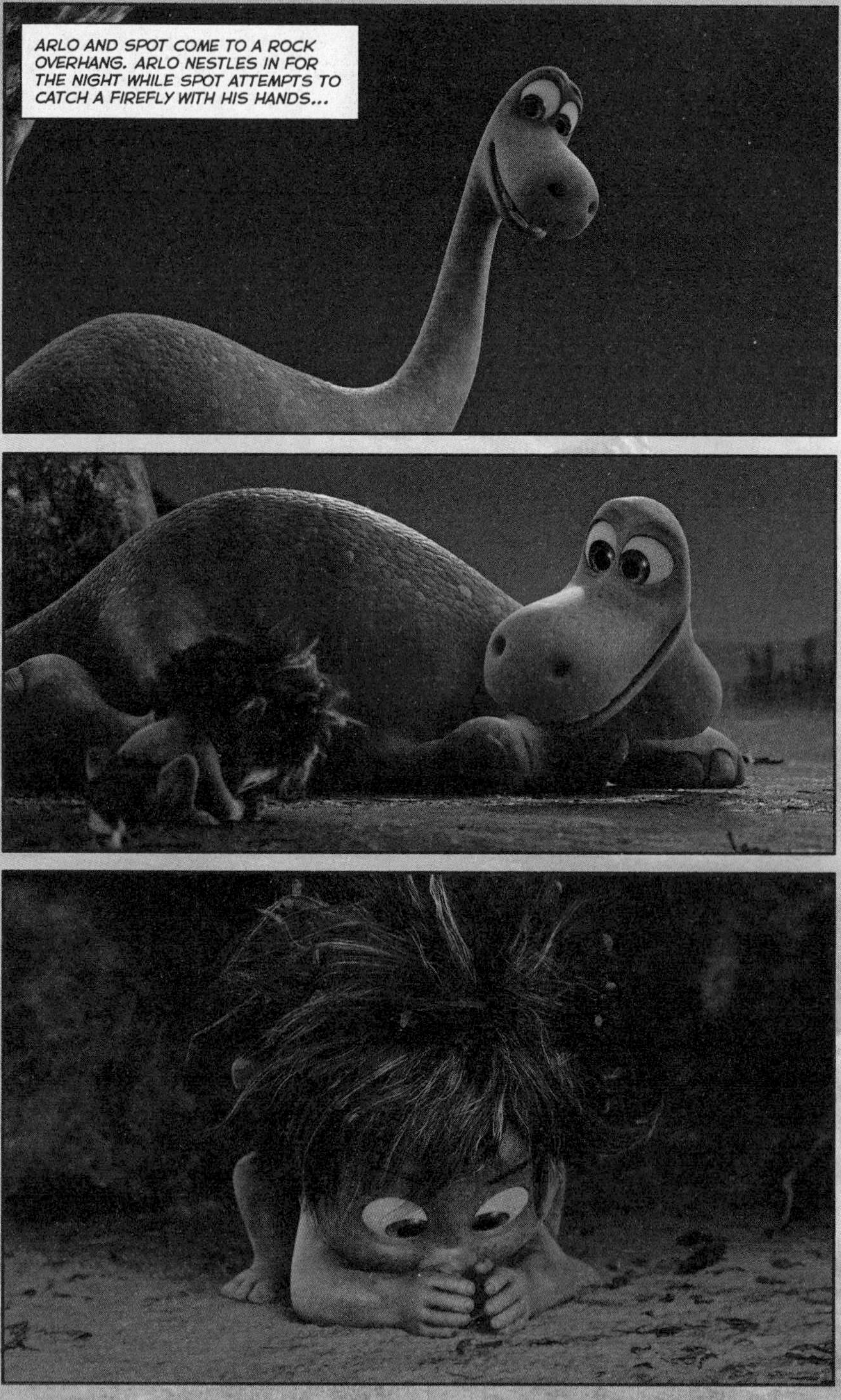
ARLO AND SPOT COME TO A ROCK OVERHANG. ARLO NESTLES IN FOR THE NIGHT WHILE SPOT ATTEMPTS TO CATCH A FIREFLY WITH HIS HANDS...

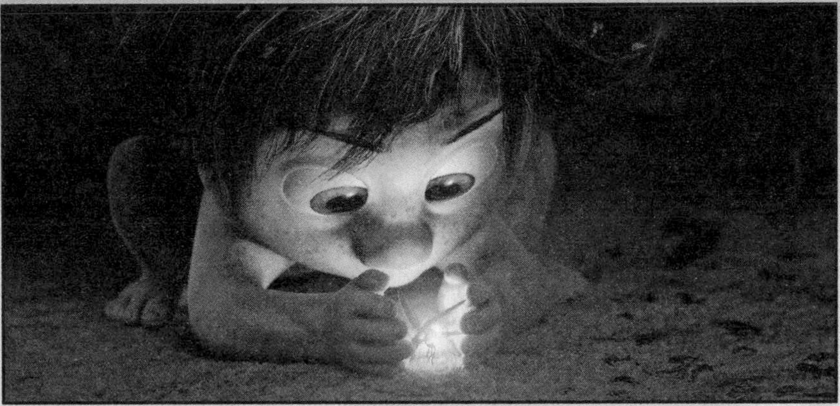
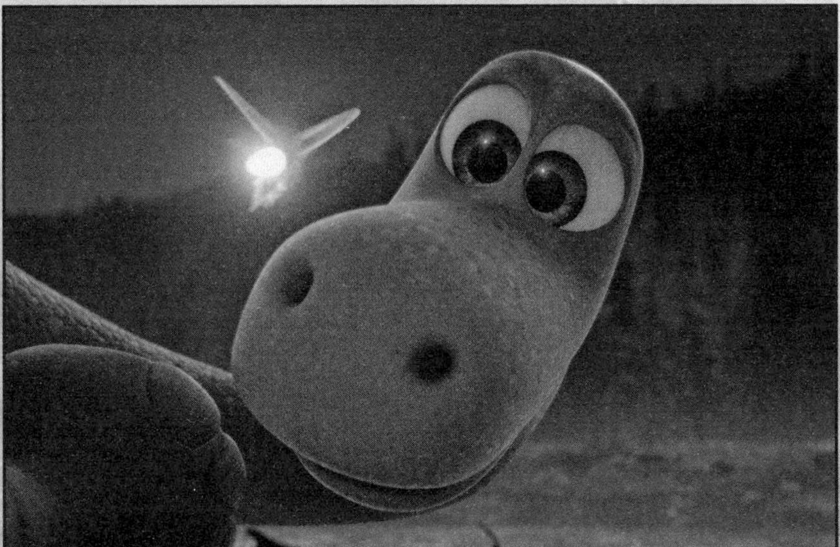
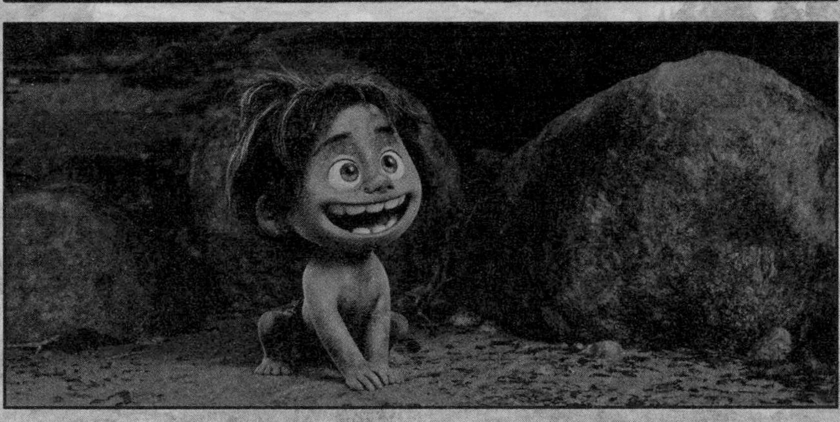

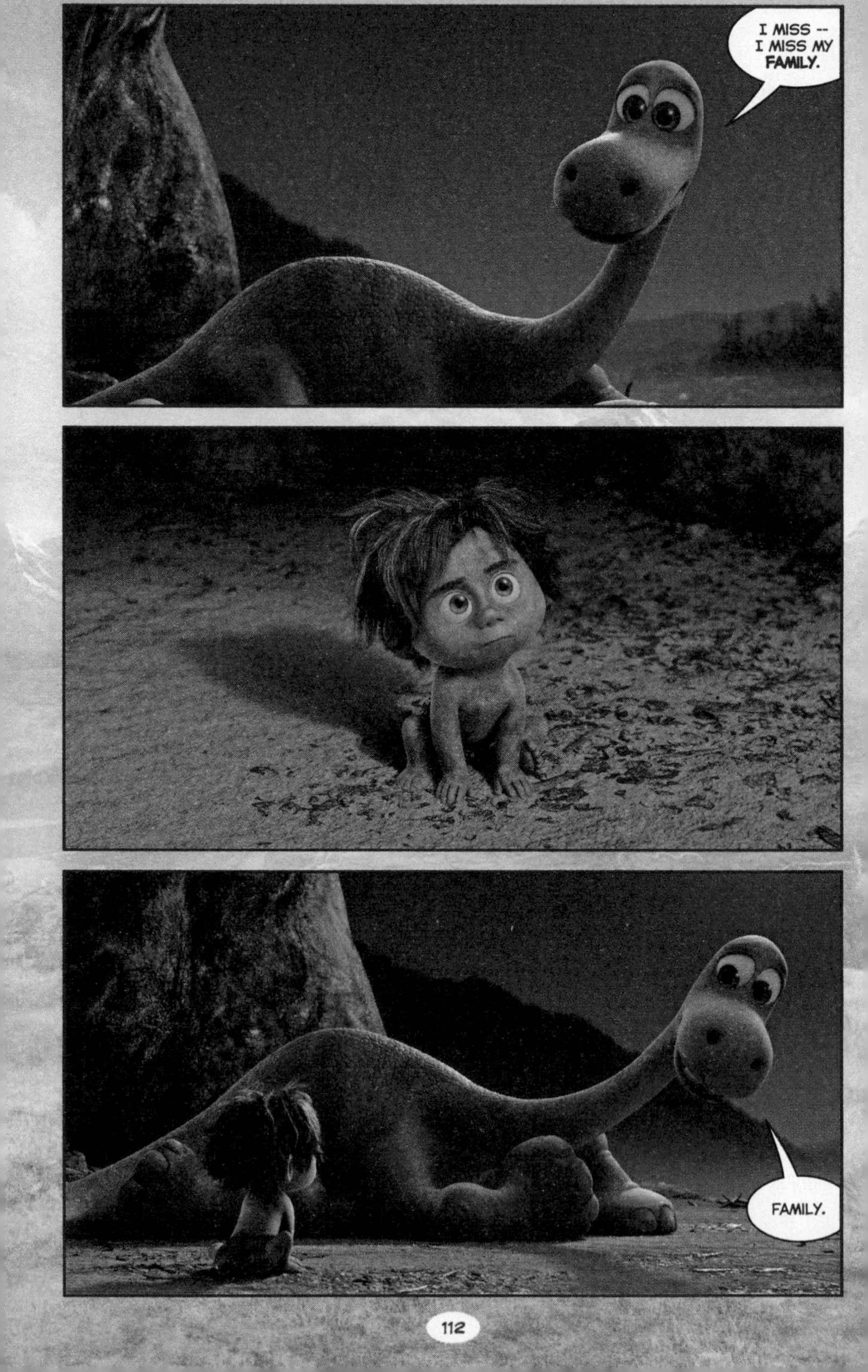
I MISS --
I MISS MY
FAMILY.
FAMILY.

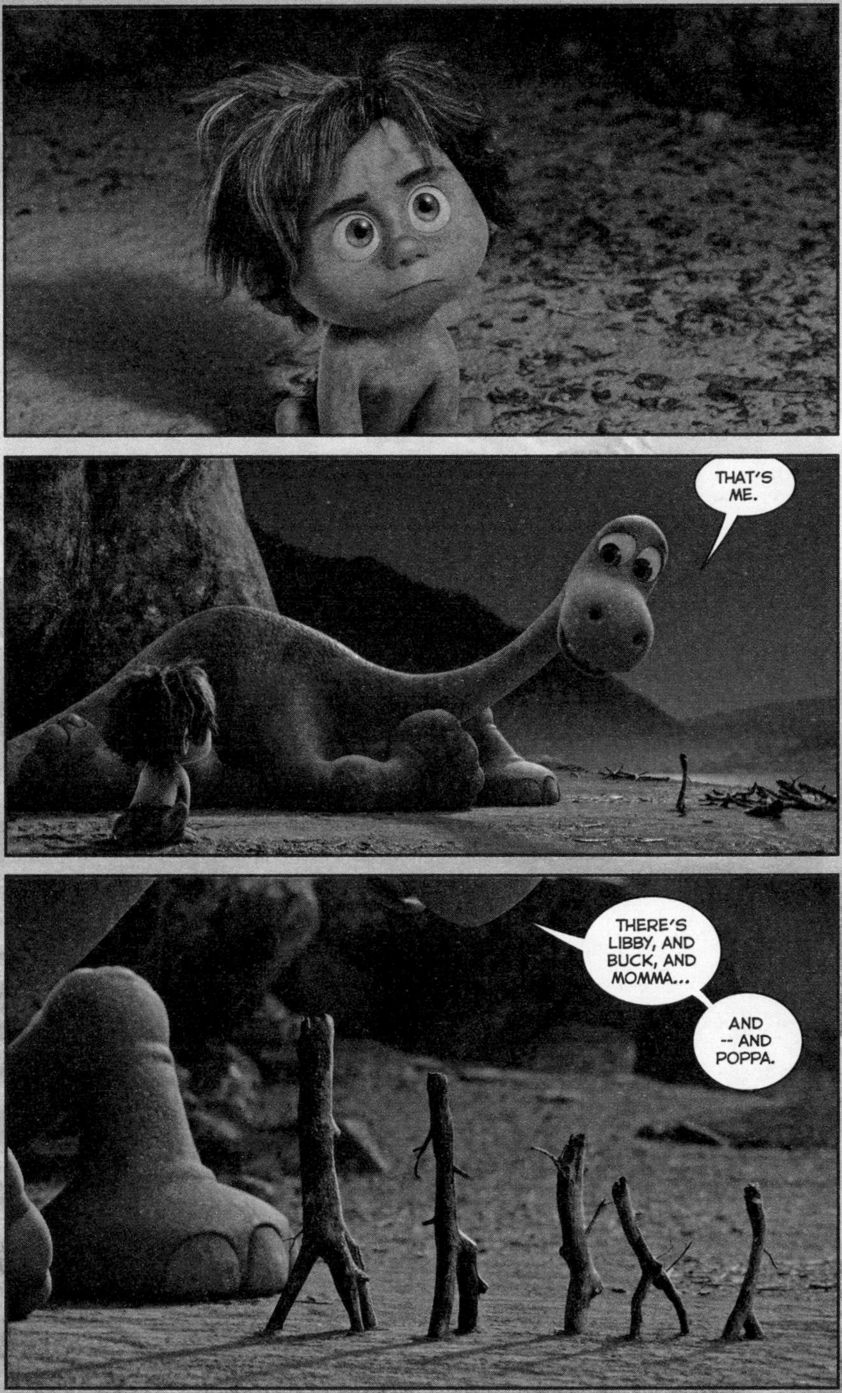
THAT'S ME.
THERE'S LIBBY, AND BUCK, AND MOMMA...
AND -- AND POPPA.

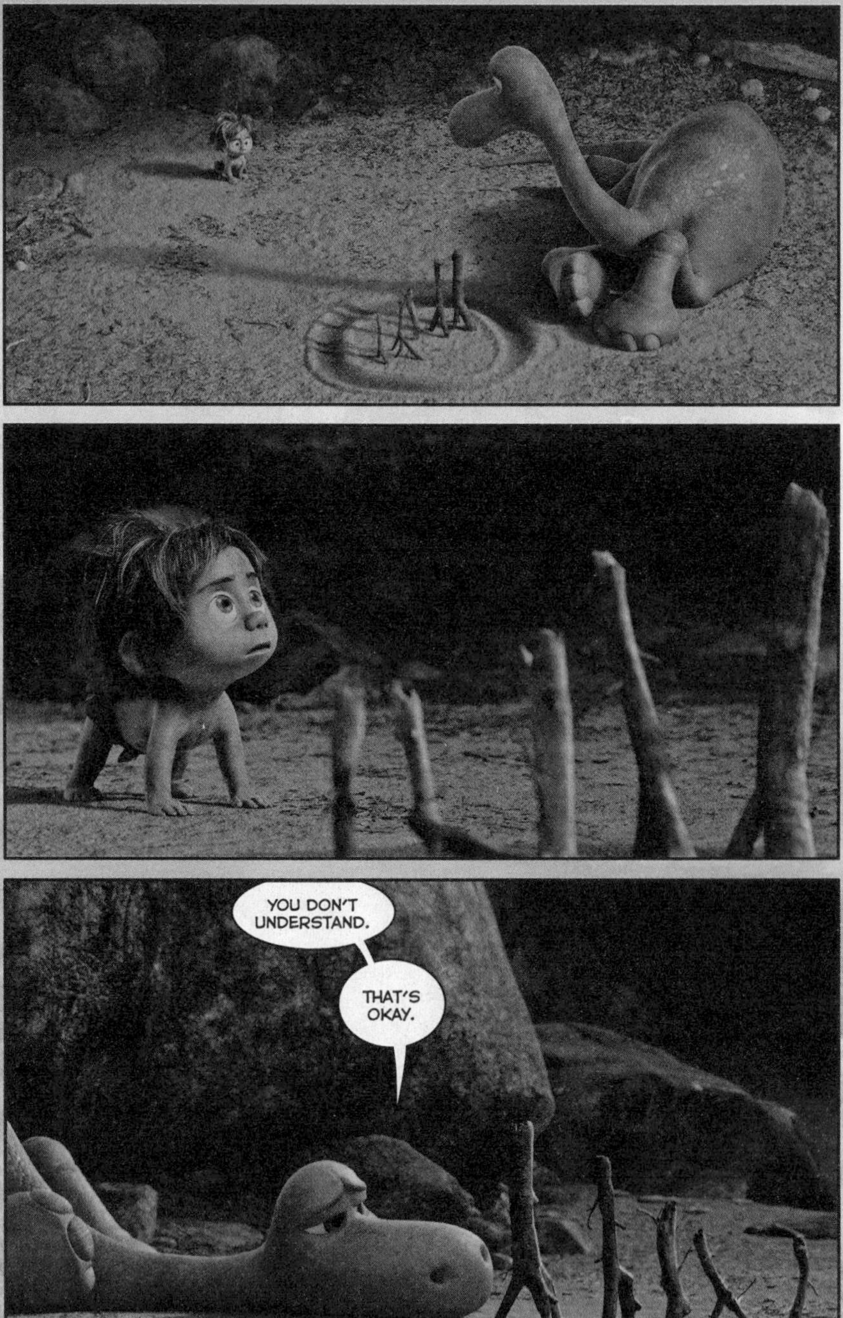
YOU DON'T UNDERSTAND.
THAT'S OKAY.

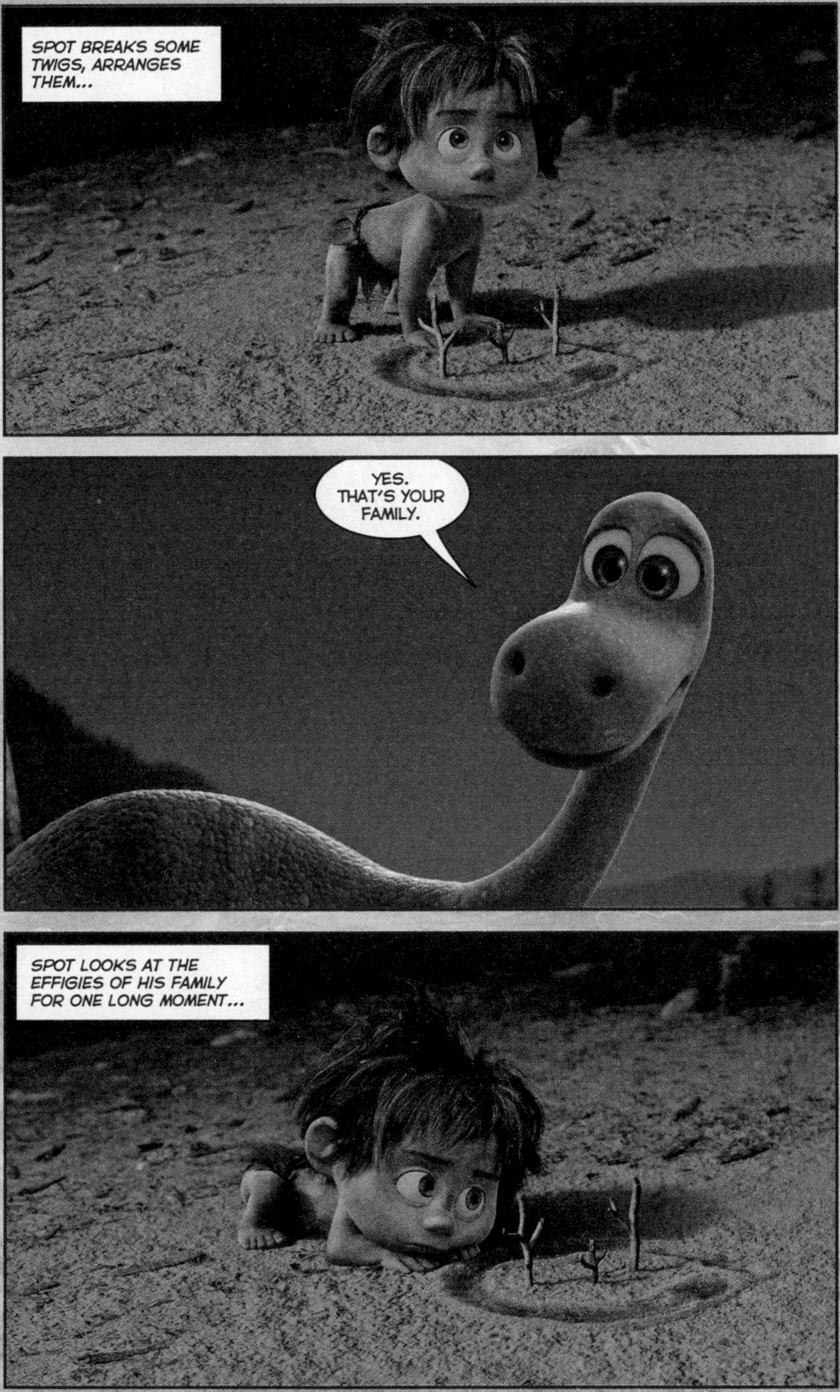
SPOT BREAKS SOME TWIGS, ARRANGES THEM...
YES. THAT'S YOUR FAMILY.
SPOT LOOKS AT THE EFFIGIES OF HIS FAMILY FOR ONE LONG MOMENT...

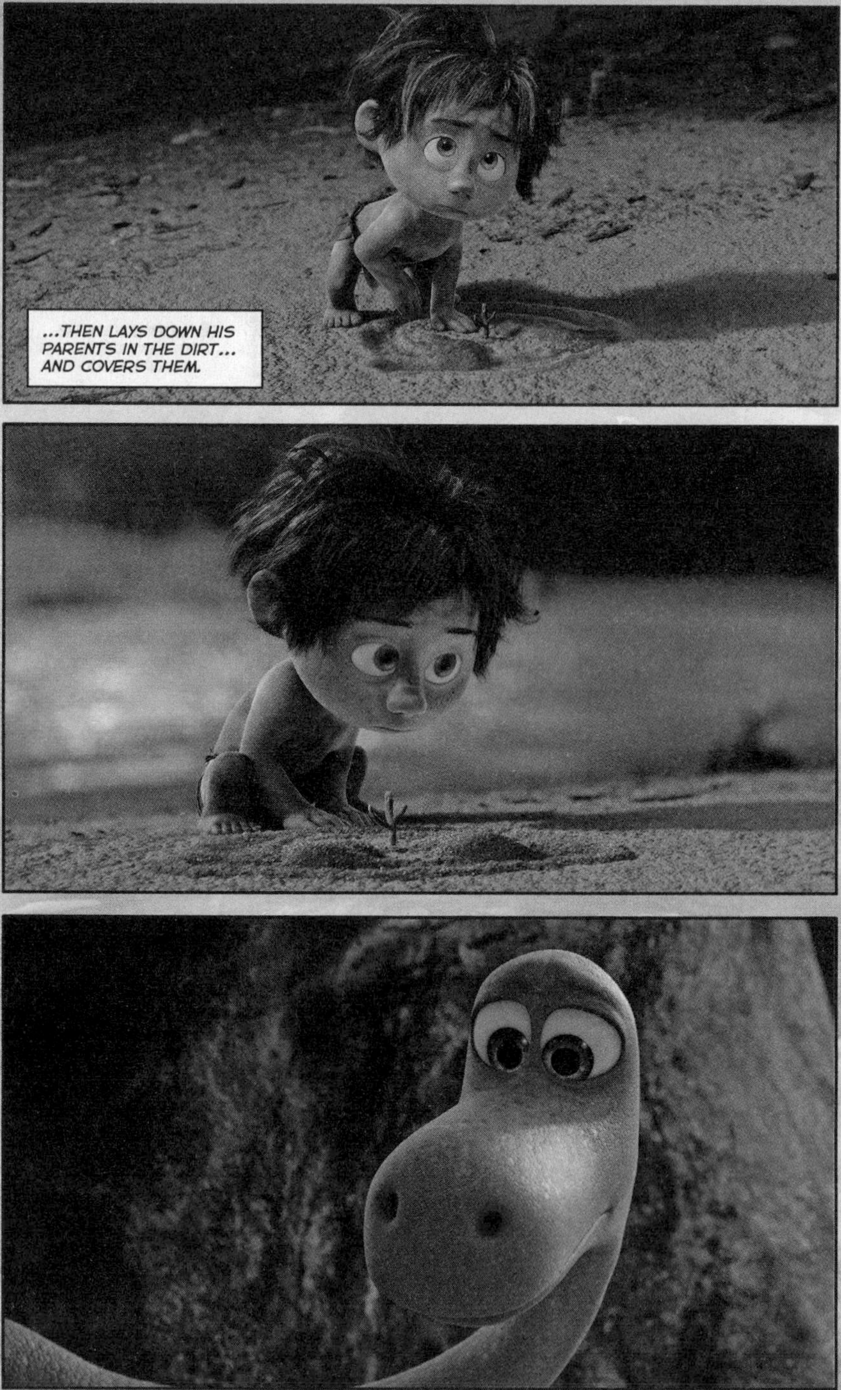
...THEN LAYS DOWN HIS PARENTS IN THE DIRT... AND COVERS THEM.

ARLO TURNS OVER
POPPA'S EFFIGY.
HE COVERS IT.

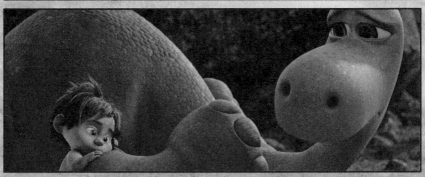

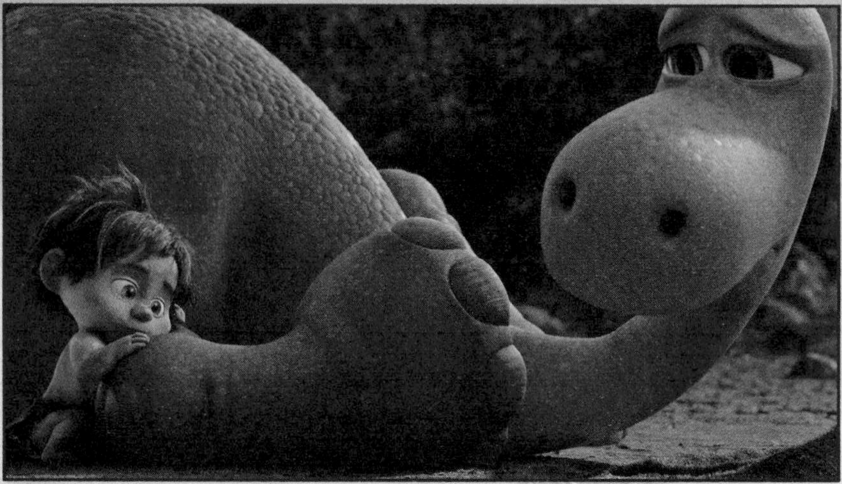

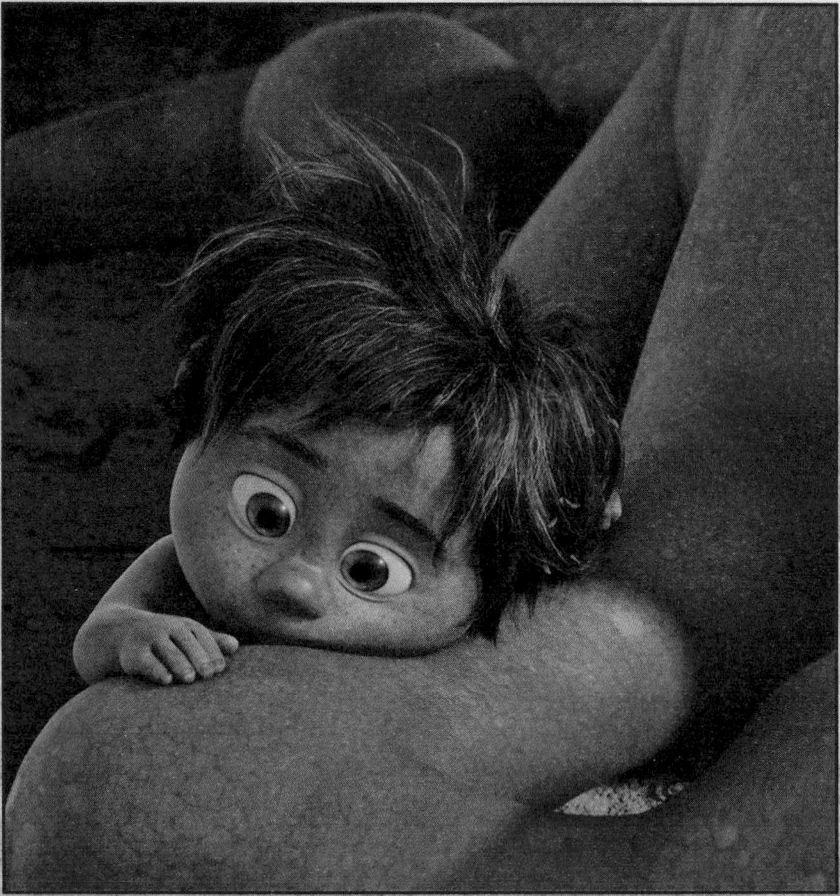

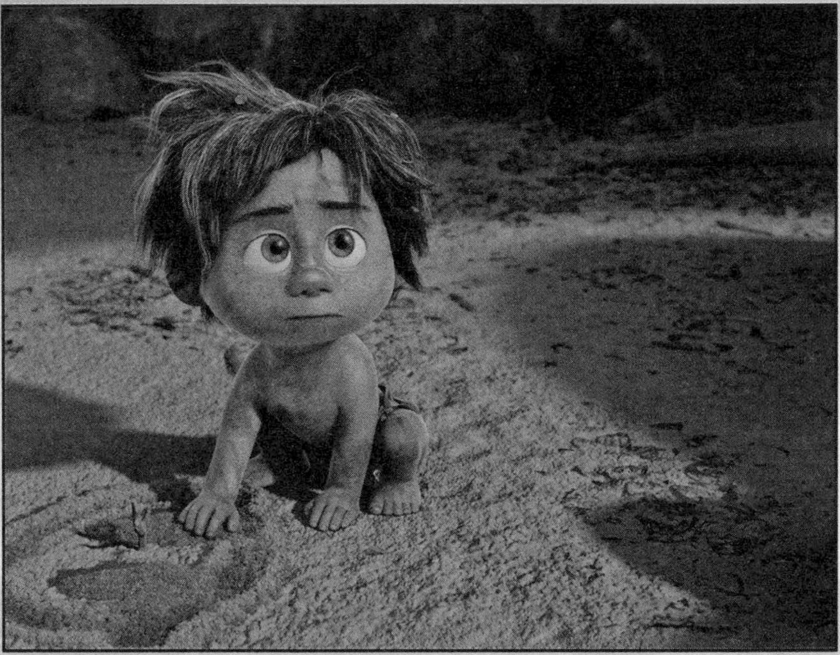

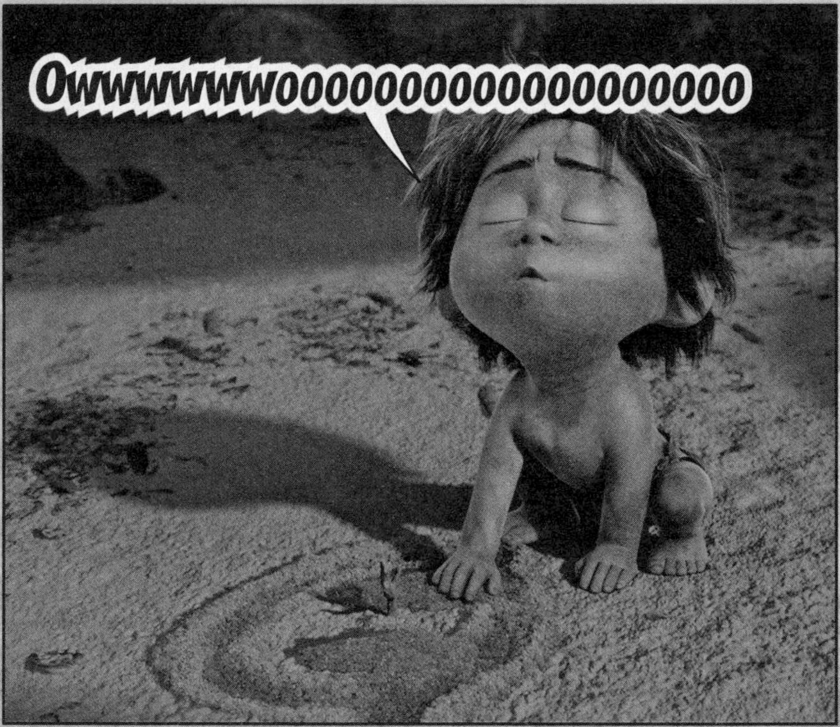
Owwwwwwooooooooooooooooooo

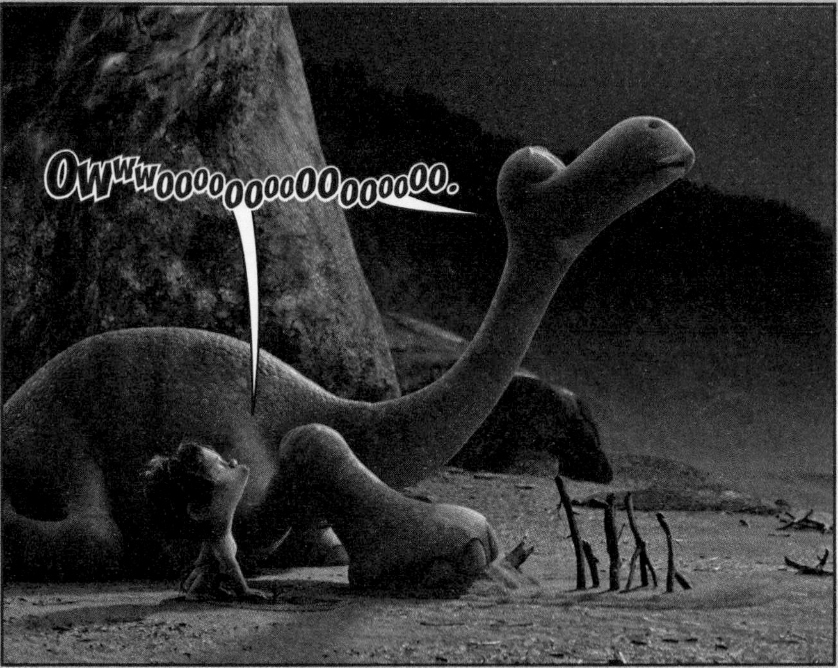
OWWWWOOOOOOOOOOOOOOOO.

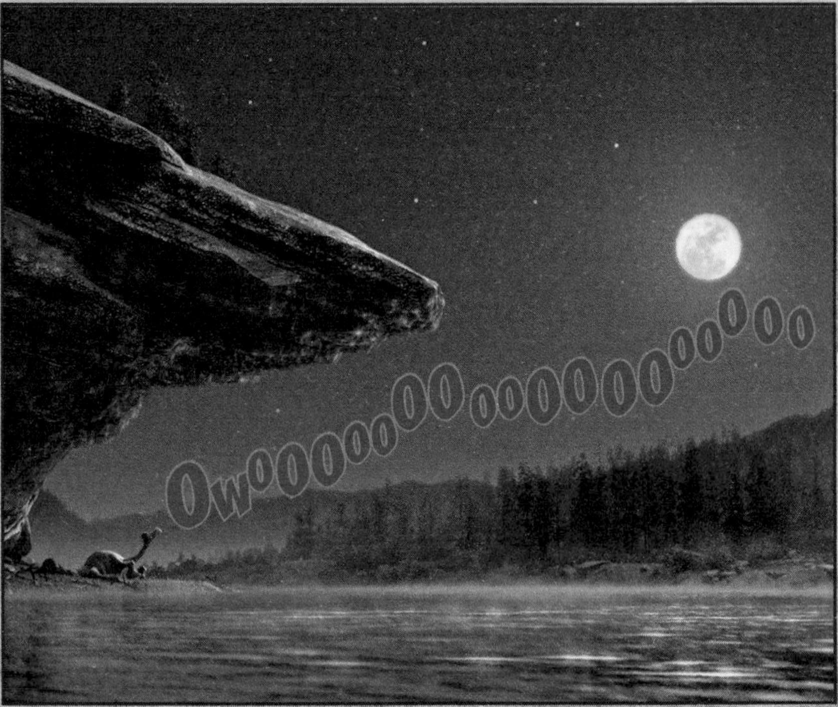
OwOOOOOOOOOOOOOOOOOO

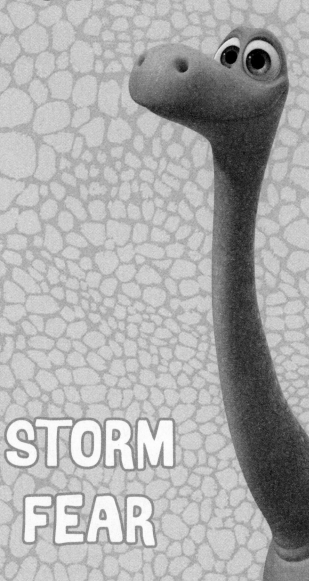

Disney · PIXAR

THE GOOD
DINOSAUR

STORM
FEAR

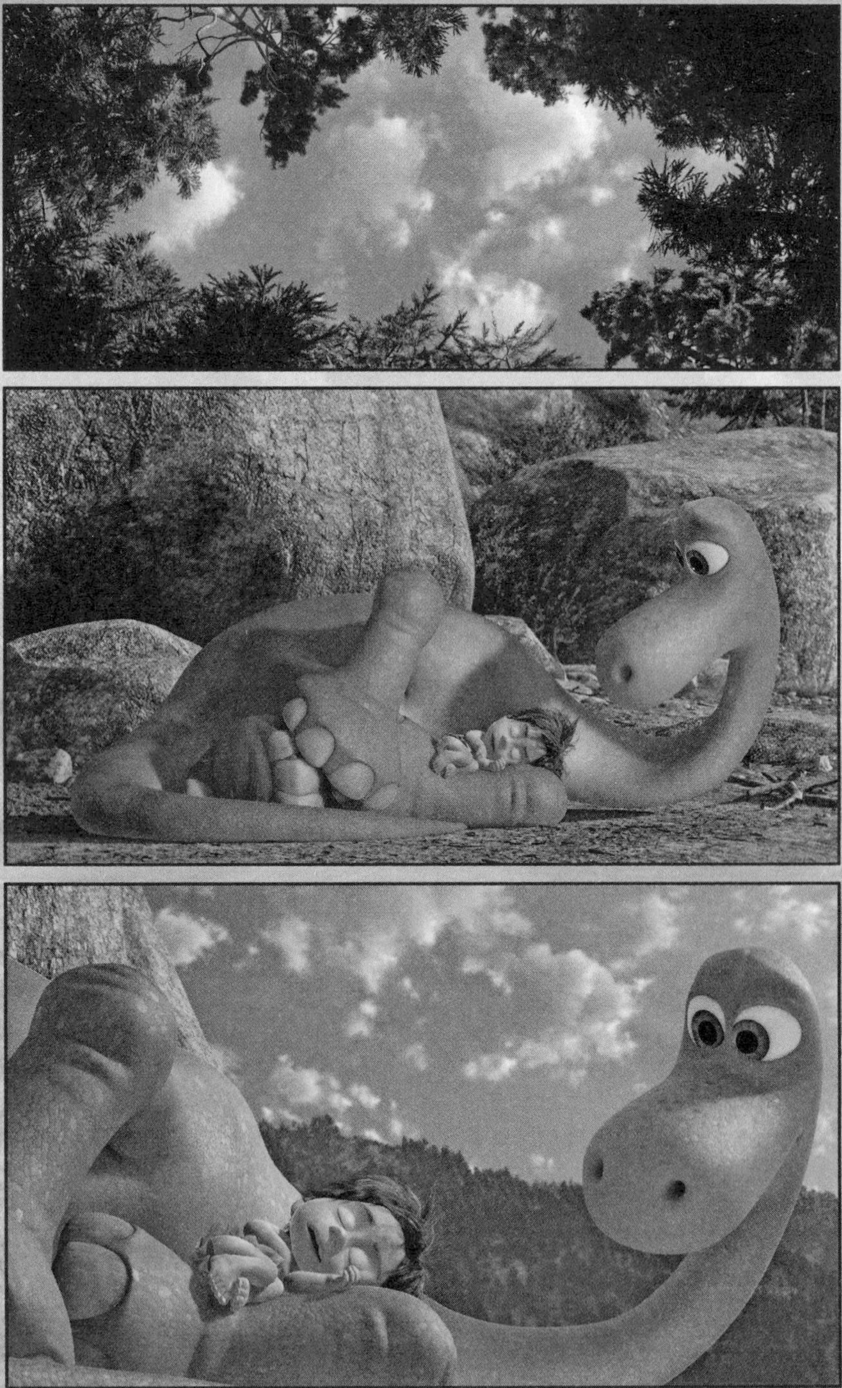

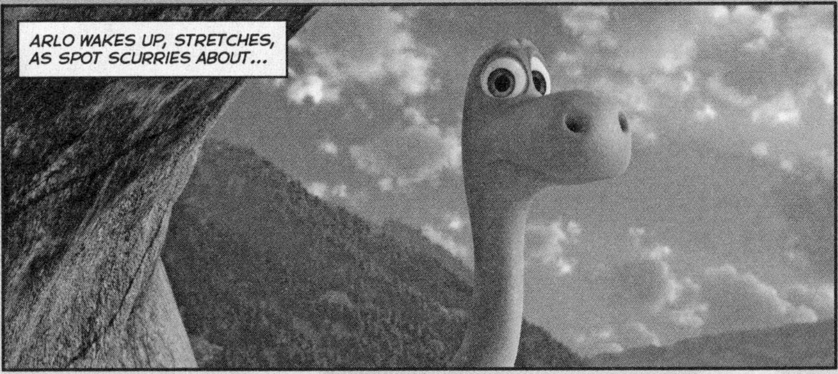
ARLO WAKES UP, STRETCHES, AS SPOT SCURRIES ABOUT...

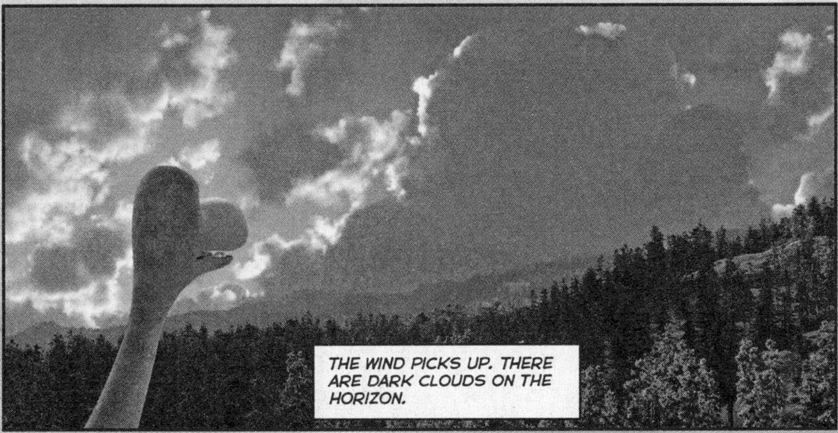
THE WIND PICKS UP. THERE ARE DARK CLOUDS ON THE HORIZON.

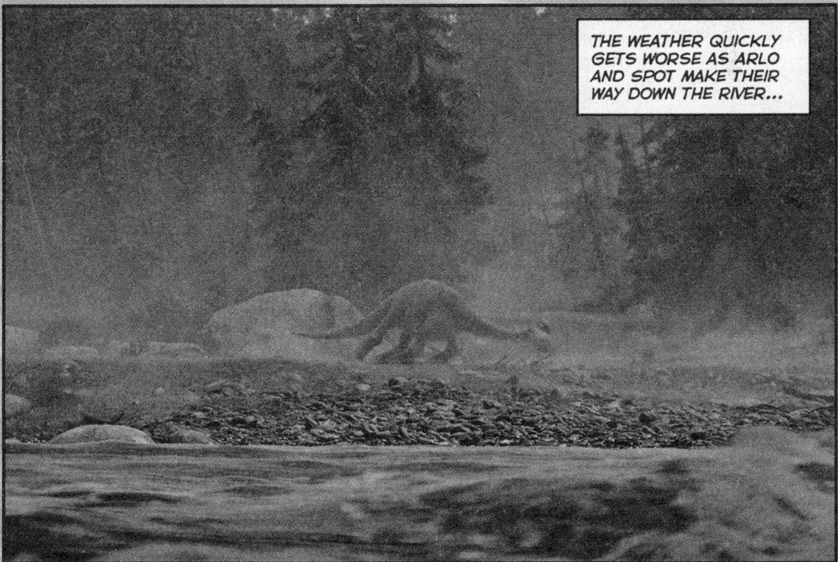
THE WEATHER QUICKLY GETS WORSE AS ARLO AND SPOT MAKE THEIR WAY DOWN THE RIVER...

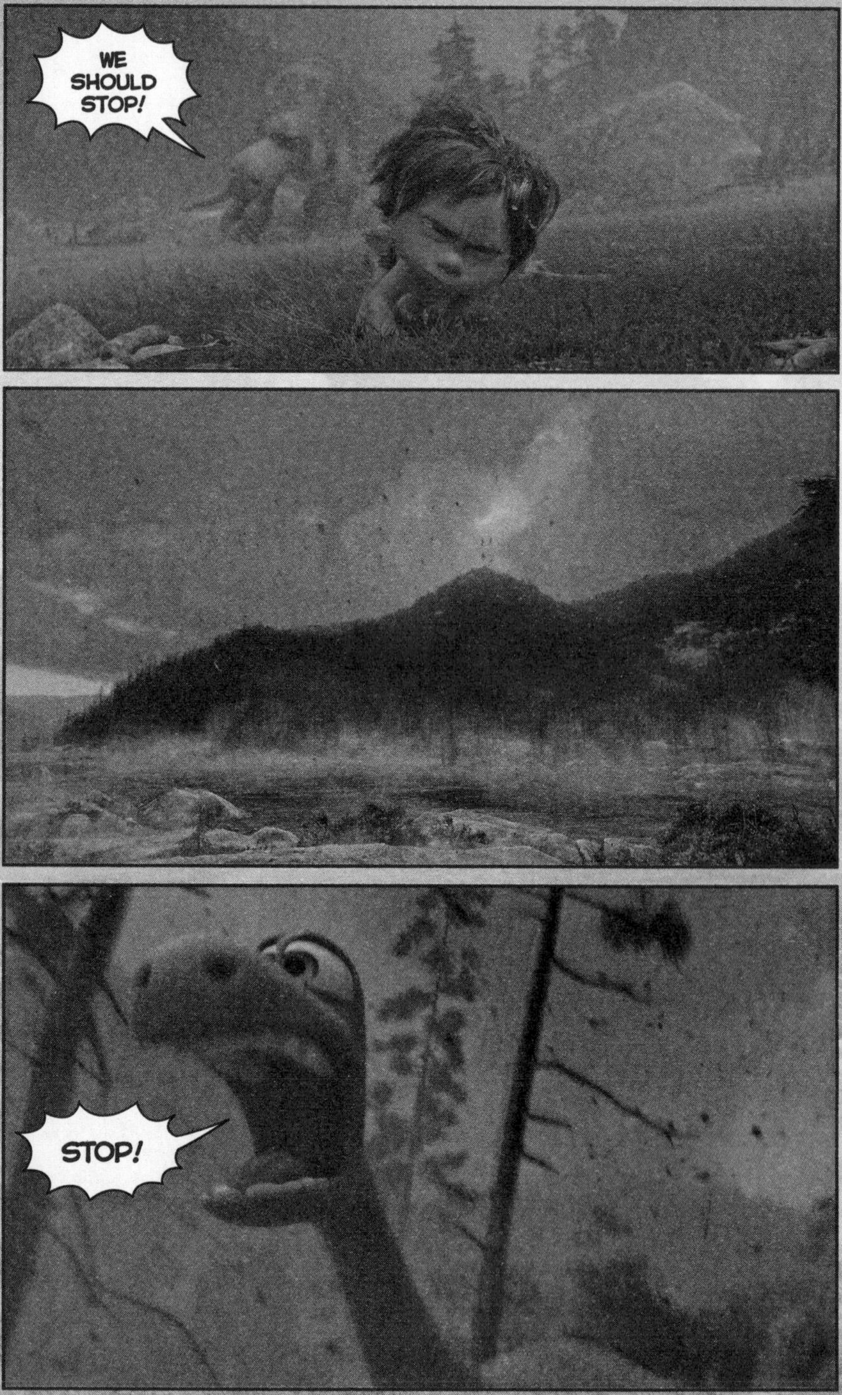
WE SHOULD STOP!
STOP!

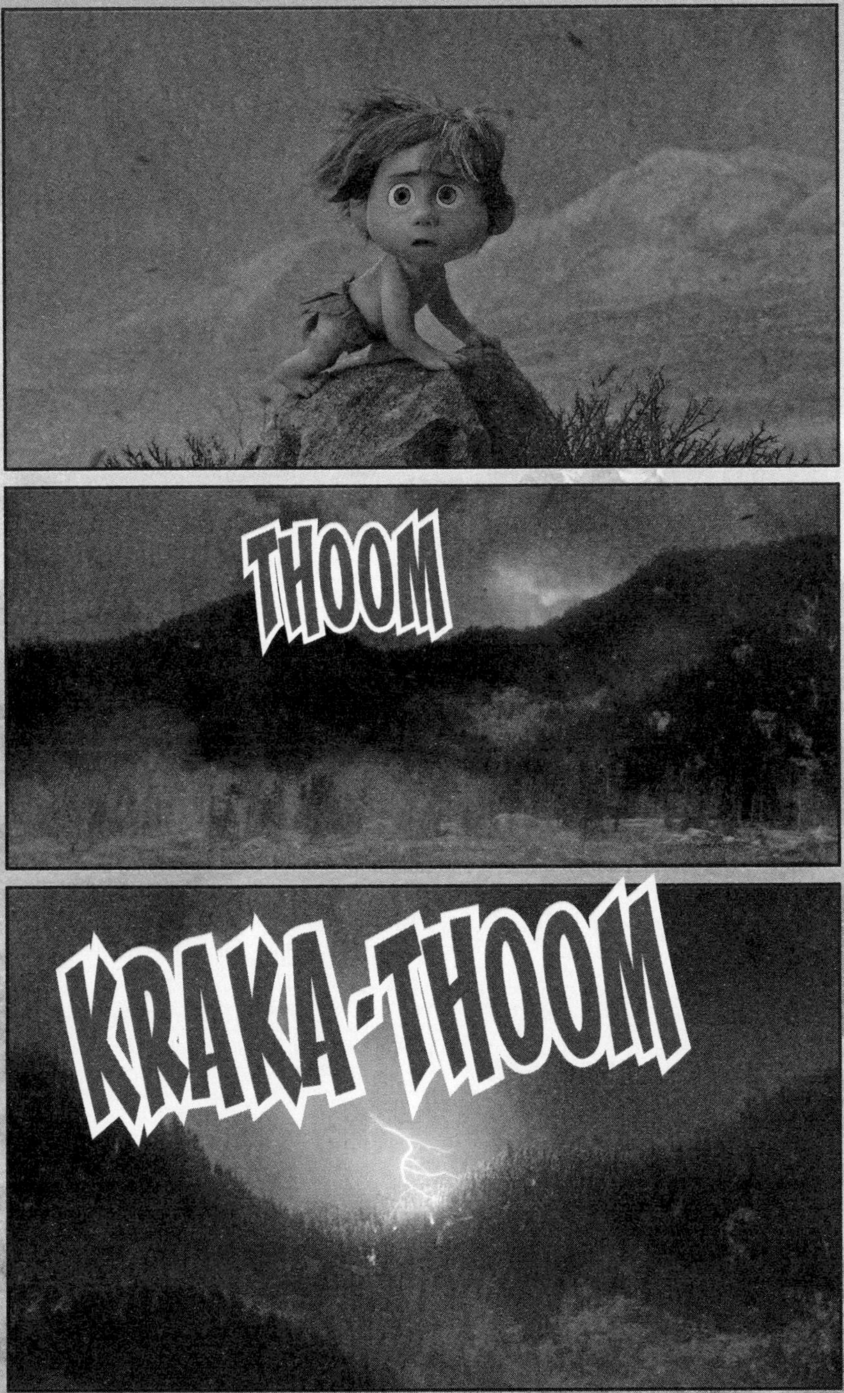
THOOM
KRAKA-THOOM

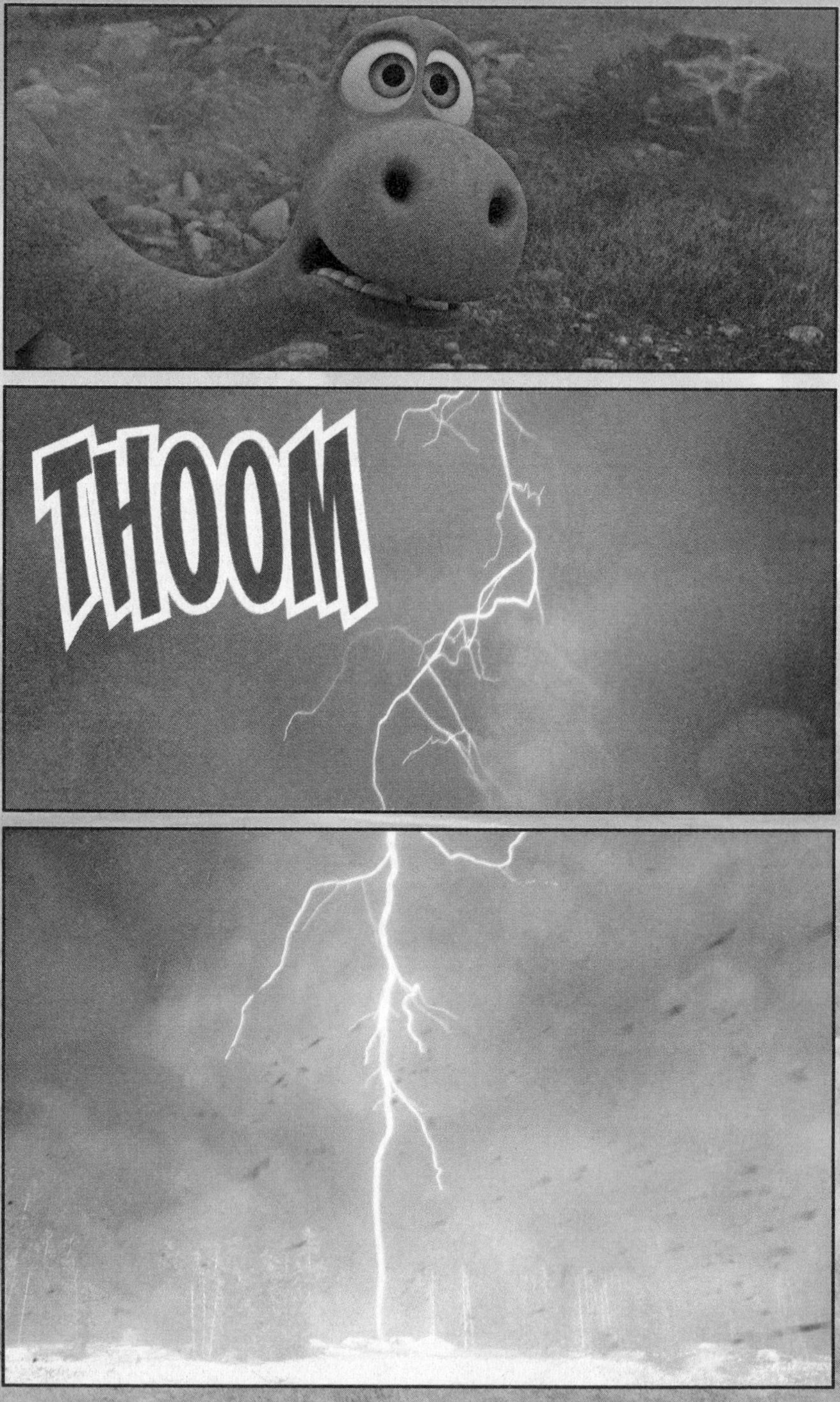
THOOM

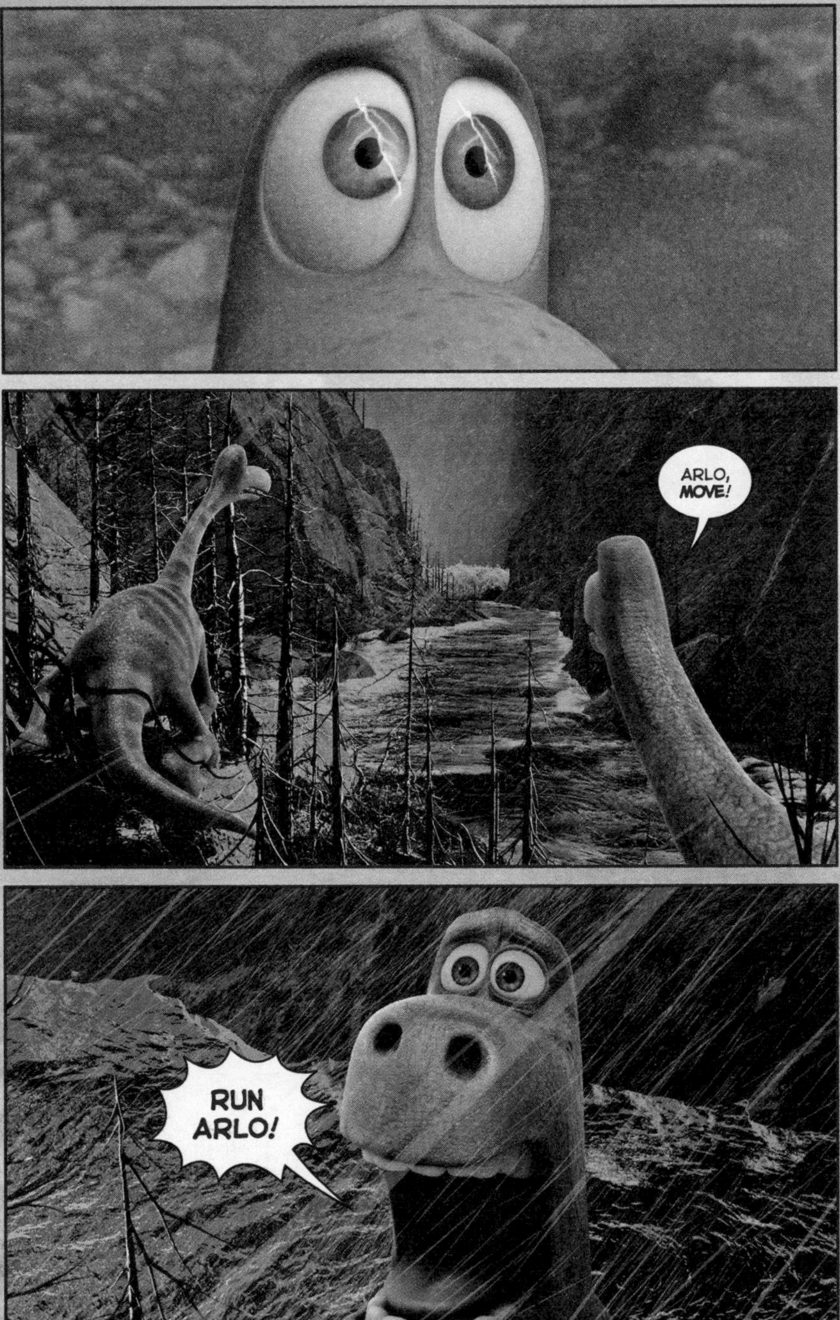
ARLO, MOVE!
RUN ARLO!

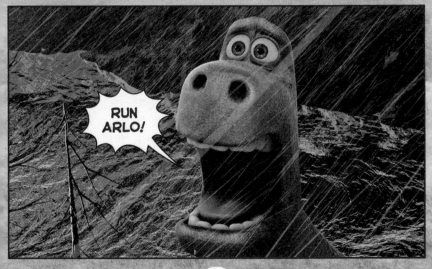

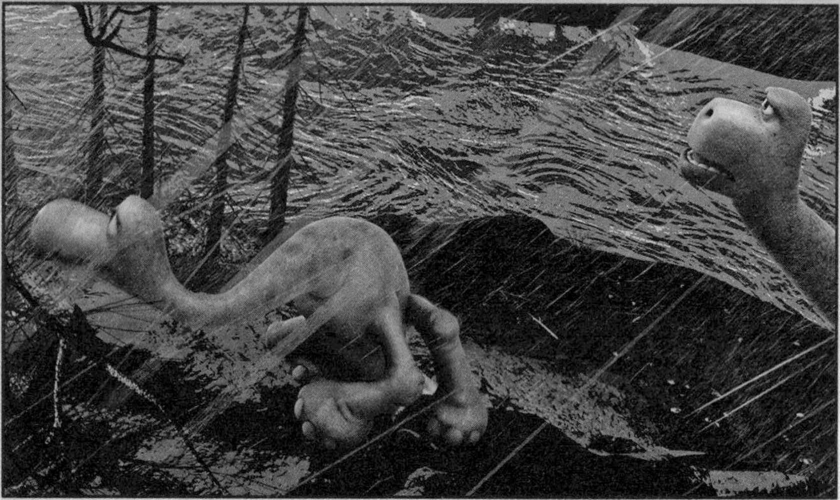

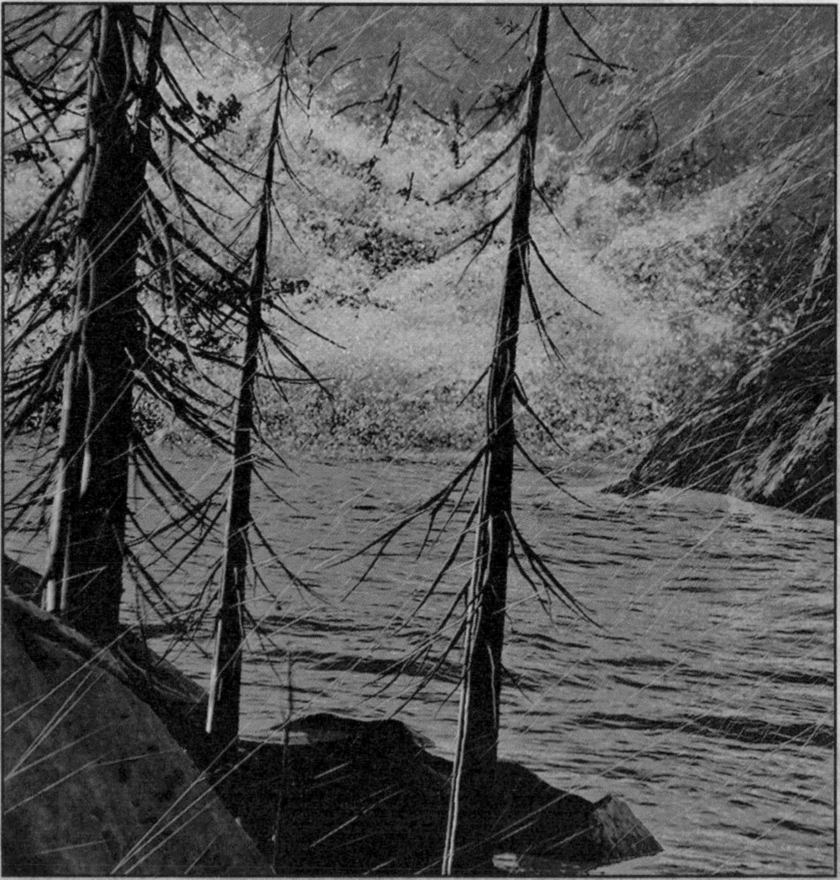

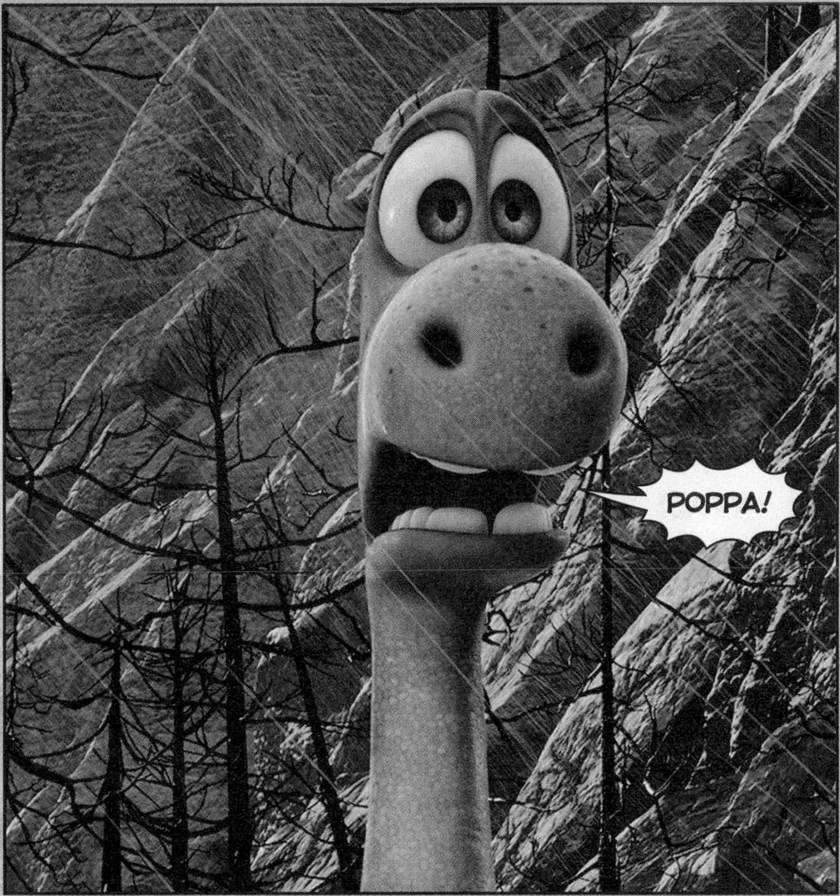
POPPA!

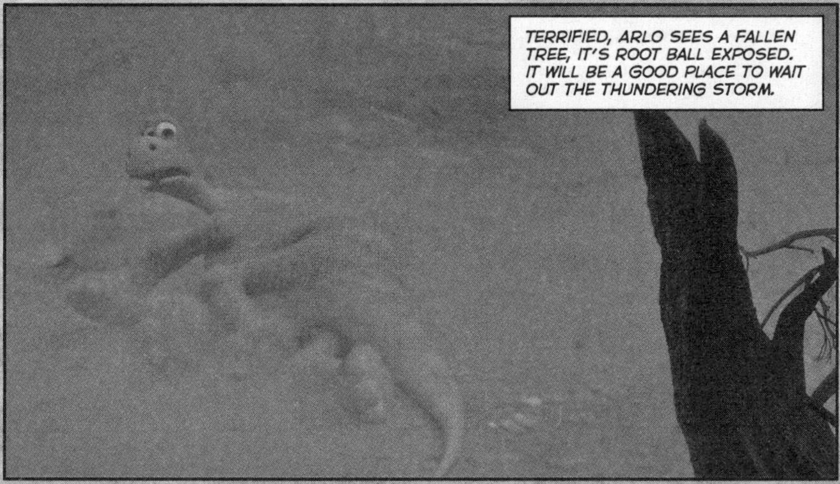
TERRIFIED, ARLO SEES A FALLEN TREE, IT'S ROOT BALL EXPOSED. IT WILL BE A GOOD PLACE TO WAIT OUT THE THUNDERING STORM.

Disney · PIXAR

THE GOOD
DINOSAUR

AMBUSH

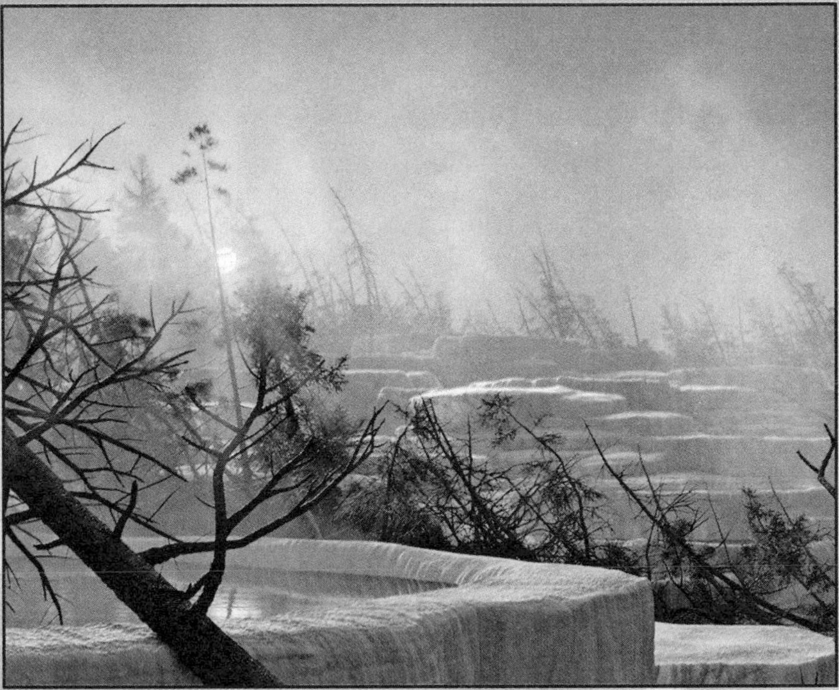

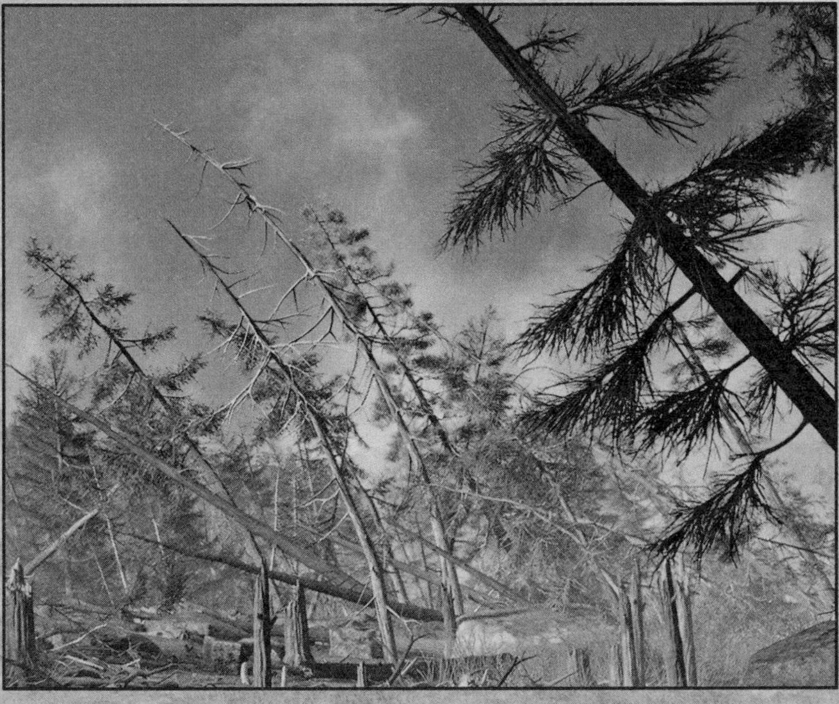

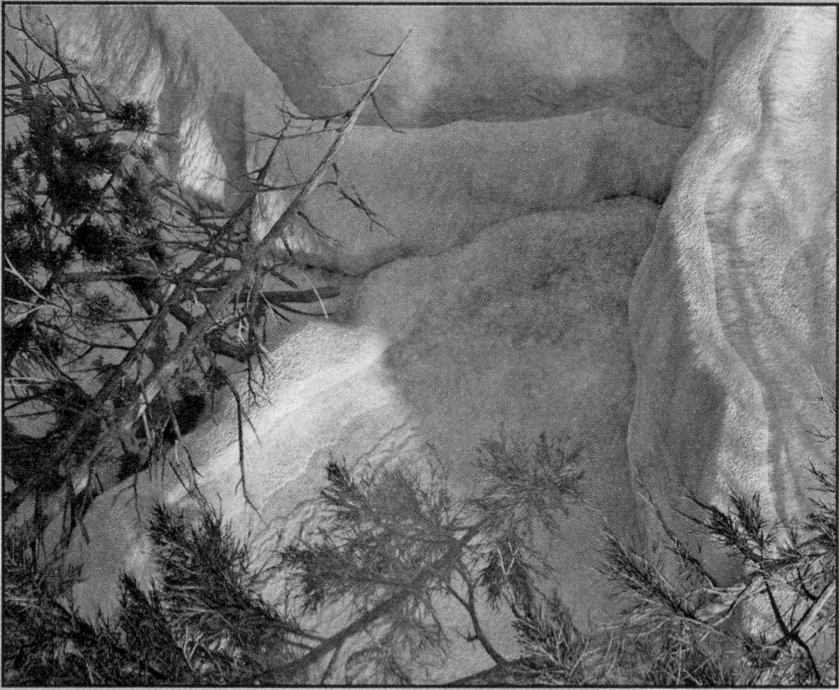

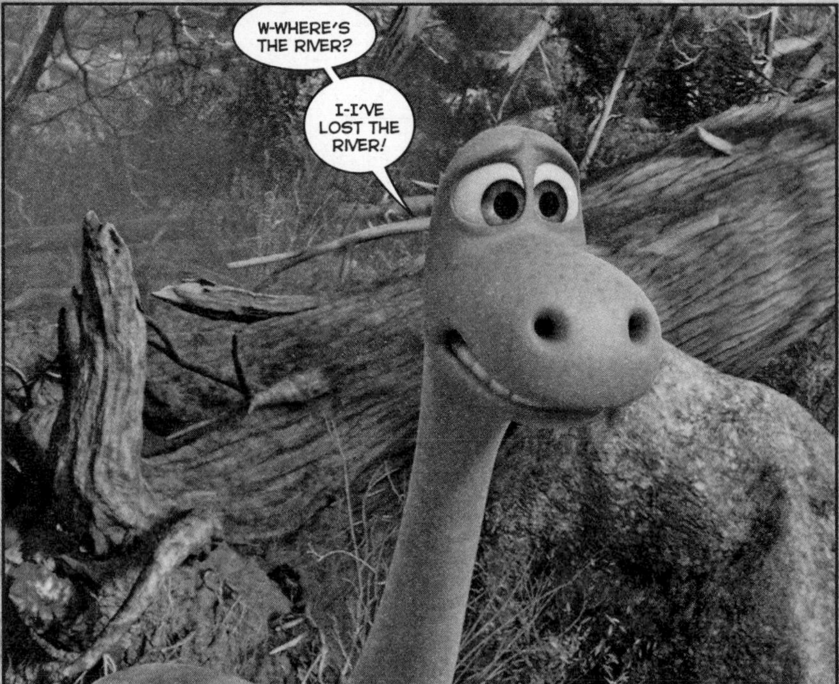
W-WHERE'S THE RIVER?
I-I'VE LOST THE RIVER!

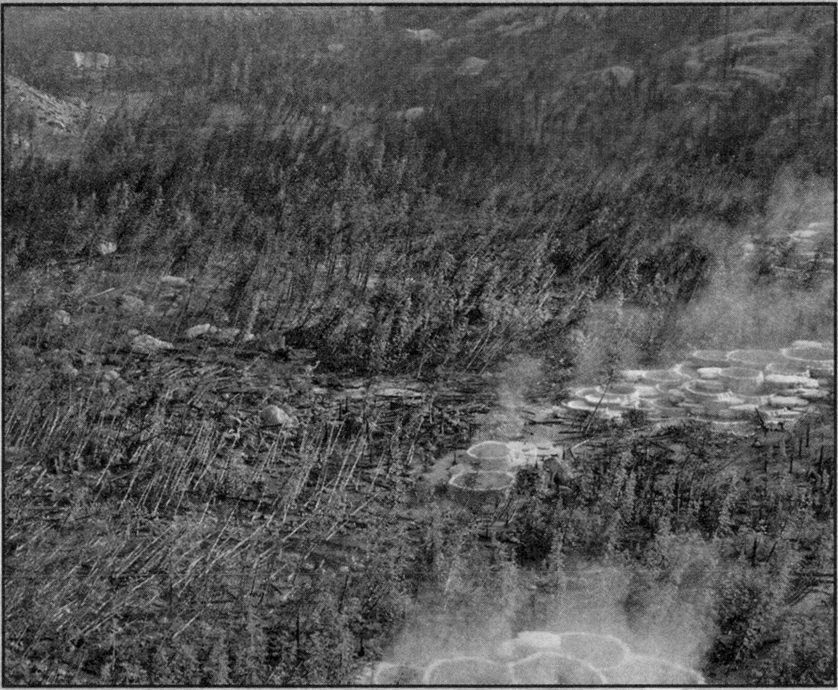

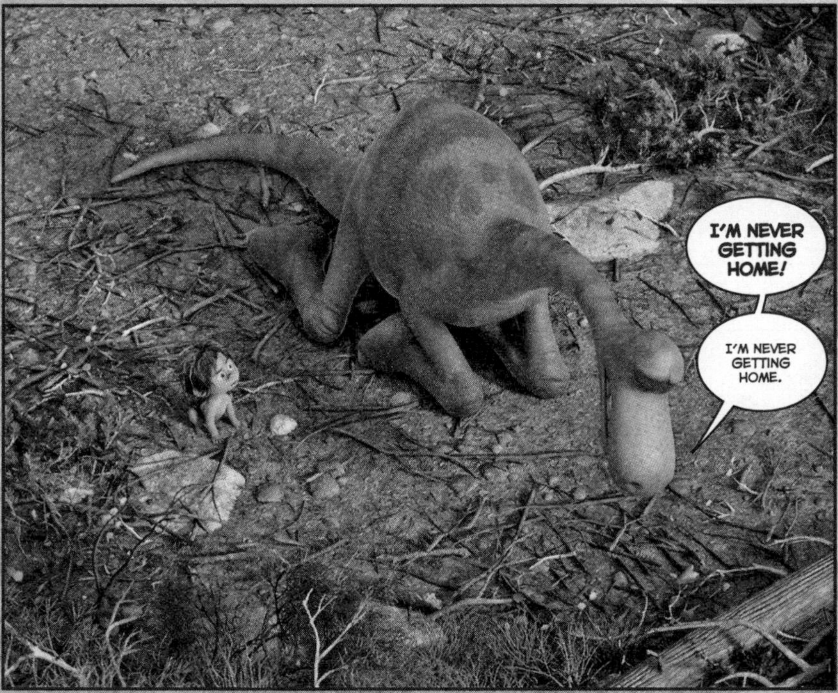
I'M NEVER GETTING HOME!
I'M NEVER GETTING HOME.

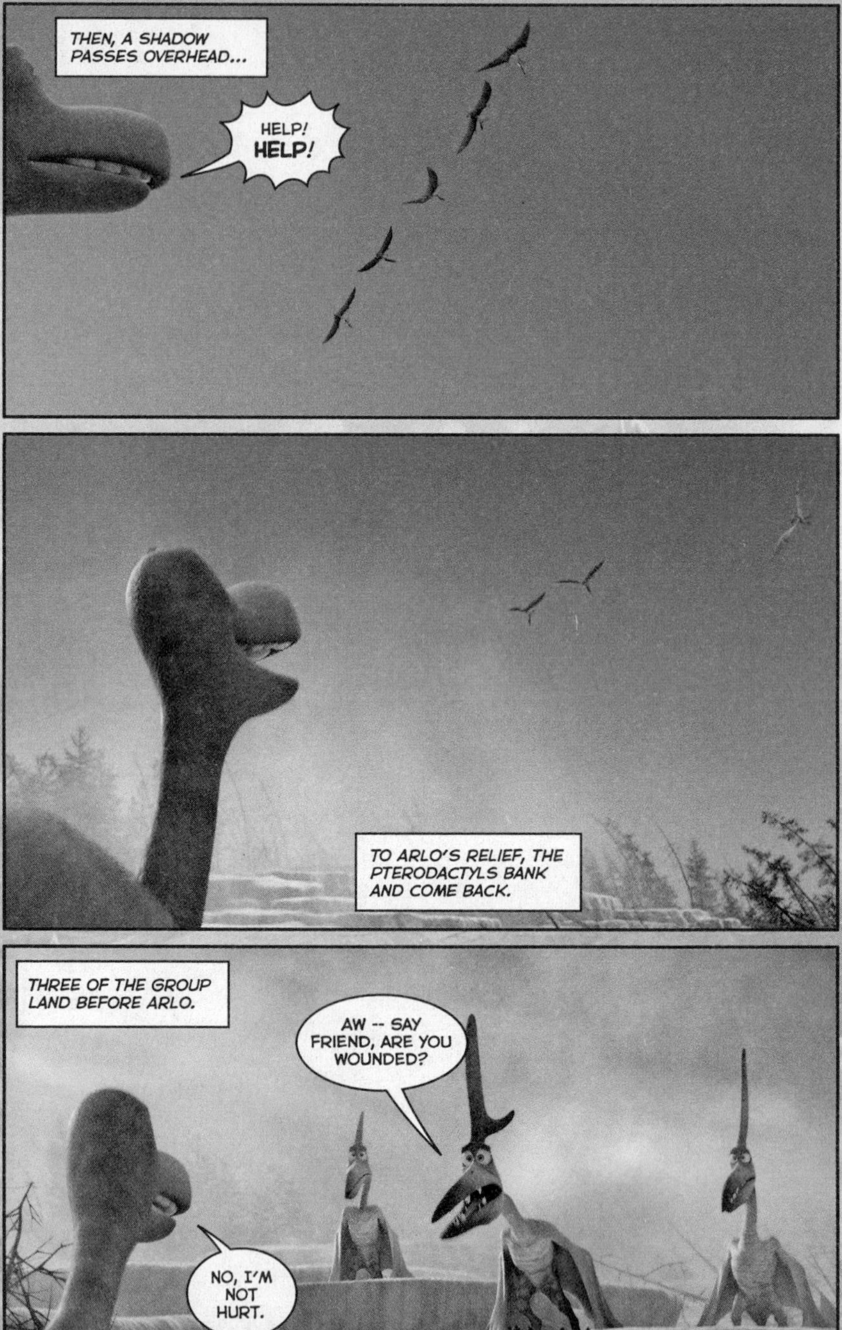
THEN, A SHADOW PASSES OVERHEAD...
HELP! HELP!
TO ARLO'S RELIEF, THE PTERODACTYLS BANK AND COME BACK.
THREE OF THE GROUP LAND BEFORE ARLO.
AW -- SAY FRIEND, ARE YOU WOUNDED?
NO, I'M NOT HURT.

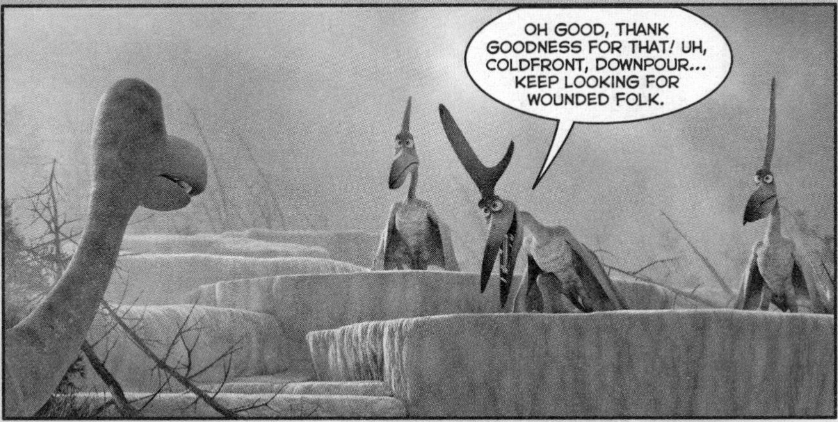
OH GOOD, THANK GOODNESS FOR THAT! UH, COLDFRONT, DOWNPOUR... KEEP LOOKING FOR WOUNDED FOLK.

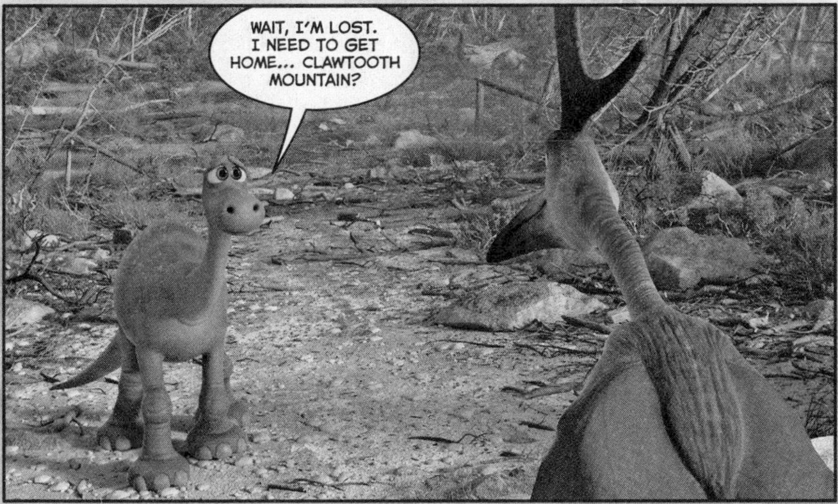
WAIT, I'M LOST. I NEED TO GET HOME... CLAWTOOTH MOUNTAIN?

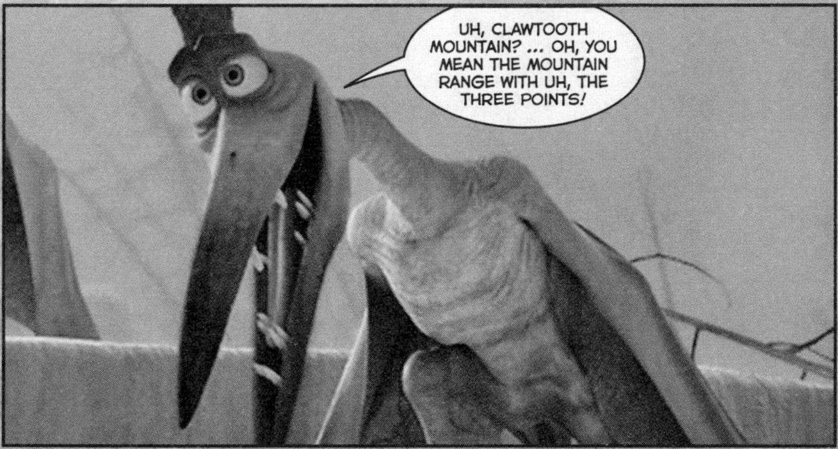
UH, CLAWTOOTH MOUNTAIN? ... OH, YOU MEAN THE MOUNTAIN RANGE WITH UH, THE THREE POINTS!

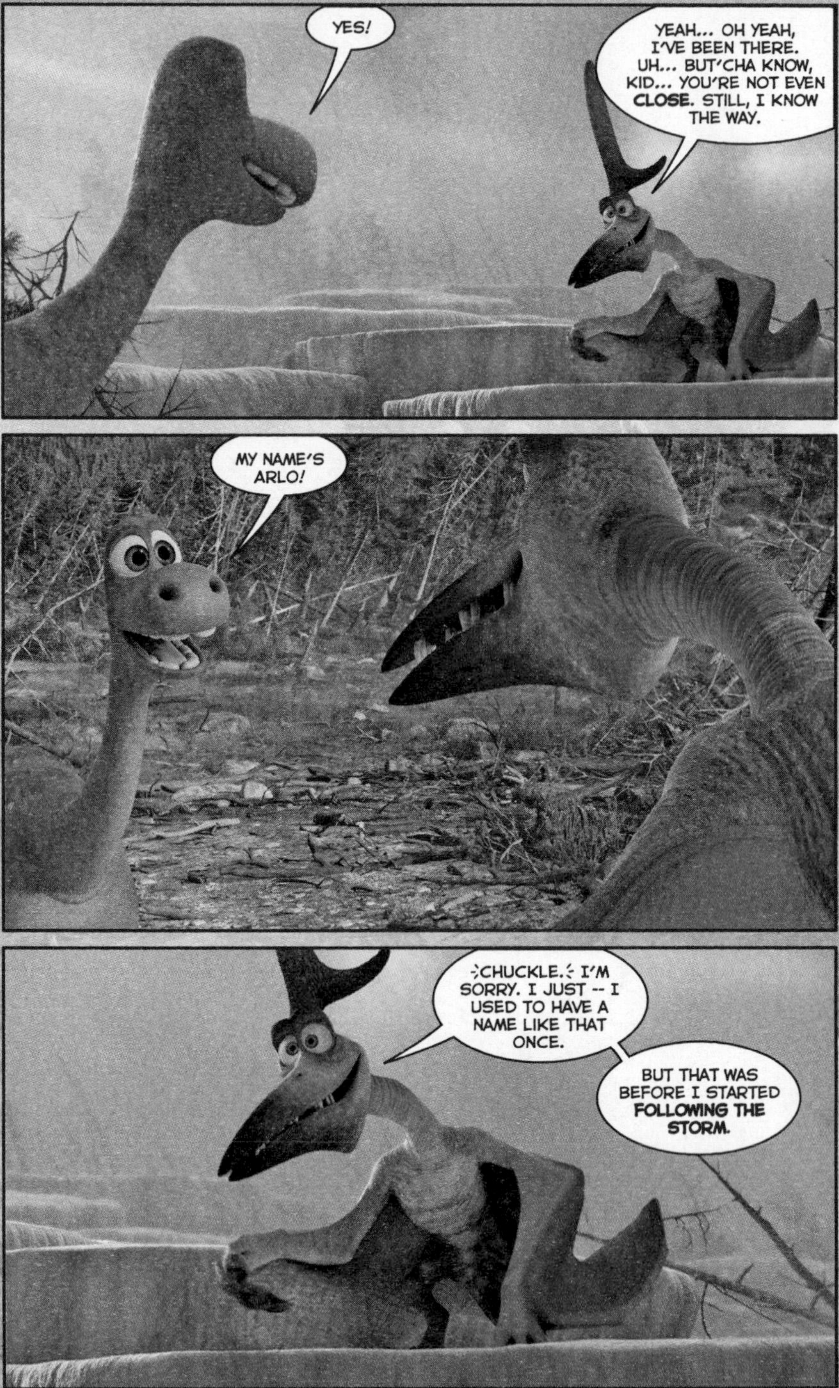
YES!
YEAH... OH YEAH, I'VE BEEN THERE. UH... BUT'CHA KNOW, KID... YOU'RE NOT EVEN **CLOSE**. STILL, I KNOW THE WAY.
MY NAME'S ARLO!
CHUCKLE. I'M SORRY. I JUST -- I USED TO HAVE A NAME LIKE THAT ONCE.
BUT THAT WAS BEFORE I STARTED **FOLLOWING THE STORM.**

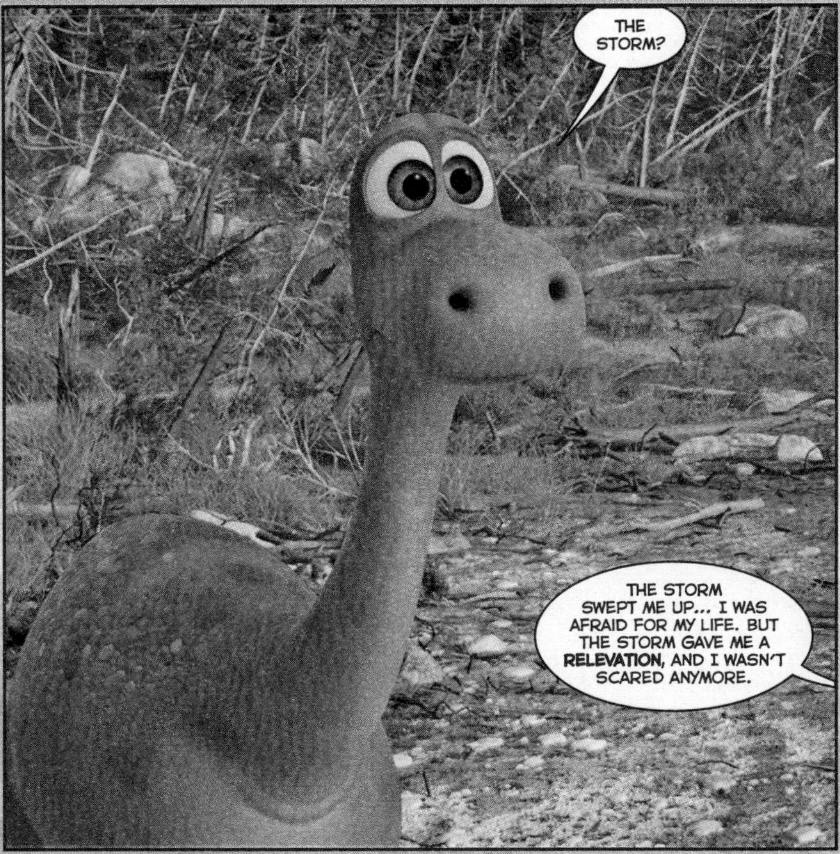
THE STORM?
THE STORM SWEPT ME UP... I WAS AFRAID FOR MY LIFE. BUT THE STORM GAVE ME A **RELEVATION**, AND I WASN'T SCARED ANYMORE.

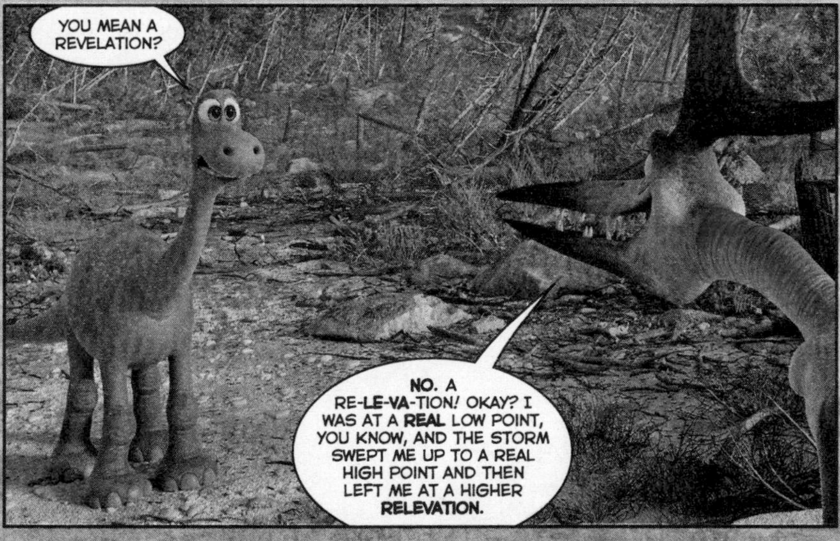
YOU MEAN A REVELATION?
NO. A RE-**LE**-**VA**-TION! OKAY? I WAS AT A **REAL** LOW POINT, YOU KNOW, AND THE STORM SWEPT ME UP TO A REAL HIGH POINT AND THEN LEFT ME AT A HIGHER **RELEVATION.**

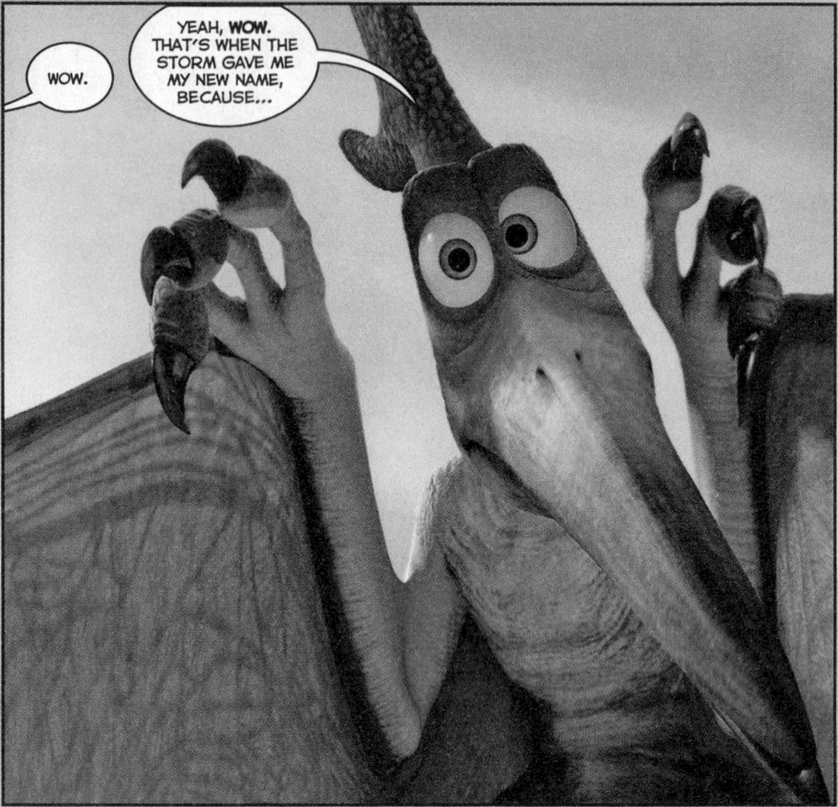
WOW.
YEAH, WOW. THAT'S WHEN THE STORM GAVE ME MY NEW NAME, BECAUSE...

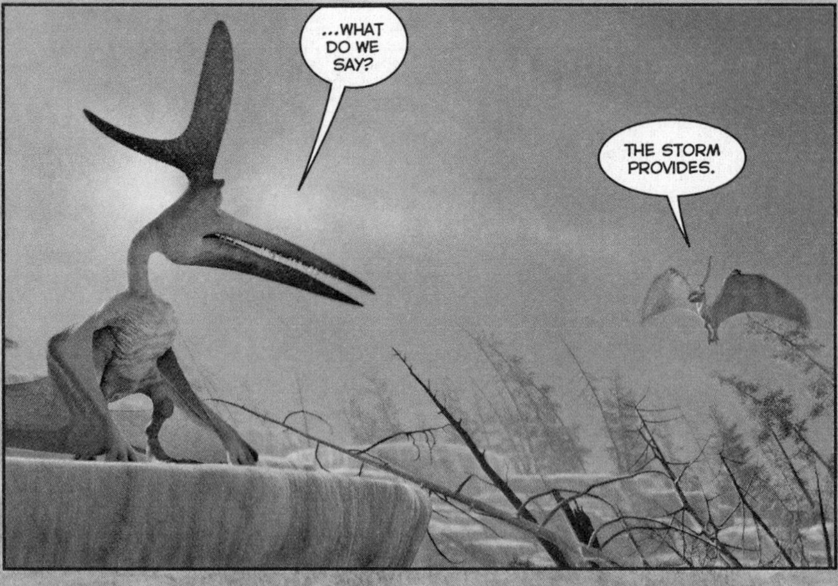
...WHAT DO WE SAY?
THE STORM PROVIDES.

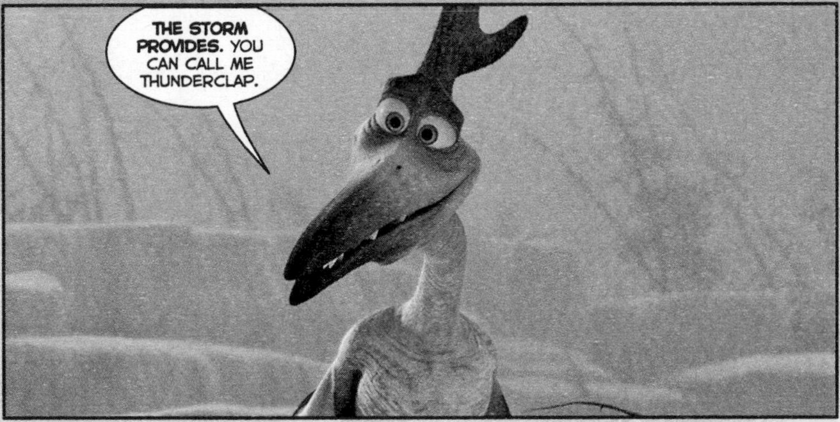
THE STORM PROVIDES. YOU CAN CALL ME THUNDERCLAP.

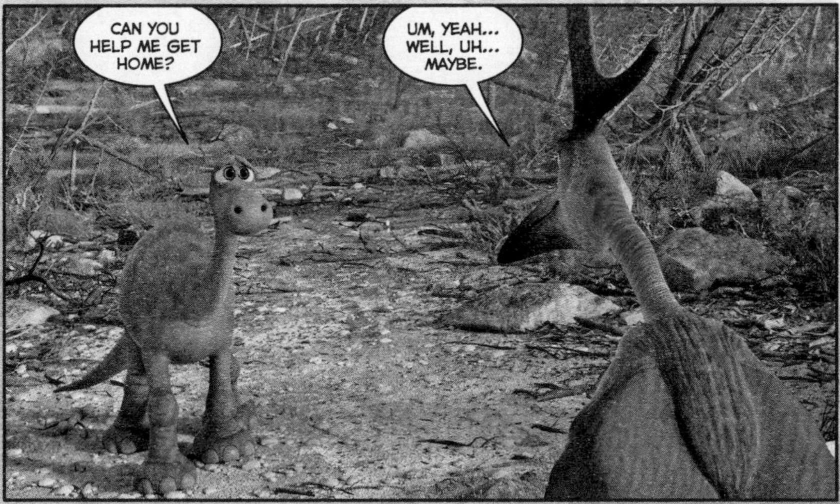
CAN YOU HELP ME GET HOME?
UM, YEAH... WELL, UH... MAYBE.

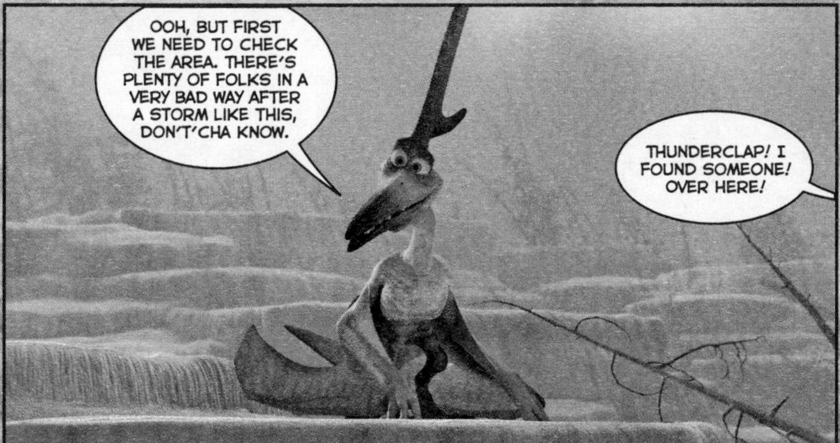
OOH, BUT FIRST WE NEED TO CHECK THE AREA. THERE'S PLENTY OF FOLKS IN A VERY BAD WAY AFTER A STORM LIKE THIS, DON'T'CHA KNOW.
THUNDERCLAP! I FOUND SOMEONE! OVER HERE!

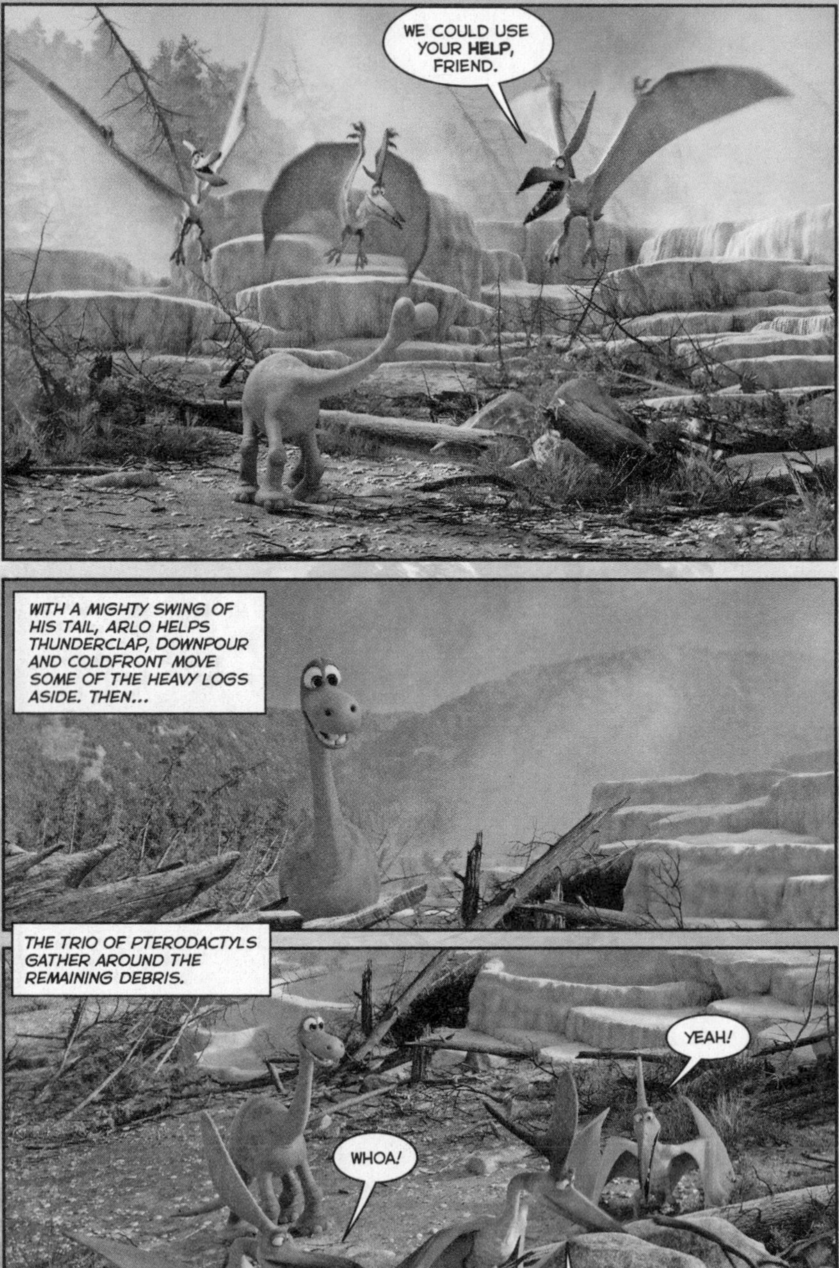
WE COULD USE YOUR **HELP**, FRIEND.
WITH A MIGHTY SWING OF HIS TAIL, ARLO HELPS THUNDERCLAP, DOWNPOUR AND COLDFRONT MOVE SOME OF THE HEAVY LOGS ASIDE. THEN...
THE TRIO OF PTERODACTYLS GATHER AROUND THE REMAINING DEBRIS.
YEAH!
WHOA!
WHOA... THAT IS GREAT!

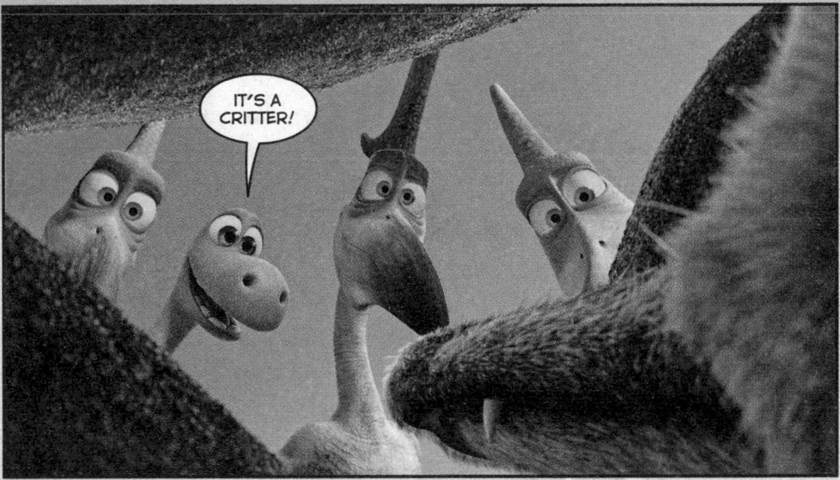
IT'S A CRITTER!

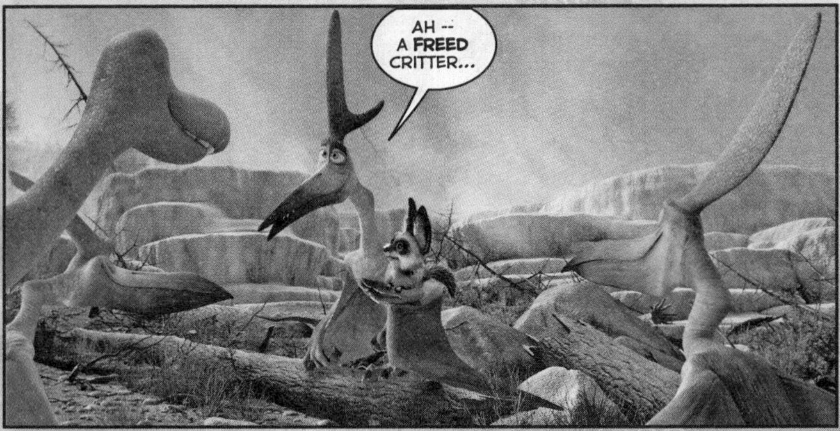
AH -- A **FREED** CRITTER...

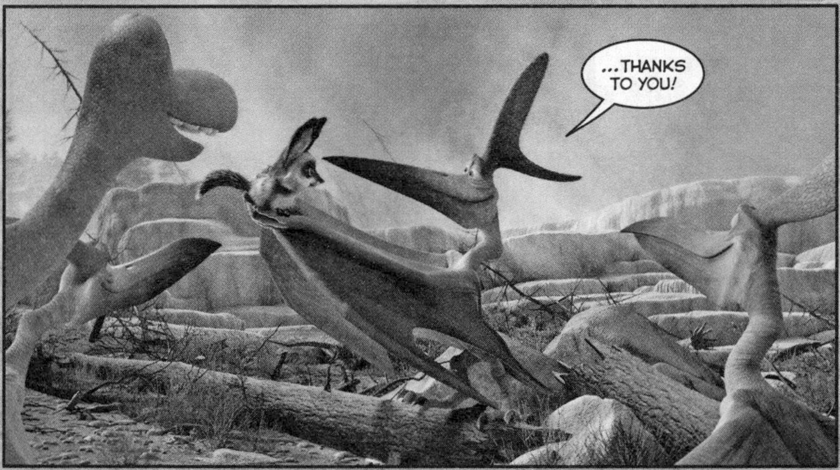
...THANKS TO YOU!

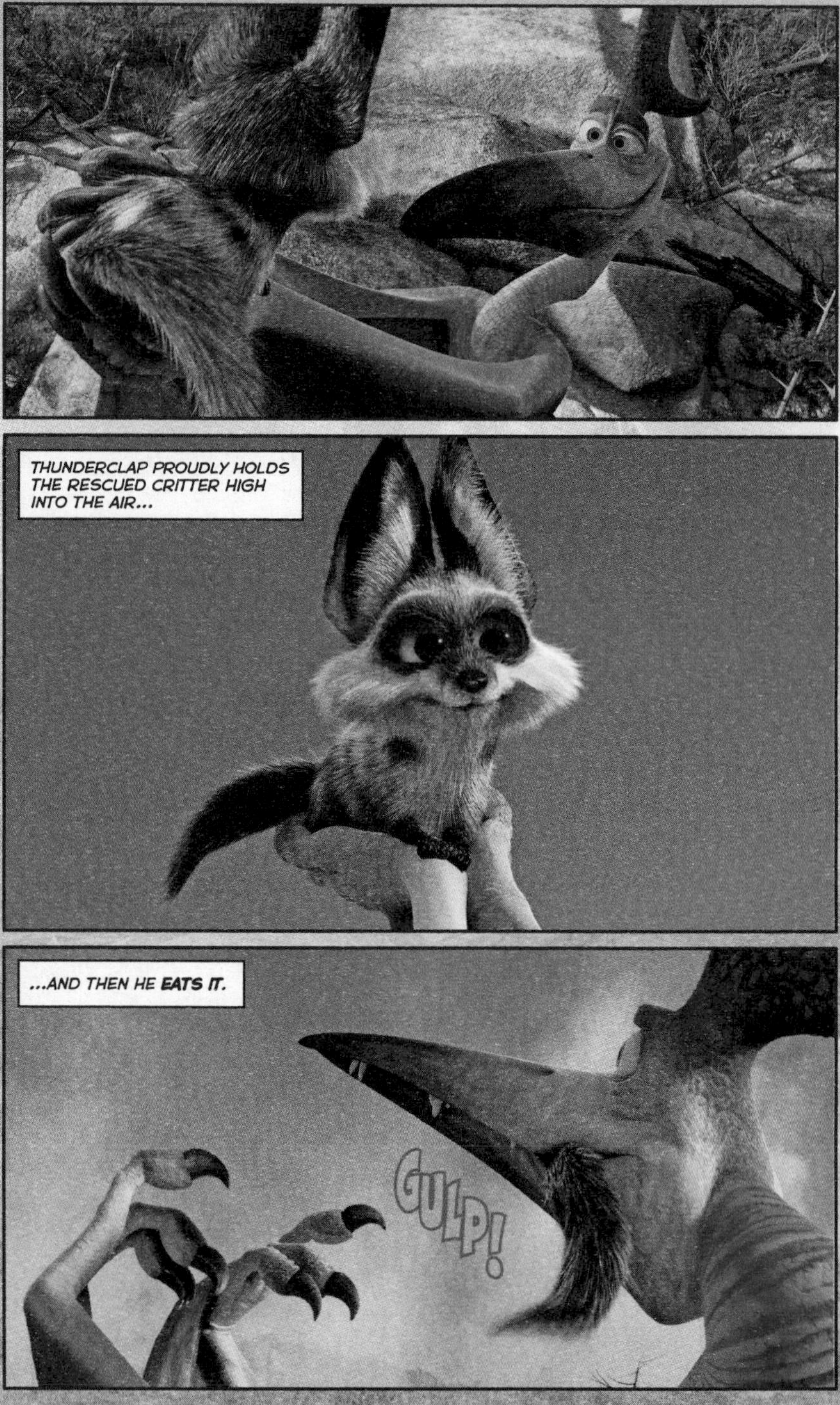
THUNDERCLAP PROUDLY HOLDS THE RESCUED CRITTER HIGH INTO THE AIR...
...AND THEN HE EATS IT.
GULP!

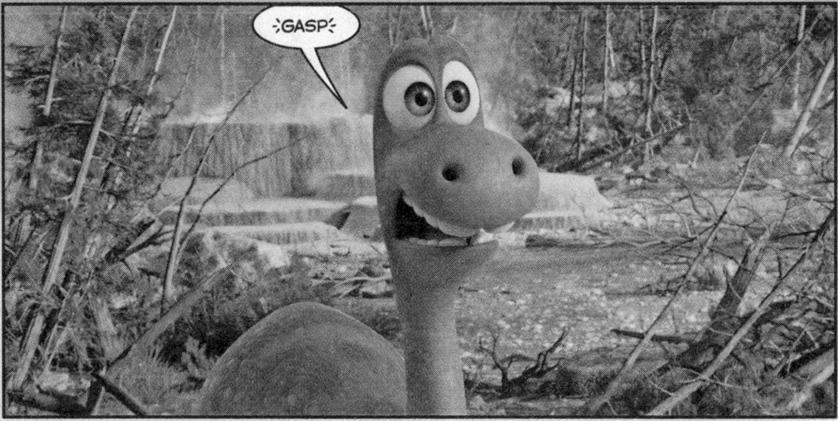
GASP

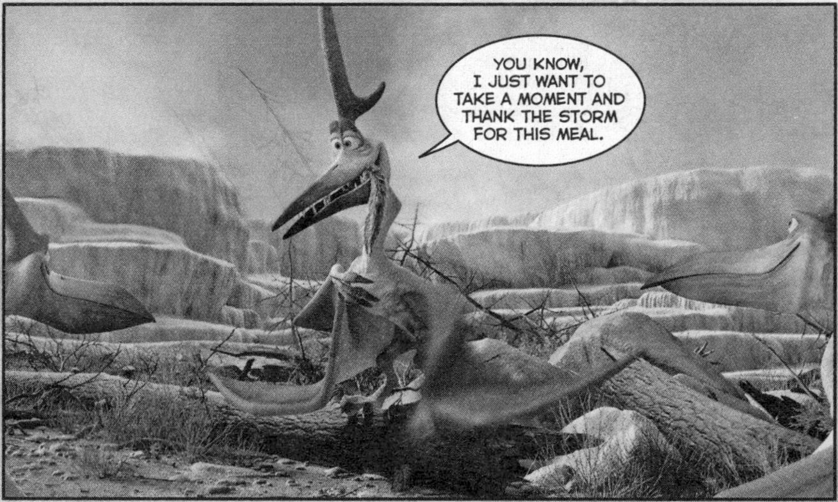
YOU KNOW, I JUST WANT TO TAKE A MOMENT AND THANK THE STORM FOR THIS MEAL.

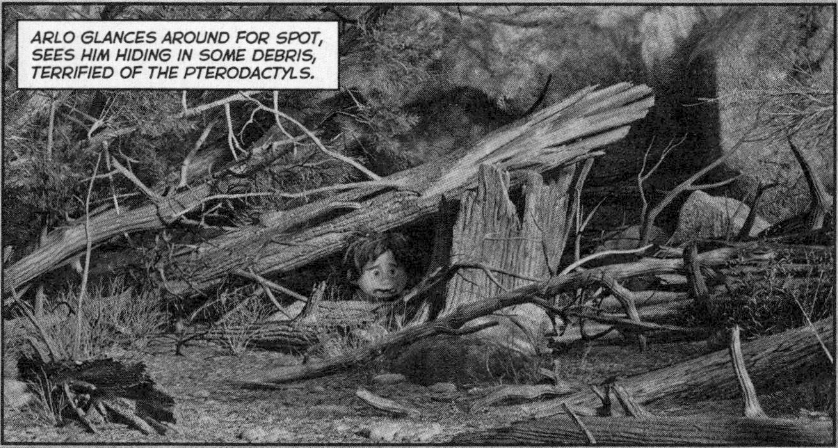
ARLO GLANCES AROUND FOR SPOT, SEES HIM HIDING IN SOME DEBRIS, TERRIFIED OF THE PTERODACTYLS.

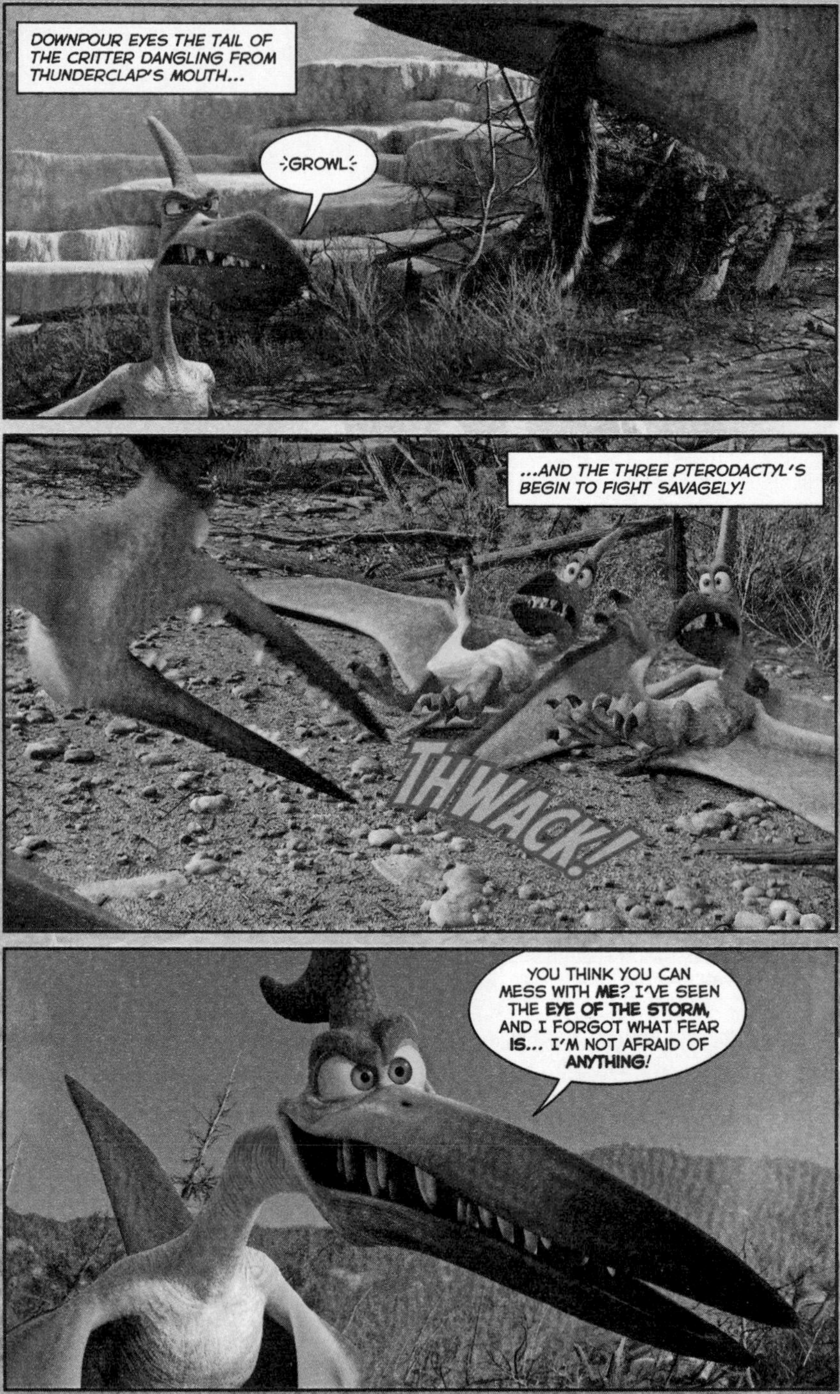
DOWNPOUR EYES THE TAIL OF THE CRITTER DANGLING FROM THUNDERCLAP'S MOUTH...
GROWL
...AND THE THREE PTERODACTYL'S BEGIN TO FIGHT SAVAGELY!
THWACK!
YOU THINK YOU CAN MESS WITH ME? I'VE SEEN THE EYE OF THE STORM, AND I FORGOT WHAT FEAR IS... I'M NOT AFRAID OF ANYTHING!

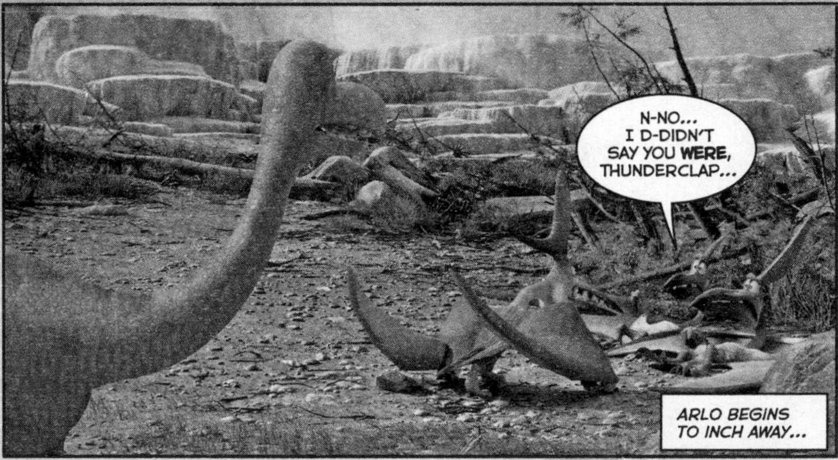
N-NO... I D-DIDN'T SAY YOU **WERE**, THUNDERCLAP...
ARLO BEGINS TO INCH AWAY...

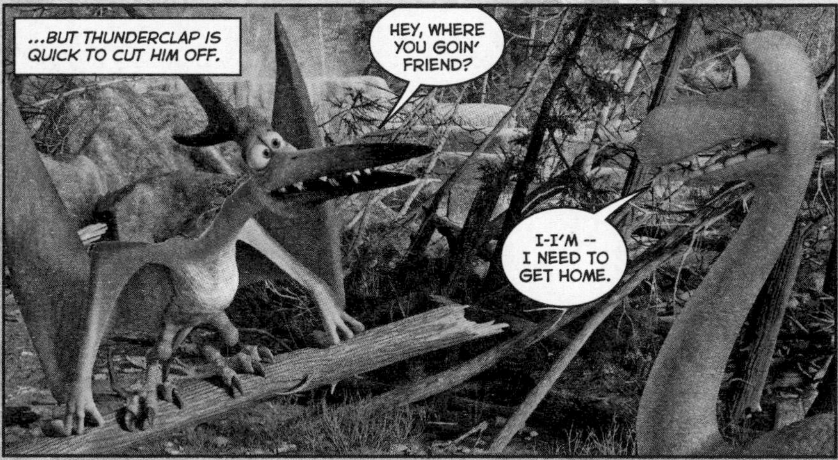
...BUT THUNDERCLAP IS QUICK TO CUT HIM OFF.
HEY, WHERE YOU GOIN' FRIEND?
I-I'M -- I NEED TO GET HOME.

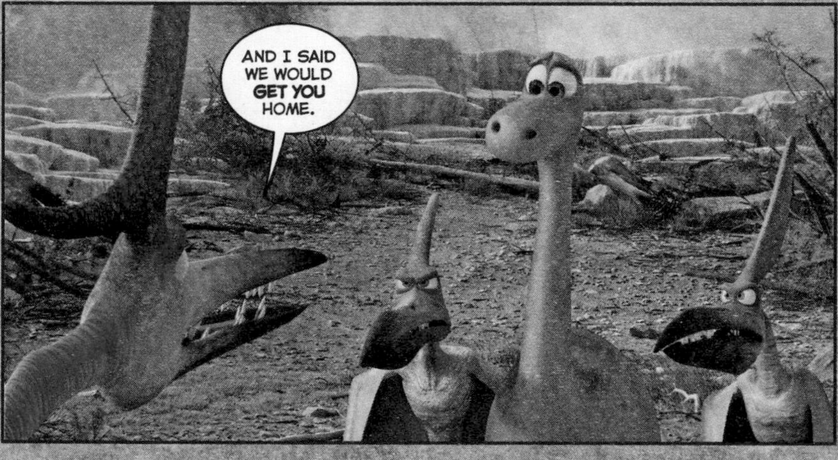
AND I SAID WE WOULD **GET YOU** HOME.

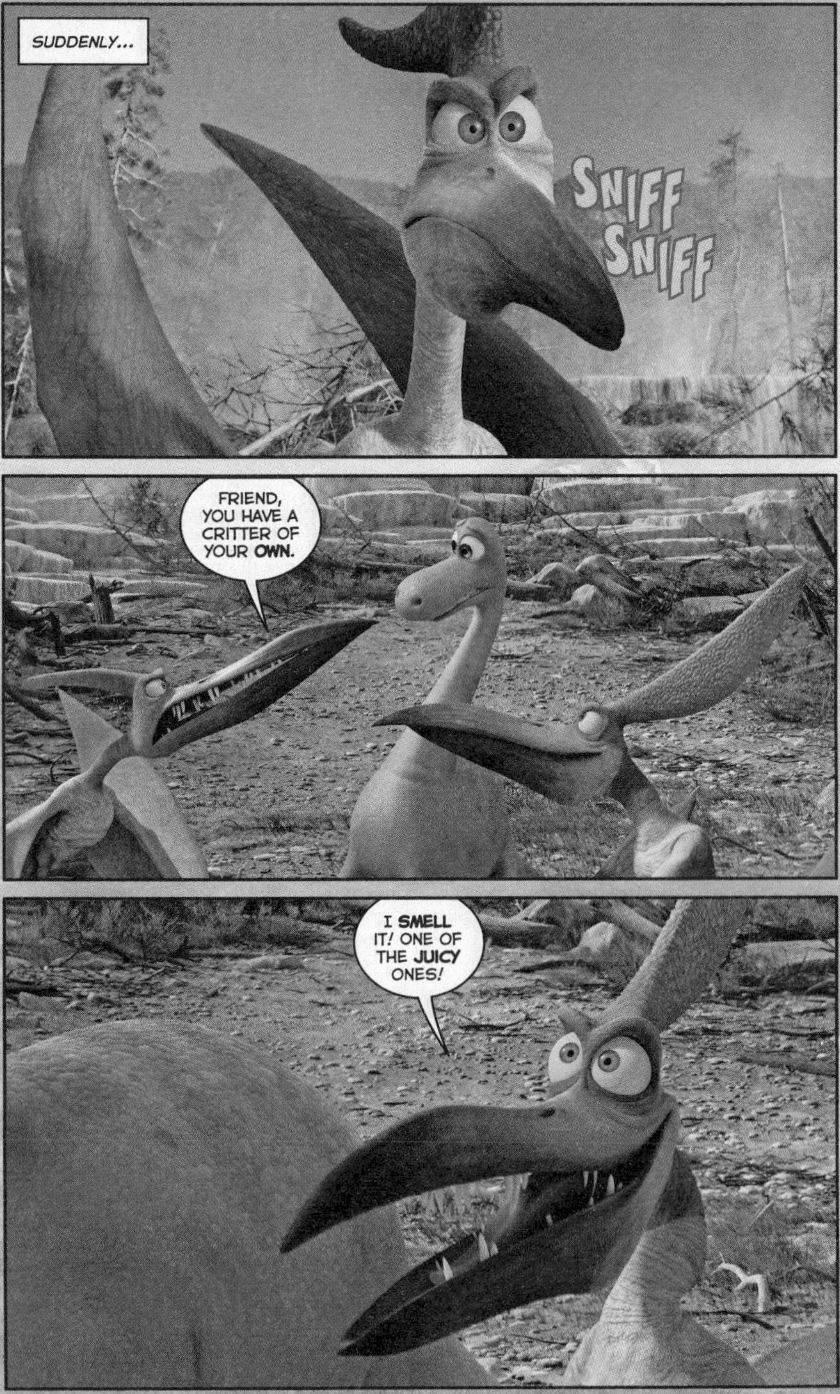
SUDDENLY...
SNIFF SNIFF
FRIEND, YOU HAVE A CRITTER OF YOUR **OWN.**
I **SMELL** IT! ONE OF THE **JUICY** ONES!

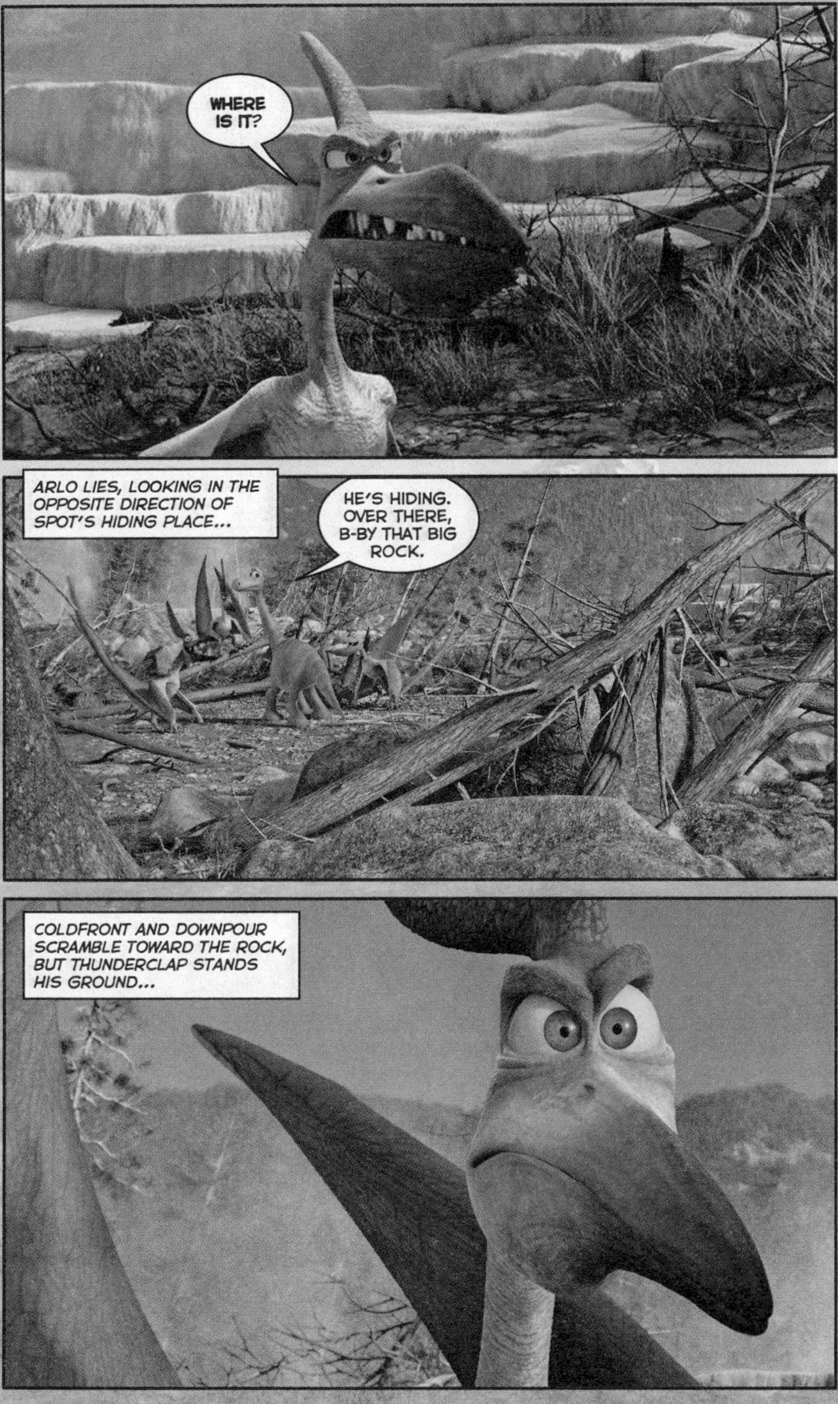
WHERE IS IT?
ARLO LIES, LOOKING IN THE OPPOSITE DIRECTION OF SPOT'S HIDING PLACE...
HE'S HIDING. OVER THERE, B-BY THAT BIG ROCK.
COLDFRONT AND DOWNPOUR SCRAMBLE TOWARD THE ROCK, BUT THUNDERCLAP STANDS HIS GROUND...

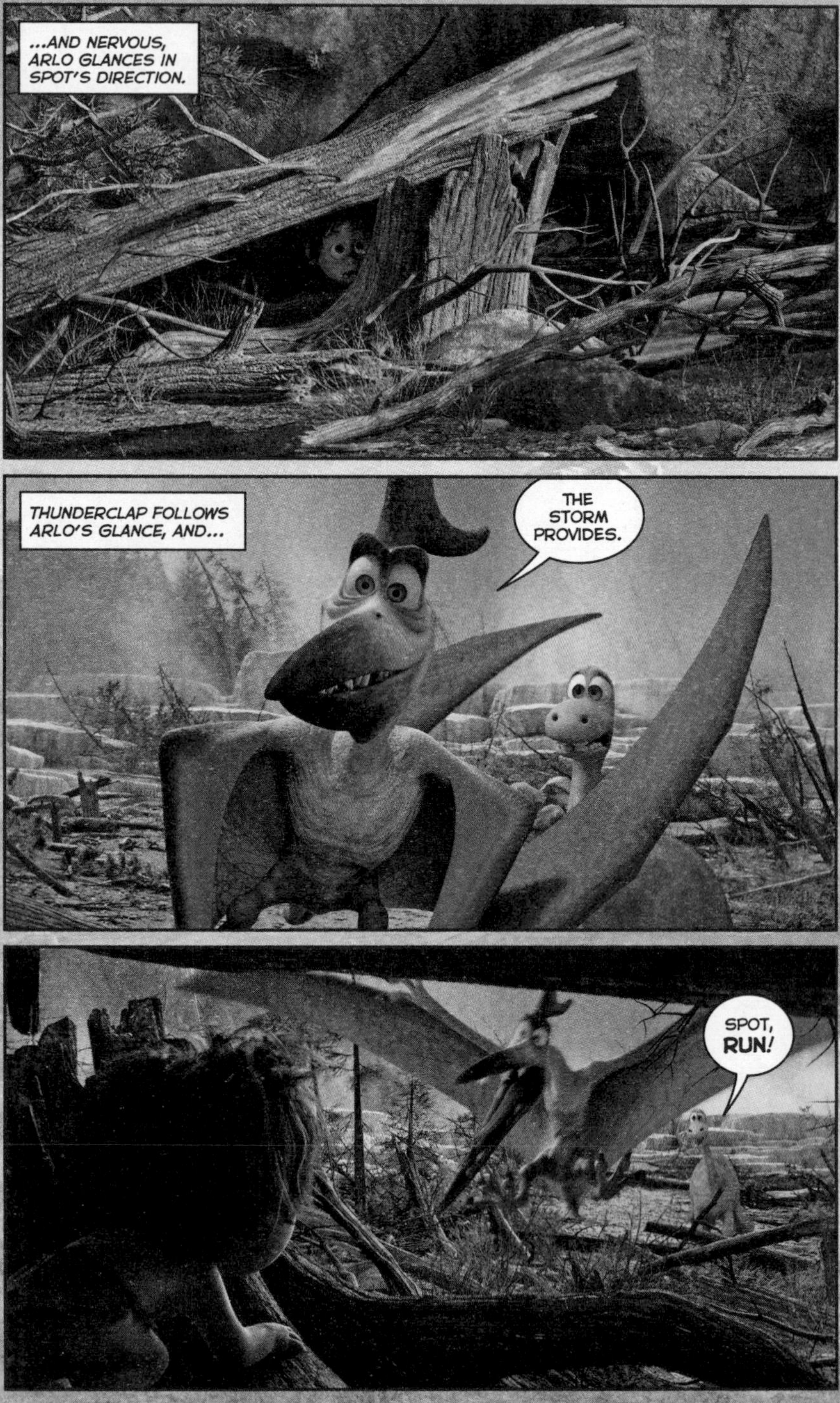
...AND NERVOUS, ARLO GLANCES IN SPOT'S DIRECTION.
THUNDERCLAP FOLLOWS ARLO'S GLANCE, AND...
THE STORM PROVIDES.
SPOT, RUN!

Disney·PIXAR

THE GOOD DINOSAUR

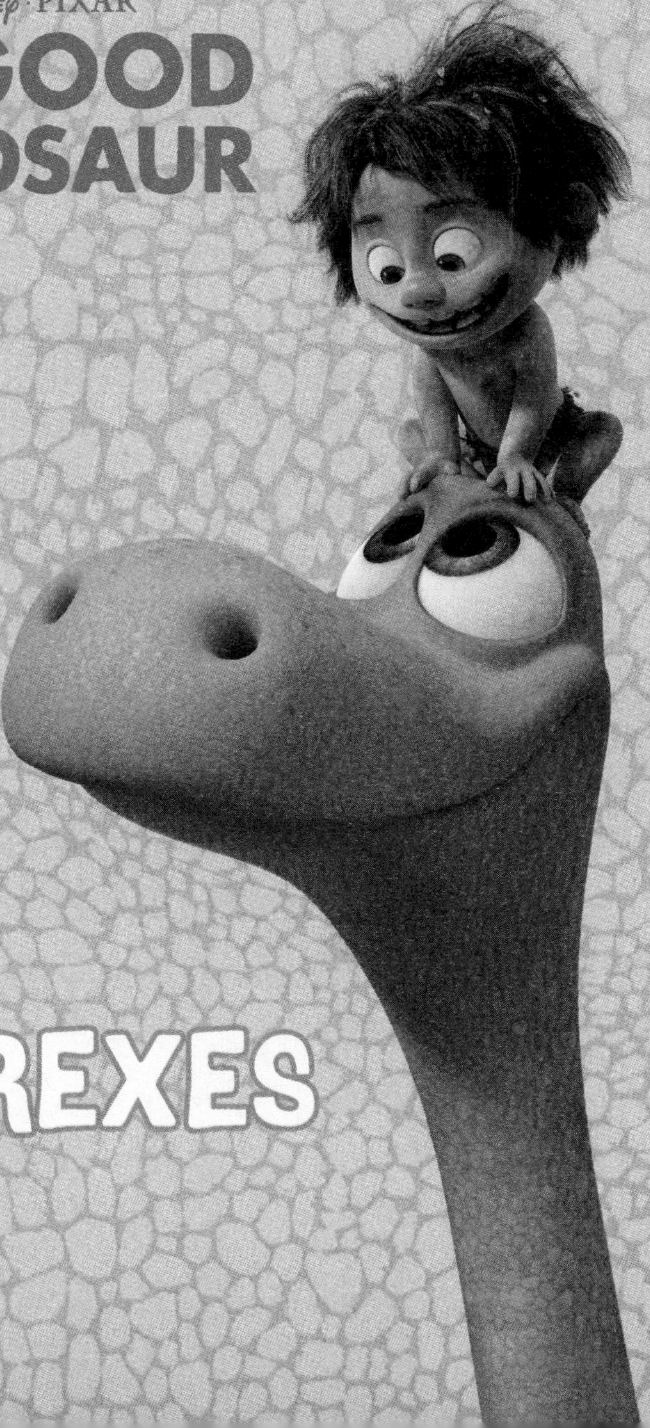

T-REXES

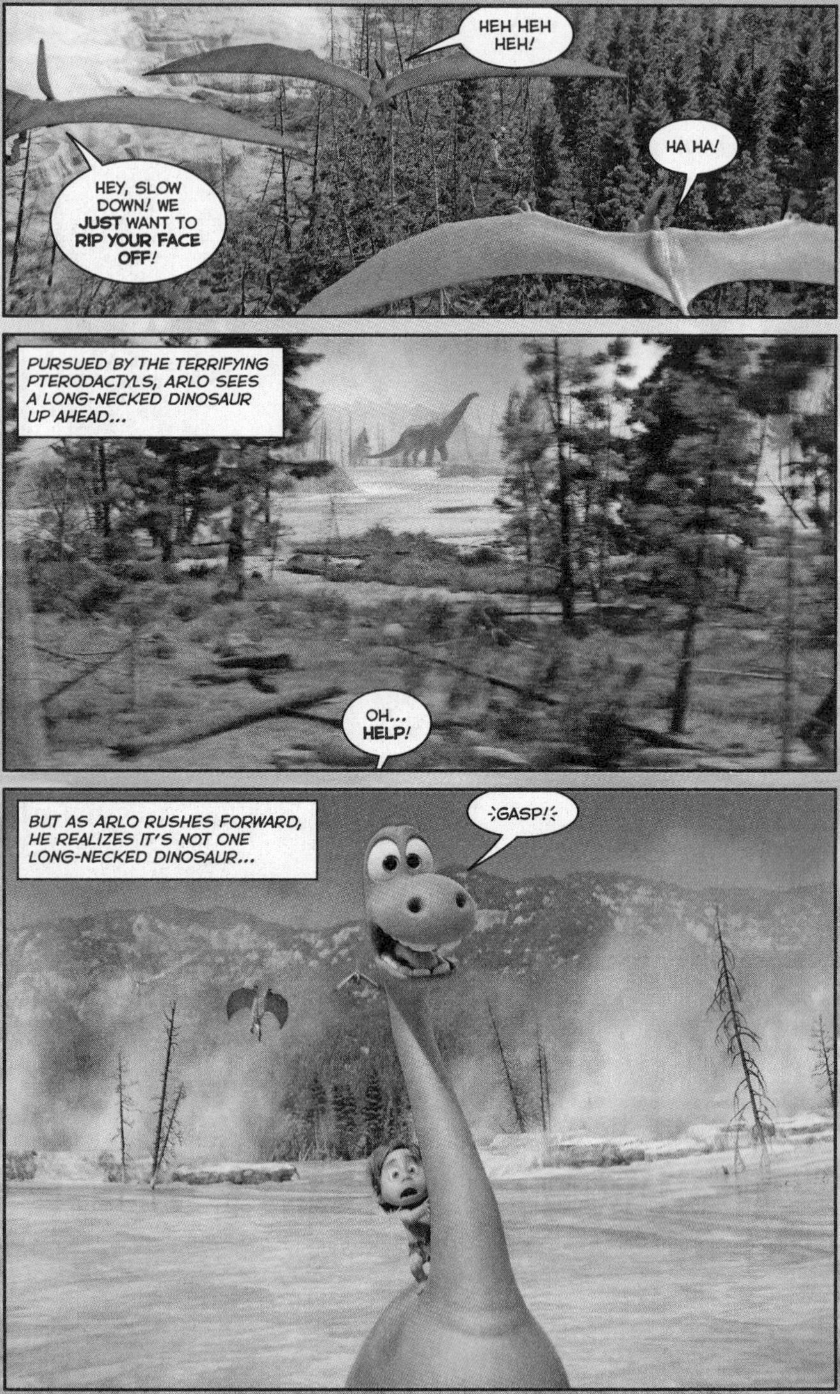
HEH HEH HEH!
HEY, SLOW DOWN! WE JUST WANT TO RIP YOUR FACE OFF!
HA HA!
PURSUED BY THE TERRIFYING PTERODACTYLS, ARLO SEES A LONG-NECKED DINOSAUR UP AHEAD...
OH... HELP!
BUT AS ARLO RUSHES FORWARD, HE REALIZES IT'S NOT ONE LONG-NECKED DINOSAUR...
GASP!

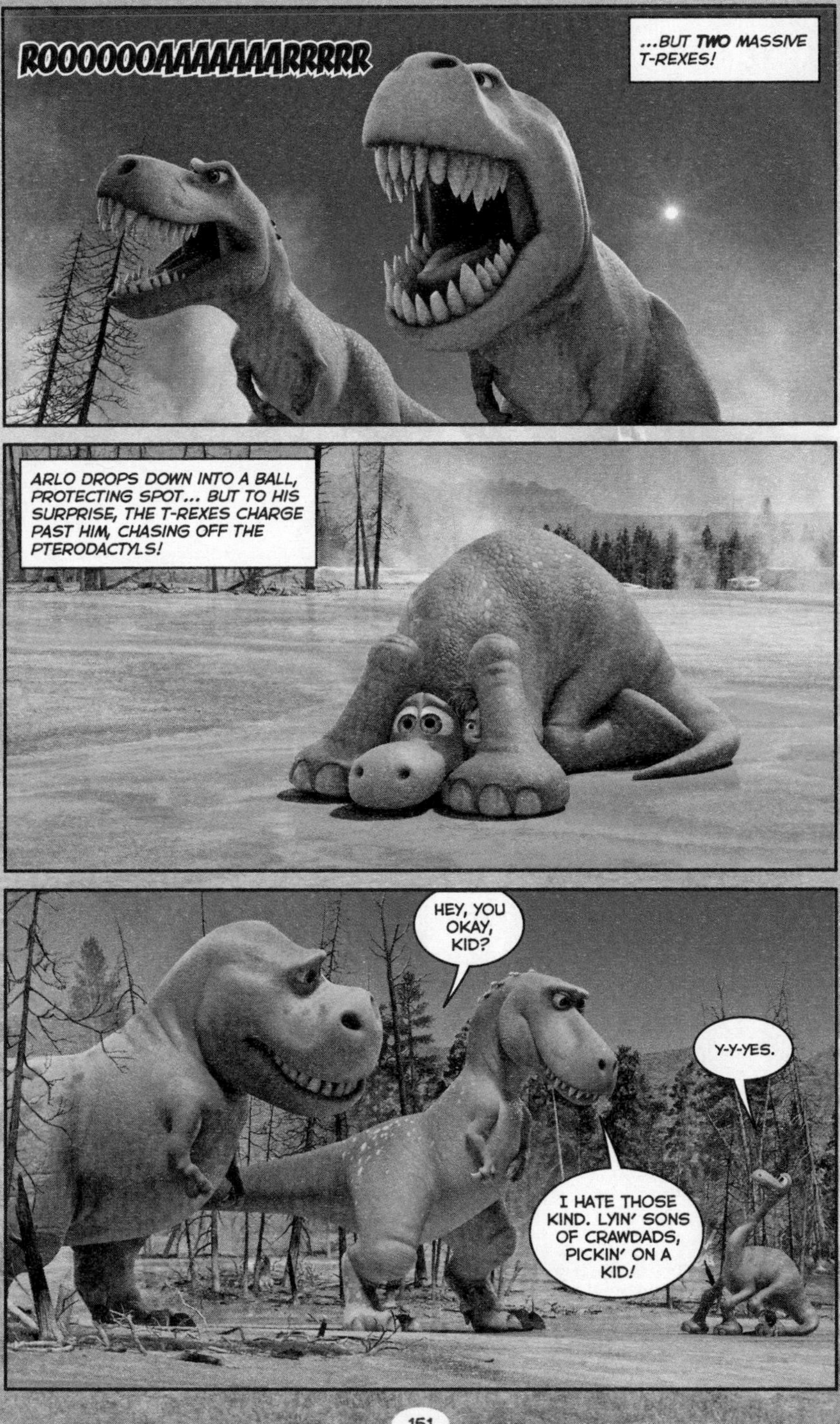
ROOOOOOOAAAAAAARRRRR
...BUT TWO MASSIVE T-REXES!
ARLO DROPS DOWN INTO A BALL, PROTECTING SPOT... BUT TO HIS SURPRISE, THE T-REXES CHARGE PAST HIM, CHASING OFF THE PTERODACTYLS!
HEY, YOU OKAY, KID?
Y-Y-YES.
I HATE THOSE KIND. LYIN' SONS OF CRAWDADS, PICKIN' ON A KID!

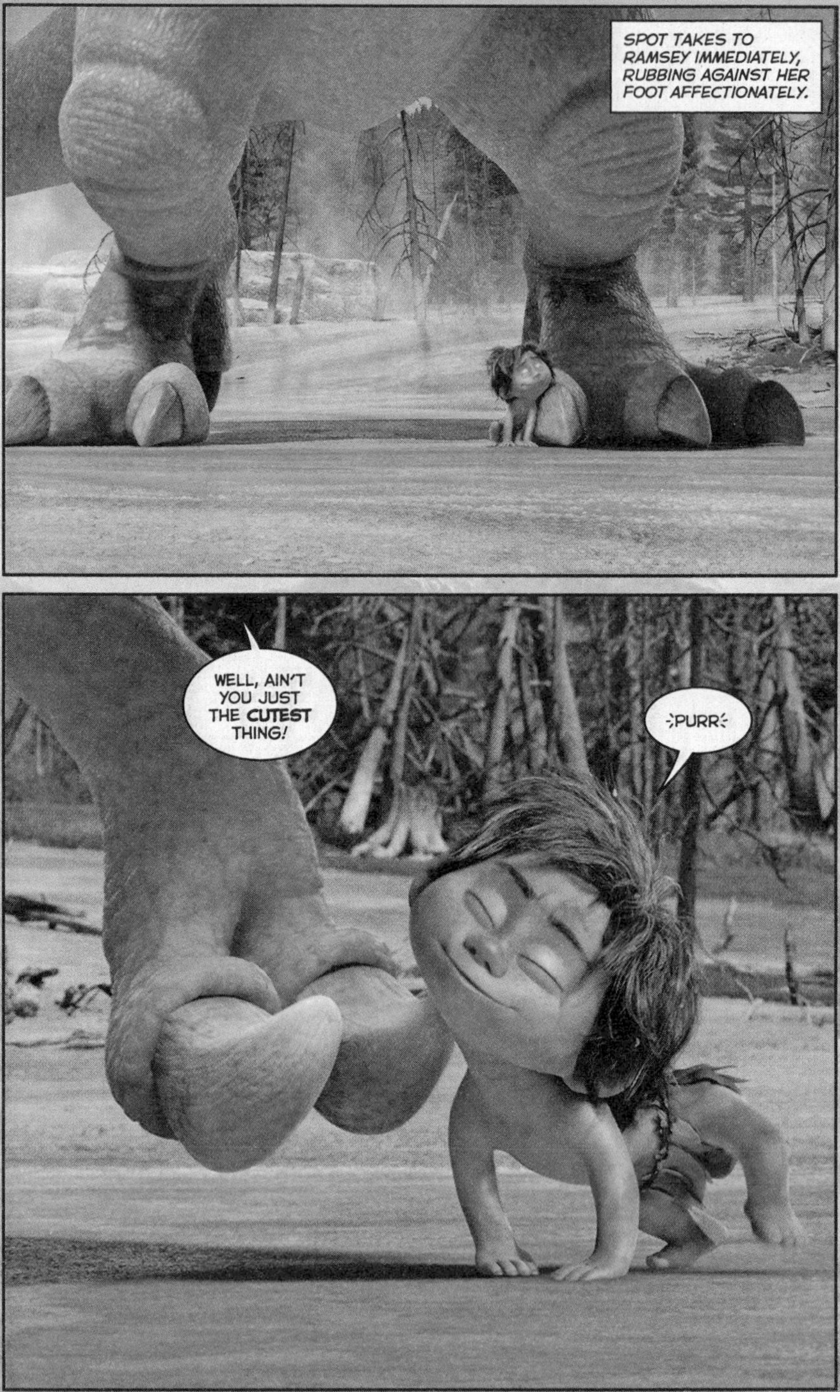
SPOT TAKES TO RAMSEY IMMEDIATELY, RUBBING AGAINST HER FOOT AFFECTIONATELY.
WELL, AIN'T YOU JUST THE **CUTEST** THING!
PURR

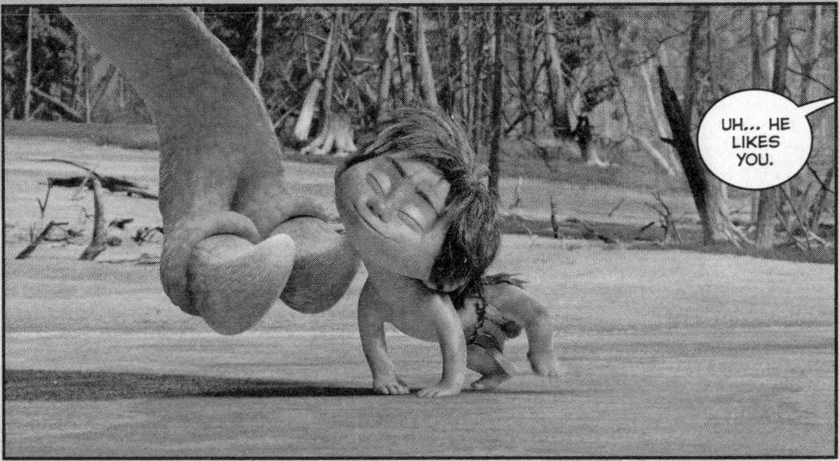
UH... HE LIKES YOU.

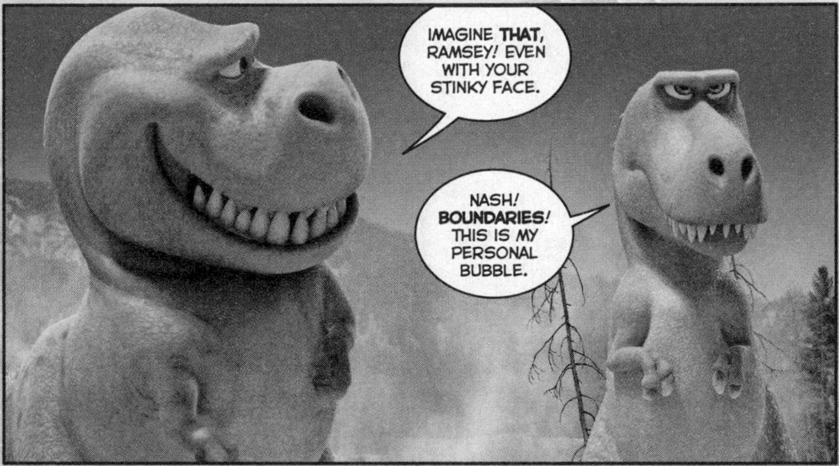
IMAGINE **THAT**, RAMSEY! EVEN WITH YOUR STINKY FACE.
NASH! **BOUNDARIES**! THIS IS MY PERSONAL BUBBLE.

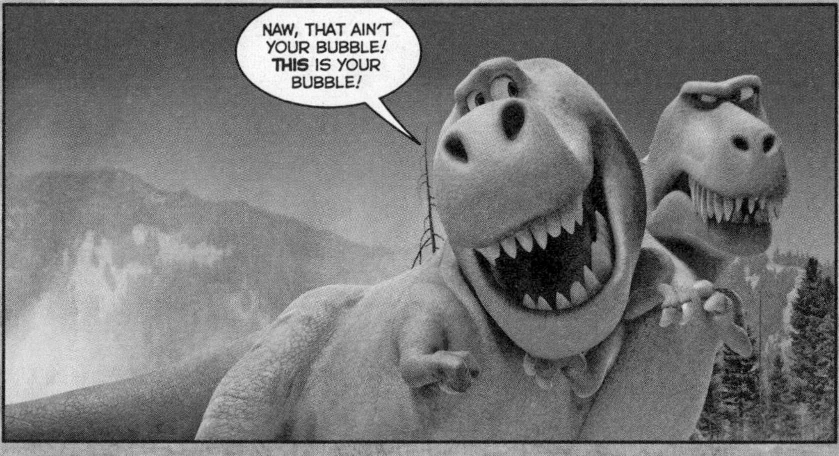
NAW, THAT AIN'T YOUR BUBBLE! **THIS** IS YOUR BUBBLE!

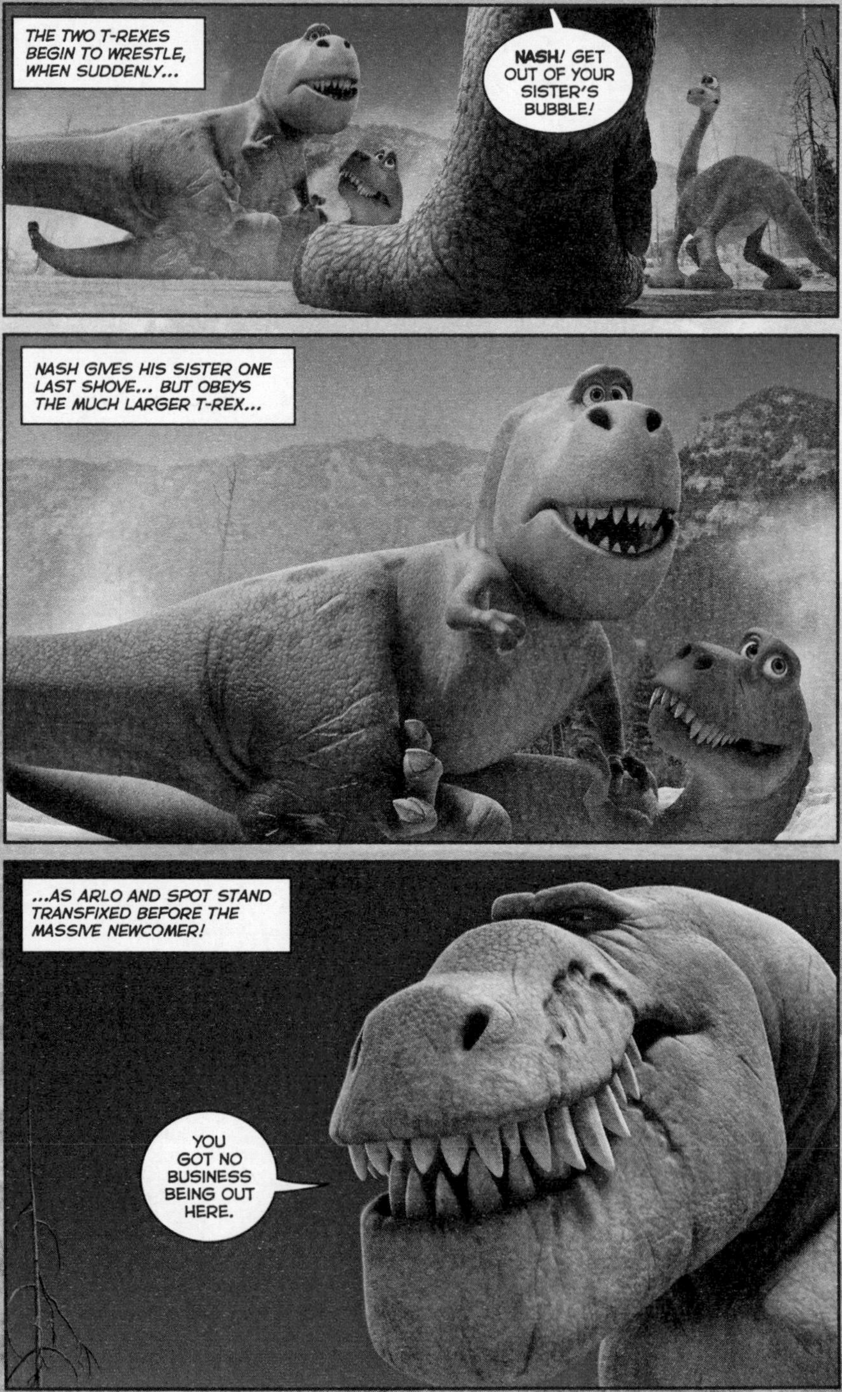
THE TWO T-REXES BEGIN TO WRESTLE, WHEN SUDDENLY...
NASH! GET OUT OF YOUR SISTER'S BUBBLE!
NASH GIVES HIS SISTER ONE LAST SHOVE... BUT OBEYS THE MUCH LARGER T-REX...
...AS ARLO AND SPOT STAND TRANSFIXED BEFORE THE MASSIVE NEWCOMER!
YOU GOT NO BUSINESS BEING OUT HERE.

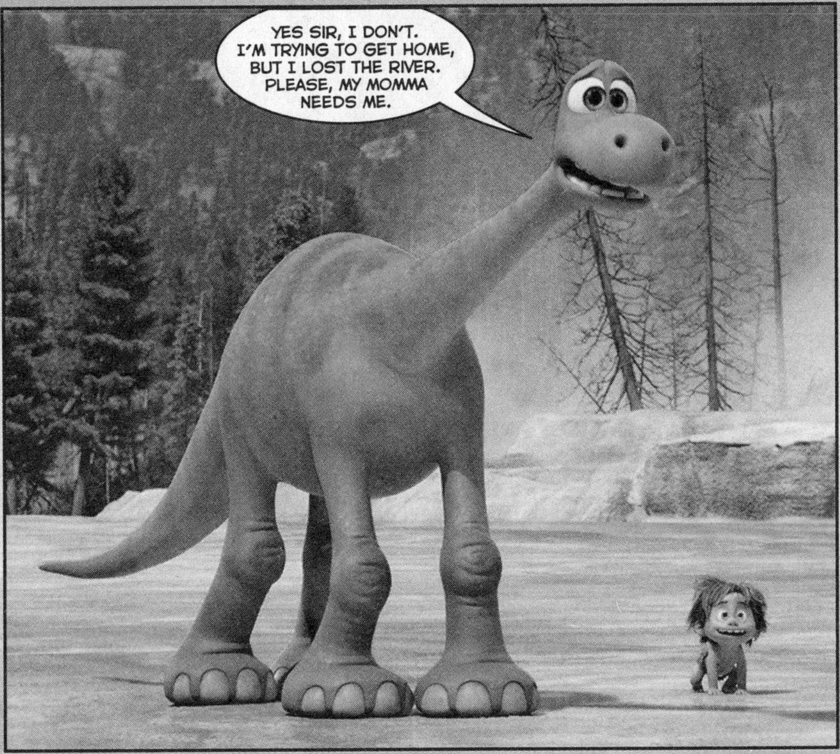
YES SIR, I DON'T. I'M TRYING TO GET HOME, BUT I LOST THE RIVER. PLEASE, MY MOMMA NEEDS ME.

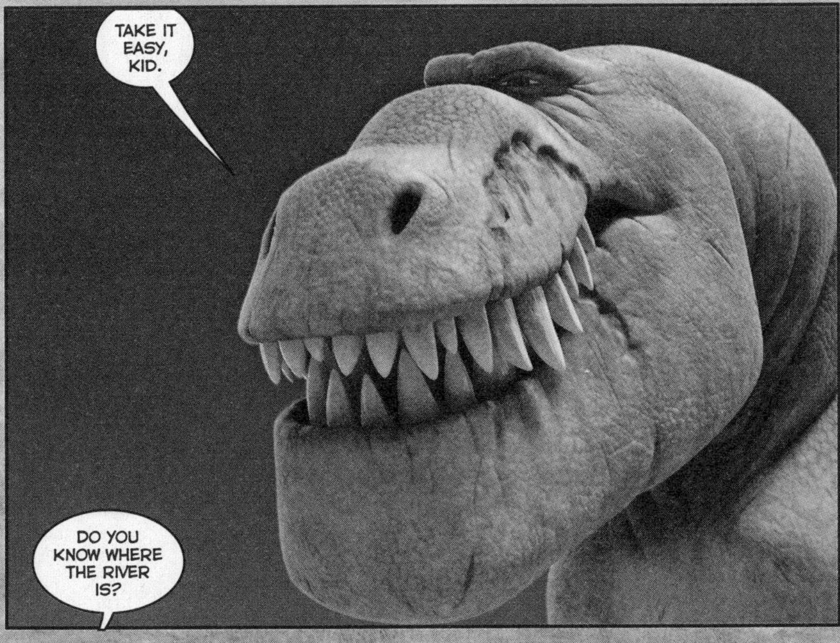
TAKE IT EASY, KID.
DO YOU KNOW WHERE THE RIVER IS?

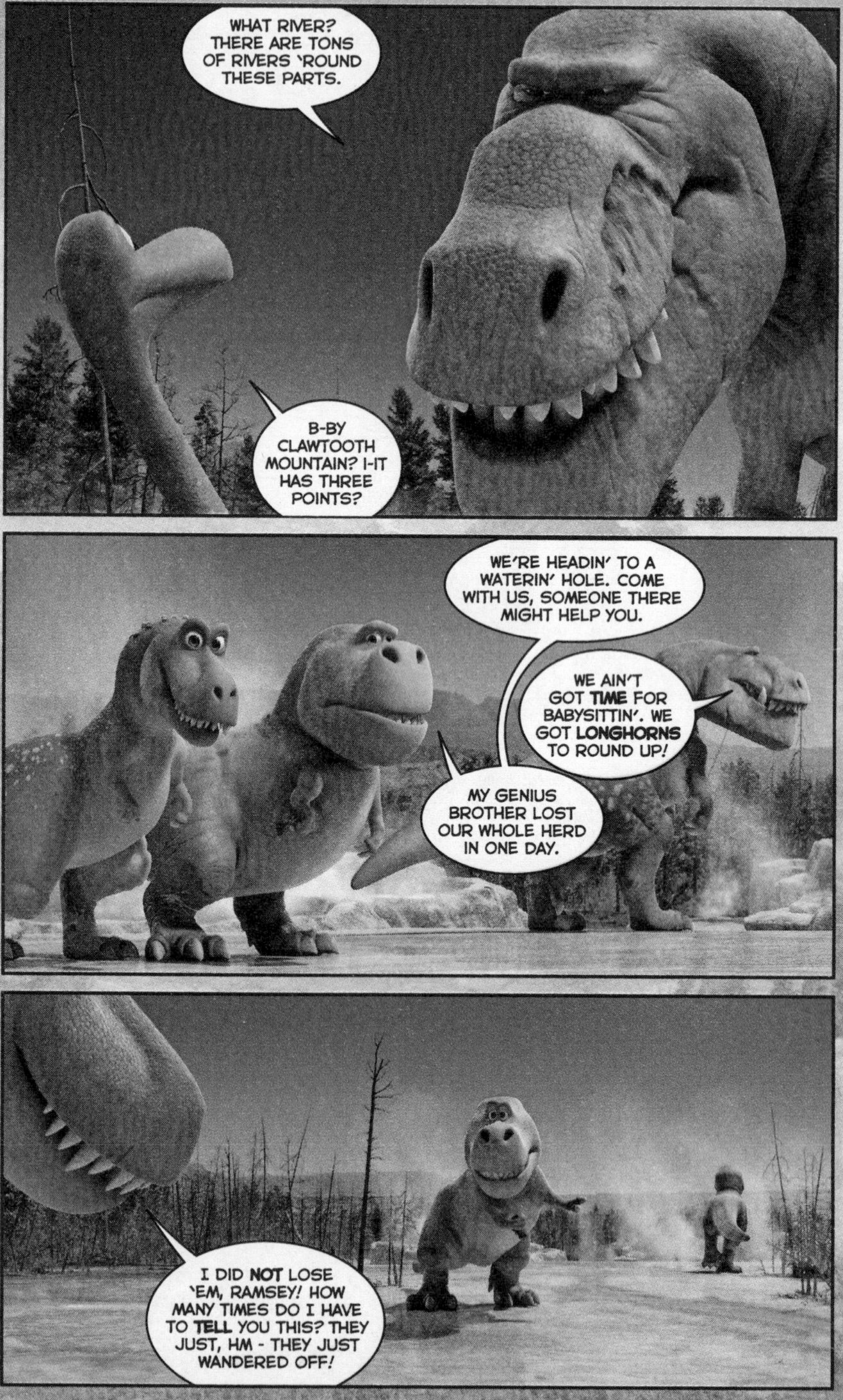
WHAT RIVER? THERE ARE TONS OF RIVERS 'ROUND THESE PARTS.
B-BY CLAWTOOTH MOUNTAIN? I-IT HAS THREE POINTS?
WE'RE HEADIN' TO A WATERIN' HOLE. COME WITH US, SOMEONE THERE MIGHT HELP YOU.
WE AIN'T GOT **TIME** FOR BABYSITTIN'. WE GOT **LONGHORNS** TO ROUND UP!
MY GENIUS BROTHER LOST OUR WHOLE HERD IN ONE DAY.
I DID **NOT** LOSE 'EM, RAMSEY! HOW MANY TIMES DO I HAVE TO **TELL** YOU THIS? THEY JUST, HM - THEY JUST WANDERED OFF!

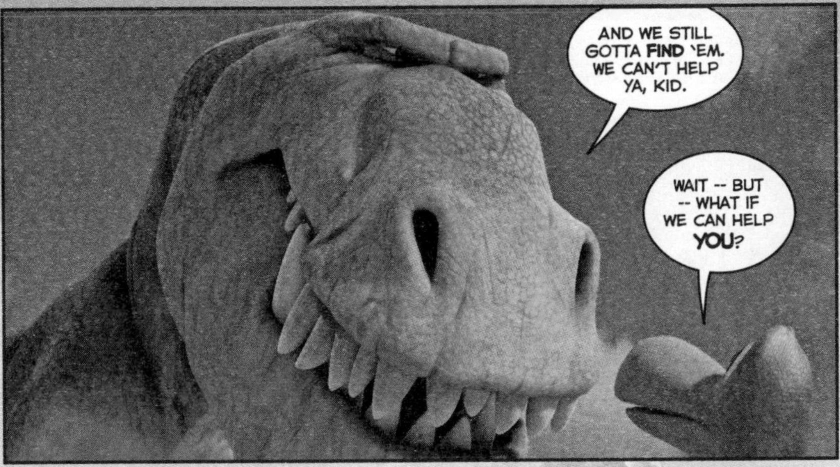
AND WE STILL GOTTA FIND 'EM. WE CAN'T HELP YA, KID.
WAIT -- BUT -- WHAT IF WE CAN HELP YOU?

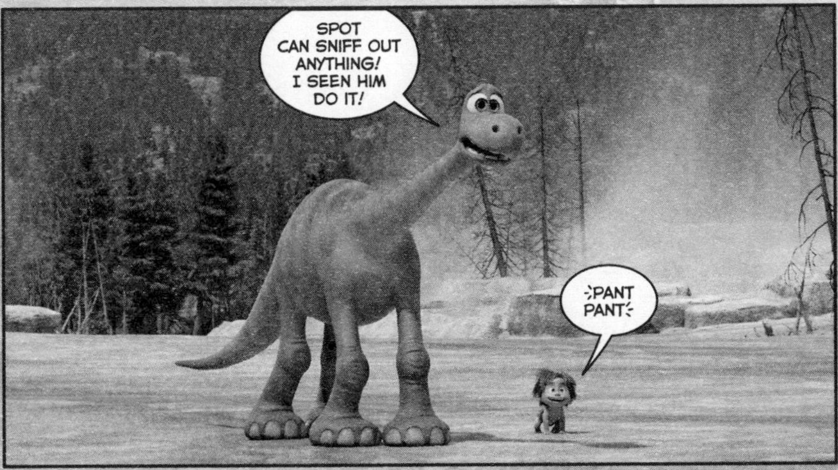
SPOT CAN SNIFF OUT ANYTHING! I SEEN HIM DO IT!
PANT PANT

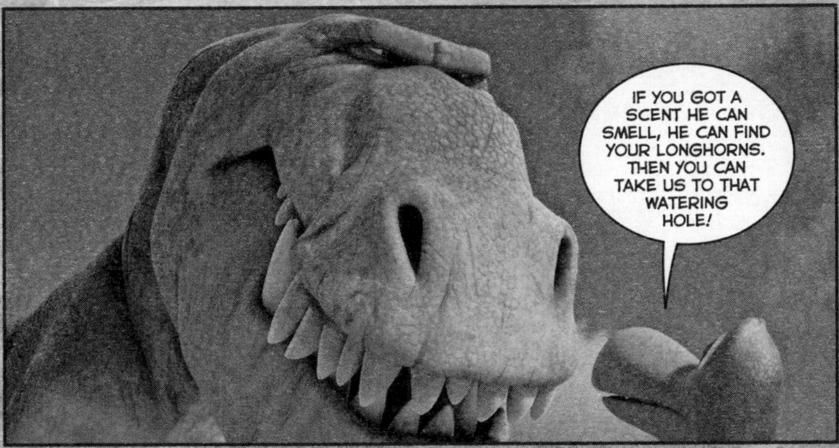
IF YOU GOT A SCENT HE CAN SMELL, HE CAN FIND YOUR LONGHORNS. THEN YOU CAN TAKE US TO THAT WATERING HOLE!

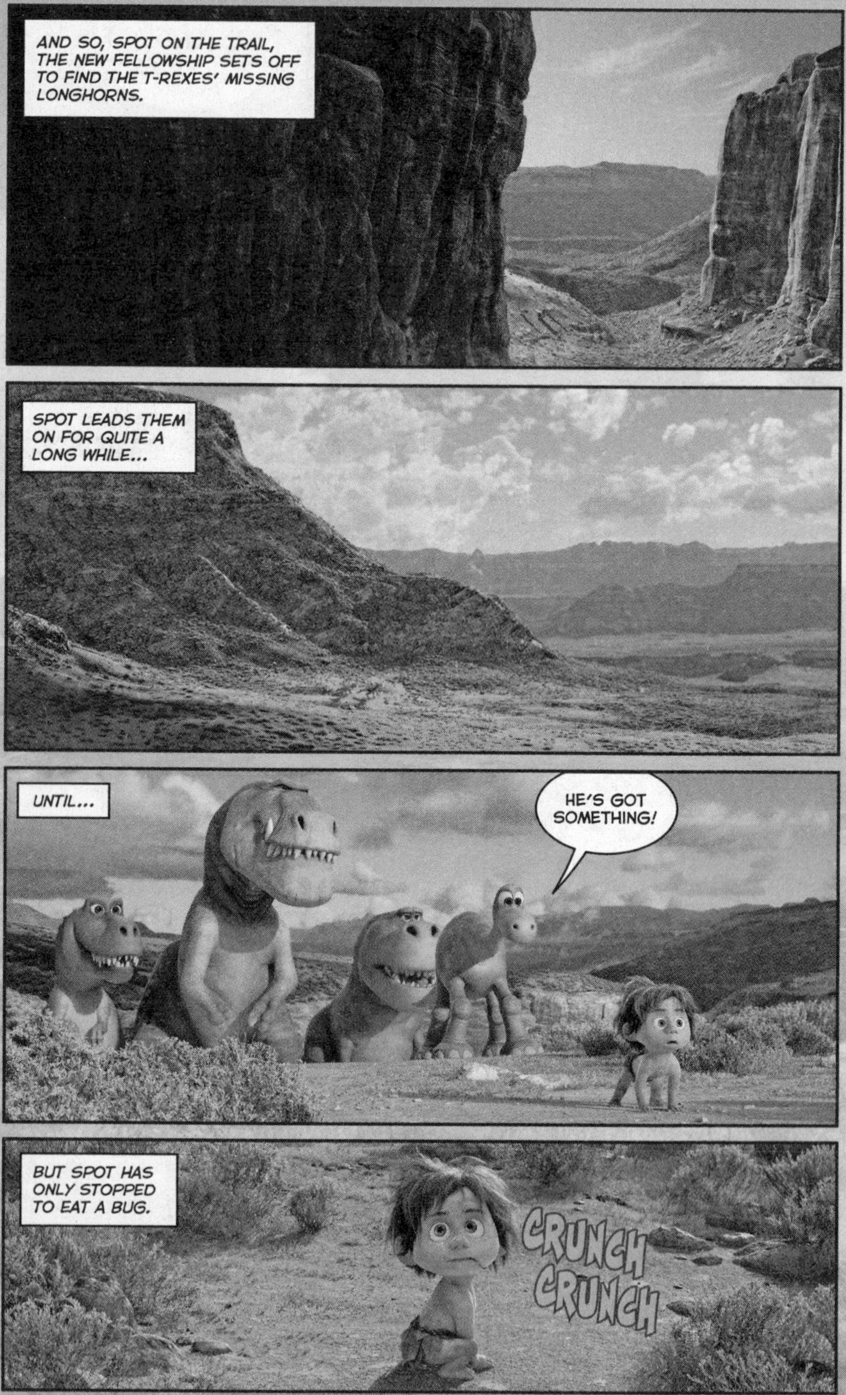
AND SO, SPOT ON THE TRAIL, THE NEW FELLOWSHIP SETS OFF TO FIND THE T-REXES' MISSING LONGHORNS.
SPOT LEADS THEM ON FOR QUITE A LONG WHILE...
UNTIL...
HE'S GOT SOMETHING!
BUT SPOT HAS ONLY STOPPED TO EAT A BUG.
CRUNCH
CRUNCH

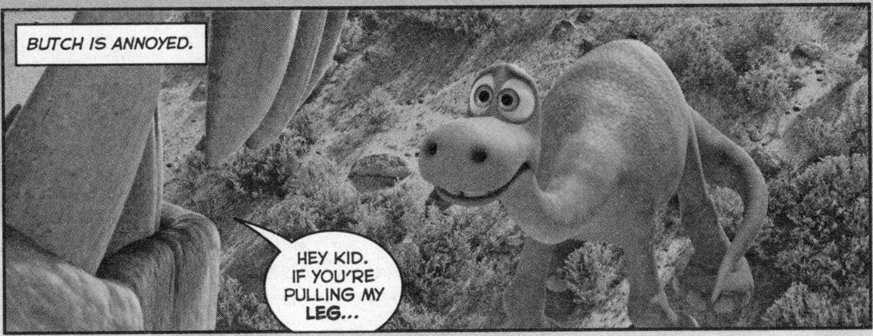
BUTCH IS ANNOYED.
HEY KID. IF YOU'RE PULLING MY **LEG**...

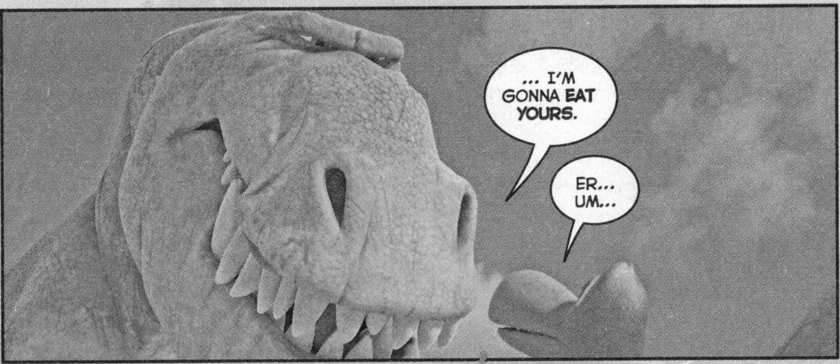
... I'M GONNA **EAT YOURS**.
ER... UM...

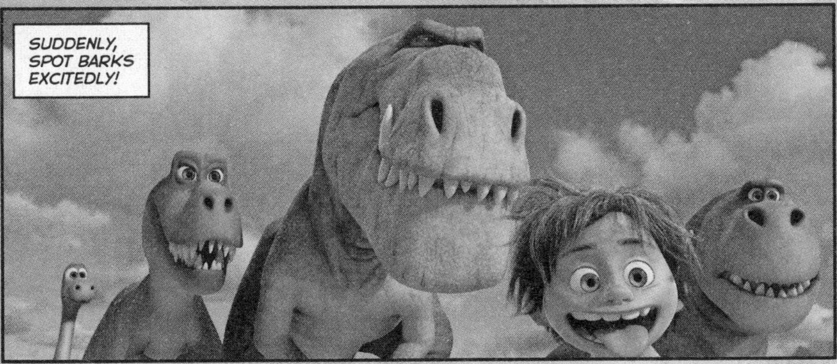
SUDDENLY, SPOT BARKS EXCITEDLY!

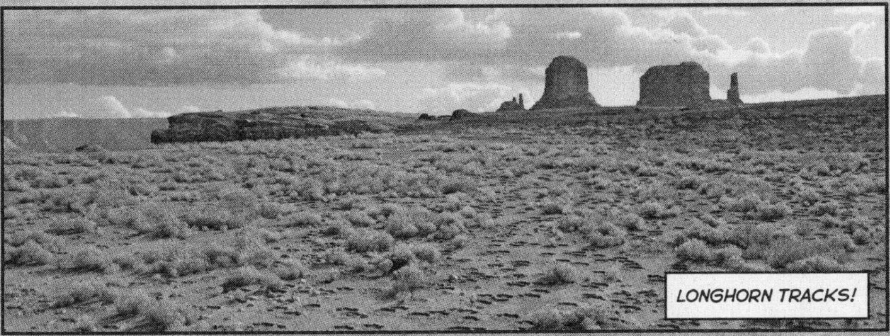
LONGHORN TRACKS!

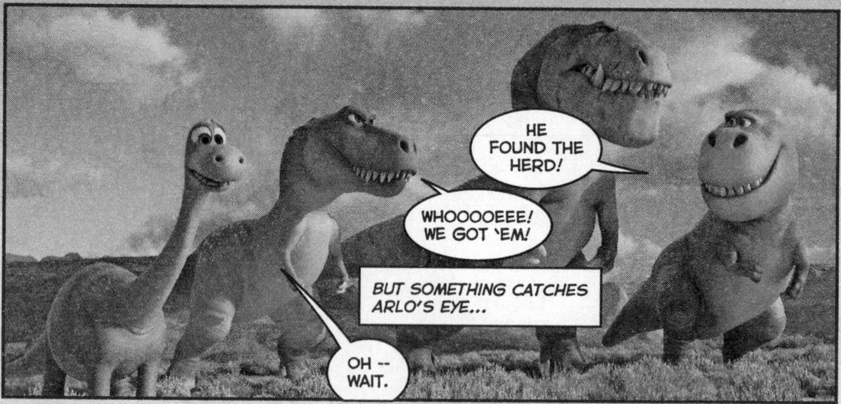
HE FOUND THE HERD!
WHOOOOEEE! WE GOT 'EM!
BUT SOMETHING CATCHES ARLO'S EYE...
OH -- WAIT.

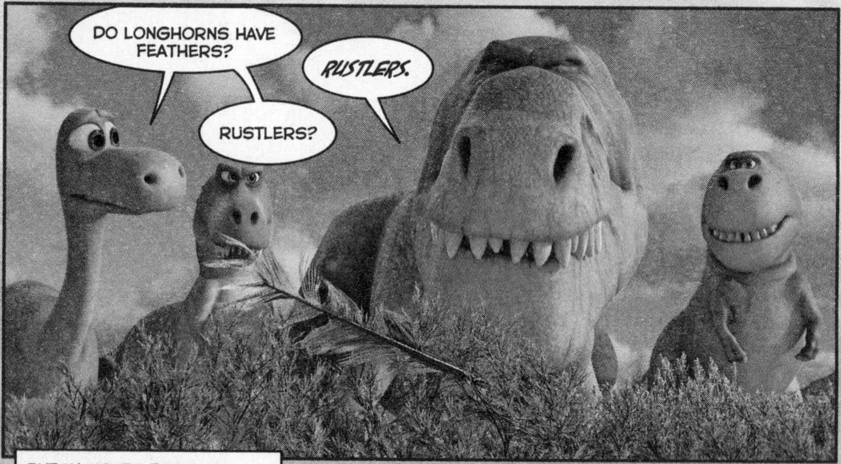
DO LONGHORNS HAVE FEATHERS?
RUSTLERS?
RUSTLERS.

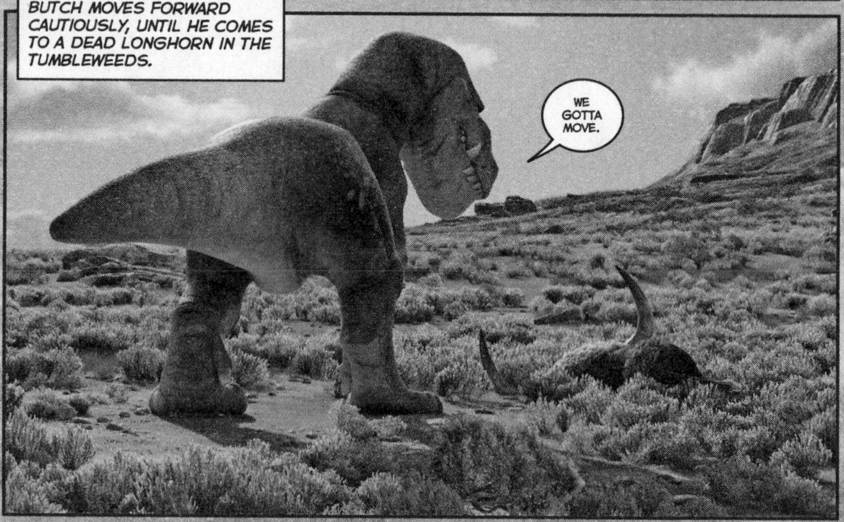
BUTCH MOVES FORWARD CAUTIOUSLY, UNTIL HE COMES TO A DEAD LONGHORN IN THE TUMBLEWEEDS.
WE GOTTA MOVE.

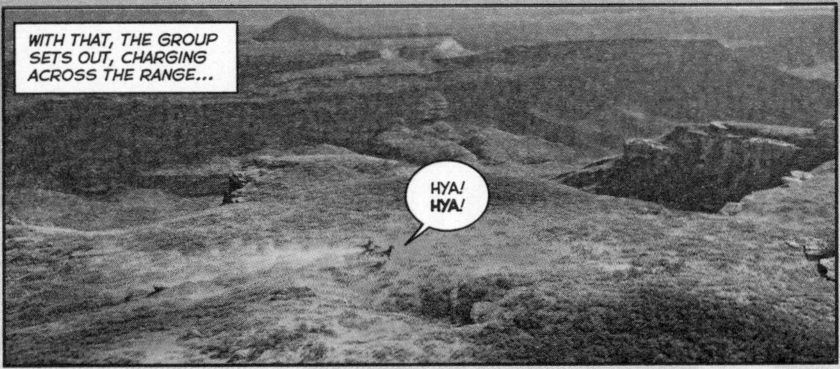
WITH THAT, THE GROUP SETS OUT, CHARGING ACROSS THE RANGE...
HYA! HYA!

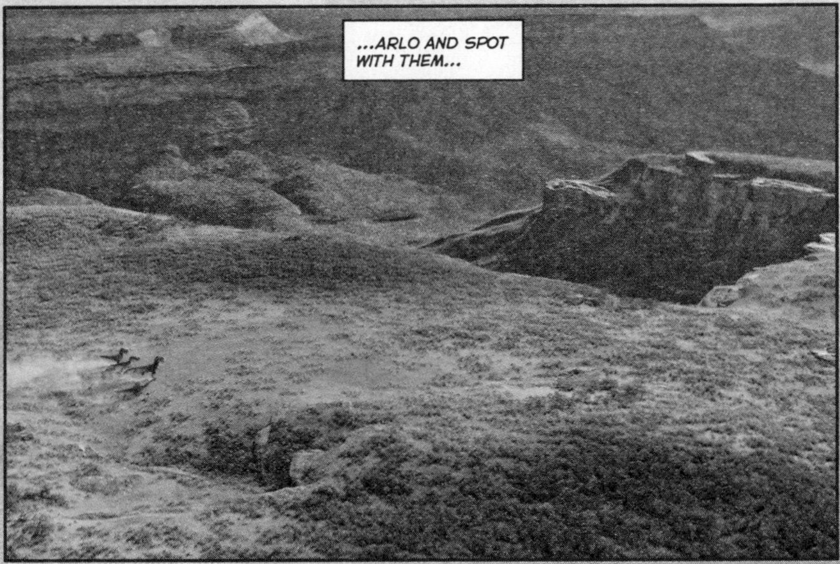
...ARLO AND SPOT WITH THEM...

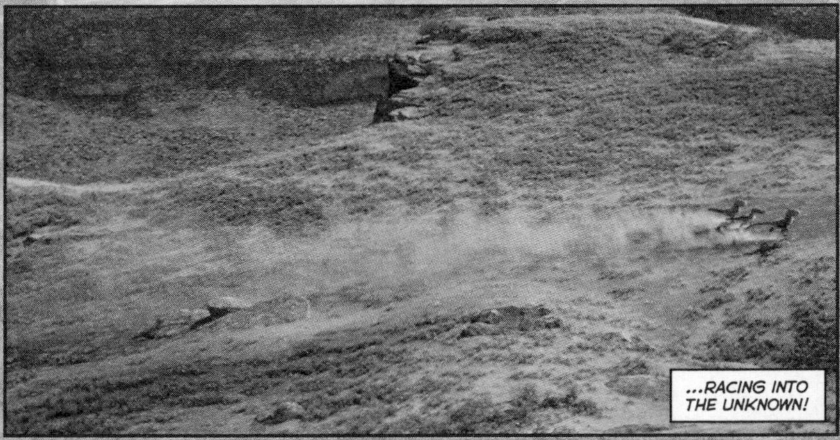
...RACING INTO THE UNKNOWN!

DISNEP · PIXAR
THE GOOD
DINOSAUR

RUSTLERS

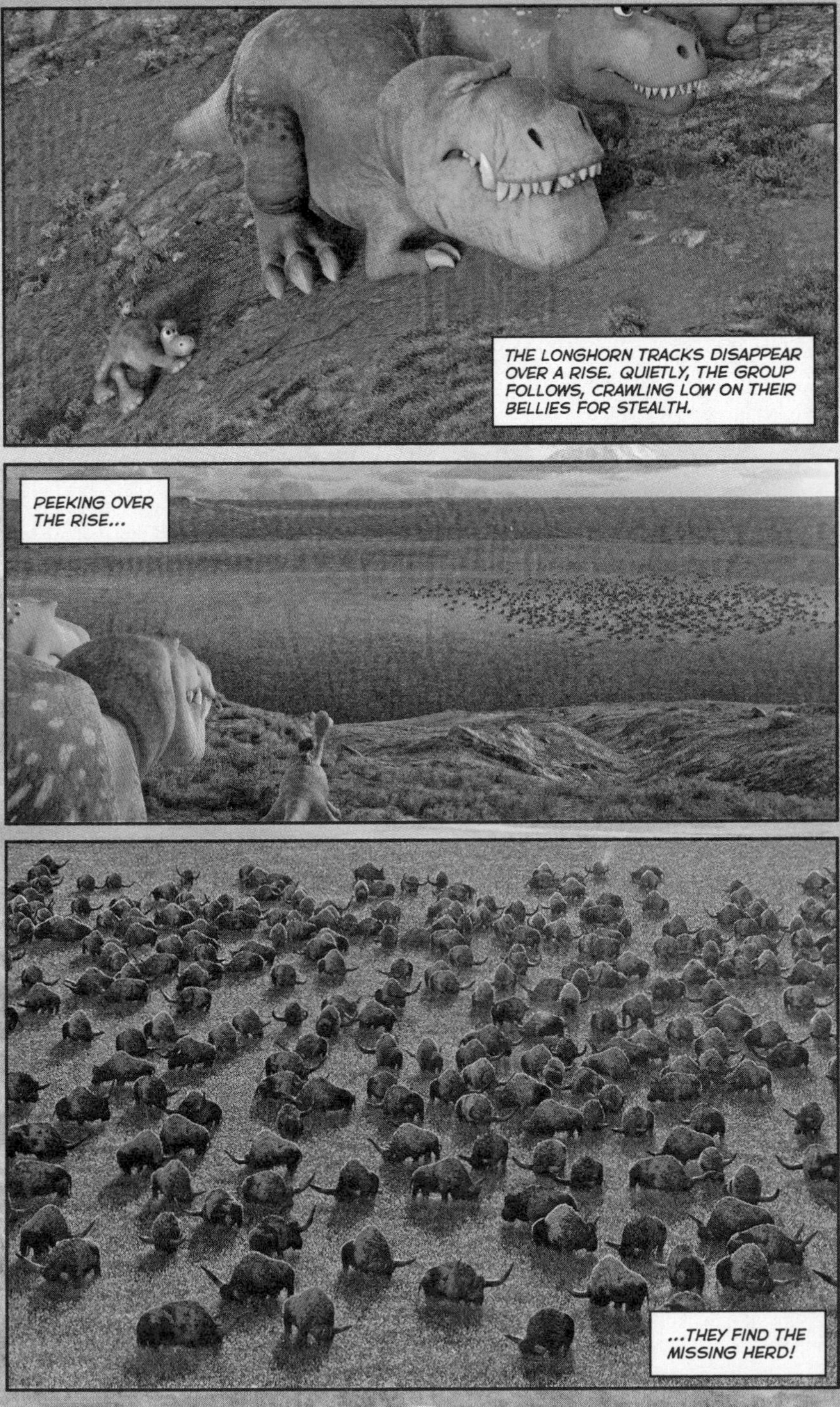
THE LONGHORN TRACKS DISAPPEAR OVER A RISE. QUIETLY, THE GROUP FOLLOWS, CRAWLING LOW ON THEIR BELLIES FOR STEALTH.
PEEKING OVER THE RISE...
...THEY FIND THE MISSING HERD!

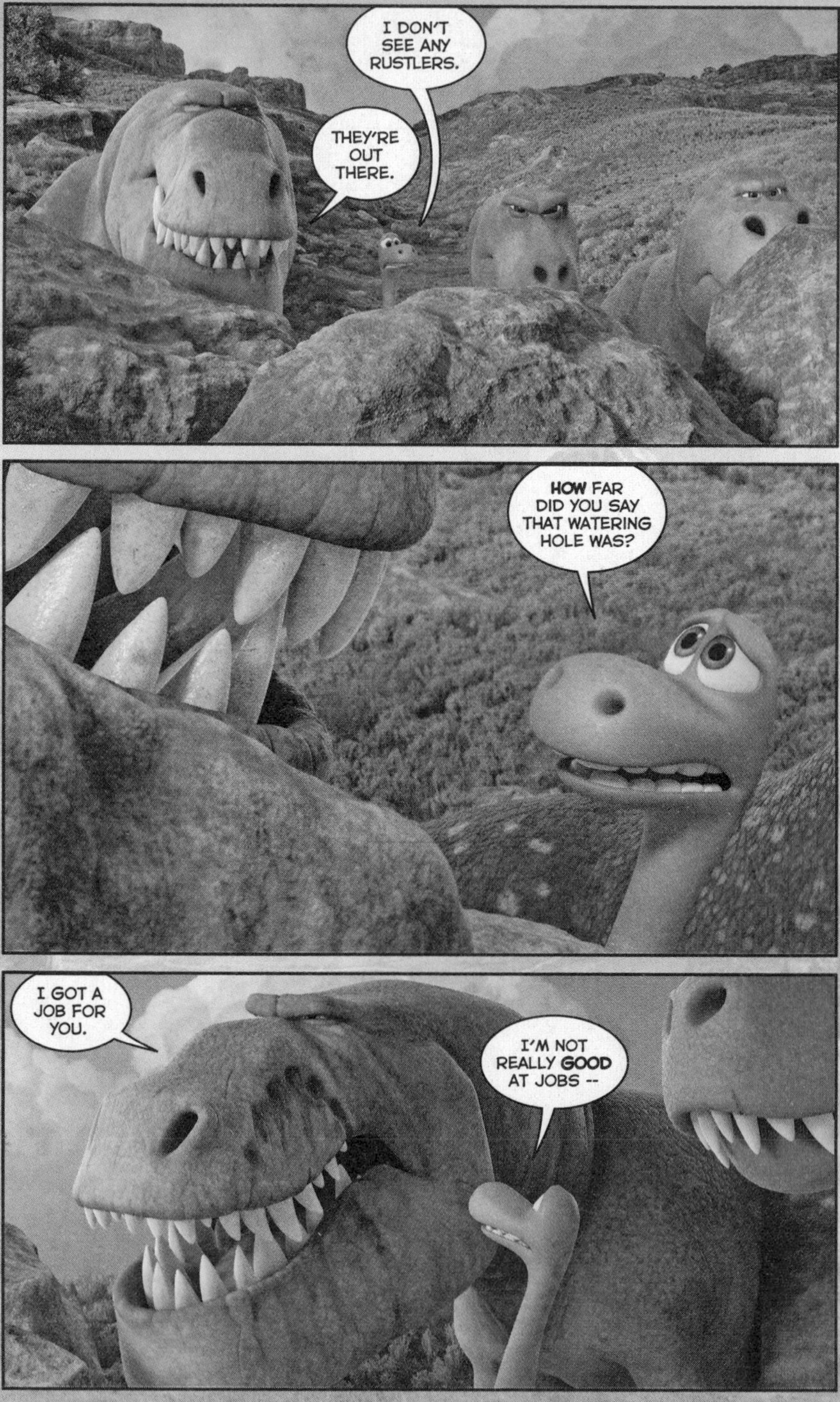
I DON'T SEE ANY RUSTLERS.
THEY'RE OUT THERE.
HOW FAR DID YOU SAY THAT WATERING HOLE WAS?
I GOT A JOB FOR YOU.
I'M NOT REALLY **GOOD** AT JOBS --

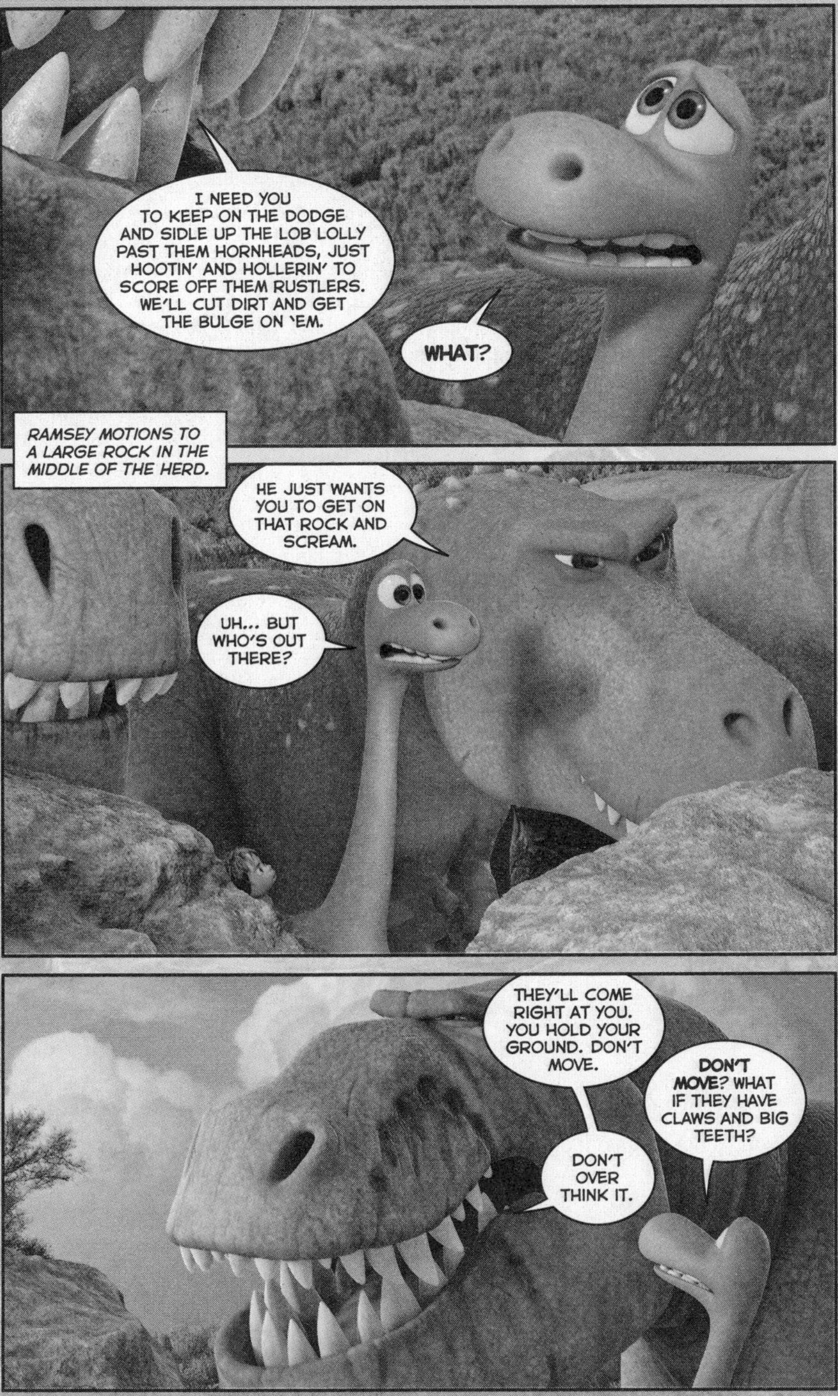
I NEED YOU TO KEEP ON THE DODGE AND SIDLE UP THE LOB LOLLY PAST THEM HORNHEADS, JUST HOOTIN' AND HOLLERIN' TO SCORE OFF THEM RUSTLERS. WE'LL CUT DIRT AND GET THE BULGE ON 'EM.
WHAT?
RAMSEY MOTIONS TO A LARGE ROCK IN THE MIDDLE OF THE HERD.
HE JUST WANTS YOU TO GET ON THAT ROCK AND SCREAM.
UH... BUT WHO'S OUT THERE?
THEY'LL COME RIGHT AT YOU. YOU HOLD YOUR GROUND. DON'T MOVE.
DON'T MOVE? WHAT IF THEY HAVE CLAWS AND BIG TEETH?
DON'T OVER THINK IT.

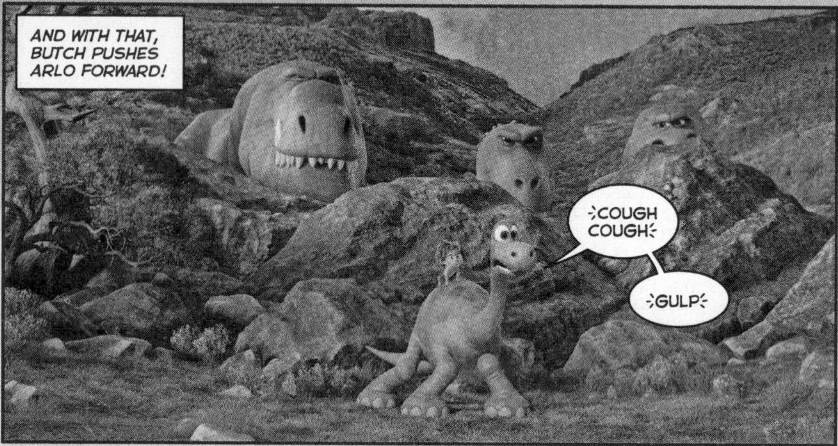
AND WITH THAT, BUTCH PUSHES ARLO FORWARD!
COUGH COUGH
GULP

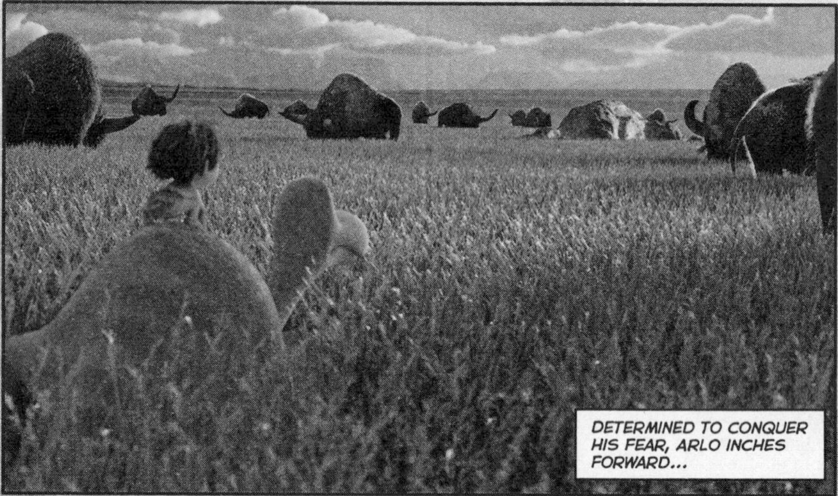
DETERMINED TO CONQUER HIS FEAR, ARLO INCHES FORWARD...

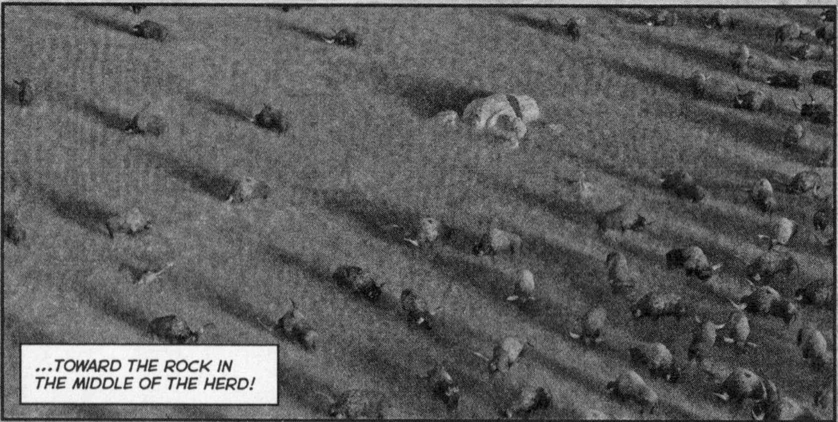
...TOWARD THE ROCK IN THE MIDDLE OF THE HERD!

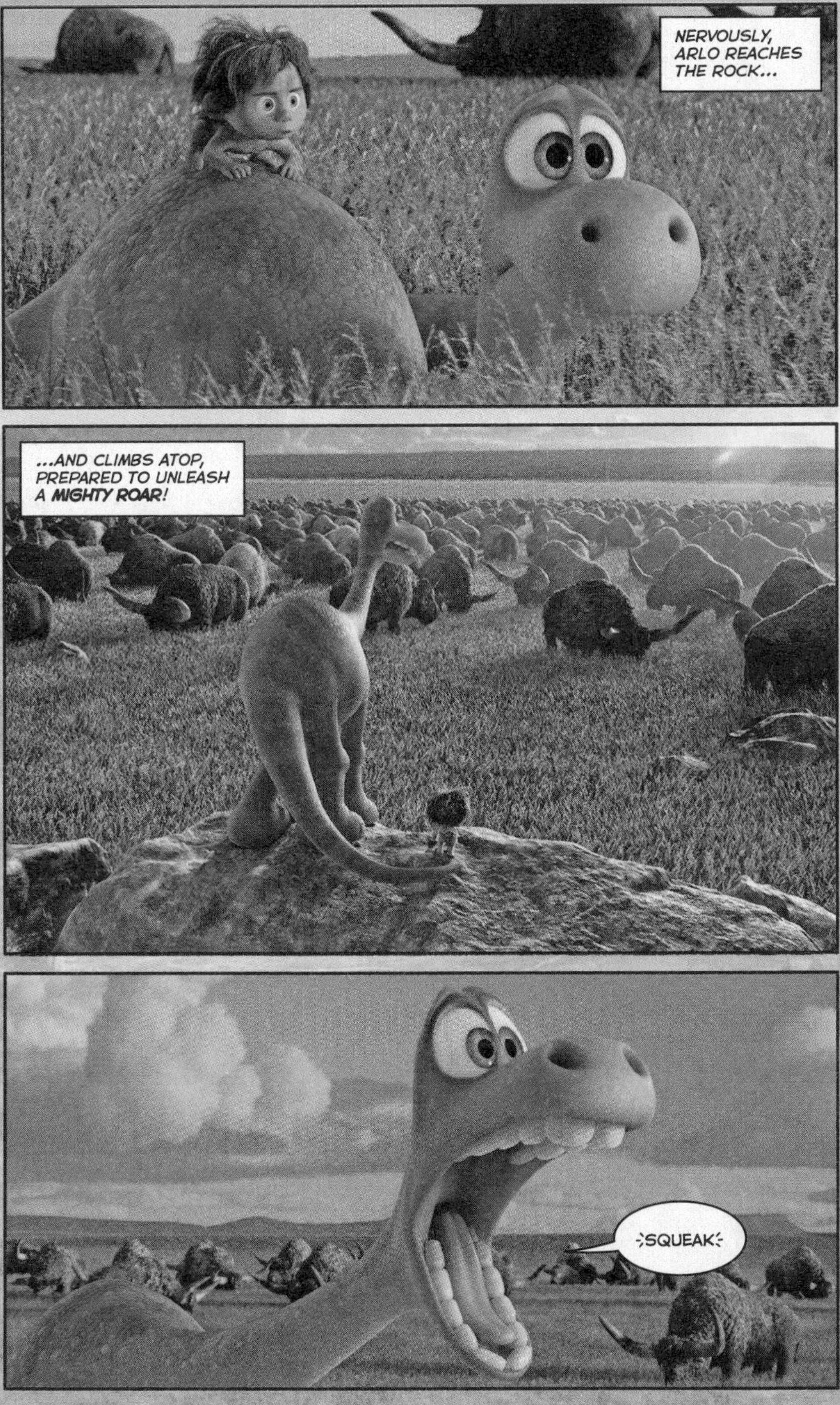
NERVOUSLY, ARLO REACHES THE ROCK...
...AND CLIMBS ATOP, PREPARED TO UNLEASH A MIGHTY ROAR!
SQUEAK

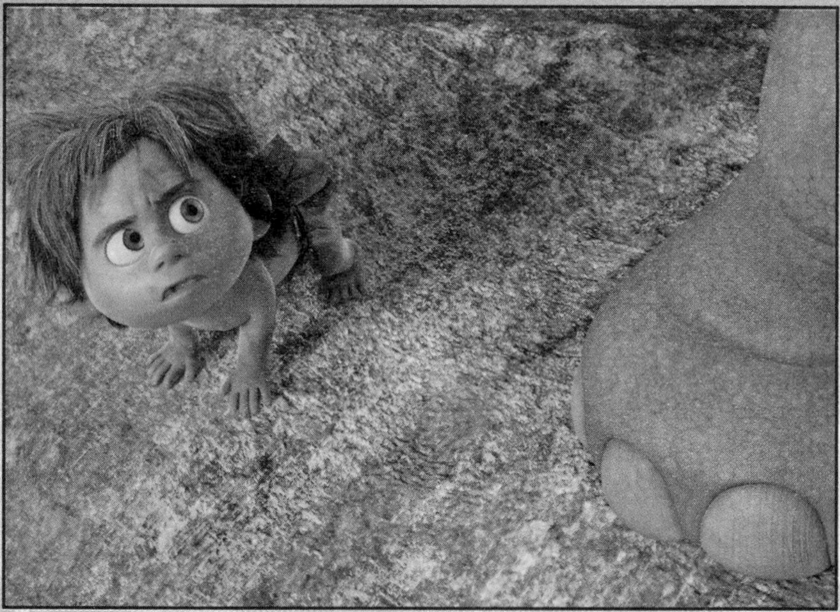

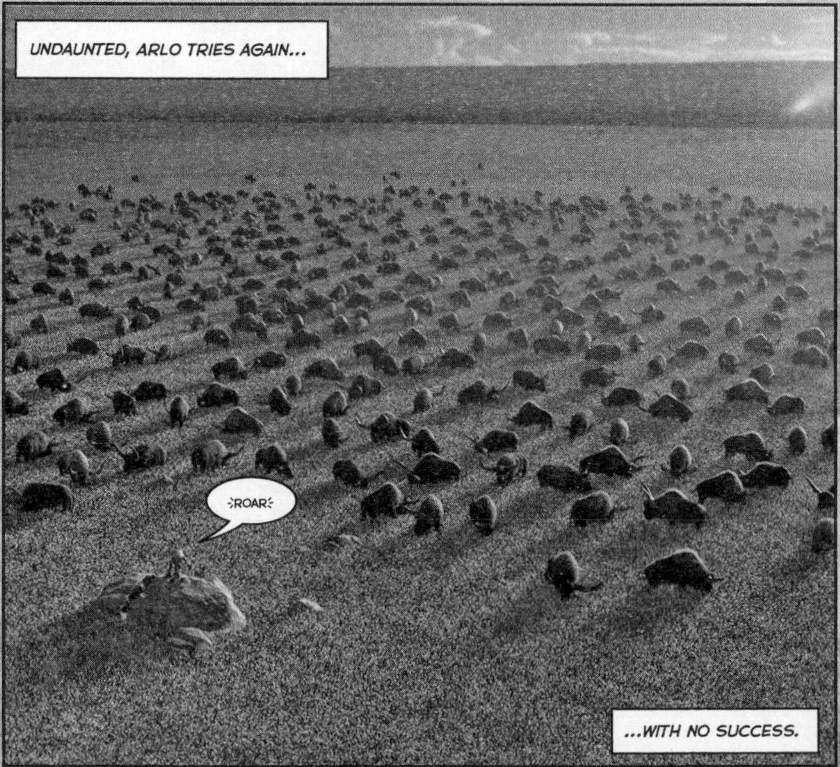

UNDAUNTED, ARLO TRIES AGAIN...
ROAR
...WITH NO SUCCESS.

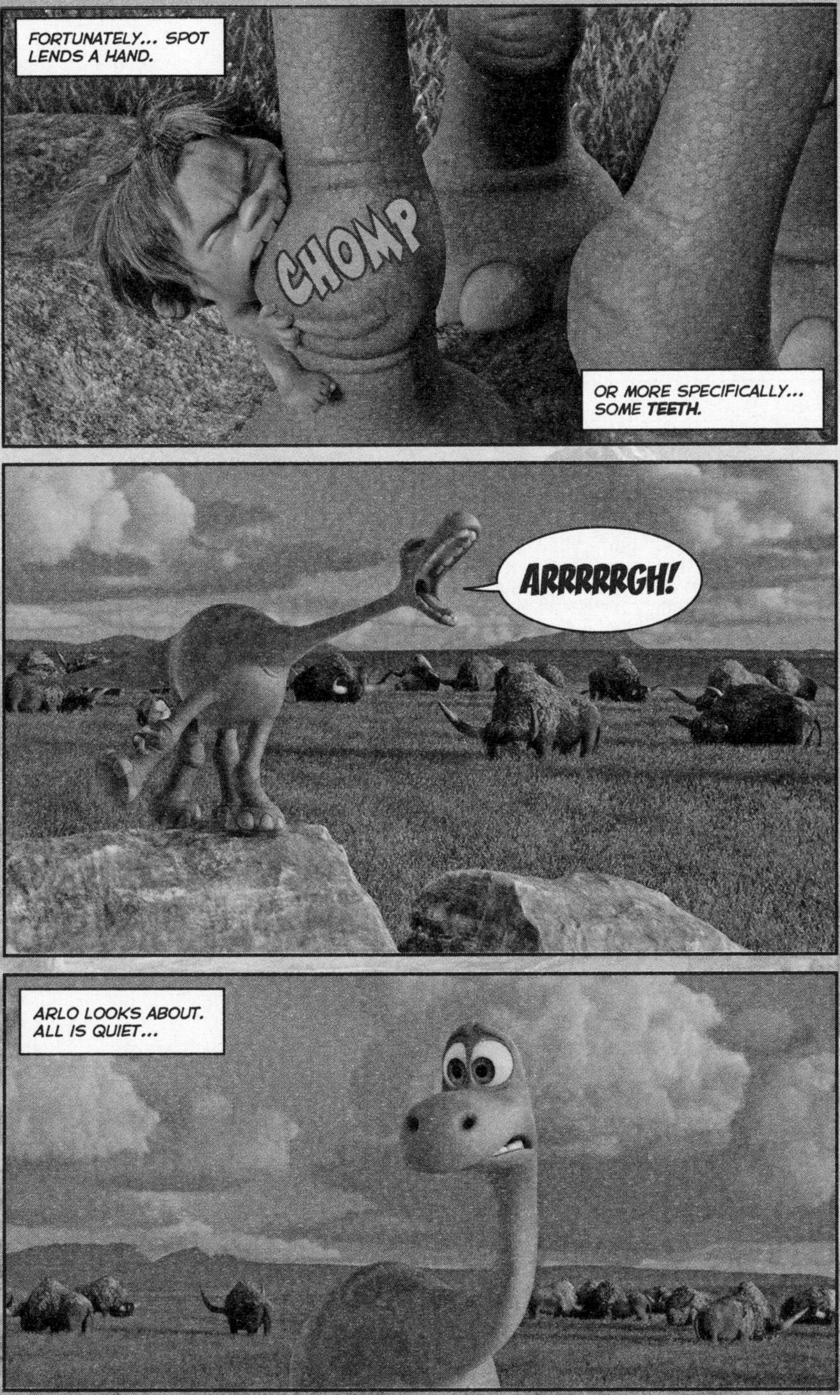
FORTUNATELY... SPOT LENDS A HAND.
CHOMP
OR MORE SPECIFICALLY... SOME **TEETH.**
ARRRRRGH!
ARLO LOOKS ABOUT. ALL IS QUIET...

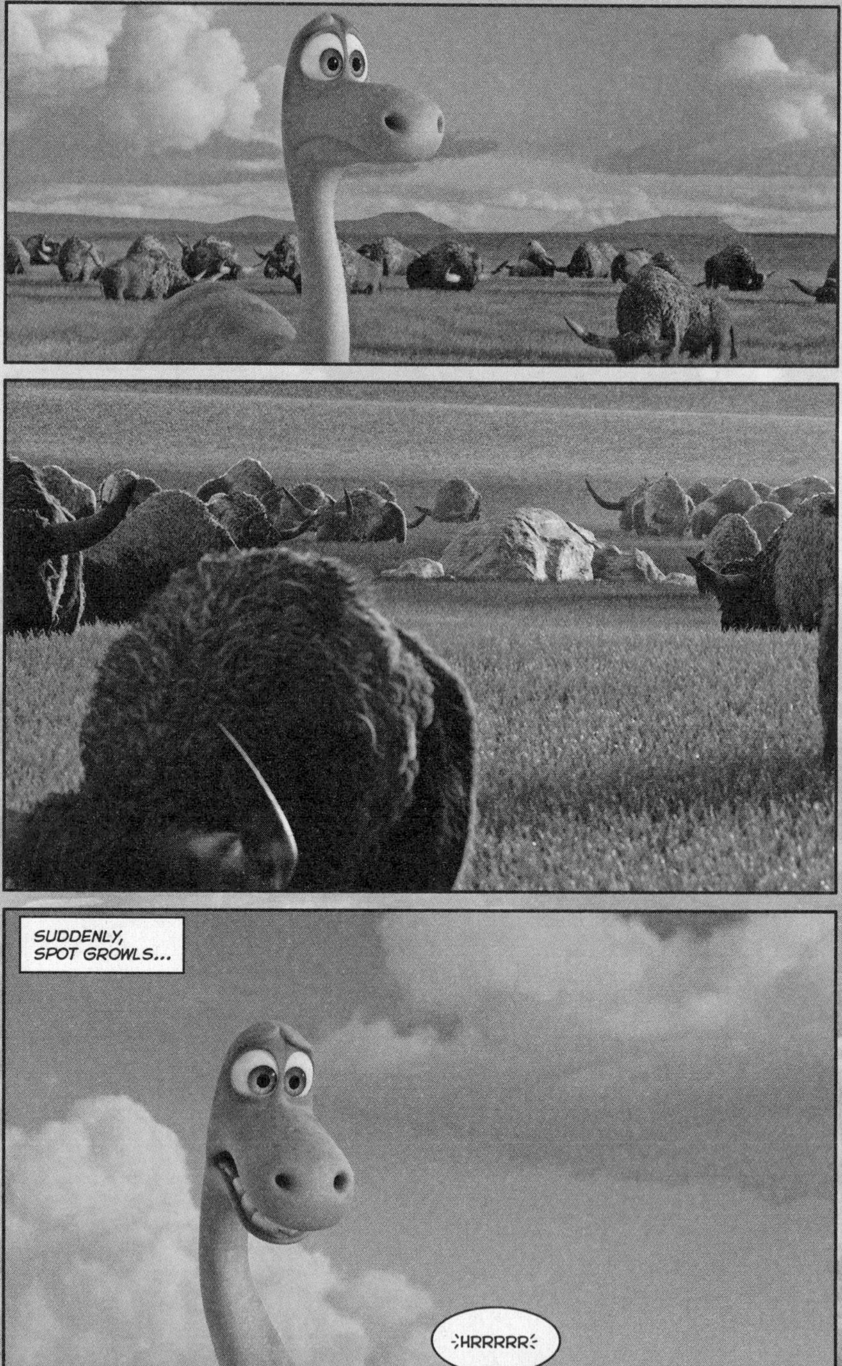
SUDDENLY, SPOT GROWLS...
HRRRRR

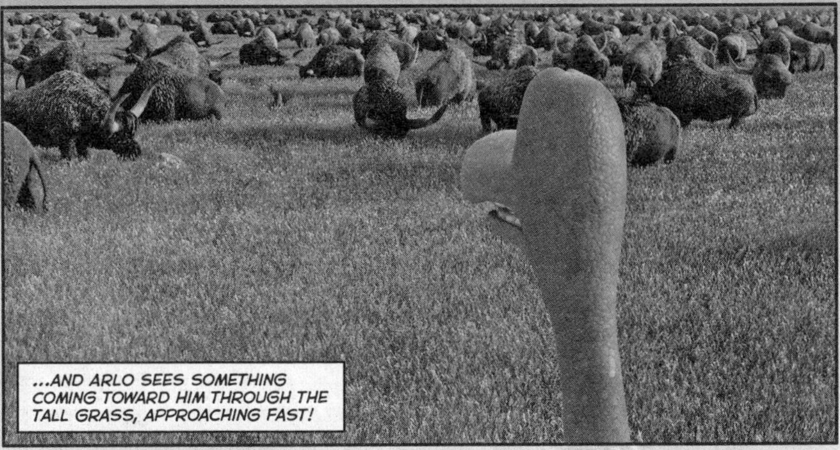
...AND ARLO SEES SOMETHING COMING TOWARD HIM THROUGH THE TALL GRASS, APPROACHING FAST!

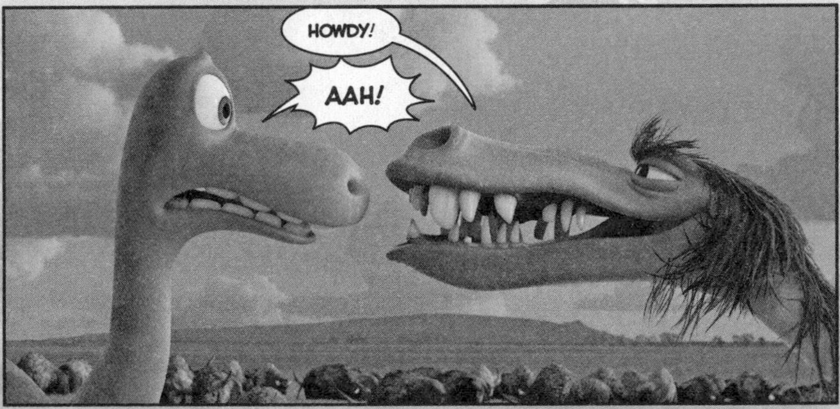
HOWDY!
AAH!

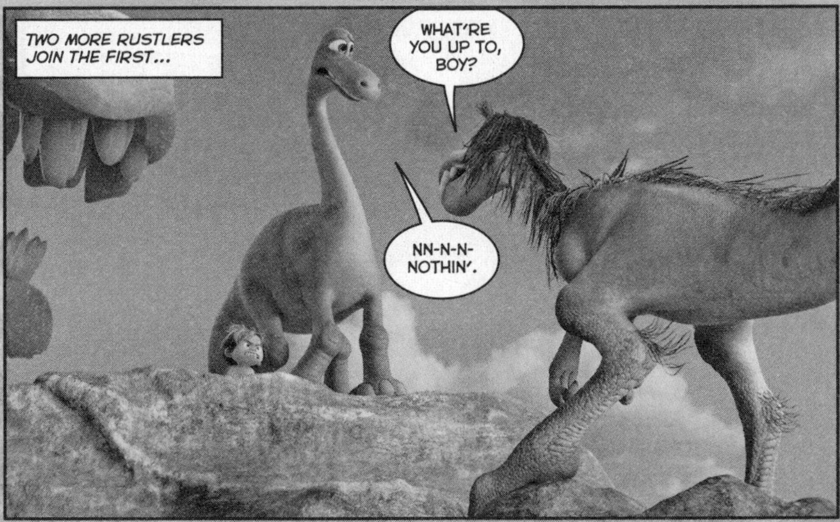
TWO MORE RUSTLERS JOIN THE FIRST...
WHAT'RE YOU UP TO, BOY?
NN-N-N-NOTHIN'.

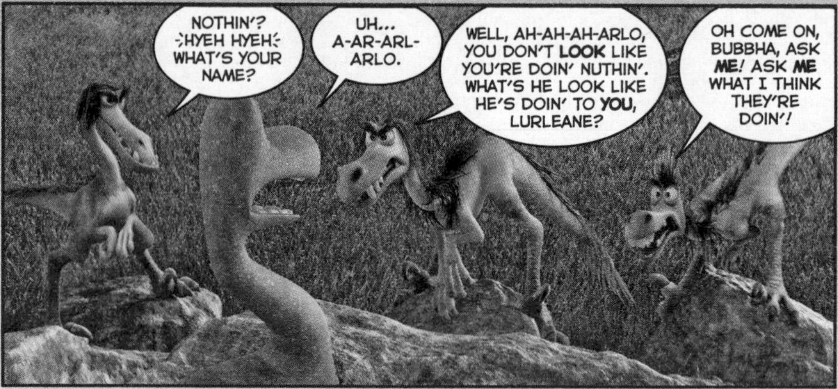
NOTHIN'? HYEH HYEH WHAT'S YOUR NAME?
UH... A-AR-ARL-ARLO.
WELL, AH-AH-AH-ARLO, YOU DON'T **LOOK** LIKE YOU'RE DOIN' NUTHIN'. WHAT'S HE LOOK LIKE HE'S DOIN' TO **YOU**, LURLEANE?
OH COME ON, BUBBHA, ASK **ME**! ASK **ME** WHAT I THINK THEY'RE DOIN'!

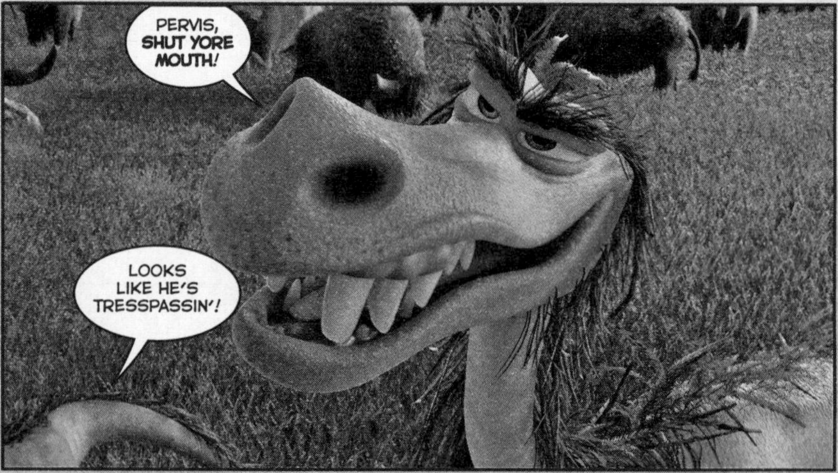
PERVIS, **SHUT YORE MOUTH**!
LOOKS LIKE HE'S TRESSPASSIN'!

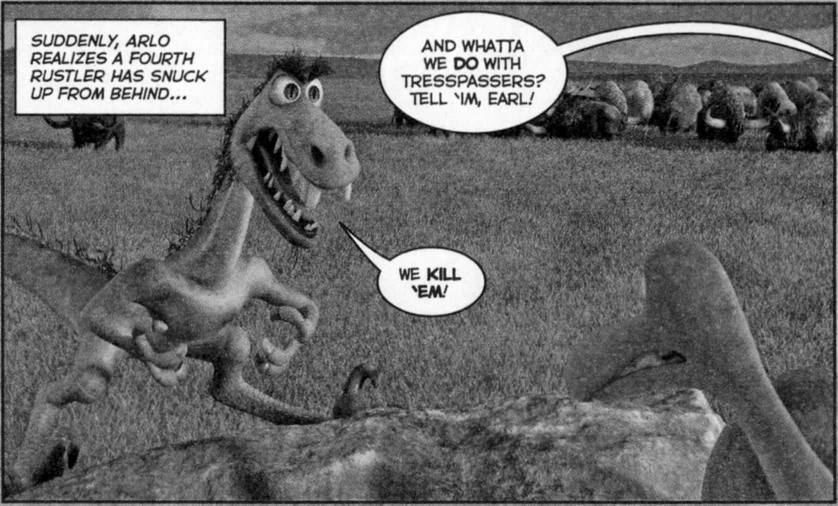
SUDDENLY, ARLO REALIZES A FOURTH RUSTLER HAS SNUCK UP FROM BEHIND...
AND WHATTA WE **DO** WITH TRESSPASSERS? TELL 'IM, EARL!
WE **KILL 'EM**!

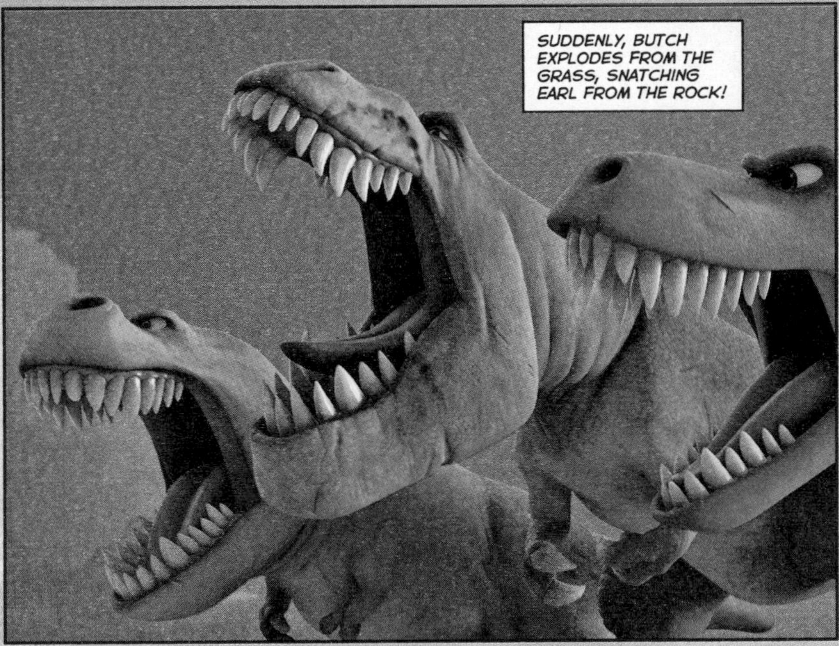
SUDDENLY, BUTCH EXPLODES FROM THE GRASS, SNATCHING EARL FROM THE ROCK!

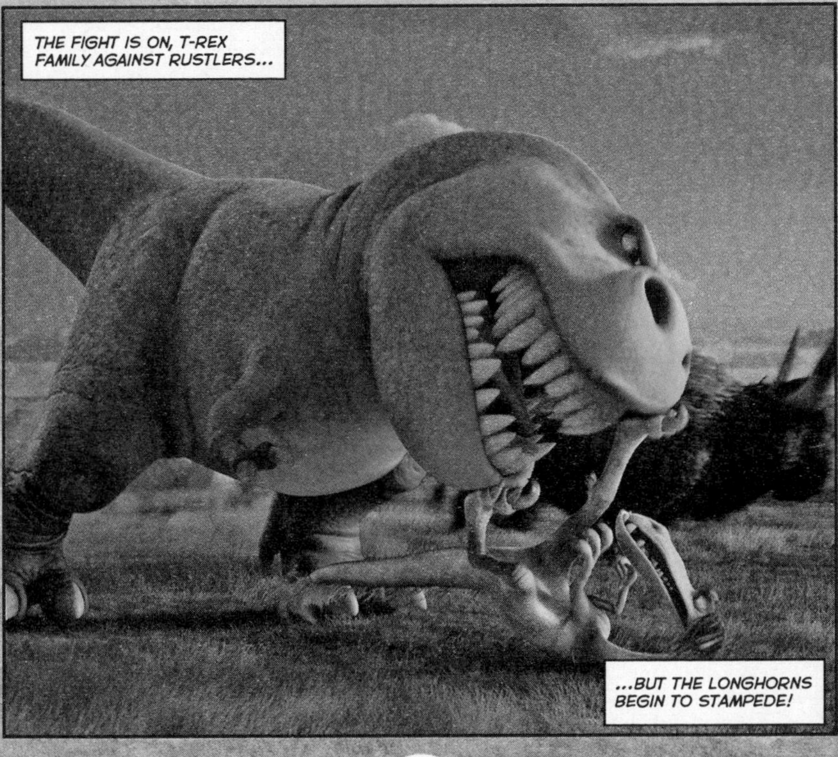
THE FIGHT IS ON, T-REX FAMILY AGAINST RUSTLERS...
...BUT THE LONGHORNS BEGIN TO STAMPEDE!

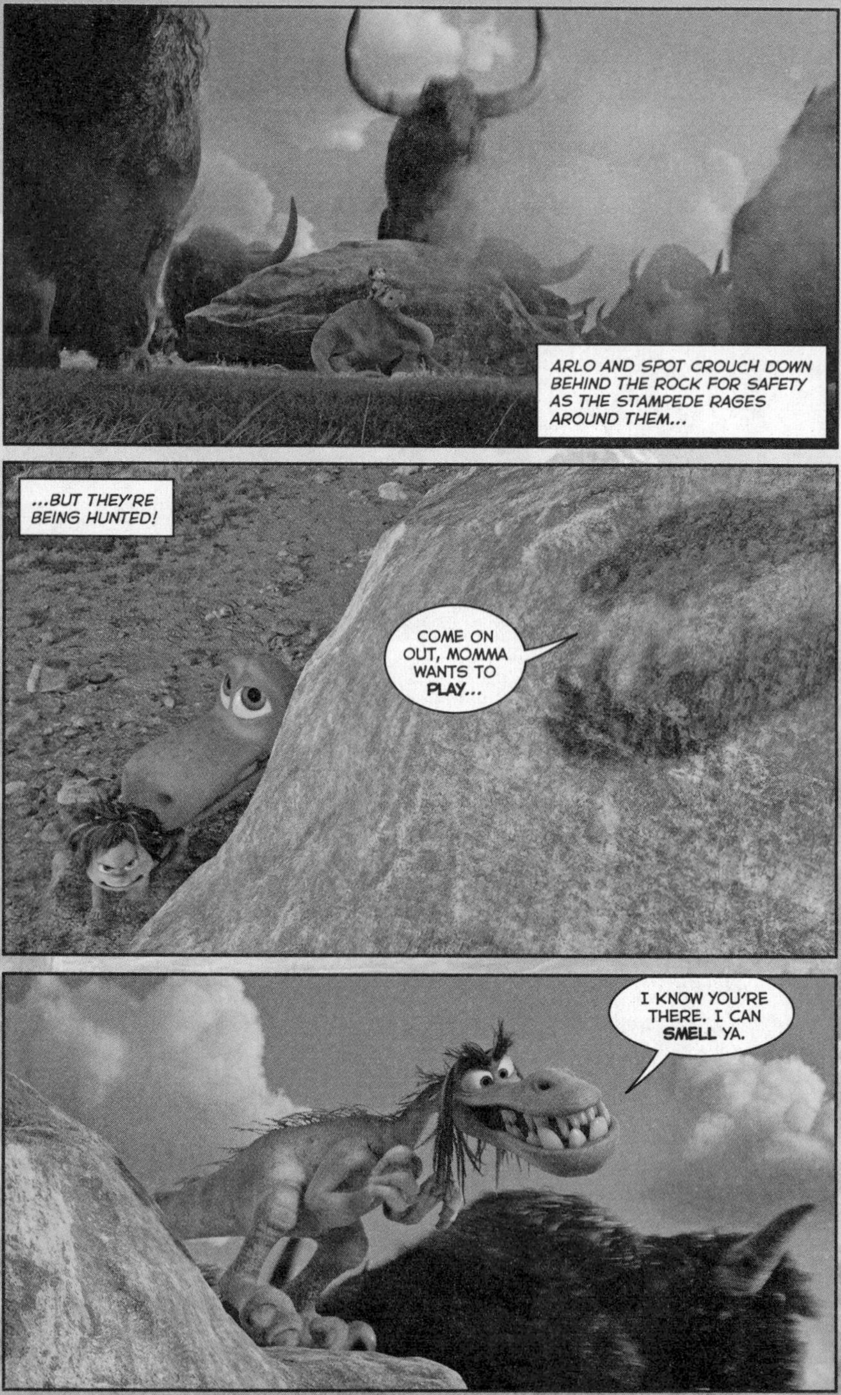
ARLO AND SPOT CROUCH DOWN BEHIND THE ROCK FOR SAFETY AS THE STAMPEDE RAGES AROUND THEM...
...BUT THEY'RE BEING HUNTED!
COME ON OUT, MOMMA WANTS TO PLAY...
I KNOW YOU'RE THERE. I CAN SMELL YA.

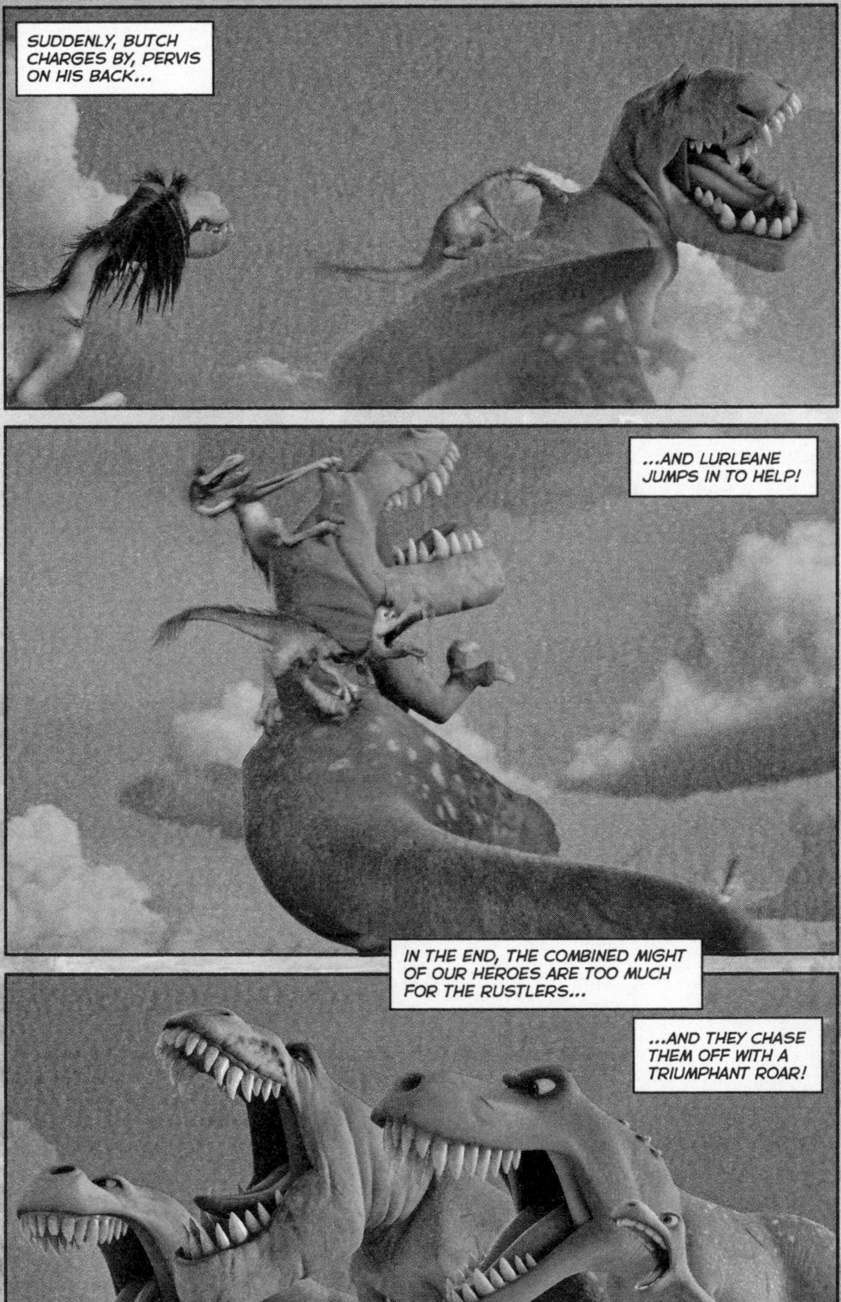
SUDDENLY, BUTCH CHARGES BY, PERVIS ON HIS BACK...
...AND LURLEANE JUMPS IN TO HELP!
IN THE END, THE COMBINED MIGHT OF OUR HEROES ARE TOO MUCH FOR THE RUSTLERS...
...AND THEY CHASE THEM OFF WITH A TRIUMPHANT ROAR!

Disney · PIXAR

THE GOOD DINOSAUR

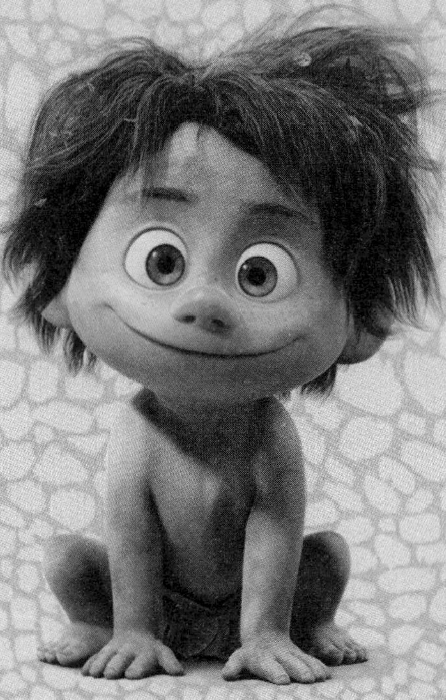

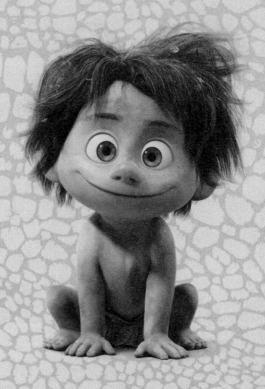

CAMPFIRE

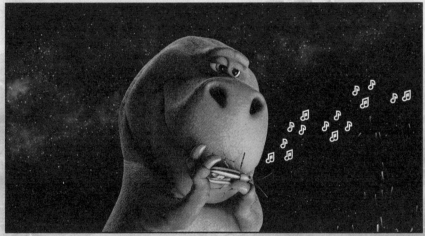

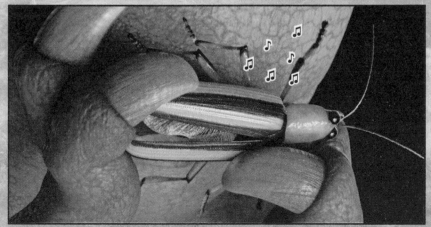

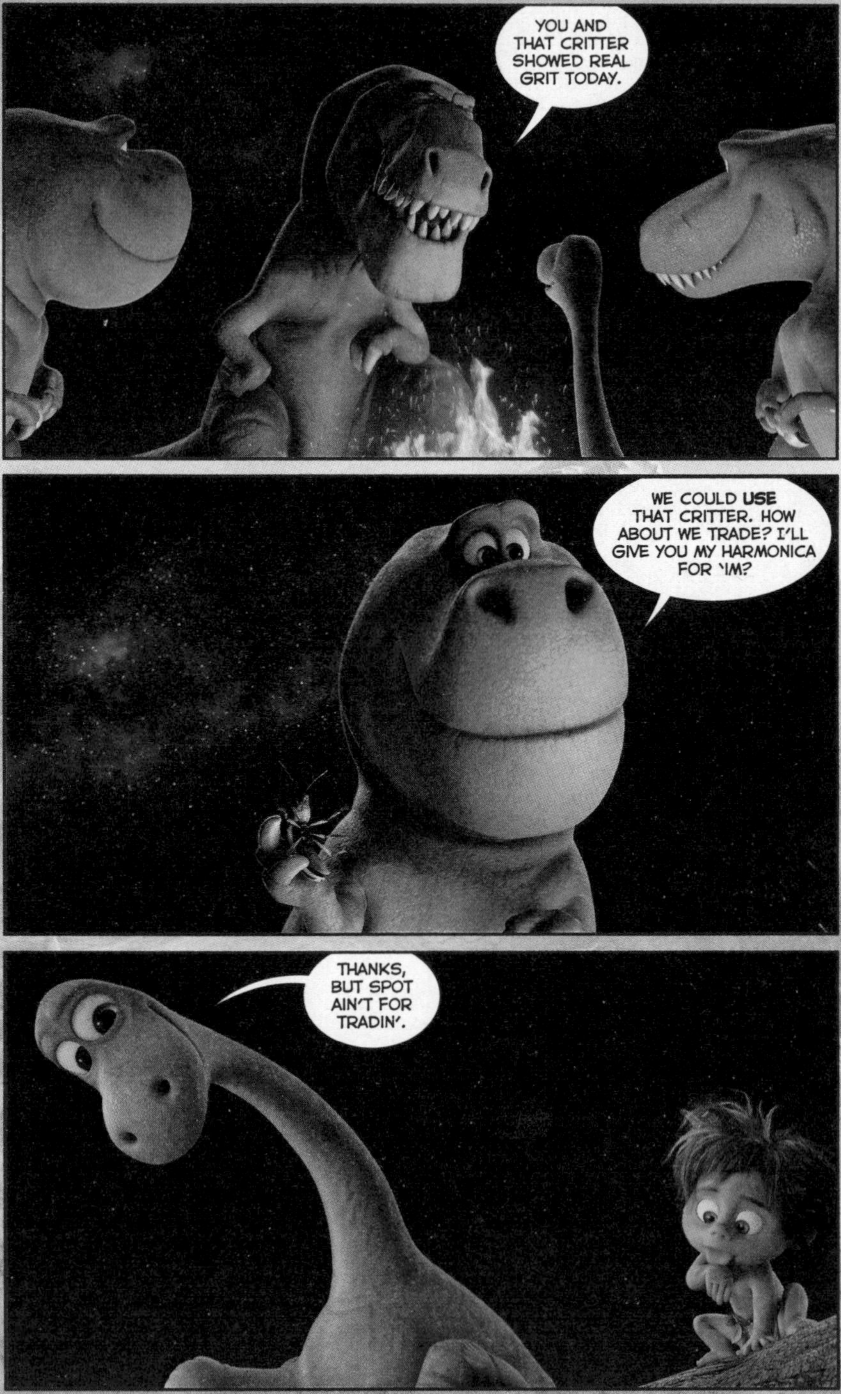
YOU AND THAT CRITTER SHOWED REAL GRIT TODAY.
WE COULD **USE** THAT CRITTER. HOW ABOUT WE TRADE? I'LL GIVE YOU MY HARMONICA FOR 'IM?
THANKS, BUT SPOT AIN'T FOR TRADIN'.

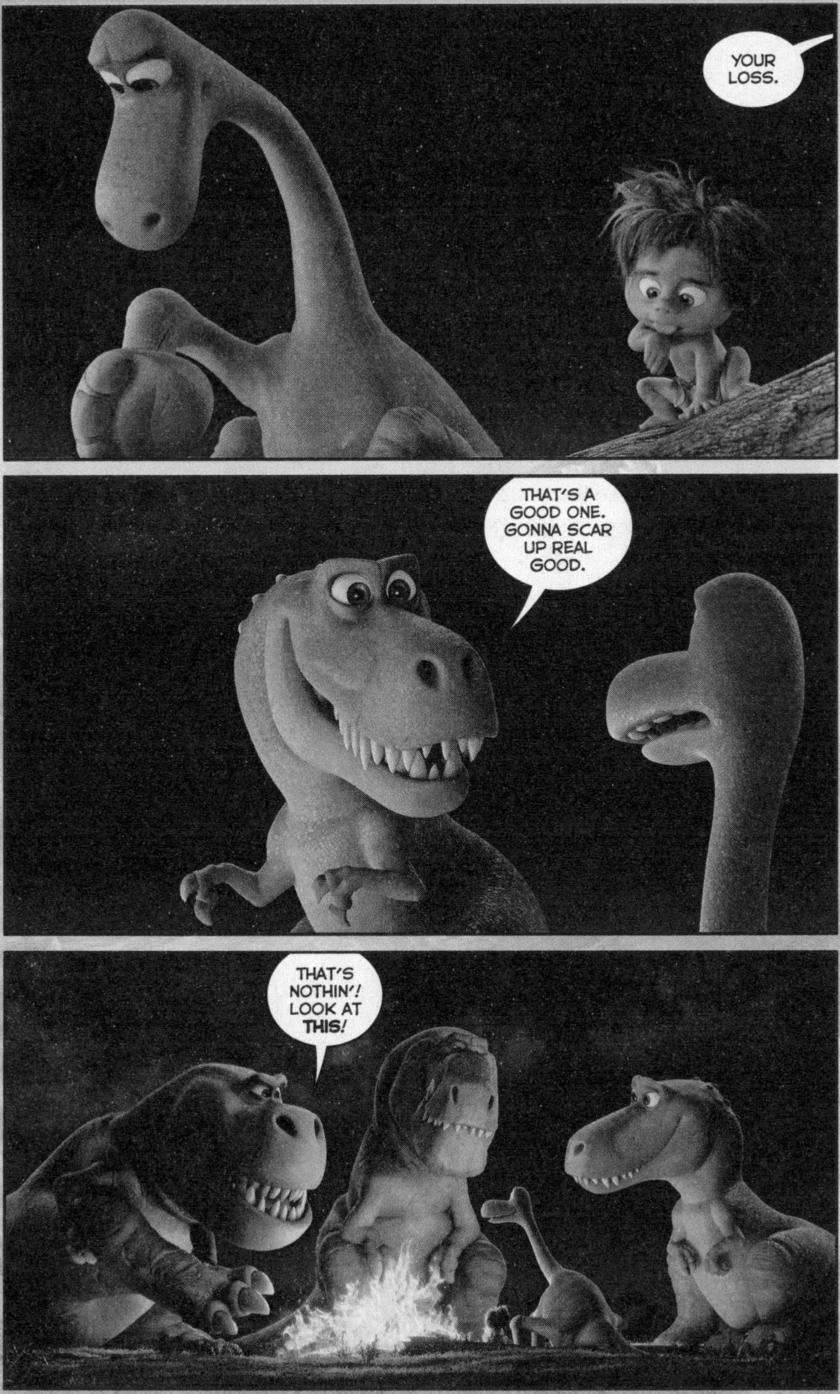
YOUR LOSS.
THAT'S A GOOD ONE. GONNA SCAR UP REAL GOOD.
THAT'S NOTHIN'! LOOK AT THIS!

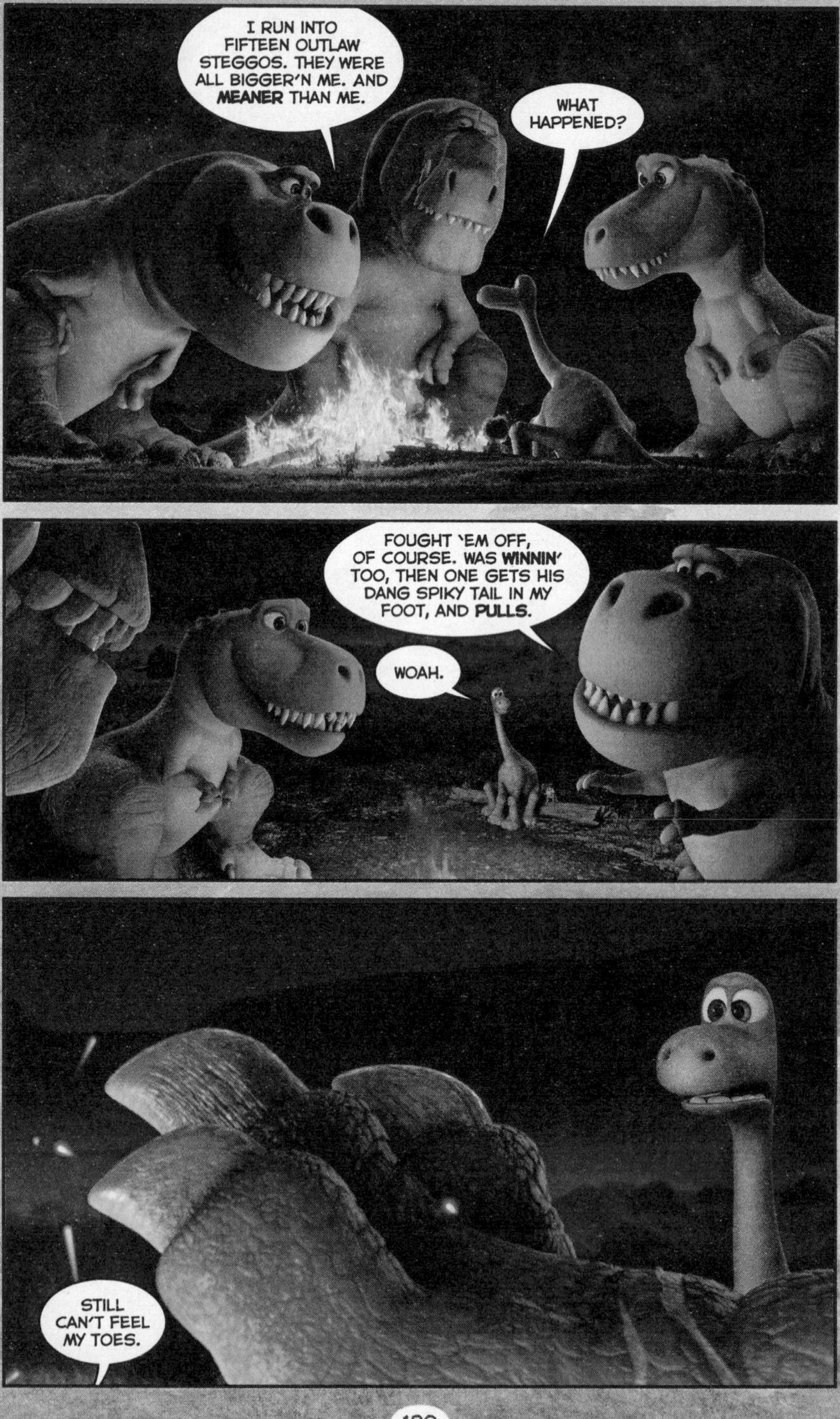
I RUN INTO FIFTEEN OUTLAW STEGGOS. THEY WERE ALL BIGGER'N ME. AND **MEANER** THAN ME.
WHAT HAPPENED?
FOUGHT 'EM OFF, OF COURSE. WAS **WINNIN'** TOO, THEN ONE GETS HIS DANG SPIKY TAIL IN MY FOOT, AND **PULLS**.
WOAH.
STILL CAN'T FEEL MY TOES.

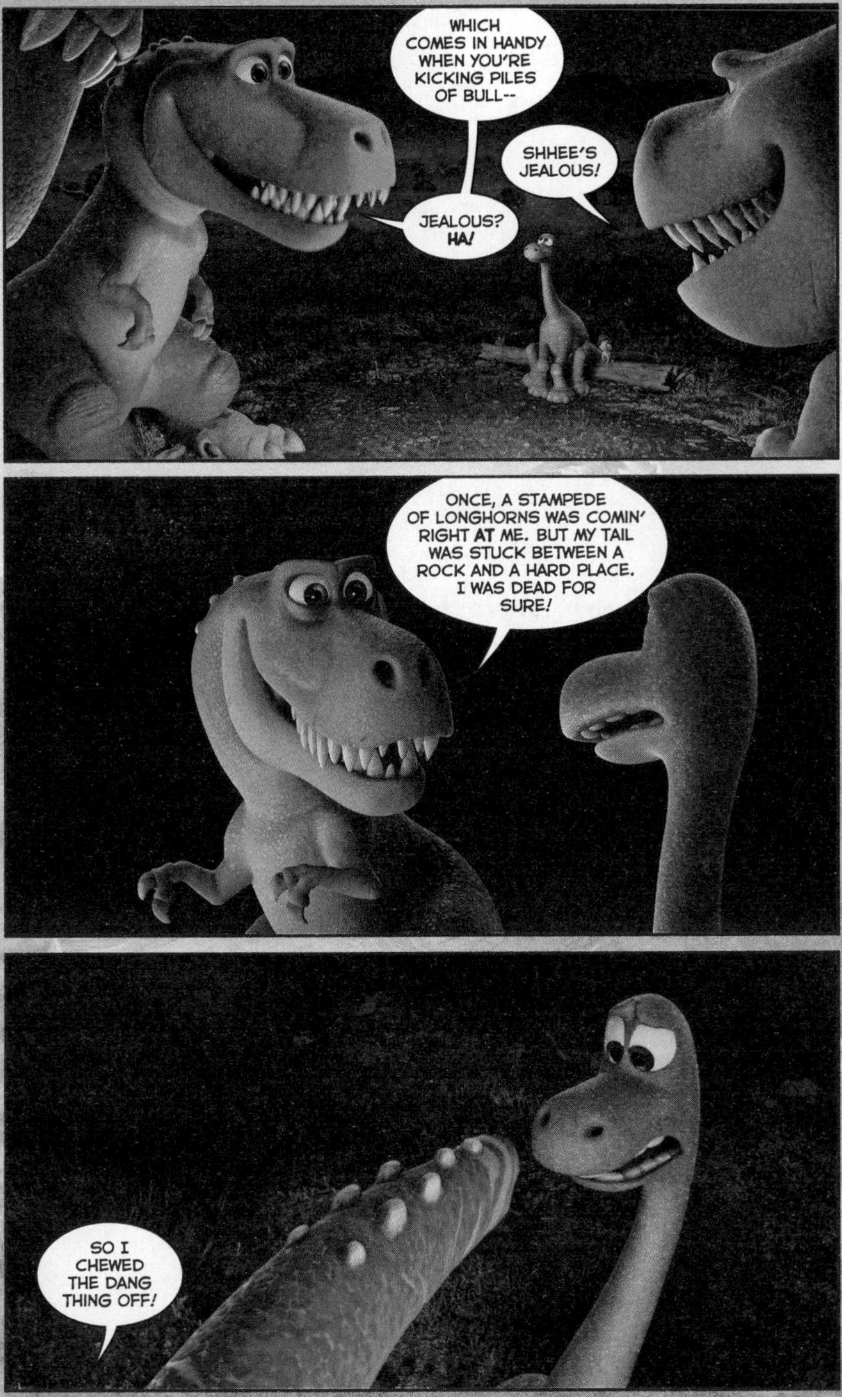
WHICH COMES IN HANDY WHEN YOU'RE KICKING PILES OF BULL--
JEALOUS? HA!
SHHEE'S JEALOUS!
ONCE, A STAMPEDE OF LONGHORNS WAS COMIN' RIGHT AT ME. BUT MY TAIL WAS STUCK BETWEEN A ROCK AND A HARD PLACE. I WAS DEAD FOR SURE!
SO I CHEWED THE DANG THING OFF!

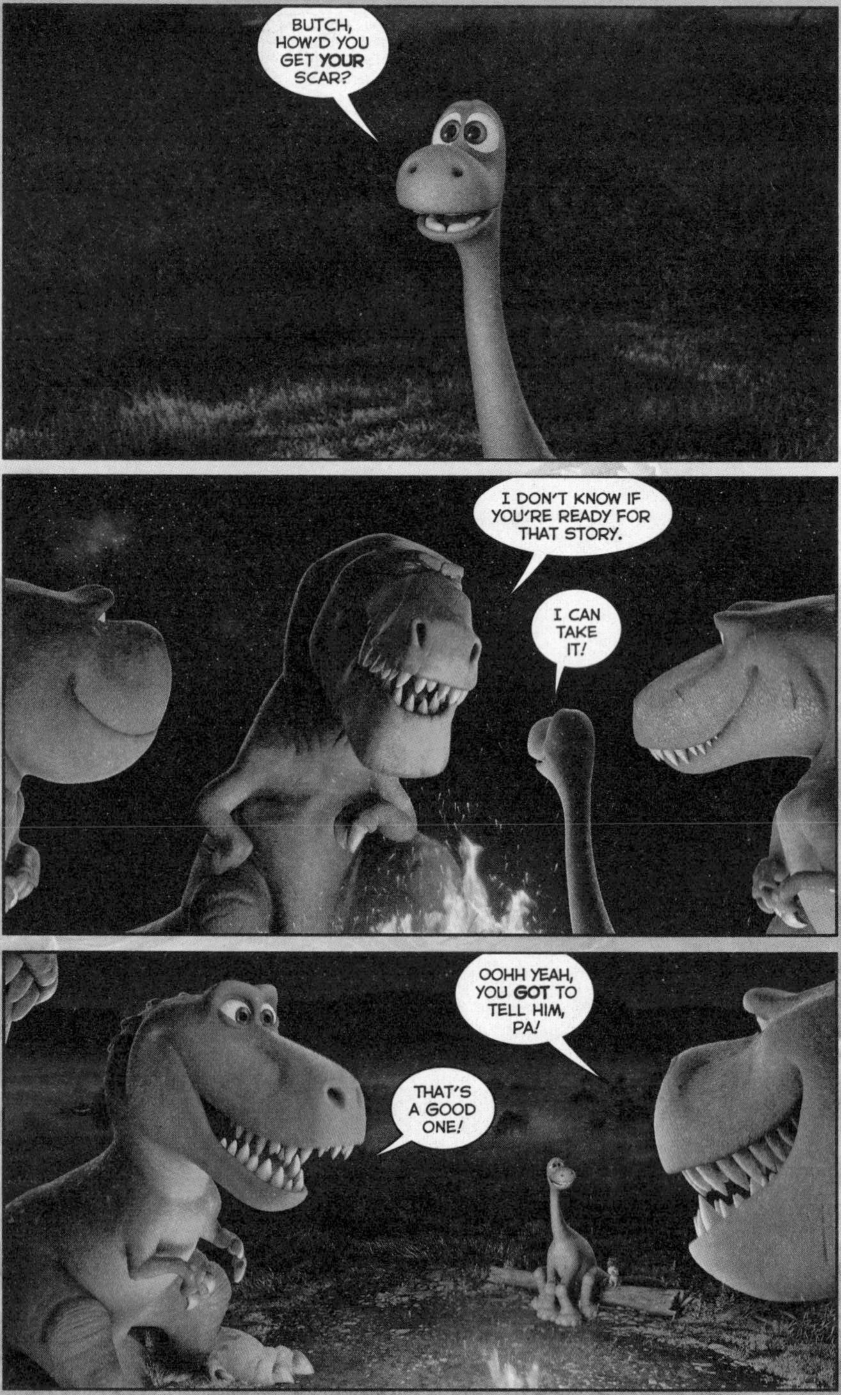
BUTCH, HOW'D YOU GET **YOUR** SCAR?
I DON'T KNOW IF YOU'RE READY FOR THAT STORY.
I CAN TAKE IT!
OOHH YEAH, YOU **GOT** TO TELL HIM, PA!
THAT'S A GOOD ONE!

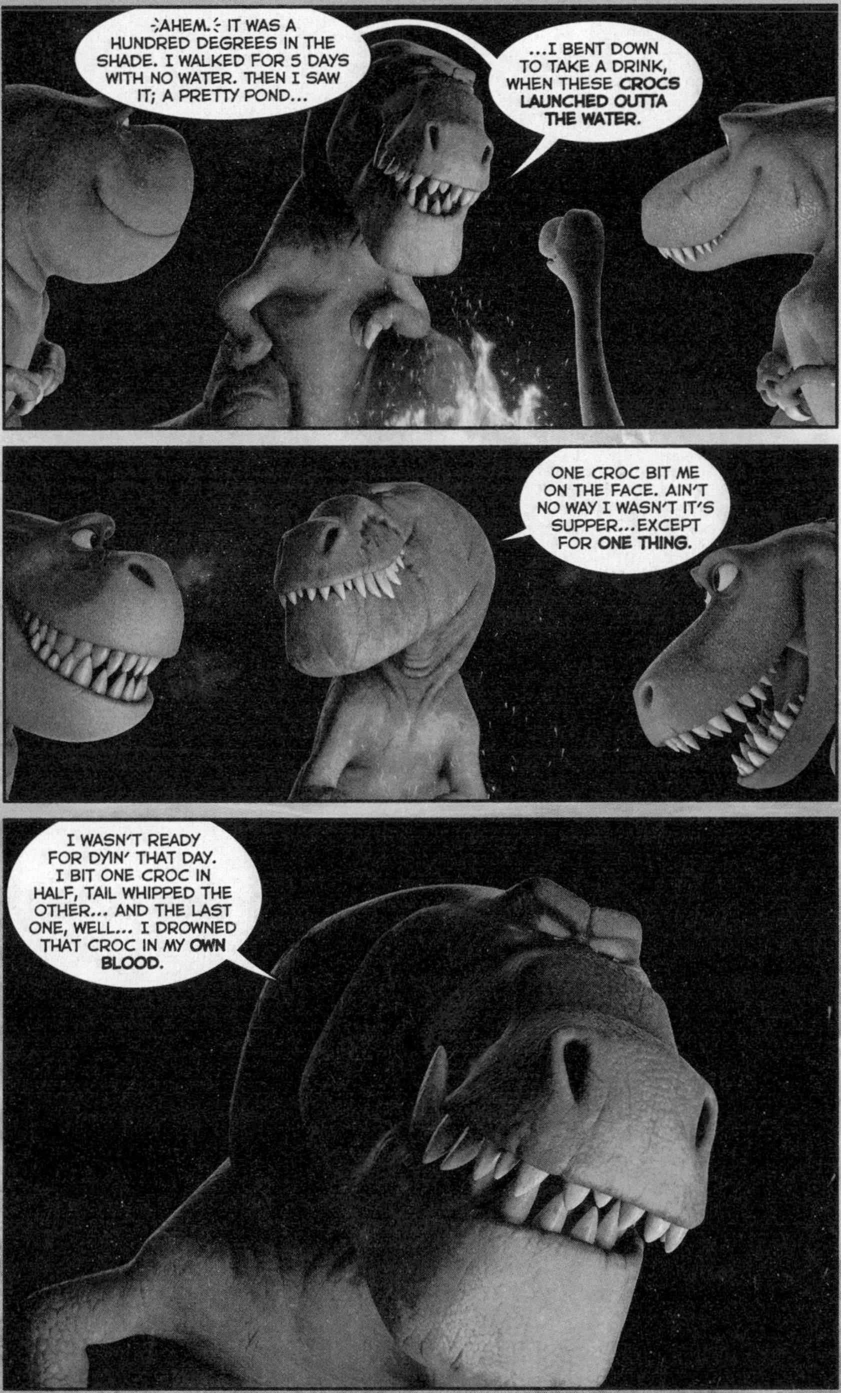
-AHEM.- IT WAS A HUNDRED DEGREES IN THE SHADE. I WALKED FOR 5 DAYS WITH NO WATER. THEN I SAW IT; A PRETTY POND...
...I BENT DOWN TO TAKE A DRINK, WHEN THESE **CROCS LAUNCHED OUTTA THE WATER.**
ONE CROC BIT ME ON THE FACE. AIN'T NO WAY I WASN'T IT'S SUPPER...EXCEPT FOR **ONE THING.**
I WASN'T READY FOR DYIN' THAT DAY. I BIT ONE CROC IN HALF, TAIL WHIPPED THE OTHER... AND THE LAST ONE, WELL... I DROWNED THAT CROC IN MY **OWN BLOOD.**

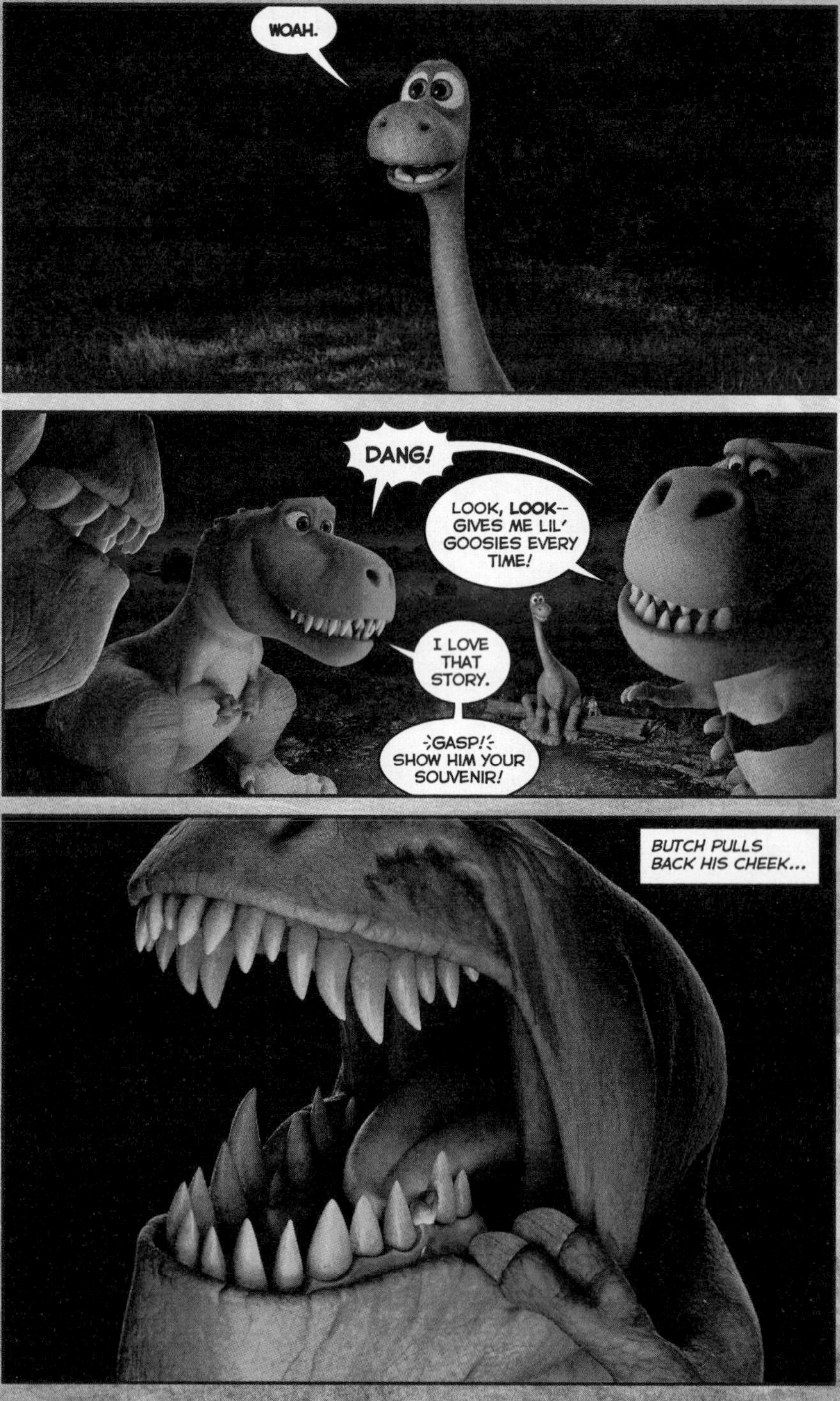
WOAH.
DANG!
LOOK, **LOOK**--
GIVES ME LIL'
GOOSIES EVERY
TIME!
I LOVE
THAT
STORY.
-GASP!-
SHOW HIM YOUR
SOUVENIR!
BUTCH PULLS
BACK HIS CHEEK...

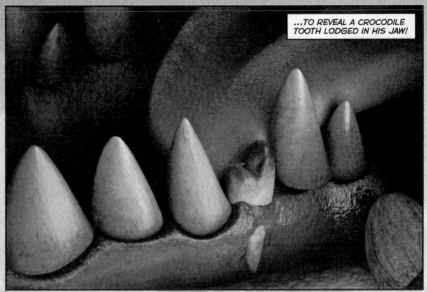

...TO REVEAL A CROCODILE TOOTH LODGED IN HIS JAW!

AIN'T THAT JUST **TOO** GOOD?

CAN I TOUCH IT THIS TIME?

NO.

⸓SIGH.⸓ YOU GUYS WOULD'VE LIKED MY POPPA.

HE WASN'T SCARED OF ANYTHING.

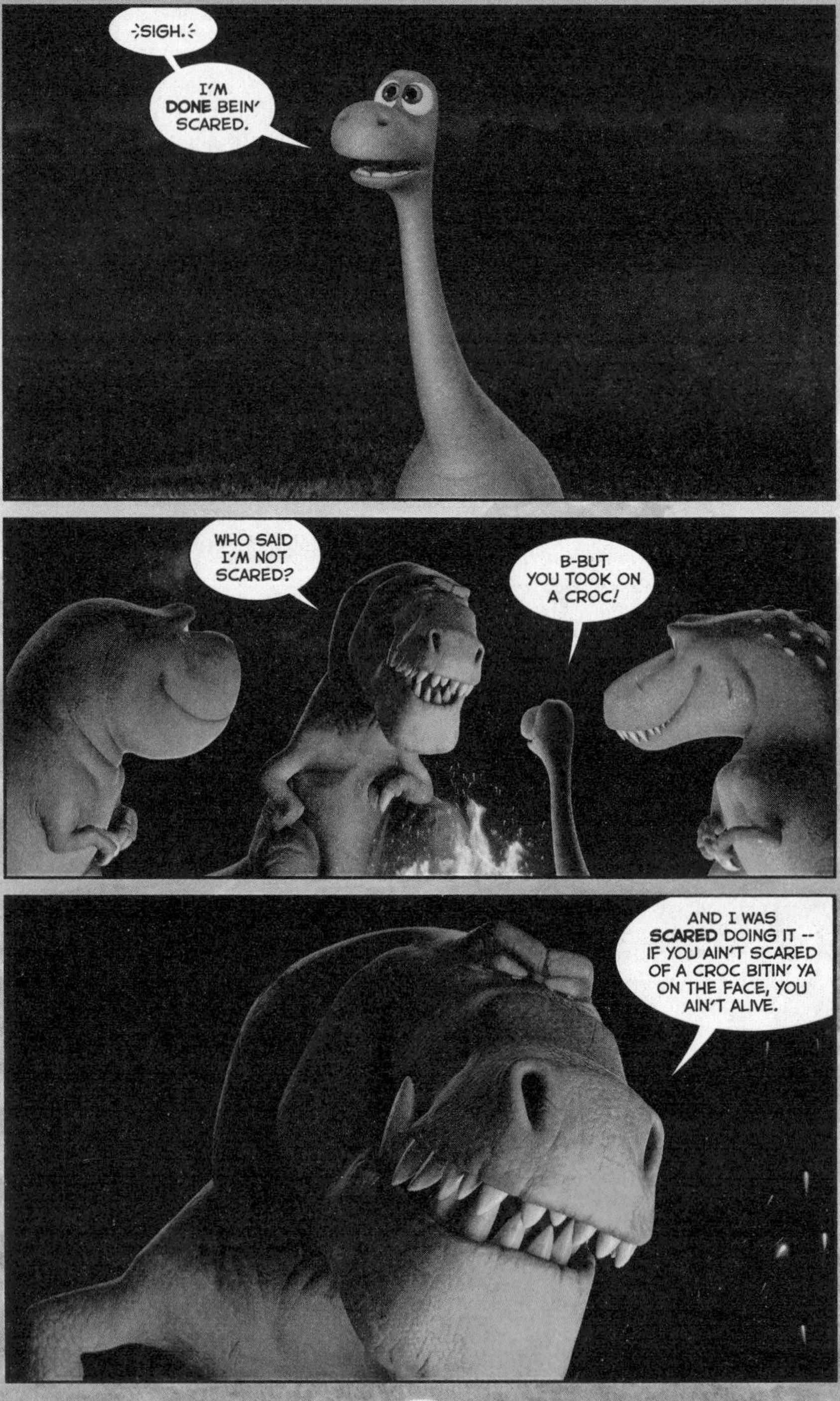

SIGH.
I'M **DONE** BEIN' SCARED.
WHO SAID I'M NOT SCARED?
B-BUT YOU TOOK ON A CROC!
AND I WAS **SCARED** DOING IT -- IF YOU AIN'T SCARED OF A CROC BITIN' YA ON THE FACE, YOU AIN'T ALIVE.

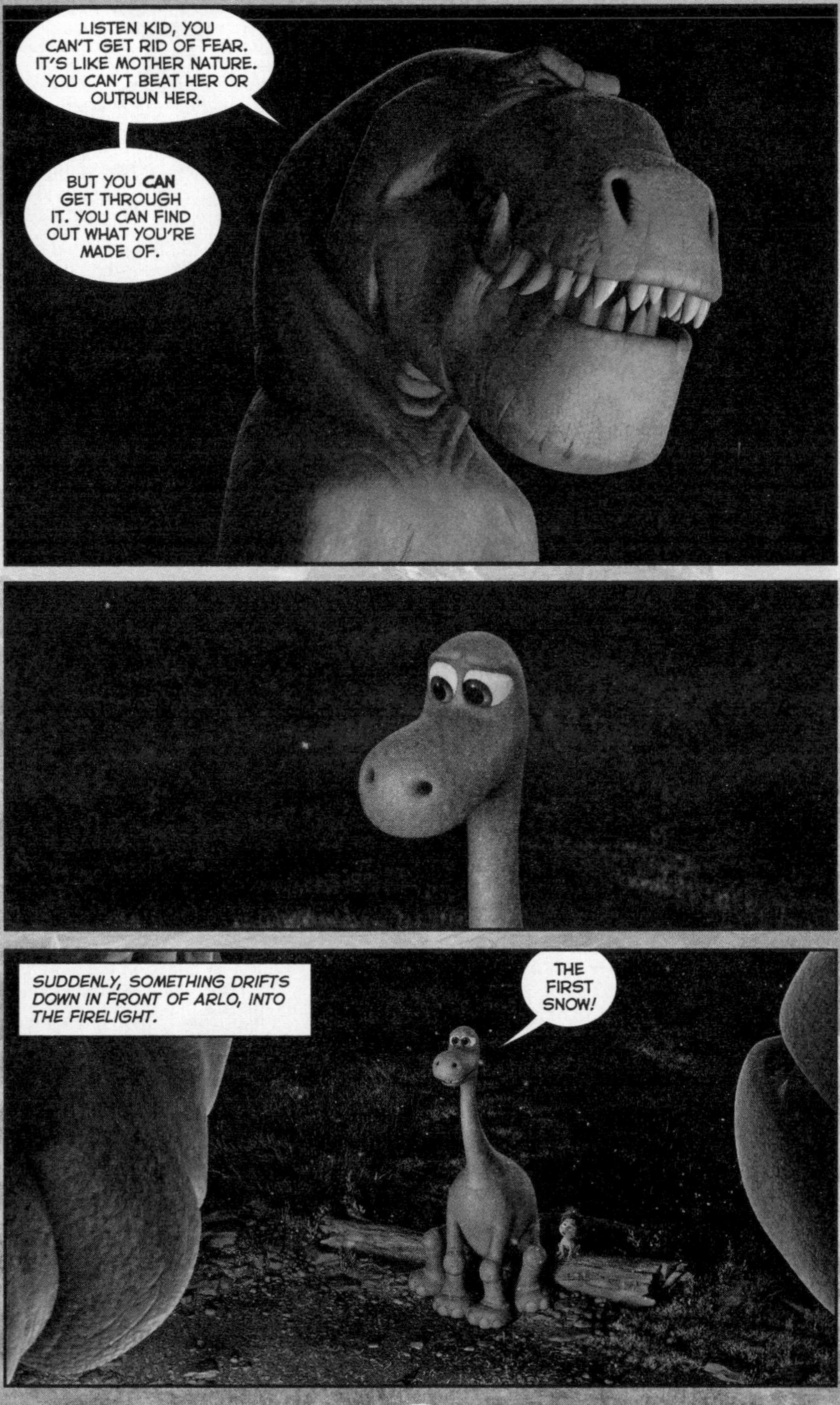
LISTEN KID, YOU CAN'T GET RID OF FEAR. IT'S LIKE MOTHER NATURE. YOU CAN'T BEAT HER OR OUTRUN HER.
BUT YOU **CAN** GET THROUGH IT. YOU CAN FIND OUT WHAT YOU'RE MADE OF.
SUDDENLY, SOMETHING DRIFTS DOWN IN FRONT OF ARLO, INTO THE FIRELIGHT.
THE FIRST SNOW!

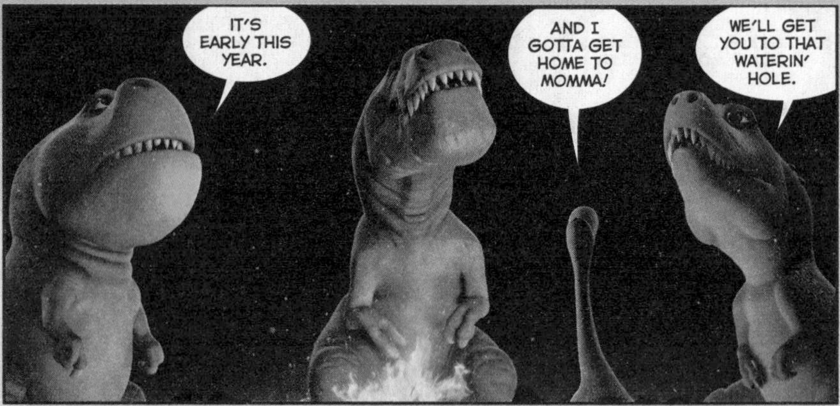
IT'S EARLY THIS YEAR.
AND I GOTTA GET HOME TO MOMMA!
WE'LL GET YOU TO THAT WATERIN' HOLE.

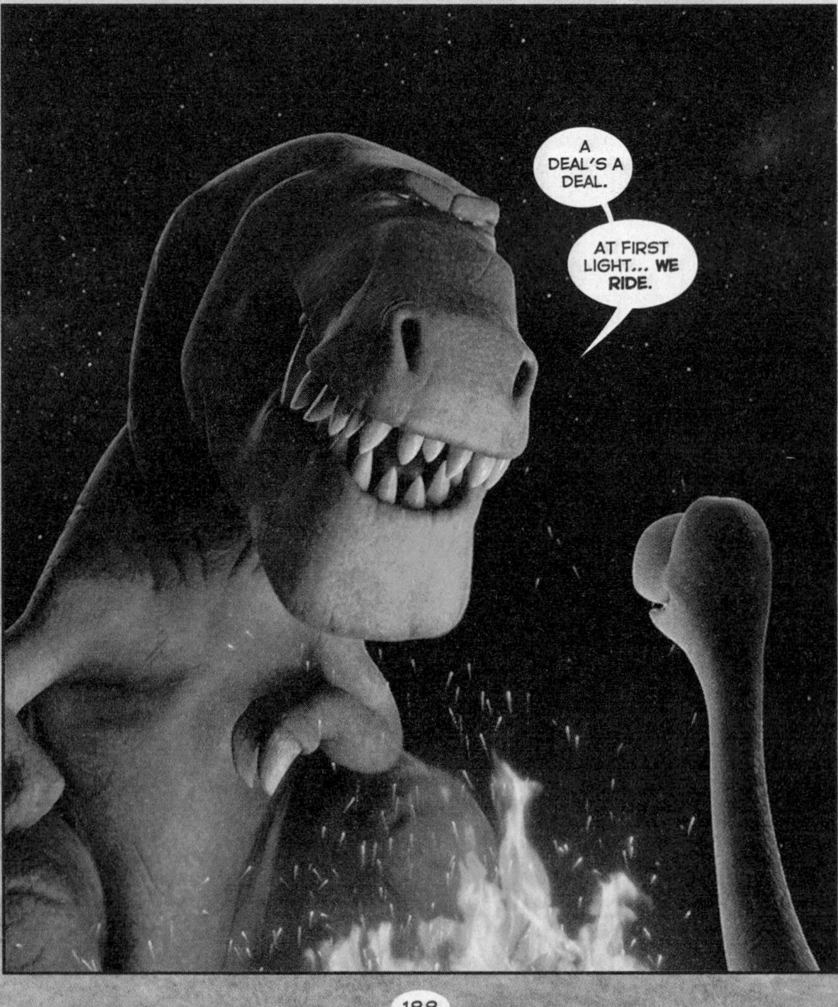
A DEAL'S A DEAL.
AT FIRST LIGHT... WE RIDE.

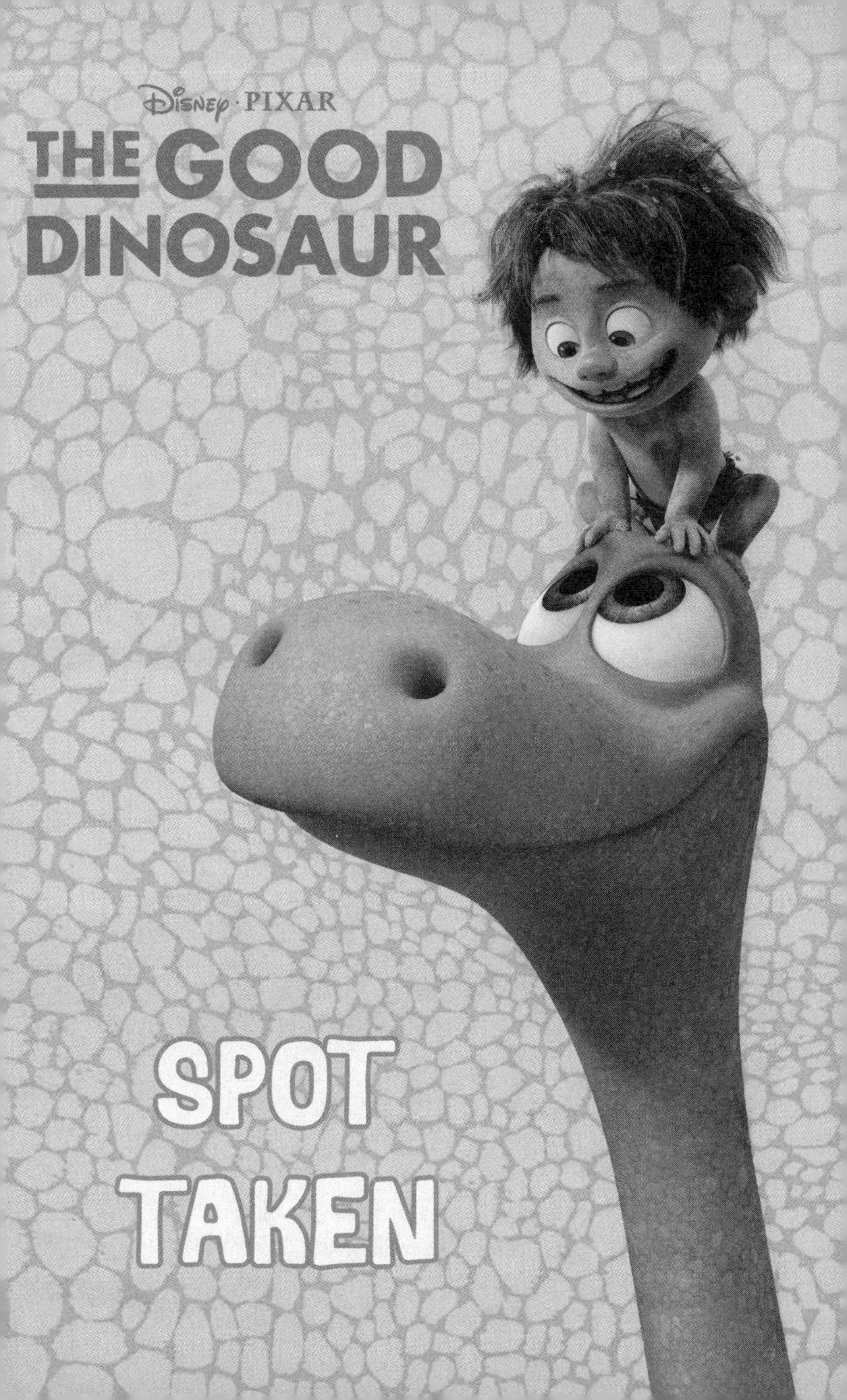
Disney · PIXAR
THE GOOD DINOSAUR
SPOT TAKEN

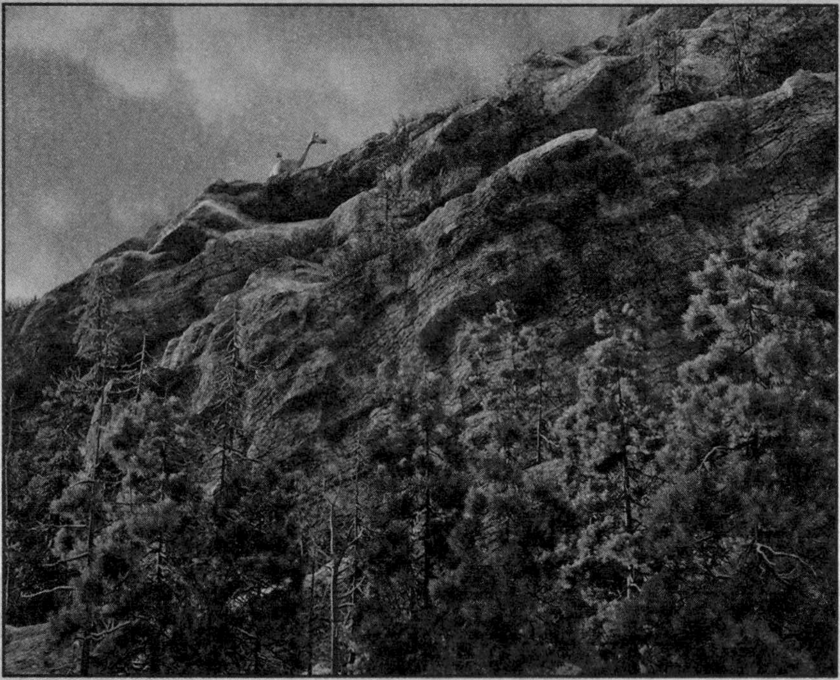

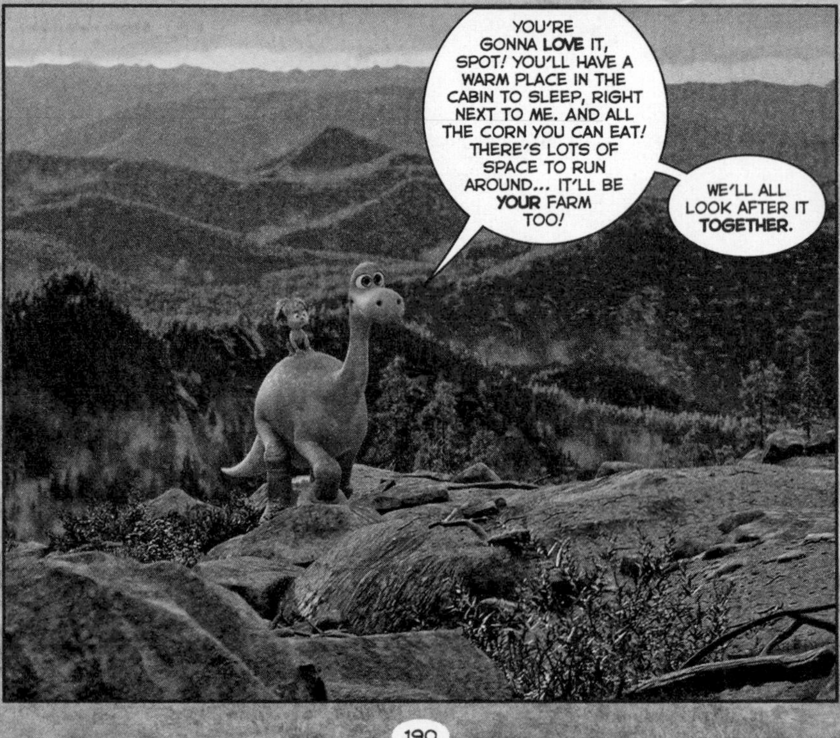
YOU'RE GONNA **LOVE** IT, SPOT! YOU'LL HAVE A WARM PLACE IN THE CABIN TO SLEEP, RIGHT NEXT TO ME. AND ALL THE CORN YOU CAN EAT! THERE'S LOTS OF SPACE TO RUN AROUND... IT'LL BE **YOUR** FARM TOO!
WE'LL ALL LOOK AFTER IT **TOGETHER.**

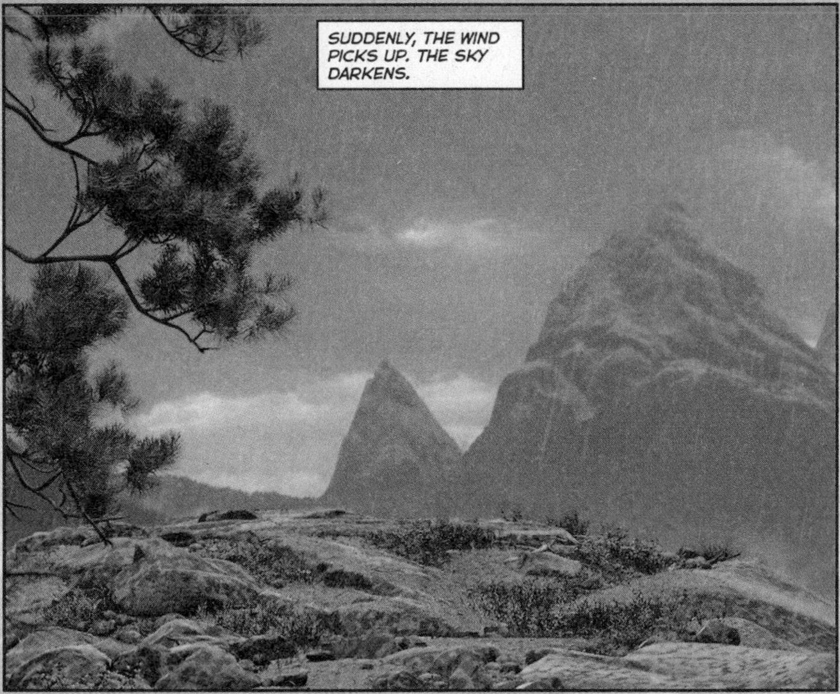
SUDDENLY, THE WIND PICKS UP. THE SKY DARKENS.

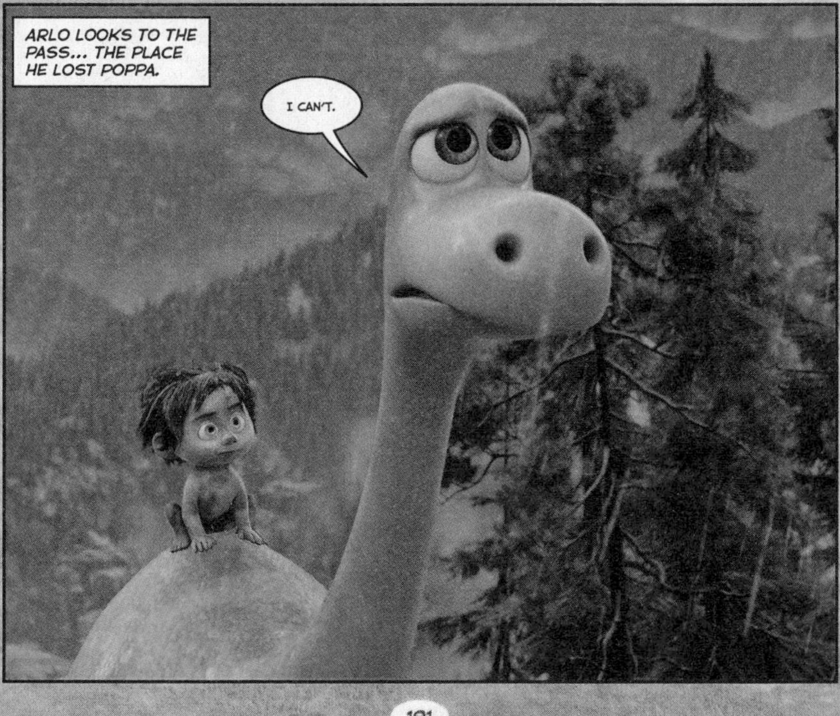
ARLO LOOKS TO THE PASS... THE PLACE HE LOST POPPA.
I CAN'T.

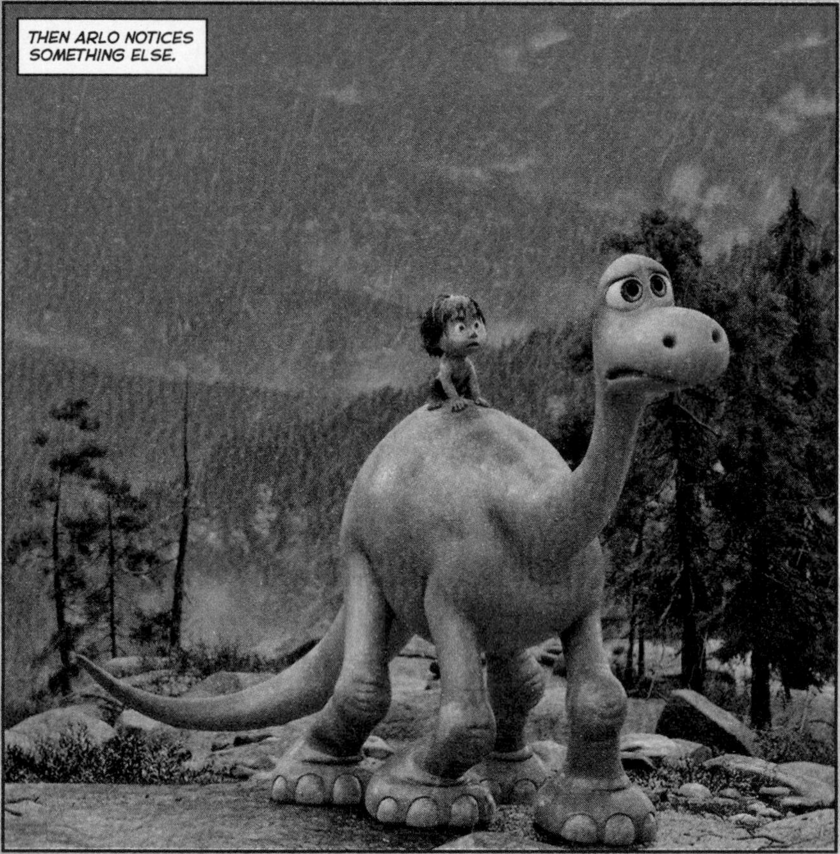
THEN ARLO NOTICES SOMETHING ELSE.

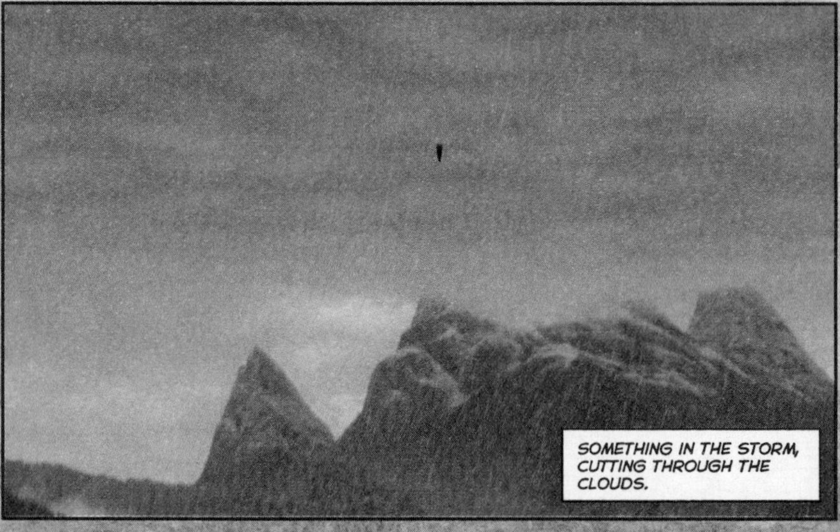
SOMETHING IN THE STORM, CUTTING THROUGH THE CLOUDS.

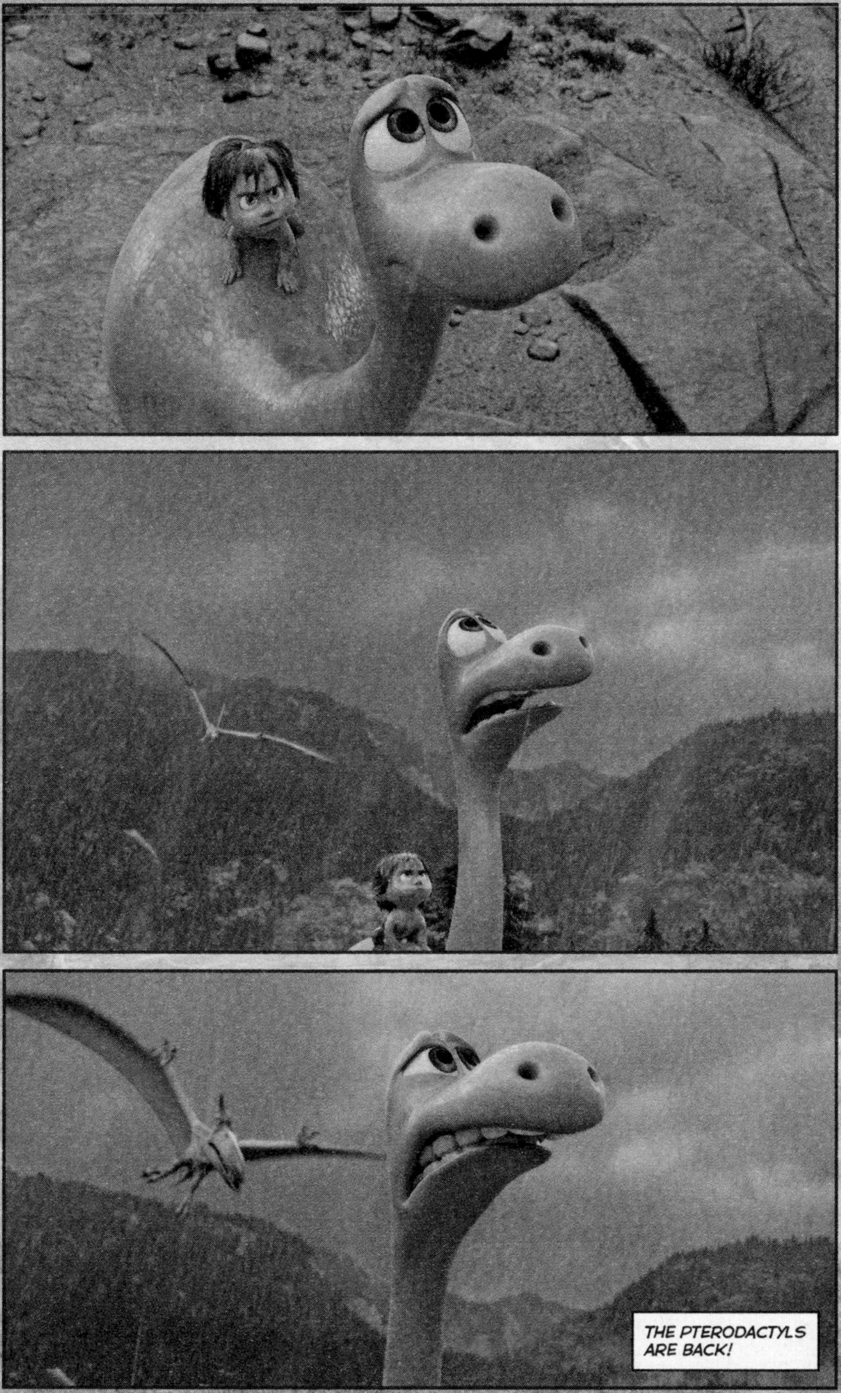
THE PTERODACTYLS
ARE BACK!

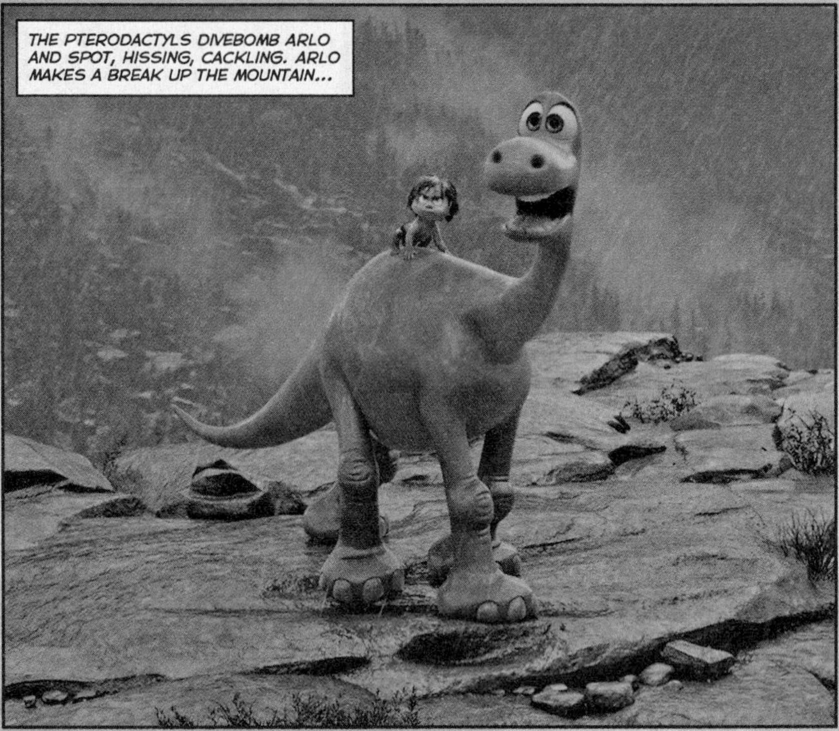
THE PTERODACTYLS DIVEBOMB ARLO AND SPOT, HISSING, CACKLING. ARLO MAKES A BREAK UP THE MOUNTAIN...

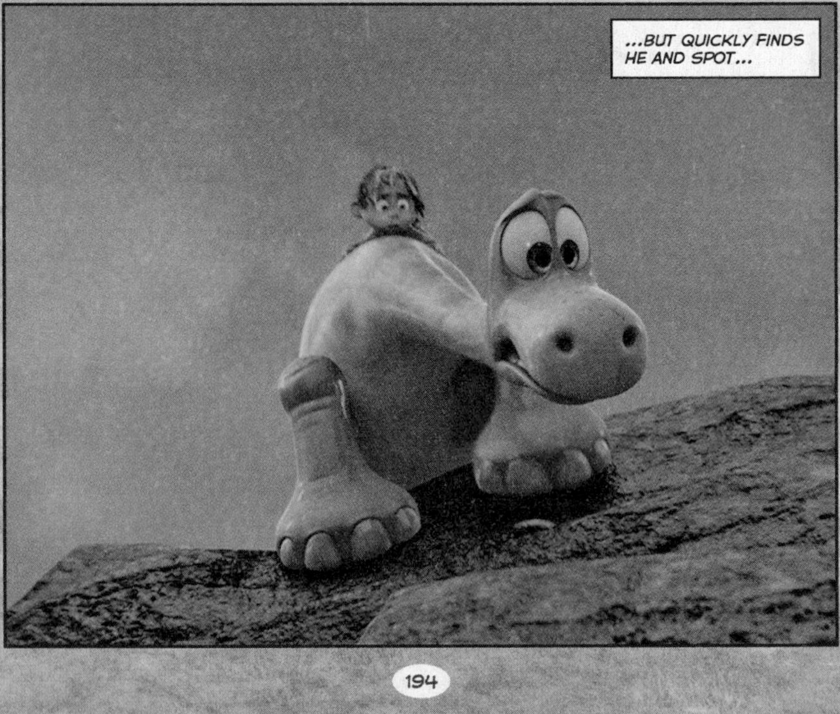
...BUT QUICKLY FINDS HE AND SPOT...

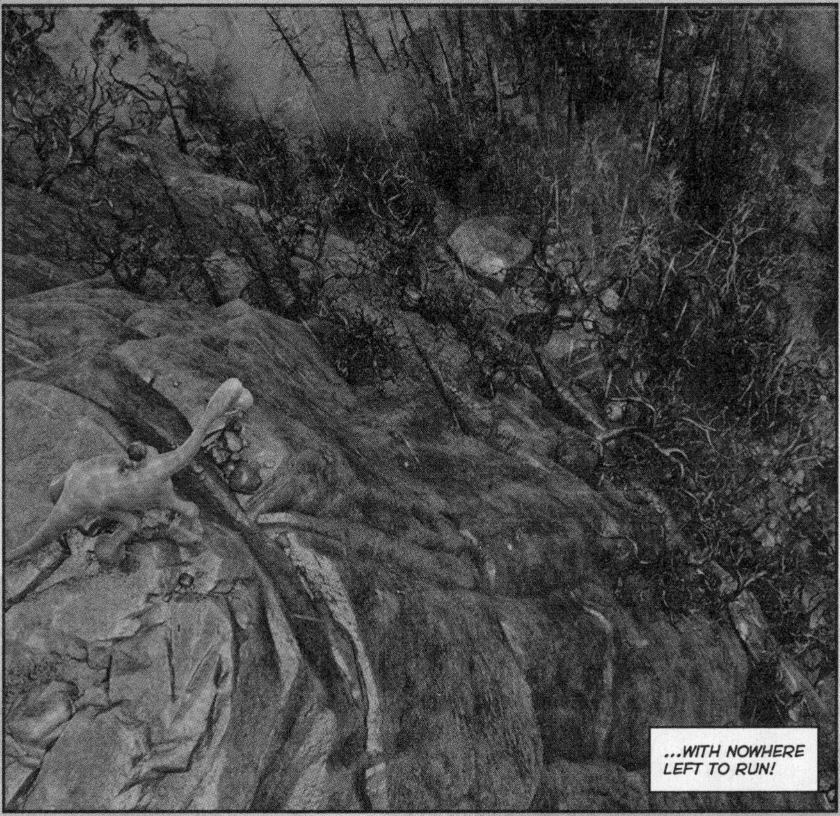
...WITH NOWHERE
LEFT TO RUN!

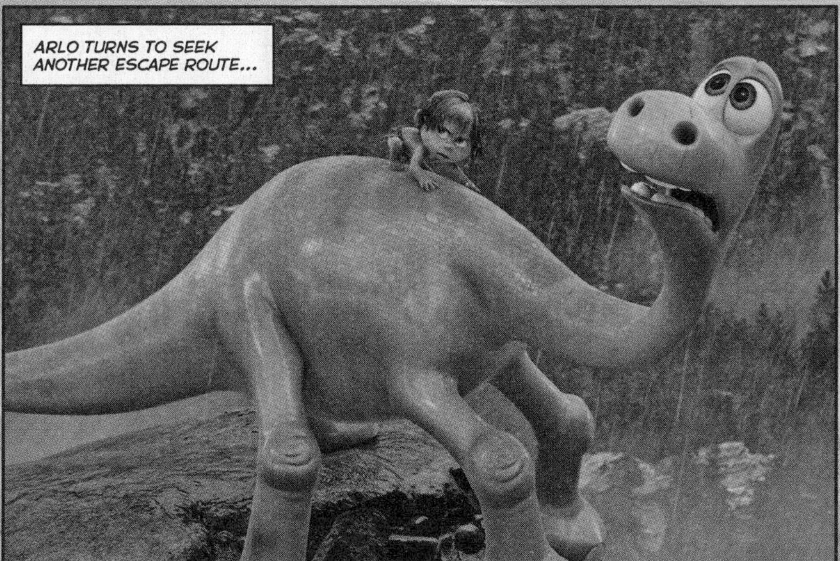
ARLO TURNS TO SEEK
ANOTHER ESCAPE ROUTE...

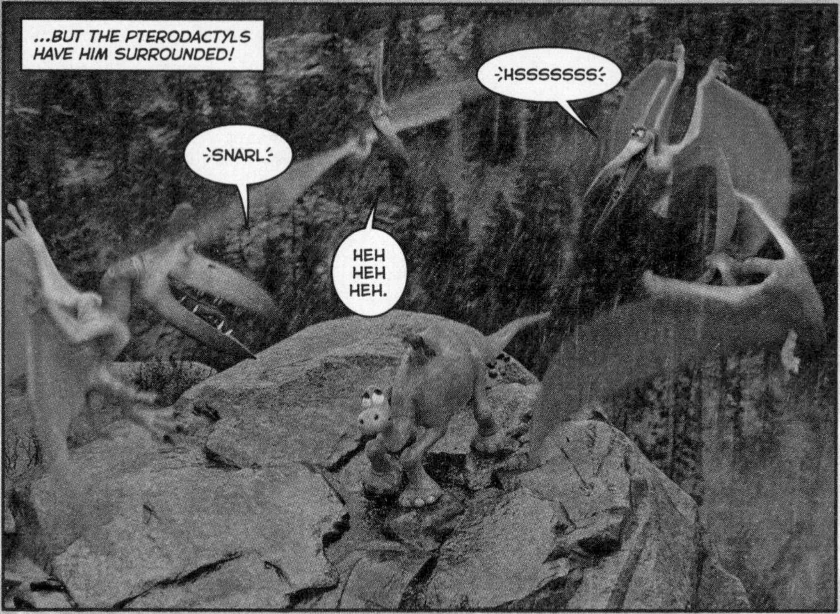
...BUT THE PTERODACTYLS HAVE HIM SURROUNDED!
HSSSSSSS
SNARL
HEH HEH HEH.

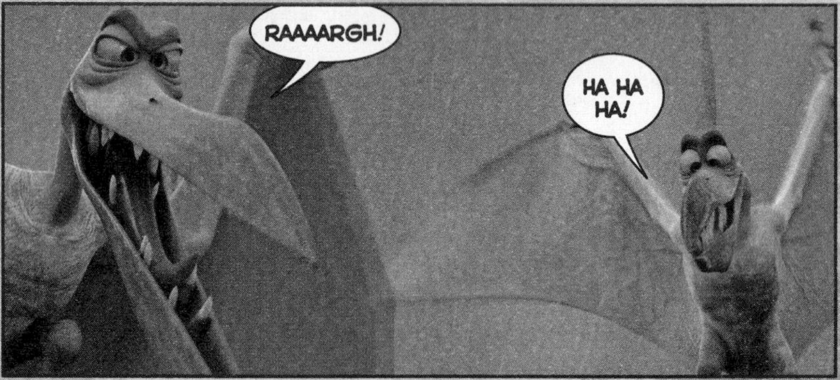
RAAAARGH!
HA HA HA!

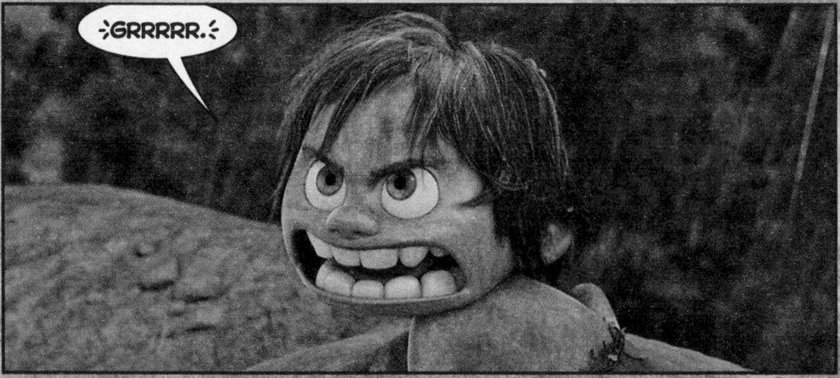
GRRRRR.

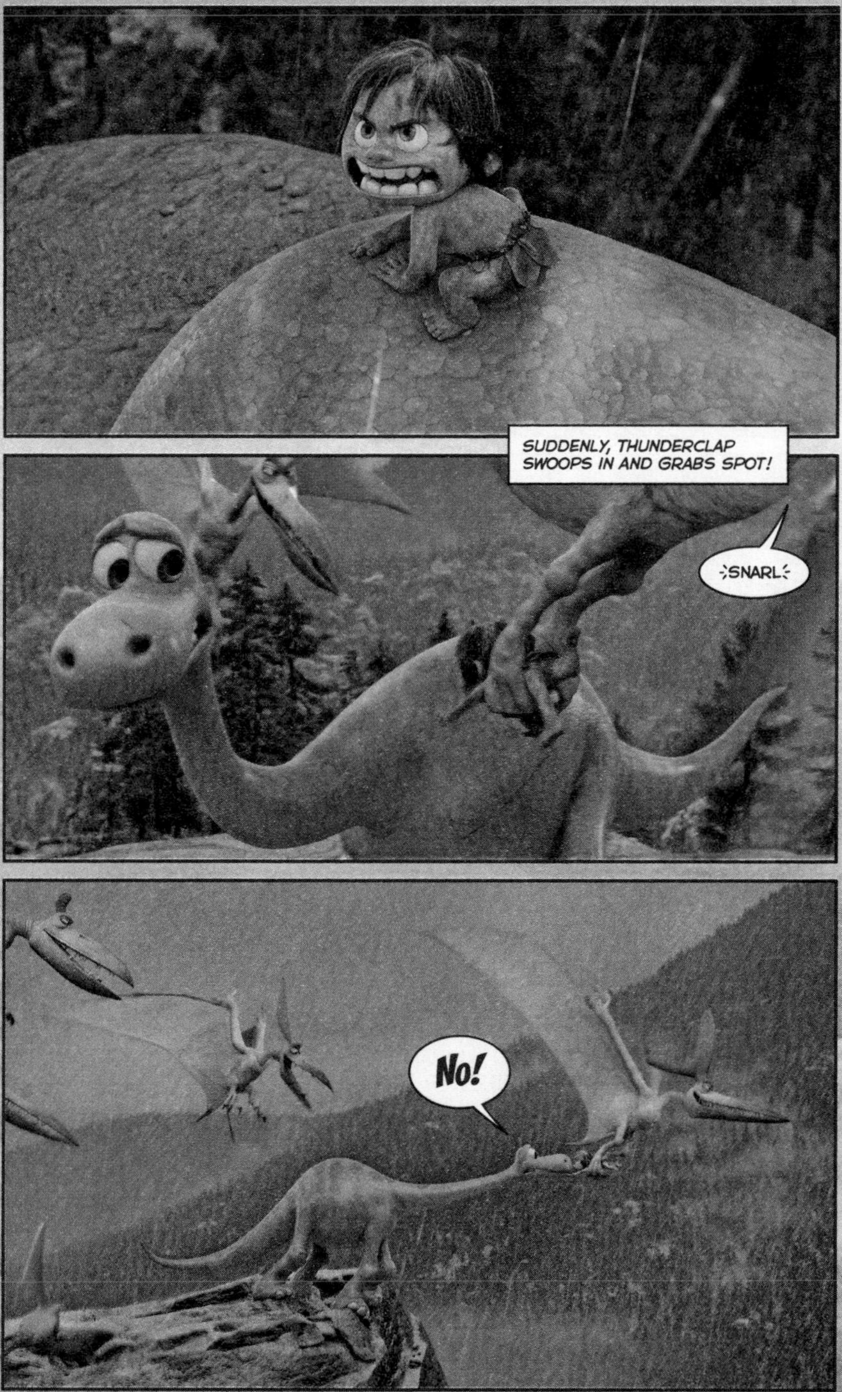
SUDDENLY, THUNDERCLAP SWOOPS IN AND GRABS SPOT!
SNARL
No!

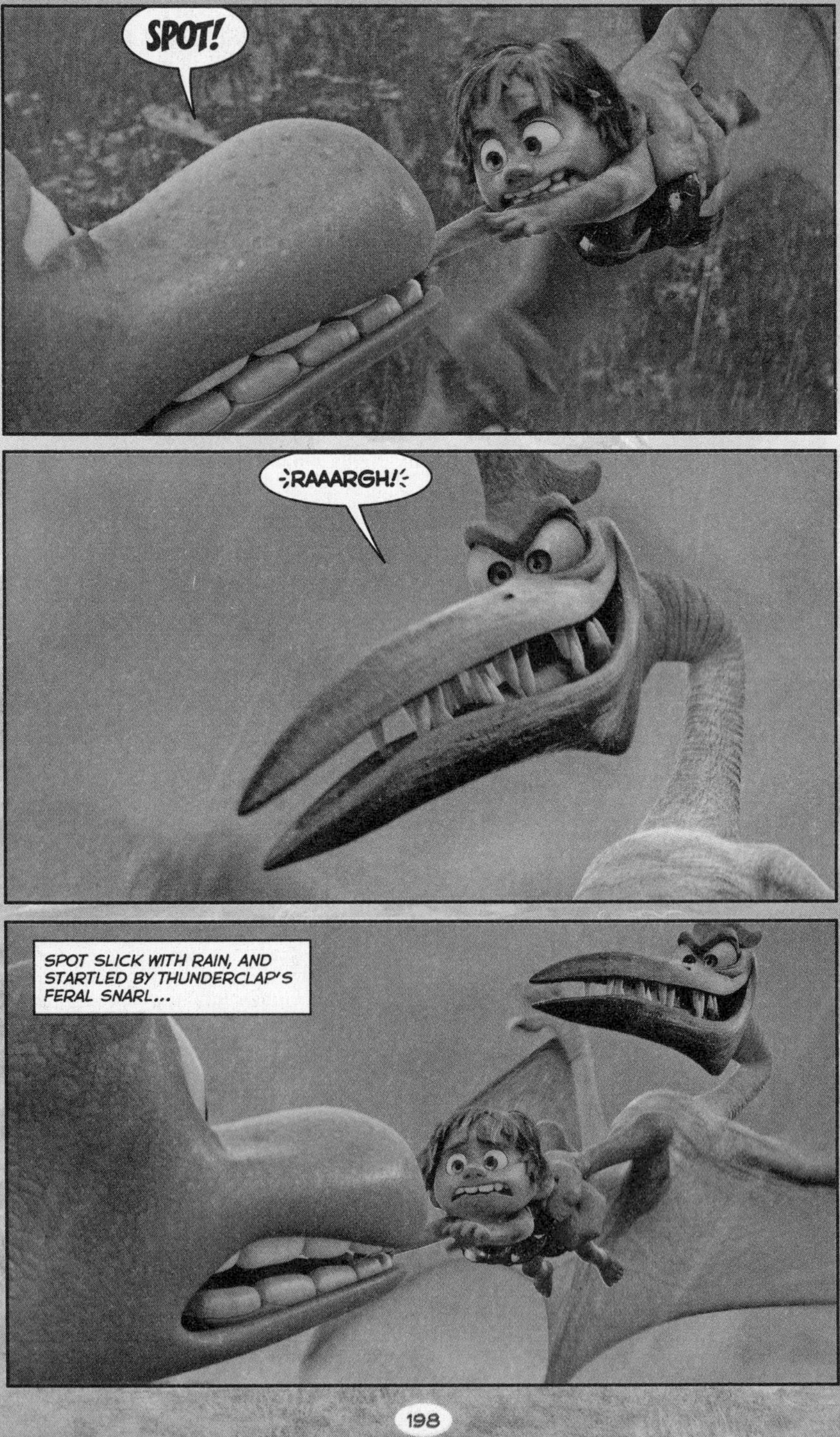
SPOT!
RAAARGH!
SPOT SLICK WITH RAIN, AND STARTLED BY THUNDERCLAP'S FERAL SNARL...

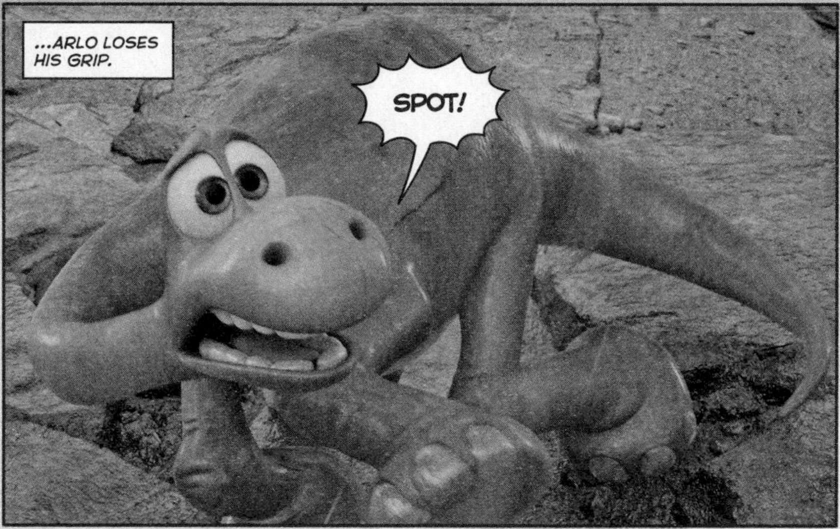
...ARLO LOSES HIS GRIP.
SPOT!

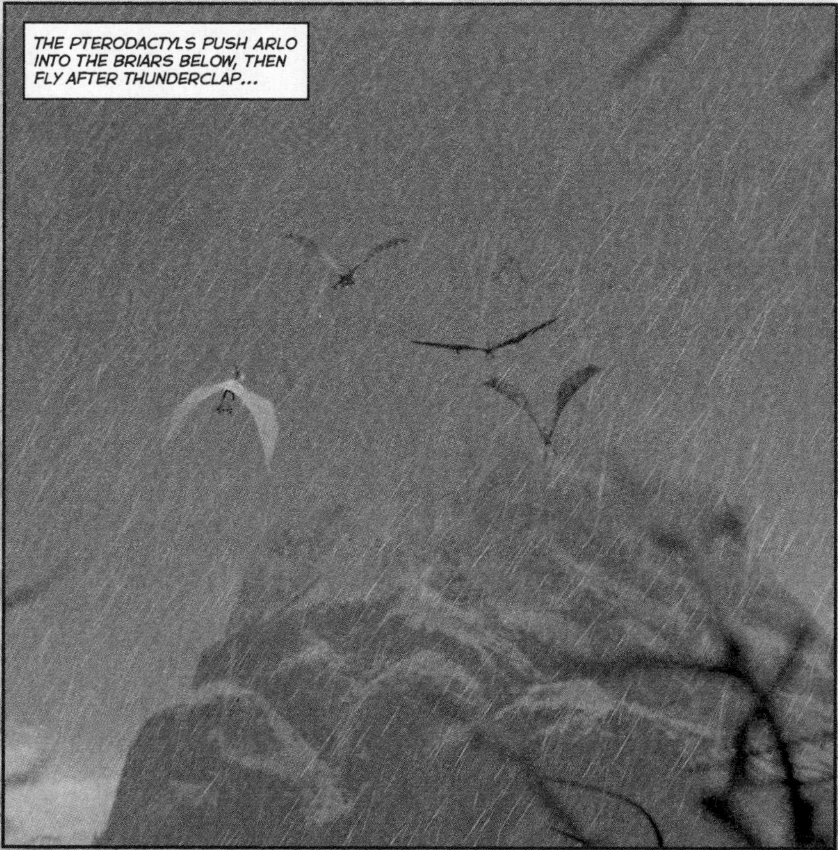
THE PTERODACTYLS PUSH ARLO INTO THE BRIARS BELOW, THEN FLY AFTER THUNDERCLAP...

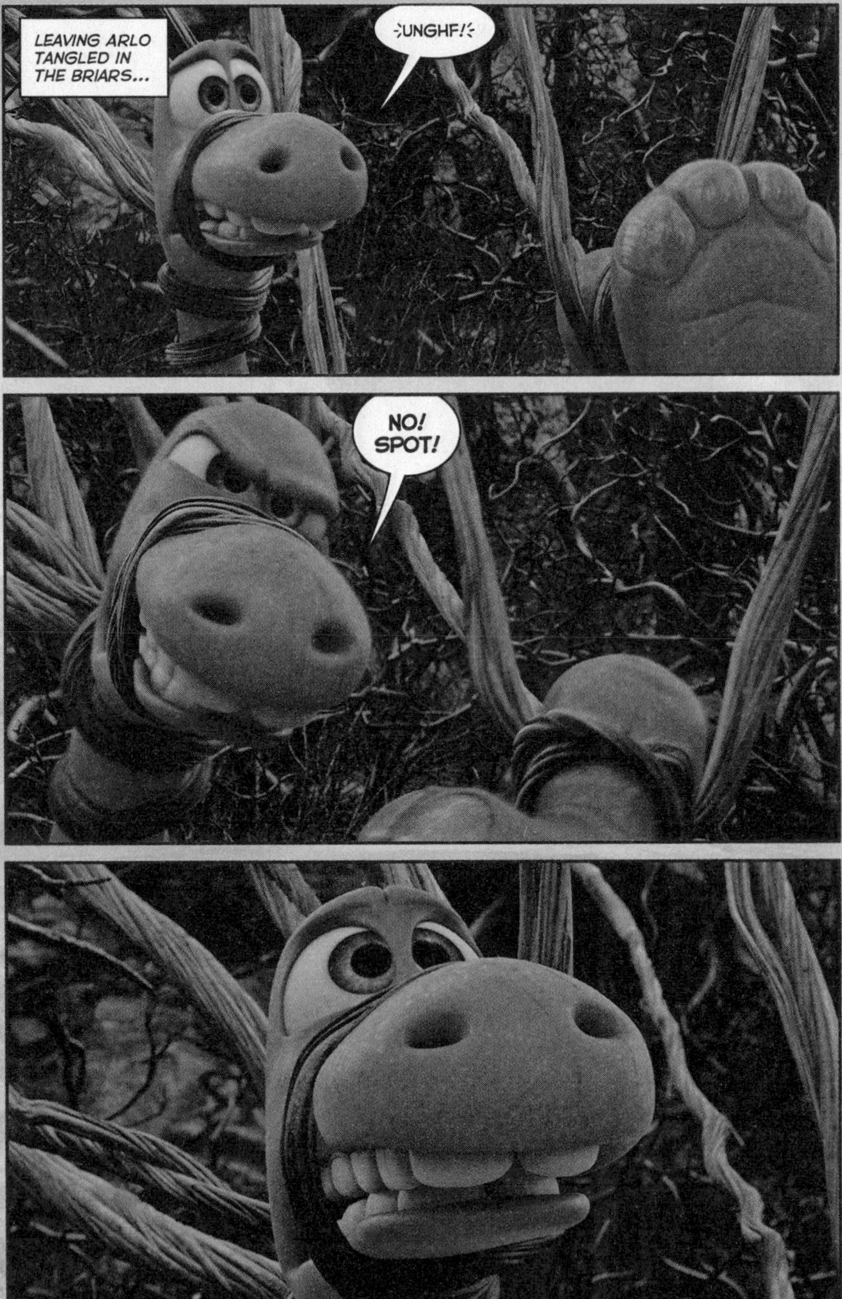
LEAVING ARLO TANGLED IN THE BRIARS...
UNGHF!
NO! SPOT!
...AND ALONE.

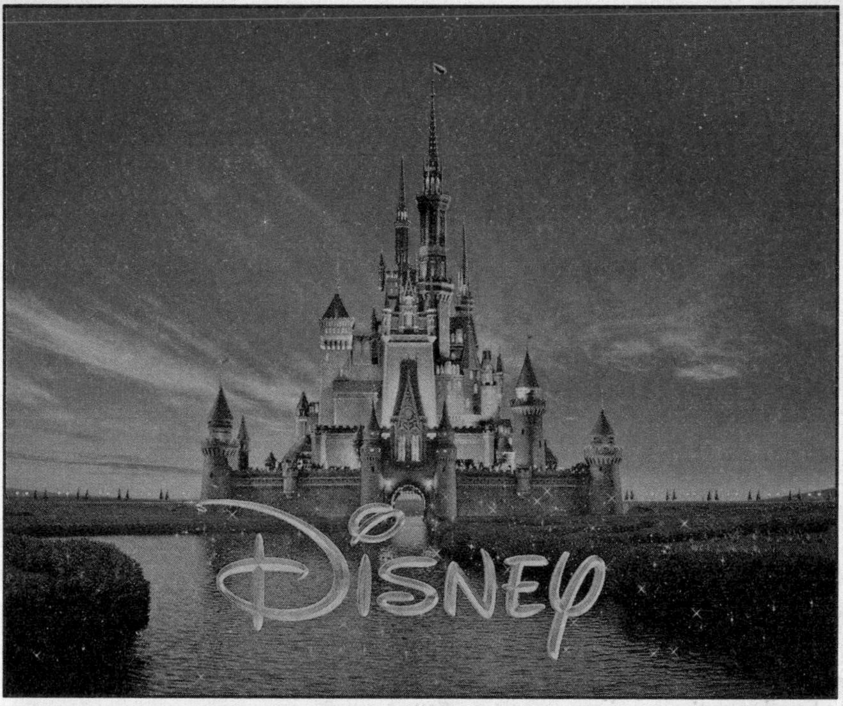
Disney

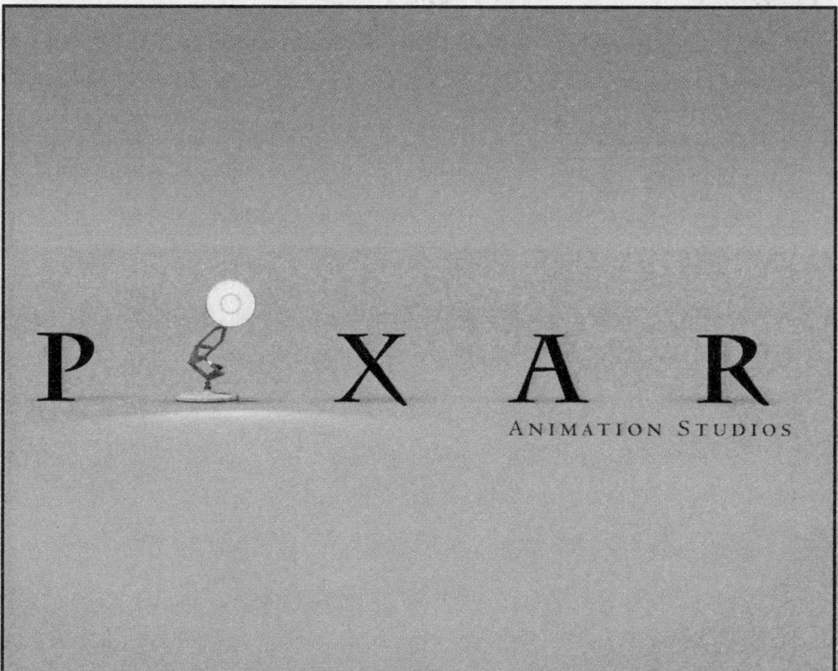
PIXAR
ANIMATION STUDIOS

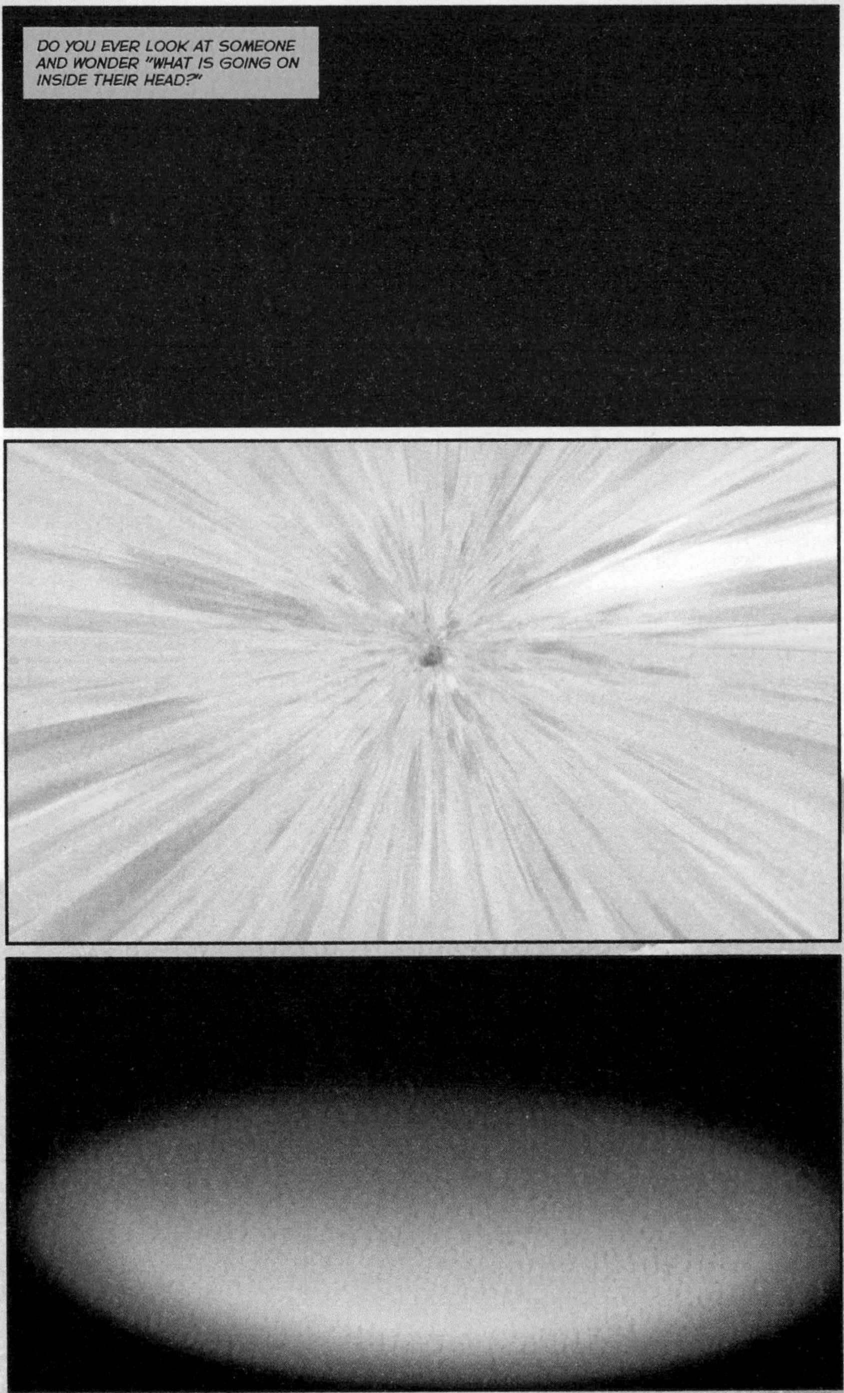
DO YOU EVER LOOK AT SOMEONE AND WONDER "WHAT IS GOING ON INSIDE THEIR HEAD?"

WELL, I KNOW.

I KNOW RILEY'S HEAD.

HMMM.

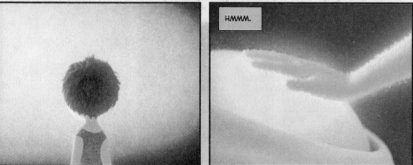

HELLO, RILEY.

OH, LOOK AT YOU. AREN'T YOU A LITTLE BUNDLE OF JOY.

AND THERE SHE WAS...

AREN'T YOU A LITTLE BUNDLE OF JOY.

WHOA.

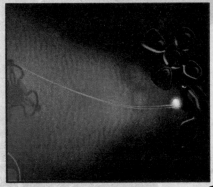

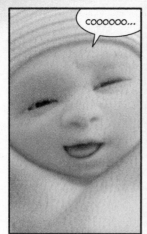

COOOOOO...

IT WAS AMAZING. JUST RILEY AND ME. FOREVER.

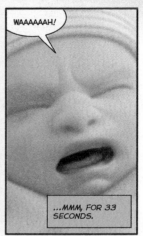

WAAAAAAH!

...MMM, FOR 33 SECONDS.

I'M SADNESS.

OH, HELLO. I'M JOY.

SO. CAN I JUST... IF YOU COULD... I JUST WANT TO FIX THAT. THANKS.

AND THAT WAS JUST THE BEGINNING. HEADQUARTERS ONLY GOT MORE CROWDED FROM THERE.

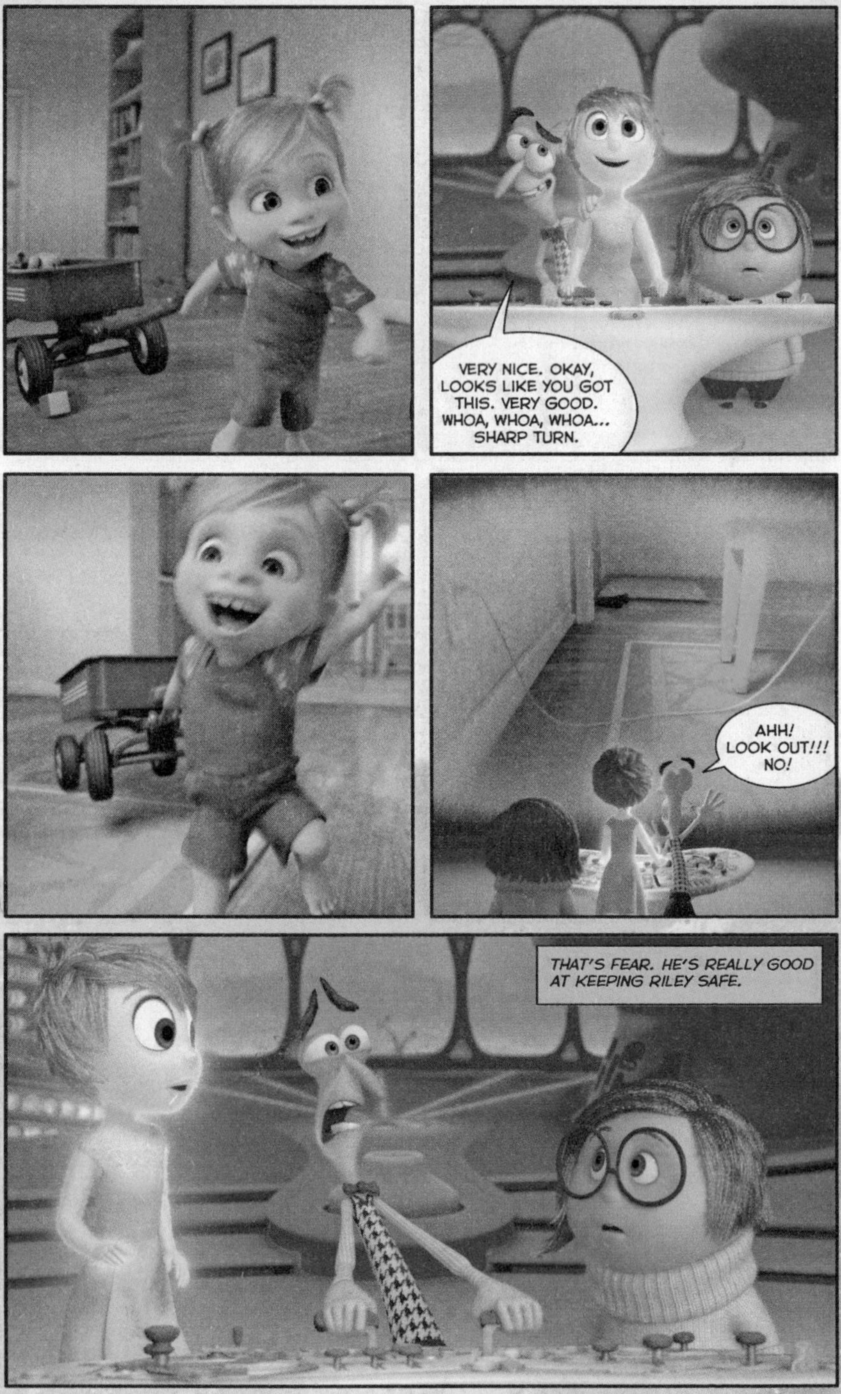
VERY NICE. OKAY, LOOKS LIKE YOU GOT THIS. VERY GOOD. WHOA, WHOA, WHOA... SHARP TURN.
AHH! LOOK OUT!!! NO!
THAT'S FEAR. HE'S REALLY GOOD AT KEEPING RILEY SAFE.

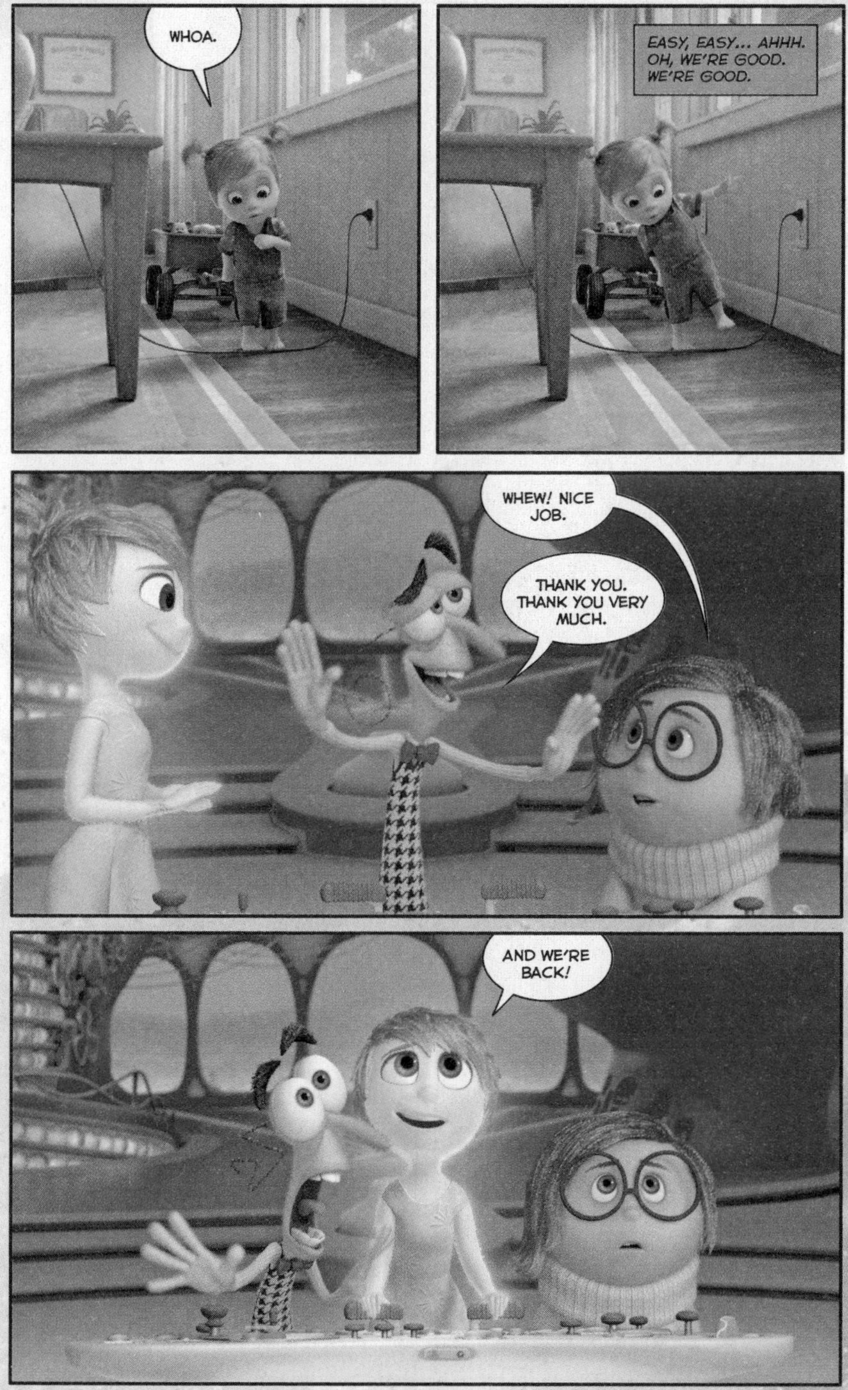
WHOA.
EASY, EASY... AHHH. OH, WE'RE GOOD. WE'RE GOOD.
WHEW! NICE JOB.
THANK YOU. THANK YOU VERY MUCH.
AND WE'RE BACK!

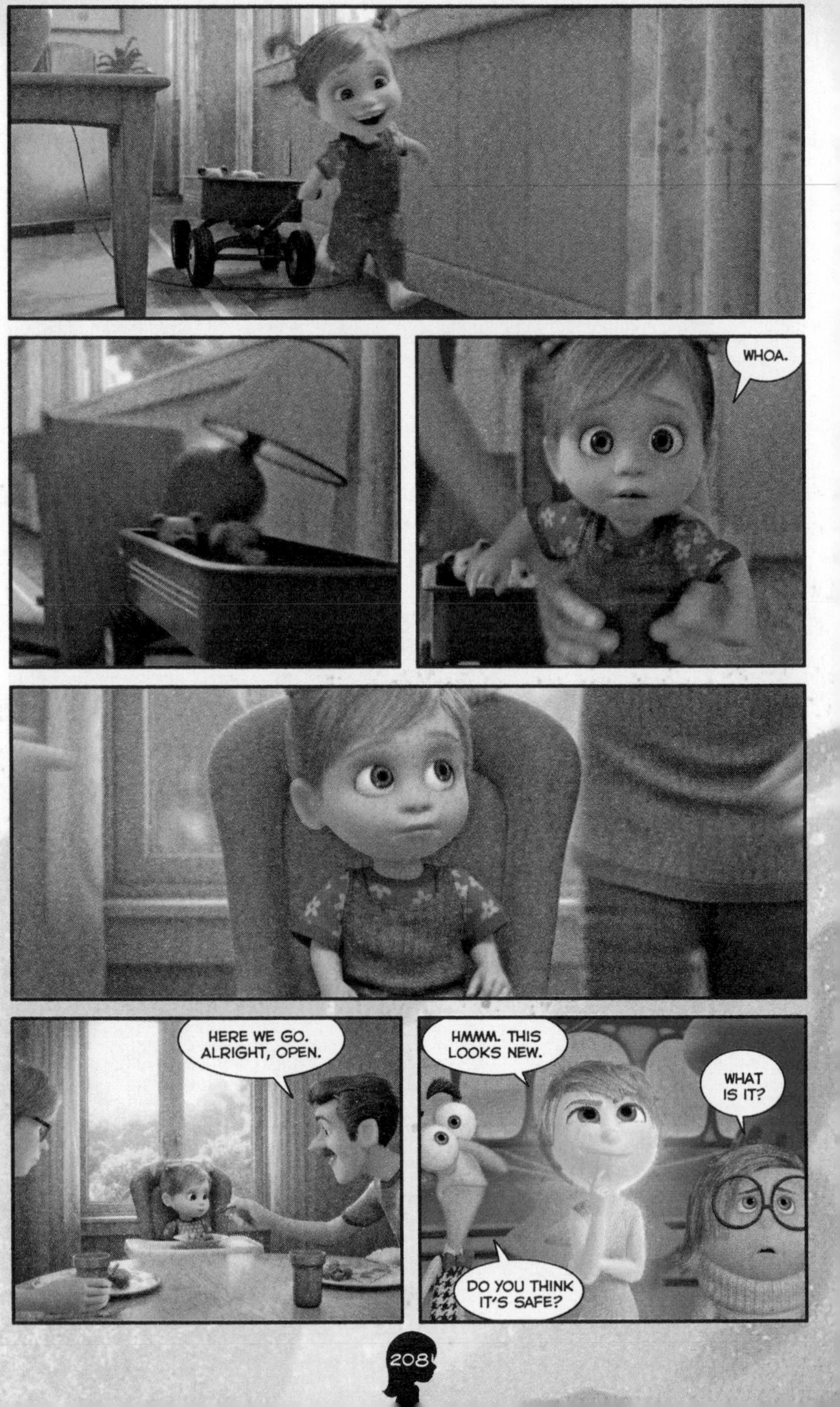
WHOA.
HERE WE GO. ALRIGHT, OPEN.
HMMM. THIS LOOKS NEW.
WHAT IS IT?
DO YOU THINK IT'S SAFE?

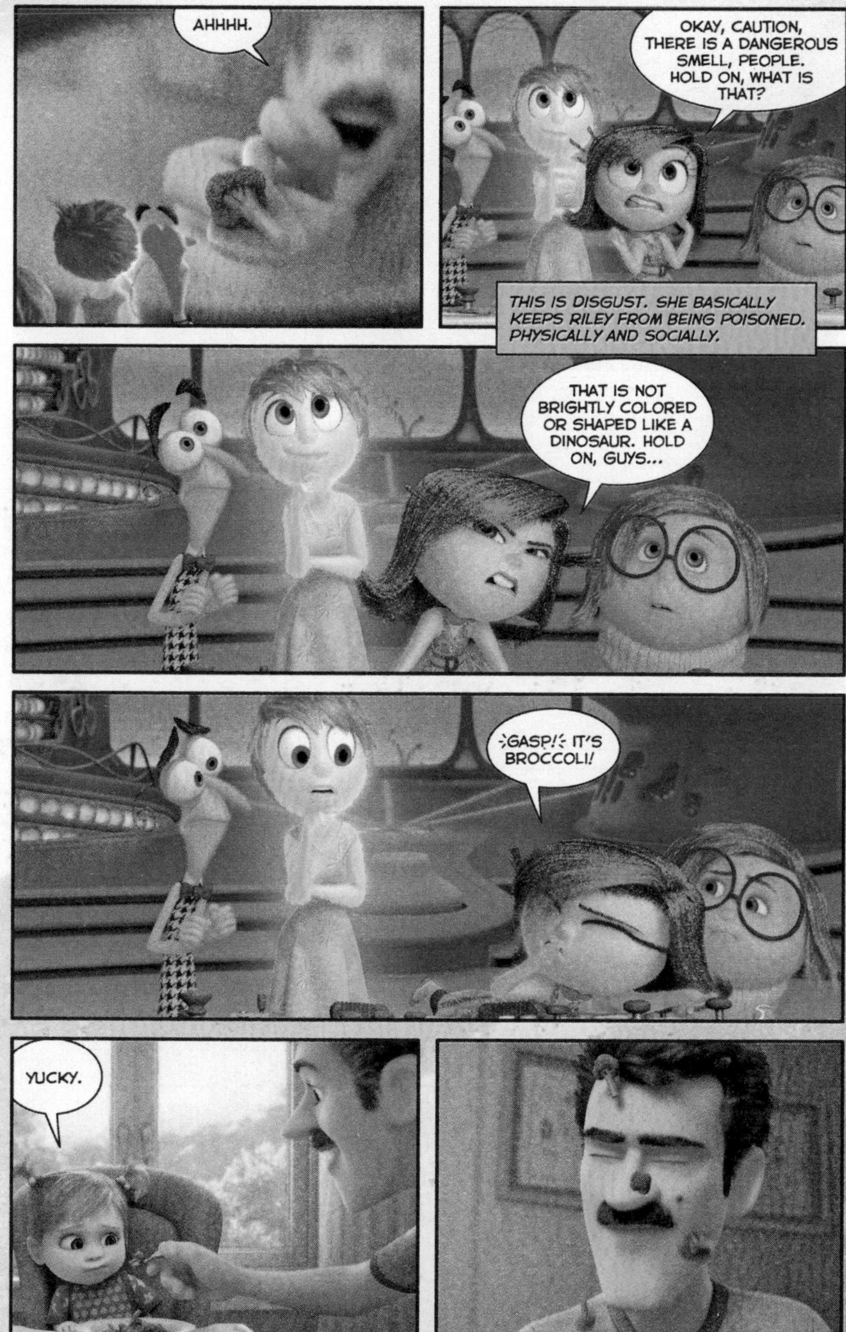
AHHHH.
OKAY, CAUTION, THERE IS A DANGEROUS SMELL, PEOPLE. HOLD ON, WHAT IS THAT?
THIS IS DISGUST. SHE BASICALLY KEEPS RILEY FROM BEING POISONED. PHYSICALLY AND SOCIALLY.
THAT IS NOT BRIGHTLY COLORED OR SHAPED LIKE A DINOSAUR. HOLD ON, GUYS...
GASP! IT'S BROCCOLI!
YUCKY.

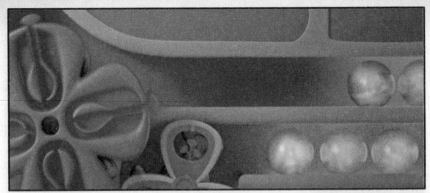

WELL, I JUST SAVED OUR LIVES. YEAH. YOU'RE WELCOME.

RILEY, IF YOU DON'T EAT YOUR DINNER, YOU'RE NOT GOING TO GET ANY DESSERT.

WAIT. DID HE JUST SAY WE COULDN'T HAVE DESSERT?

NO DESSERT!

THAT'S ANGER. HE CARES VERY DEEPLY ABOUT THINGS BEING FAIR.

NO DESSERT!

SO THAT'S HOW YOU WANT TO PLAY IT, OLD MAN? NO DESSERT.

OH, SURE, WE'LL EAT OUR DINNER...RIGHT AFTER YOU EAT THIS!

GRRRRAAAAAHH!

AAAAAAAAAH!

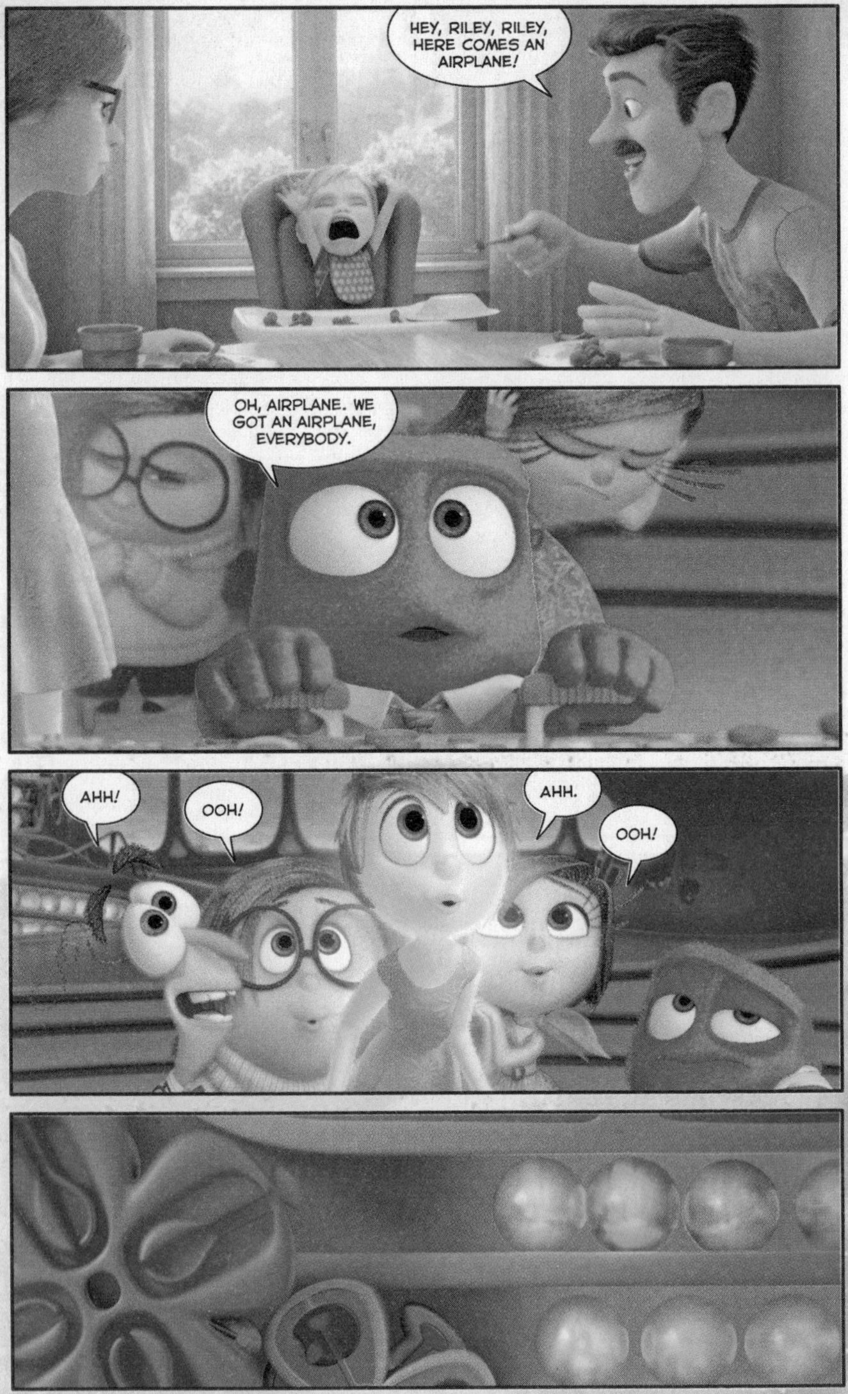
HEY, RILEY, RILEY, HERE COMES AN AIRPLANE!
OH, AIRPLANE. WE GOT AN AIRPLANE, EVERYBODY.
AHH!
OOH!
AHH.
OOH!

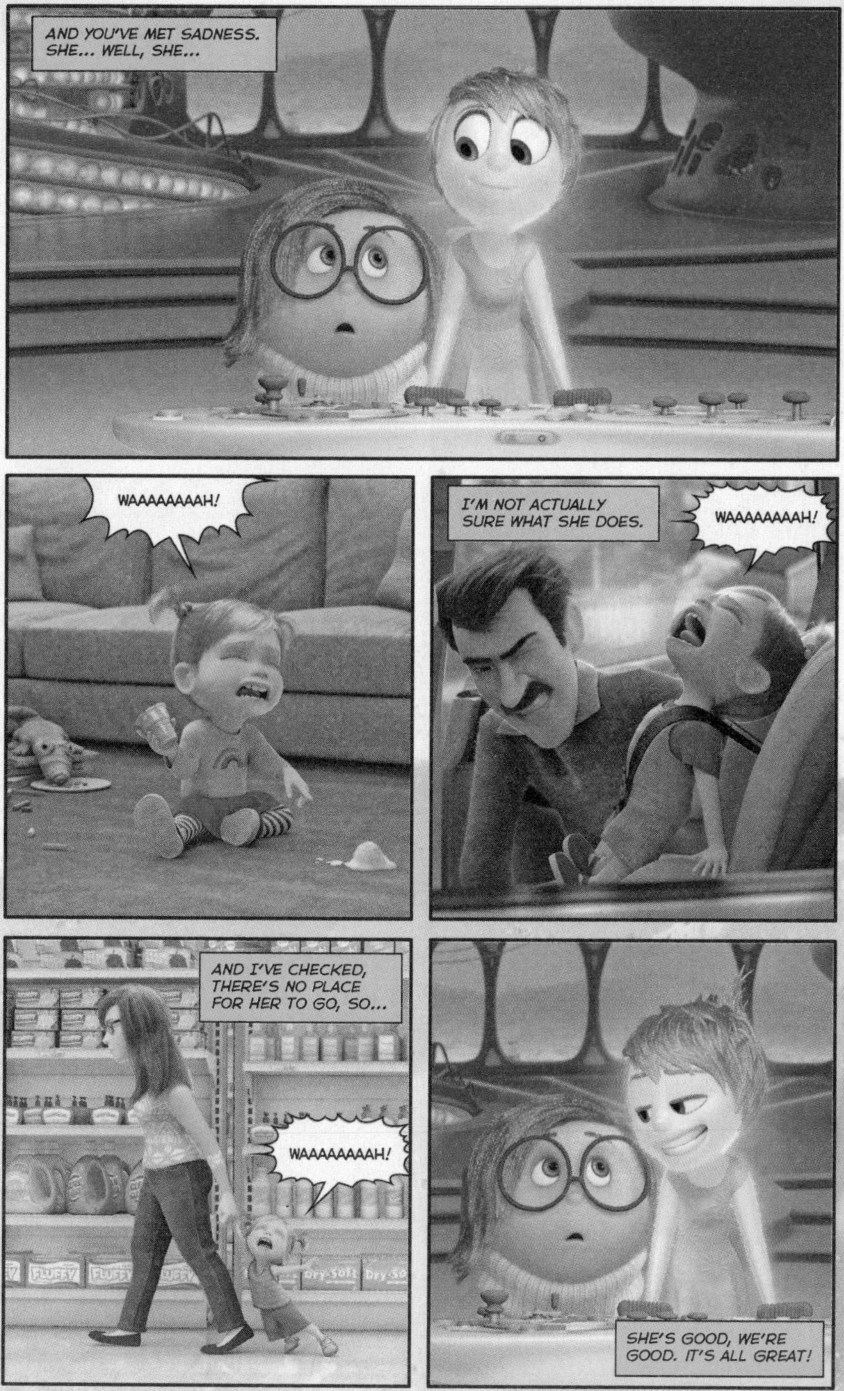
AND YOU'VE MET SADNESS. SHE... WELL, SHE...
WAAAAAAAAH!
I'M NOT ACTUALLY SURE WHAT SHE DOES.
WAAAAAAAAH!
AND I'VE CHECKED, THERE'S NO PLACE FOR HER TO GO, SO...
WAAAAAAAAH!
SHE'S GOOD, WE'RE GOOD. IT'S ALL GREAT!

ANYWAY! THESE ARE RILEY'S MEMORIES...

...AND THEY'RE MOSTLY HAPPY, YOU'LL NOTICE, NOT TO BRAG.

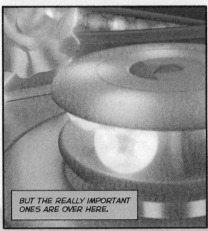

BUT THE REALLY IMPORTANT ONES ARE OVER HERE.

I DON'T WANT TO GET TOO TECHNICAL, BUT THESE ARE CALLED CORE MEMORIES.

EACH ONE CAME FROM A SUPER IMPORTANT TIME IN RILEY'S LIFE.

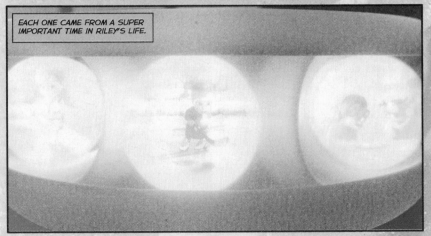

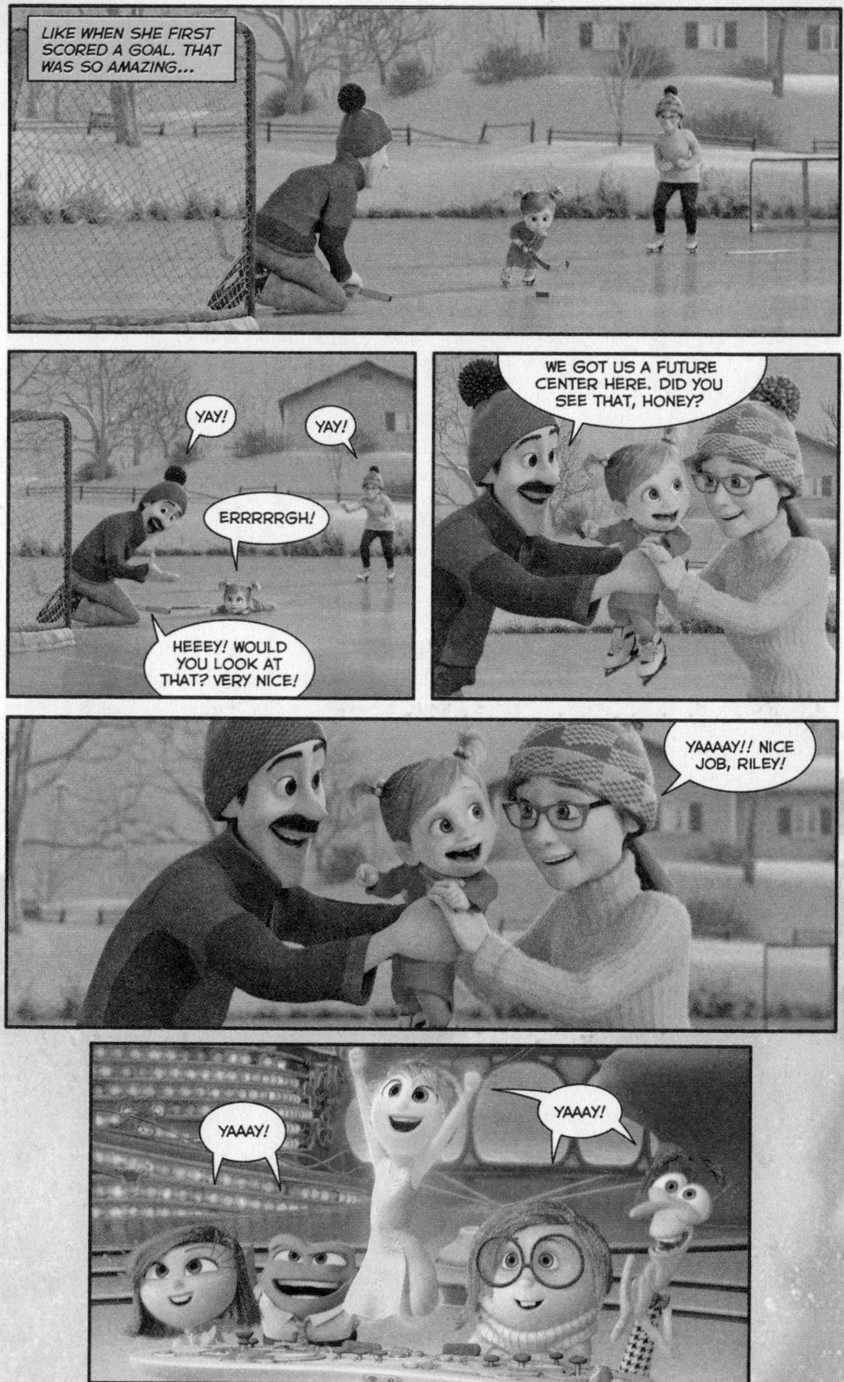
LIKE WHEN SHE FIRST SCORED A GOAL. THAT WAS SO AMAZING...
YAY!
YAY!
ERRRRRGH!
HEEEY! WOULD YOU LOOK AT THAT? VERY NICE!
WE GOT US A FUTURE CENTER HERE. DID YOU SEE THAT, HONEY?
YAAAAY!! NICE JOB, RILEY!
YAAAY!
YAAAY!

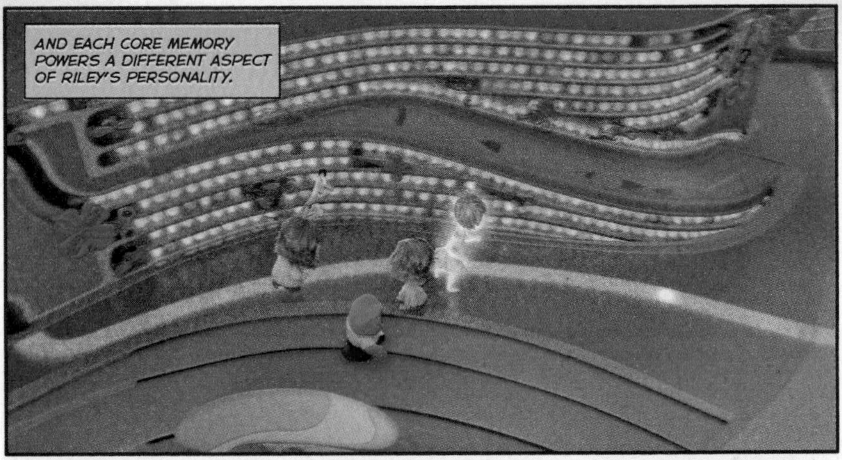
AND EACH CORE MEMORY POWERS A DIFFERENT ASPECT OF RILEY'S PERSONALITY.

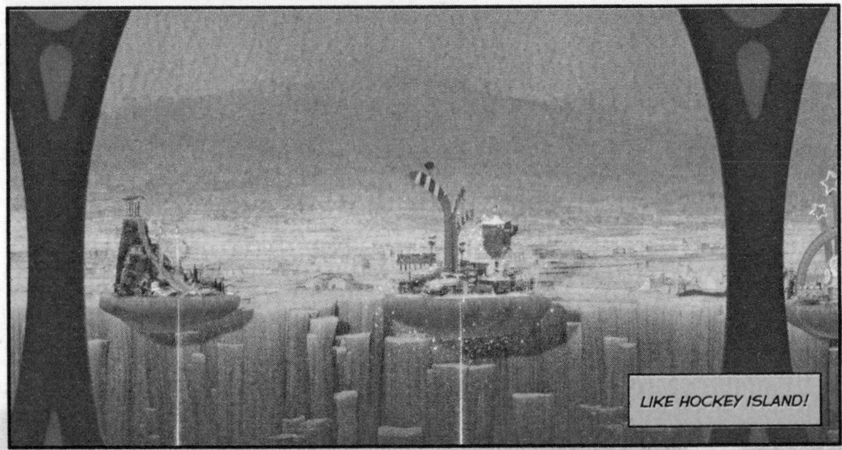
LIKE HOCKEY ISLAND!

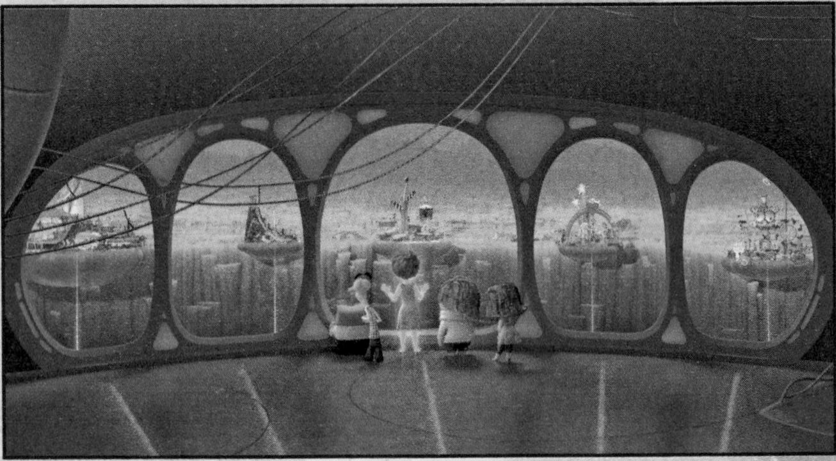

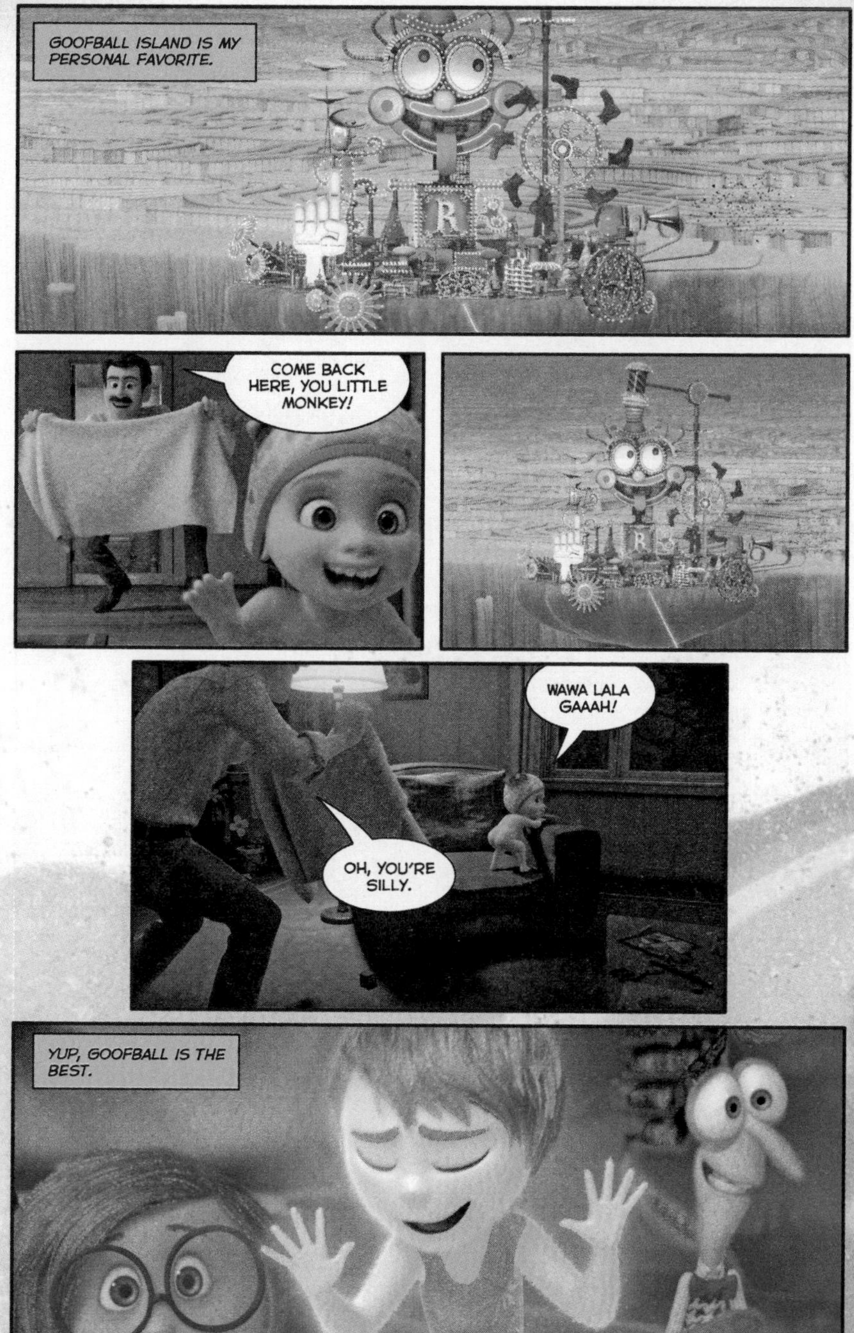
GOOFBALL ISLAND IS MY PERSONAL FAVORITE.
COME BACK HERE, YOU LITTLE MONKEY!
WAWA LALA GAAAH!
OH, YOU'RE SILLY.
YUP, GOOFBALL IS THE BEST.

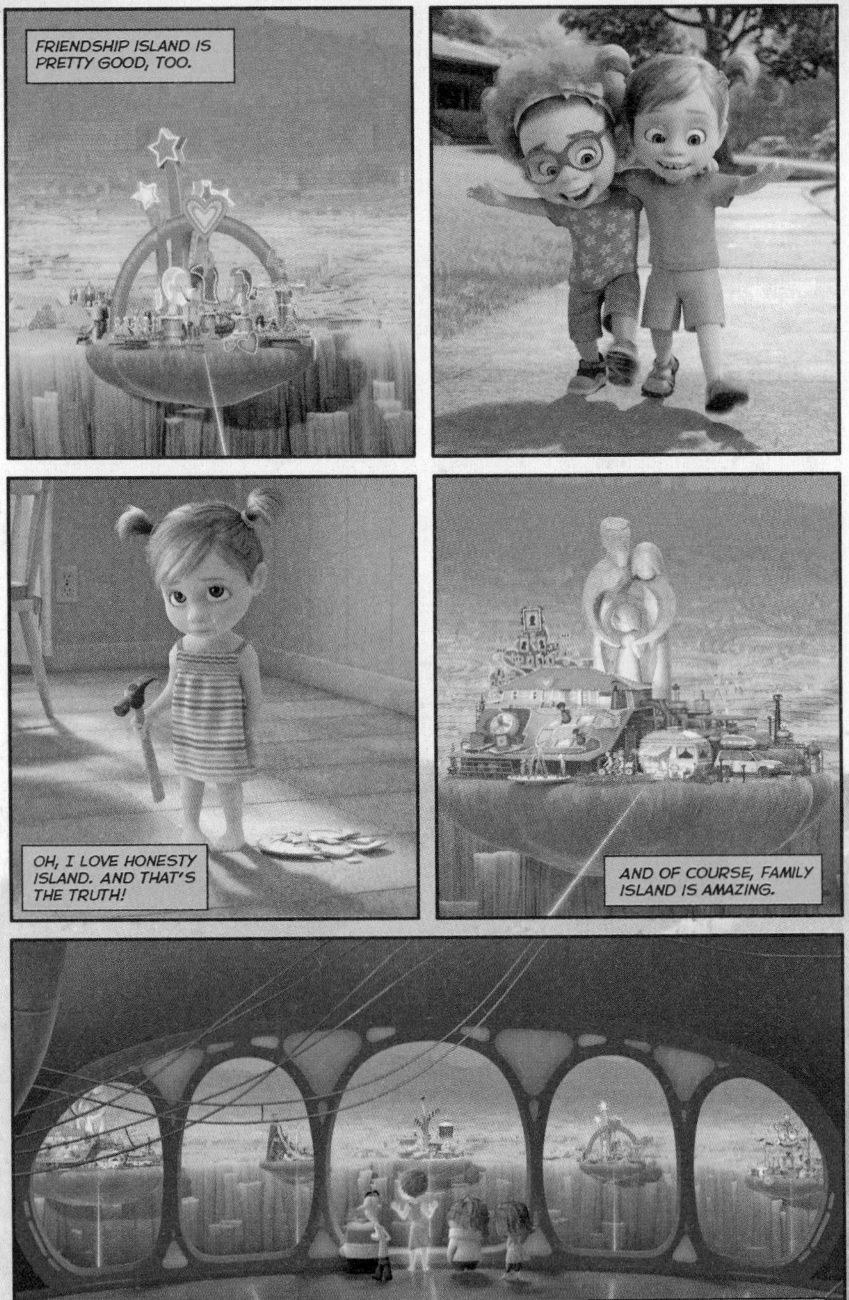
FRIENDSHIP ISLAND IS PRETTY GOOD, TOO.
OH, I LOVE HONESTY ISLAND. AND THAT'S THE TRUTH!
AND OF COURSE, FAMILY ISLAND IS AMAZING.
THE POINT IS, THE ISLANDS OF PERSONALITY ARE WHAT MAKE RILEY... RILEY!

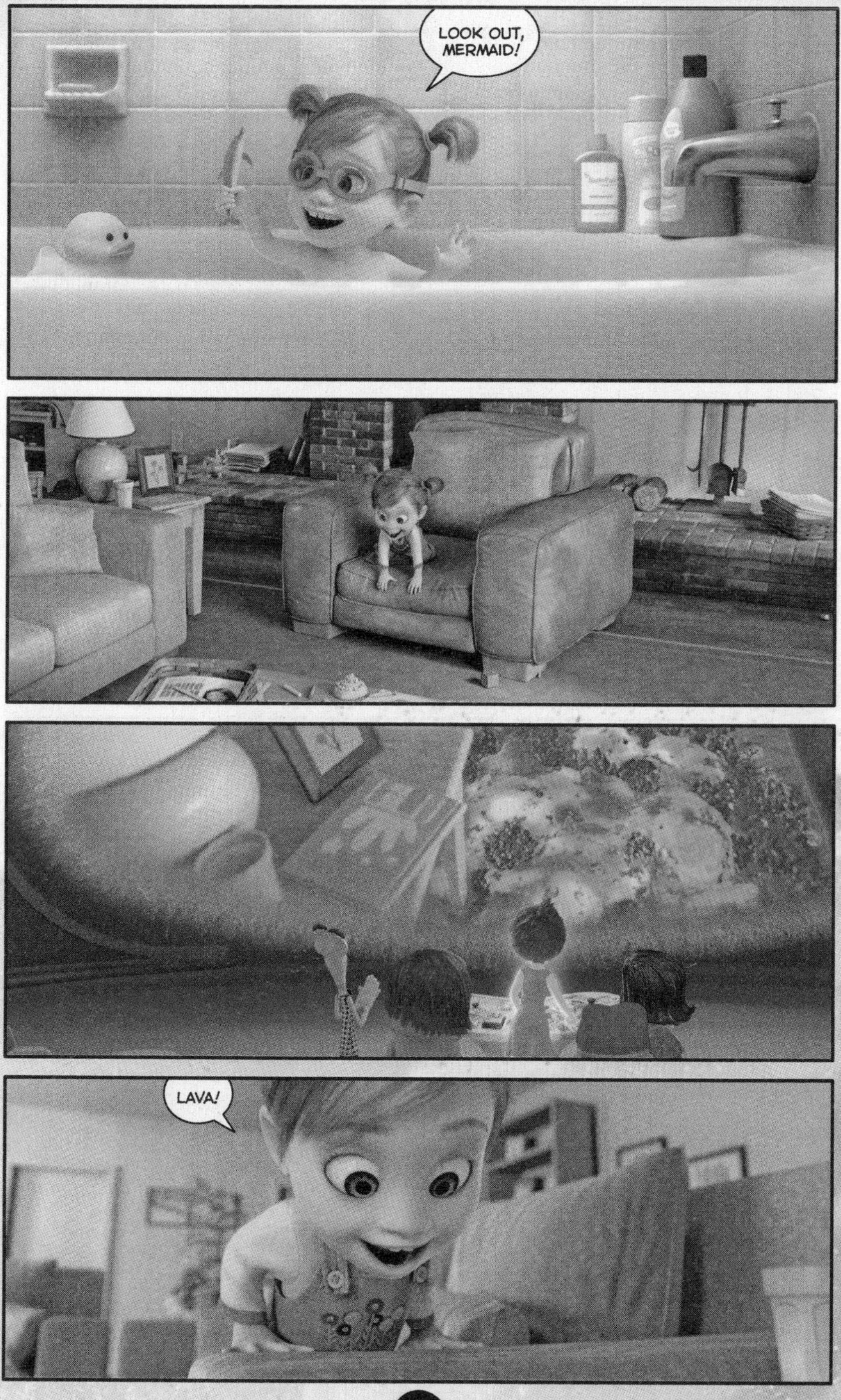
LOOK OUT, MERMAID!
LAVA!

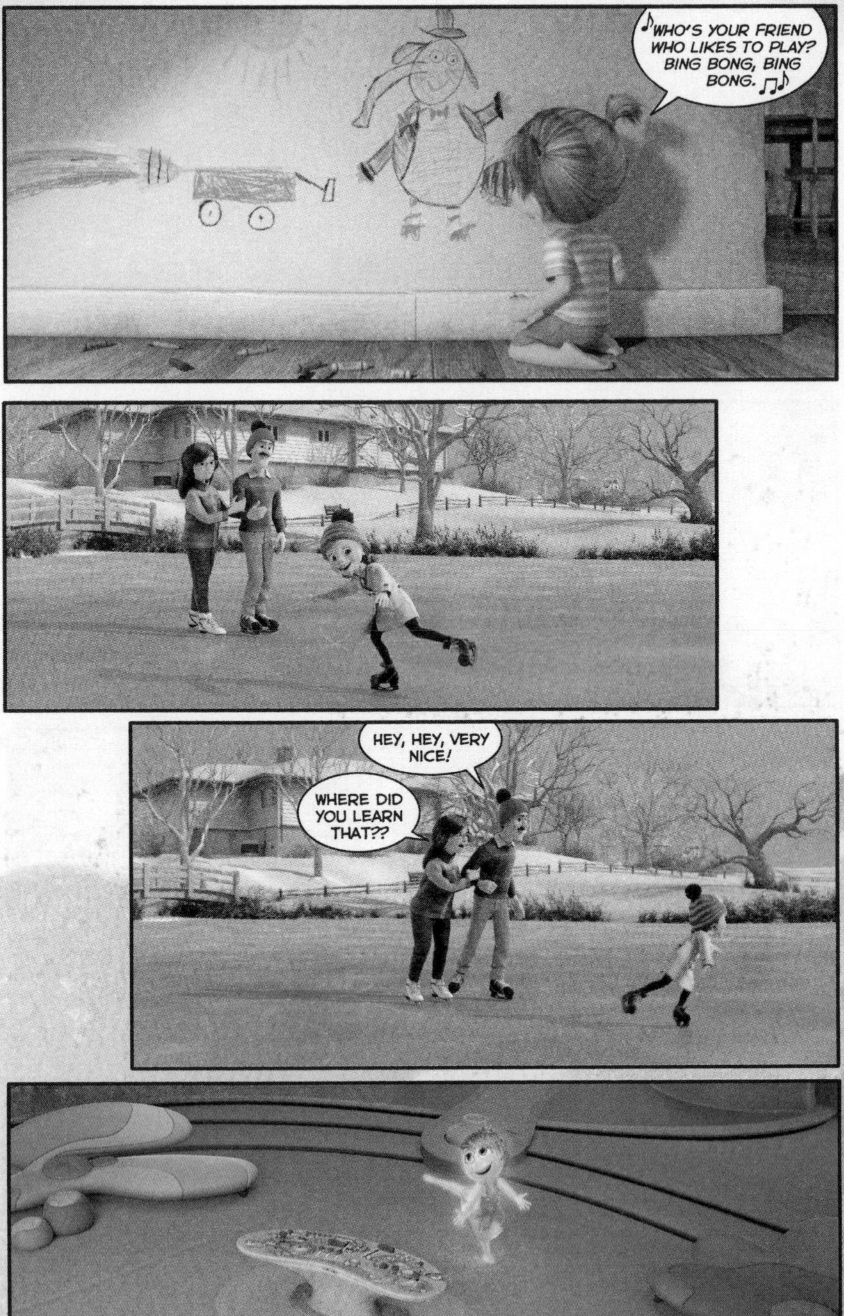
♪WHO'S YOUR FRIEND WHO LIKES TO PLAY? BING BONG, BING BONG. ♫♪
HEY, HEY, VERY NICE!
WHERE DID YOU LEARN THAT??

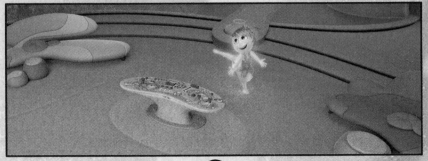

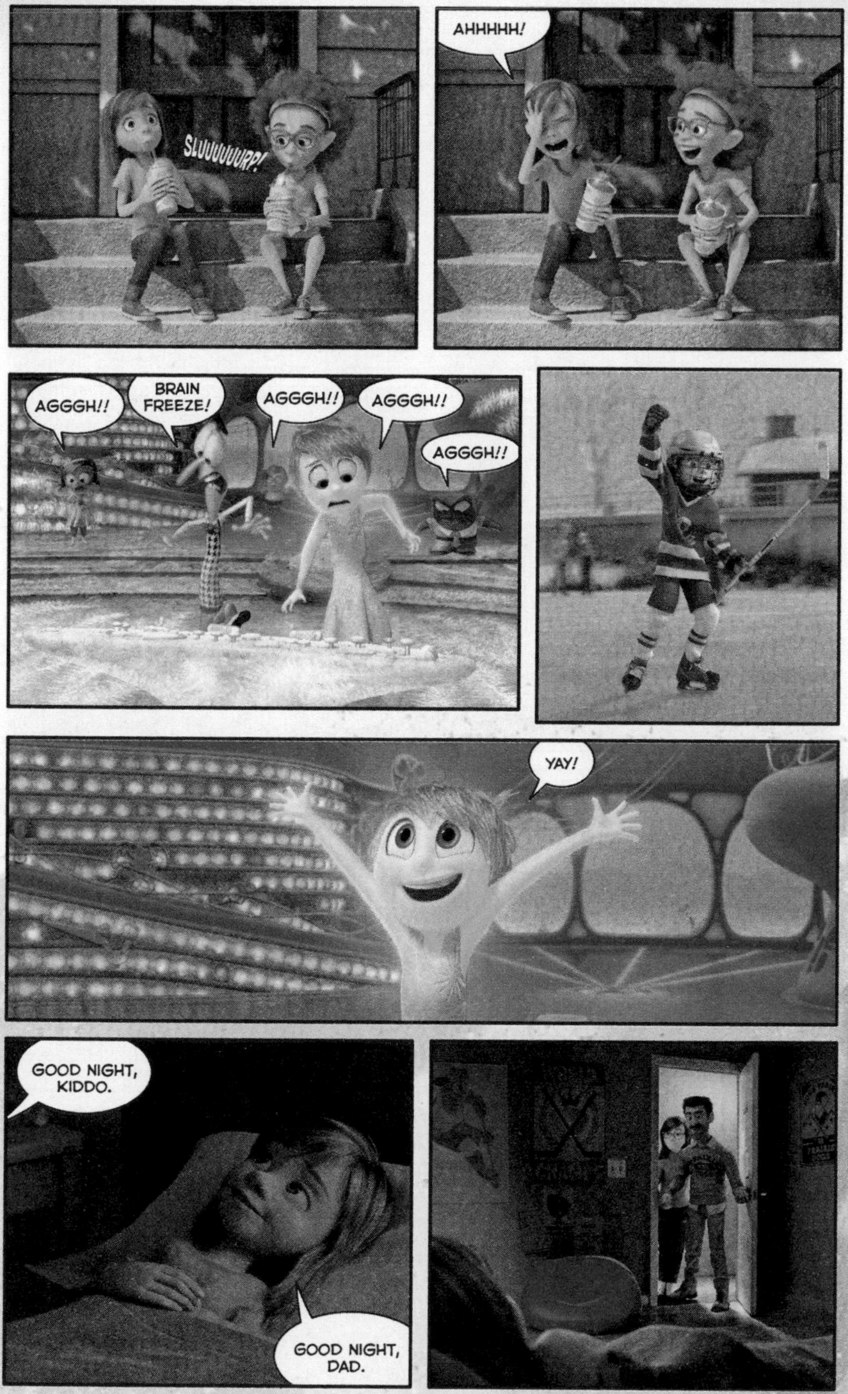
SLUUUUUURP!
AHHHHH!
AGGGH!!
BRAIN FREEZE!
AGGGH!!
AGGGH!!
AGGGH!!
YAY!
GOOD NIGHT, KIDDO.
GOOD NIGHT, DAD.

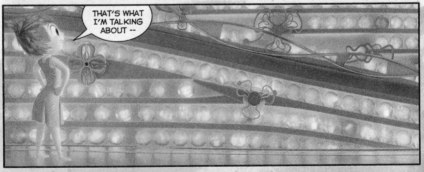

AND... WE'RE OUT!

THAT'S WHAT I'M TALKING ABOUT --

-- WOO! ANOTHER PERFECT DAY!

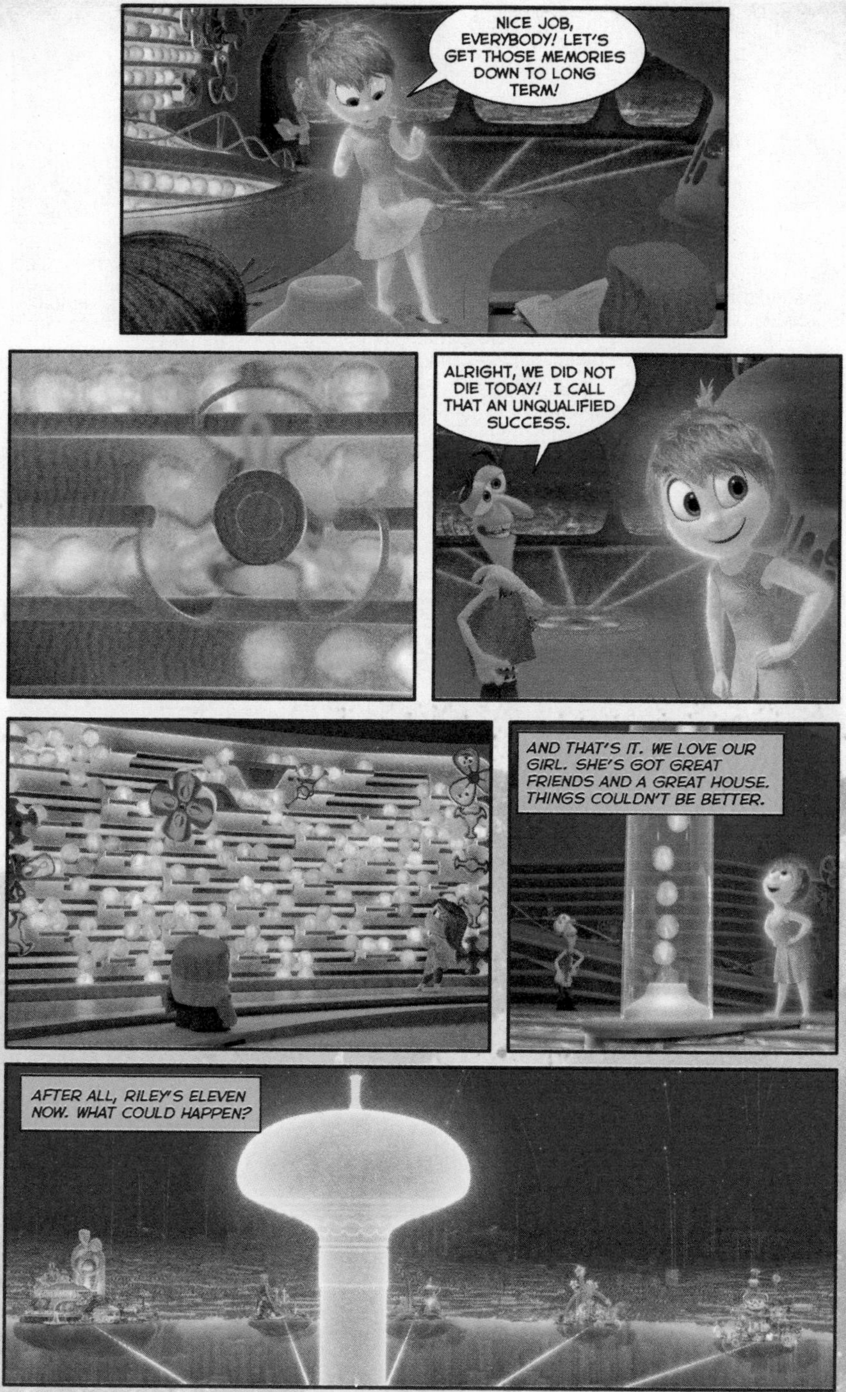

NICE JOB, EVERYBODY! LET'S GET THOSE MEMORIES DOWN TO LONG TERM!
ALRIGHT, WE DID NOT DIE TODAY! I CALL THAT AN UNQUALIFIED SUCCESS.
AND THAT'S IT. WE LOVE OUR GIRL. SHE'S GOT GREAT FRIENDS AND A GREAT HOUSE. THINGS COULDN'T BE BETTER.
AFTER ALL, RILEY'S ELEVEN NOW. WHAT COULD HAPPEN?

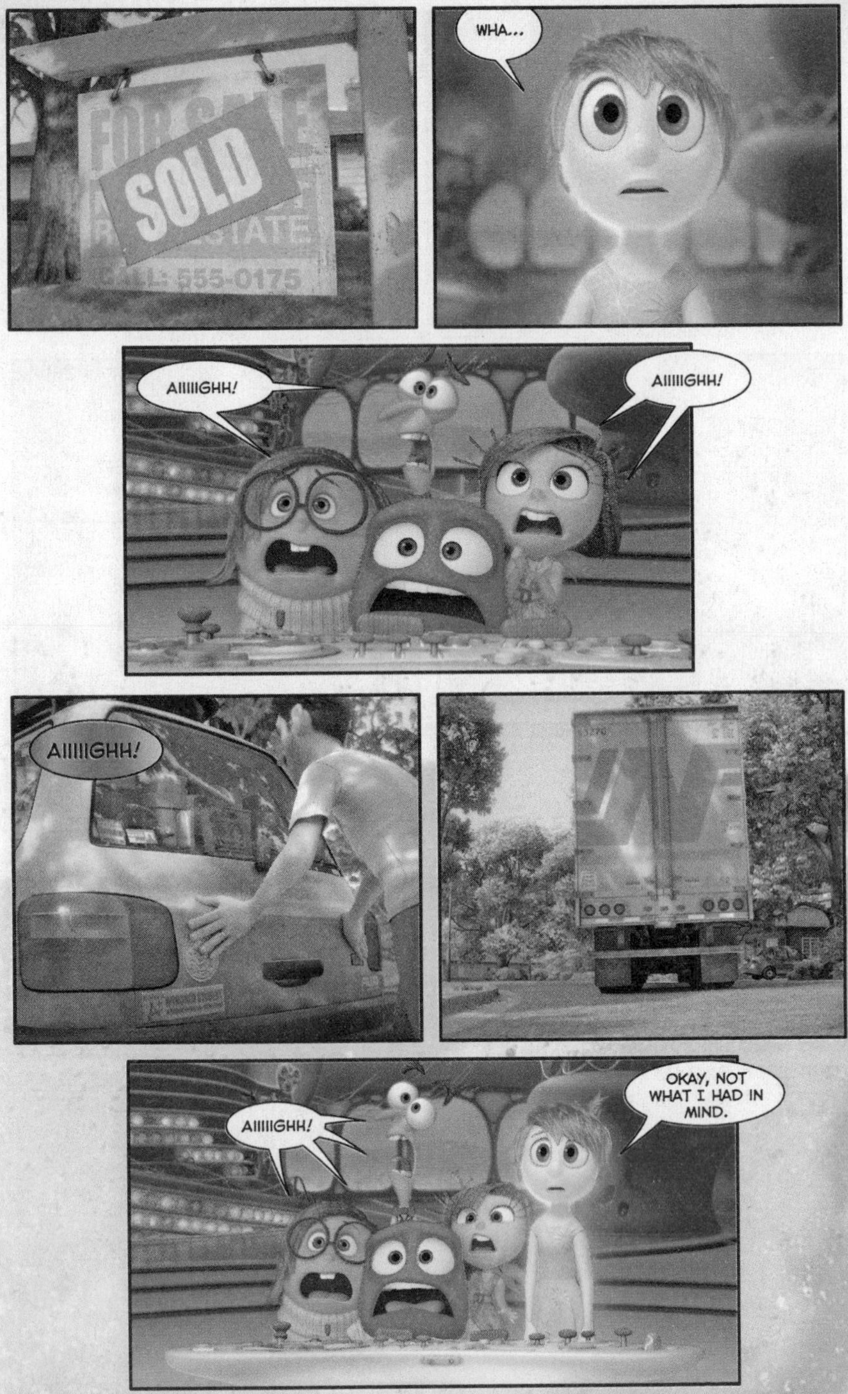
SOLD
555-0175
WHA...
AIIIIGHH!
AIIIIGHH!
AIIIIGHH!
AIIIIGHH!
OKAY, NOT WHAT I HAD IN MIND.

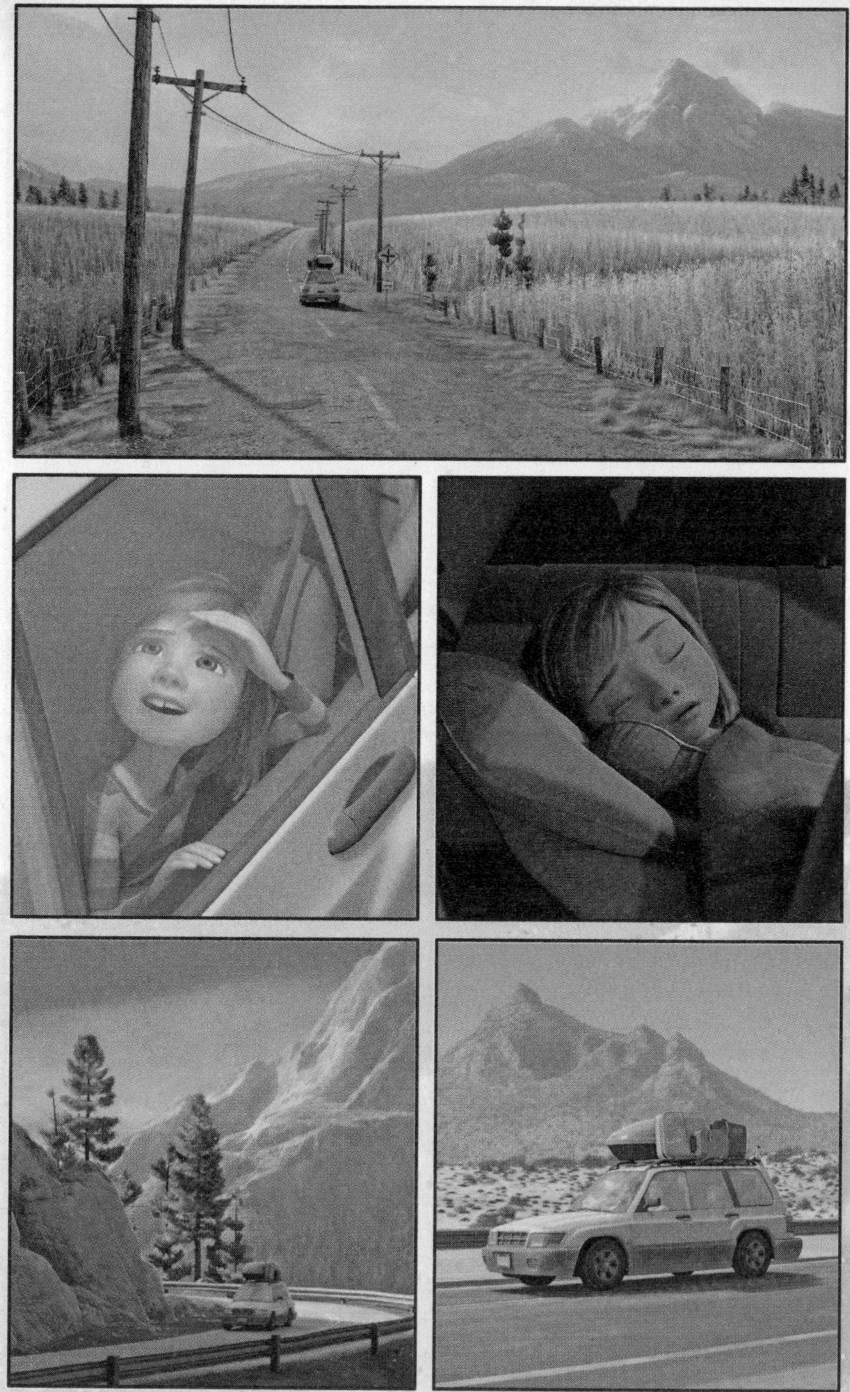

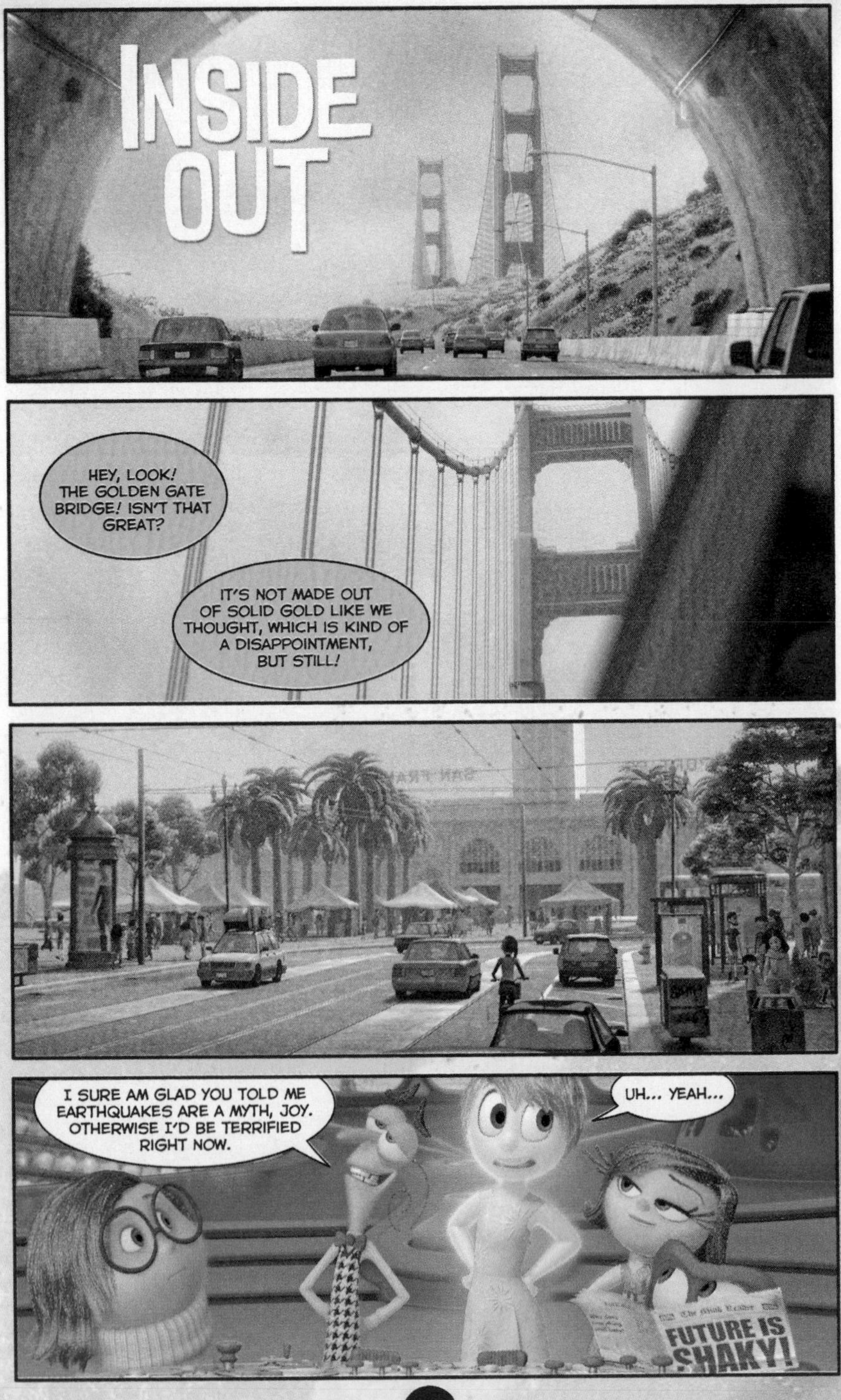
INSIDE OUT
HEY, LOOK! THE GOLDEN GATE BRIDGE! ISN'T THAT GREAT?
IT'S NOT MADE OUT OF SOLID GOLD LIKE WE THOUGHT, WHICH IS KIND OF A DISAPPOINTMENT, BUT STILL!
I SURE AM GLAD YOU TOLD ME EARTHQUAKES ARE A MYTH, JOY. OTHERWISE I'D BE TERRIFIED RIGHT NOW.
UH... YEAH...
FUTURE IS SHAKY!

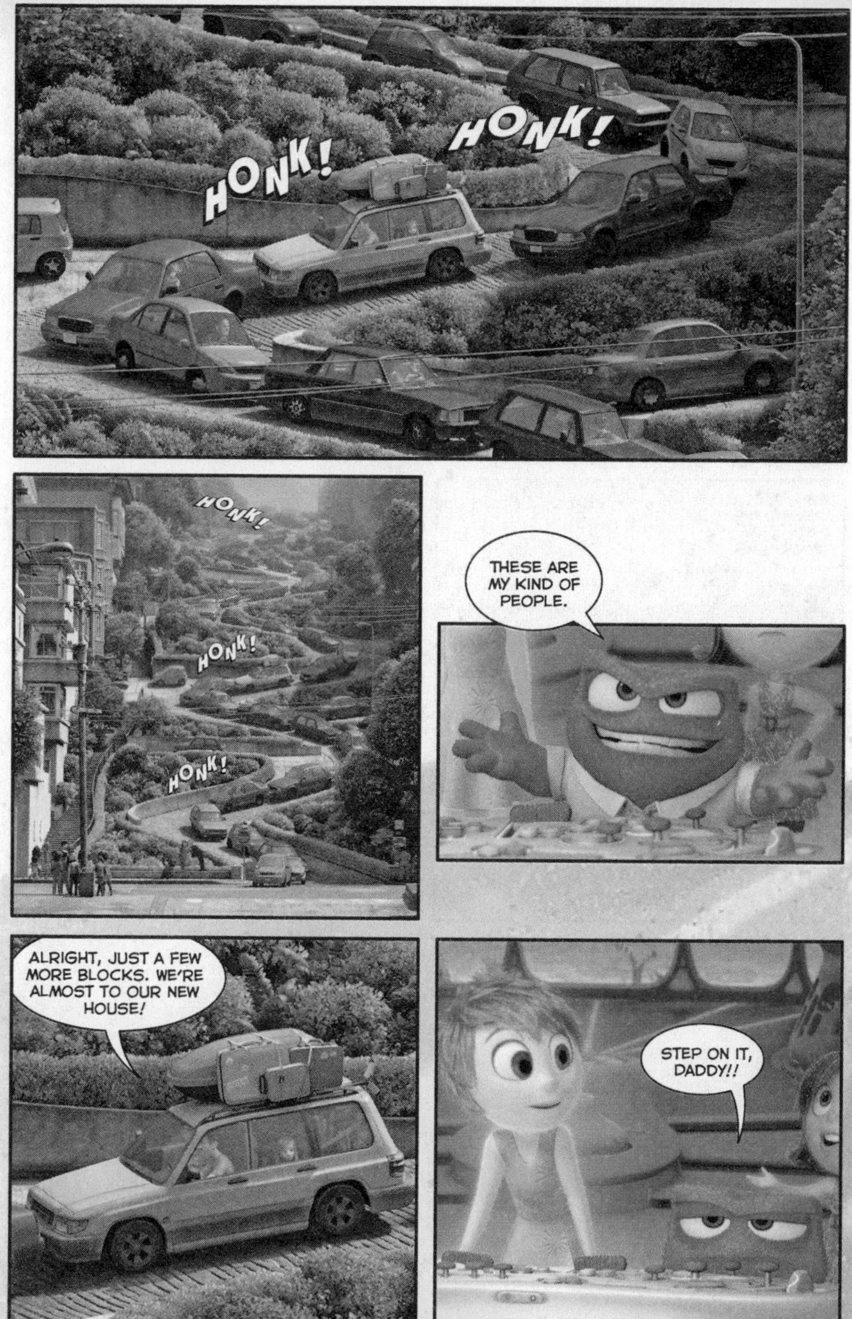
HONK!
HONK!
HONK!
HONK!
HONK!
THESE ARE MY KIND OF PEOPLE.
ALRIGHT, JUST A FEW MORE BLOCKS. WE'RE ALMOST TO OUR NEW HOUSE!
STEP ON IT, DADDY!!

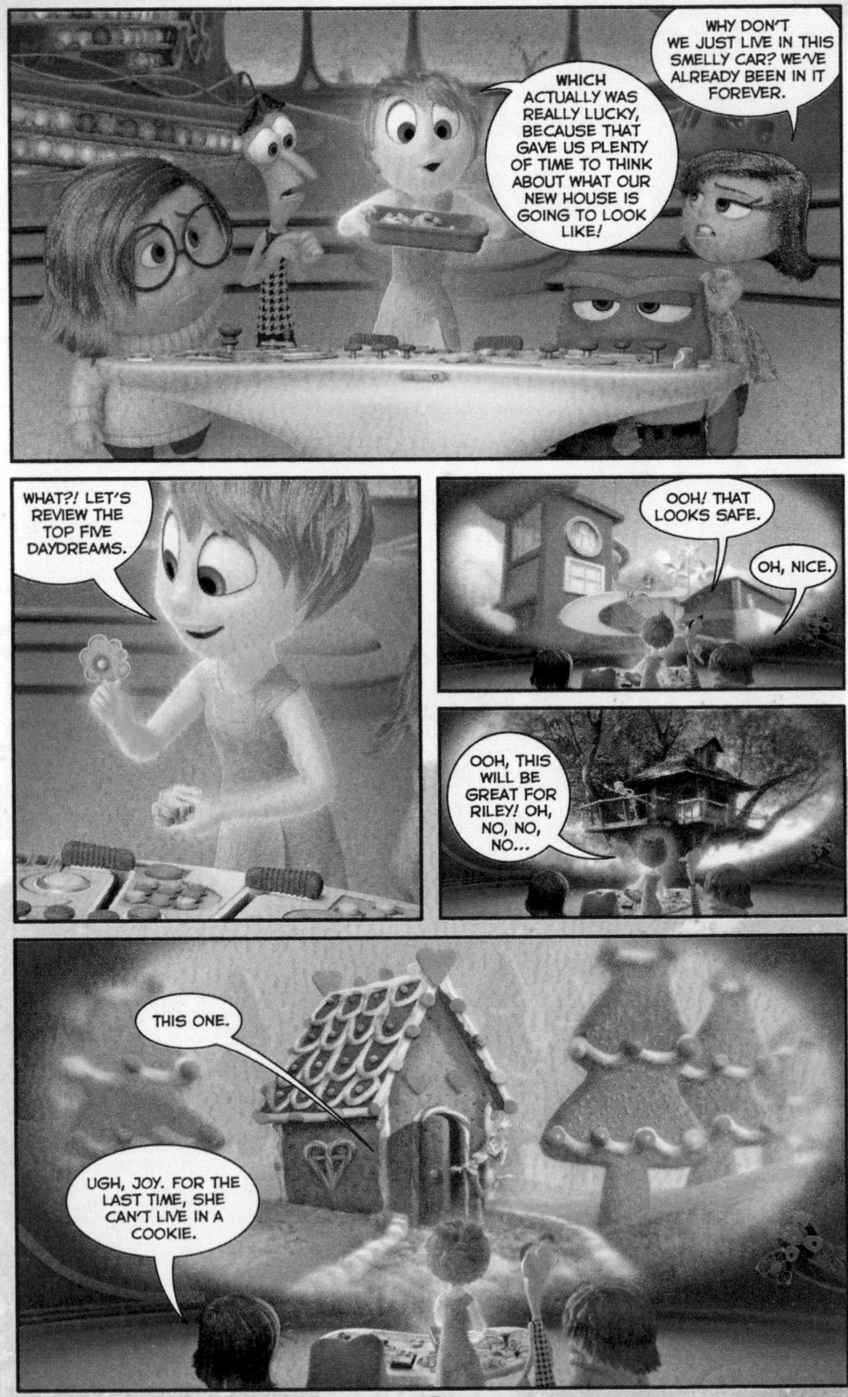
WHY DON'T WE JUST LIVE IN THIS SMELLY CAR? WE'VE ALREADY BEEN IN IT FOREVER.
WHICH ACTUALLY WAS REALLY LUCKY, BECAUSE THAT GAVE US PLENTY OF TIME TO THINK ABOUT WHAT OUR NEW HOUSE IS GOING TO LOOK LIKE!
WHAT?! LET'S REVIEW THE TOP FIVE DAYDREAMS.
OOH! THAT LOOKS SAFE.
OH, NICE.
OOH, THIS WILL BE GREAT FOR RILEY! OH, NO, NO, NO...
THIS ONE.
UGH, JOY. FOR THE LAST TIME, SHE CAN'T LIVE IN A COOKIE.

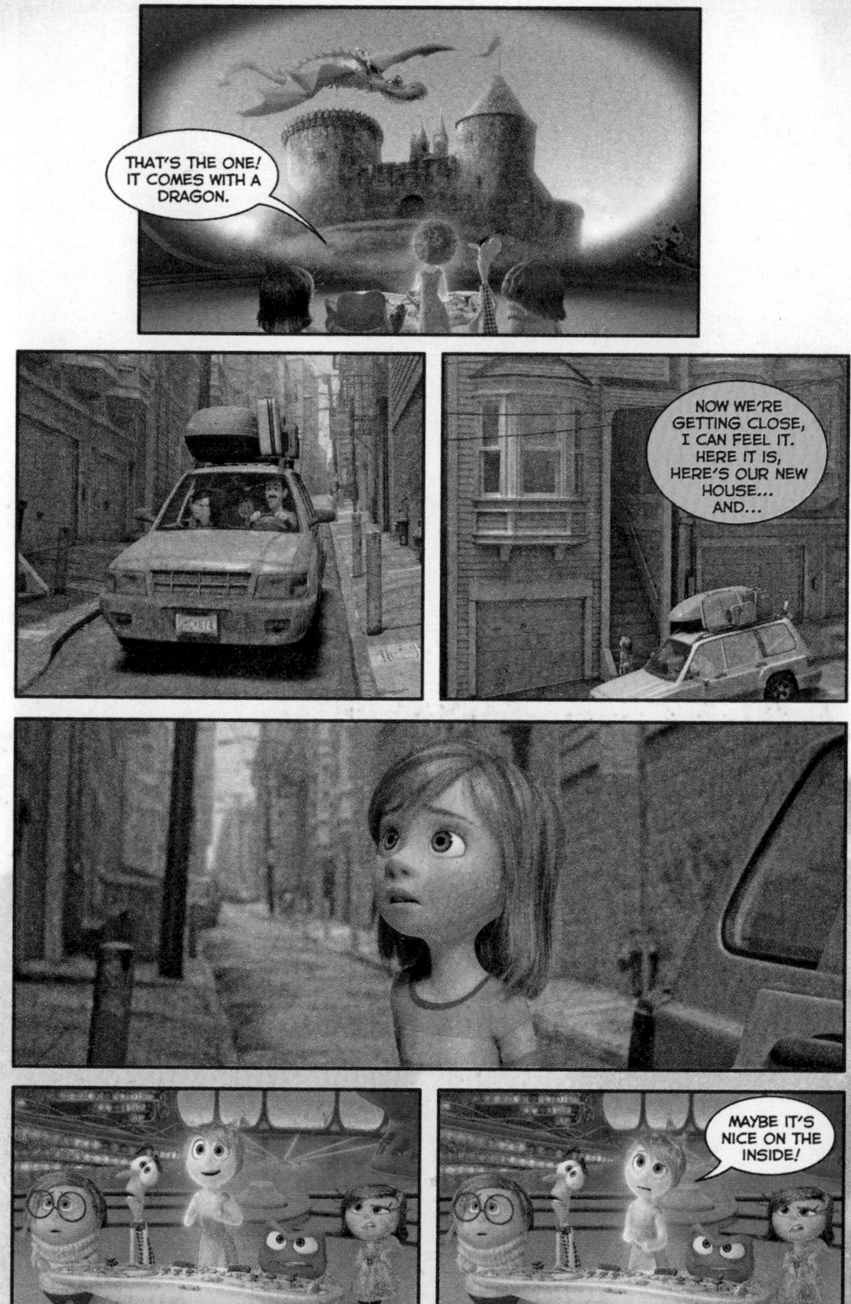
THAT'S THE ONE! IT COMES WITH A DRAGON.
NOW WE'RE GETTING CLOSE, I CAN FEEL IT. HERE IT IS, HERE'S OUR NEW HOUSE... AND...
MAYBE IT'S NICE ON THE INSIDE!

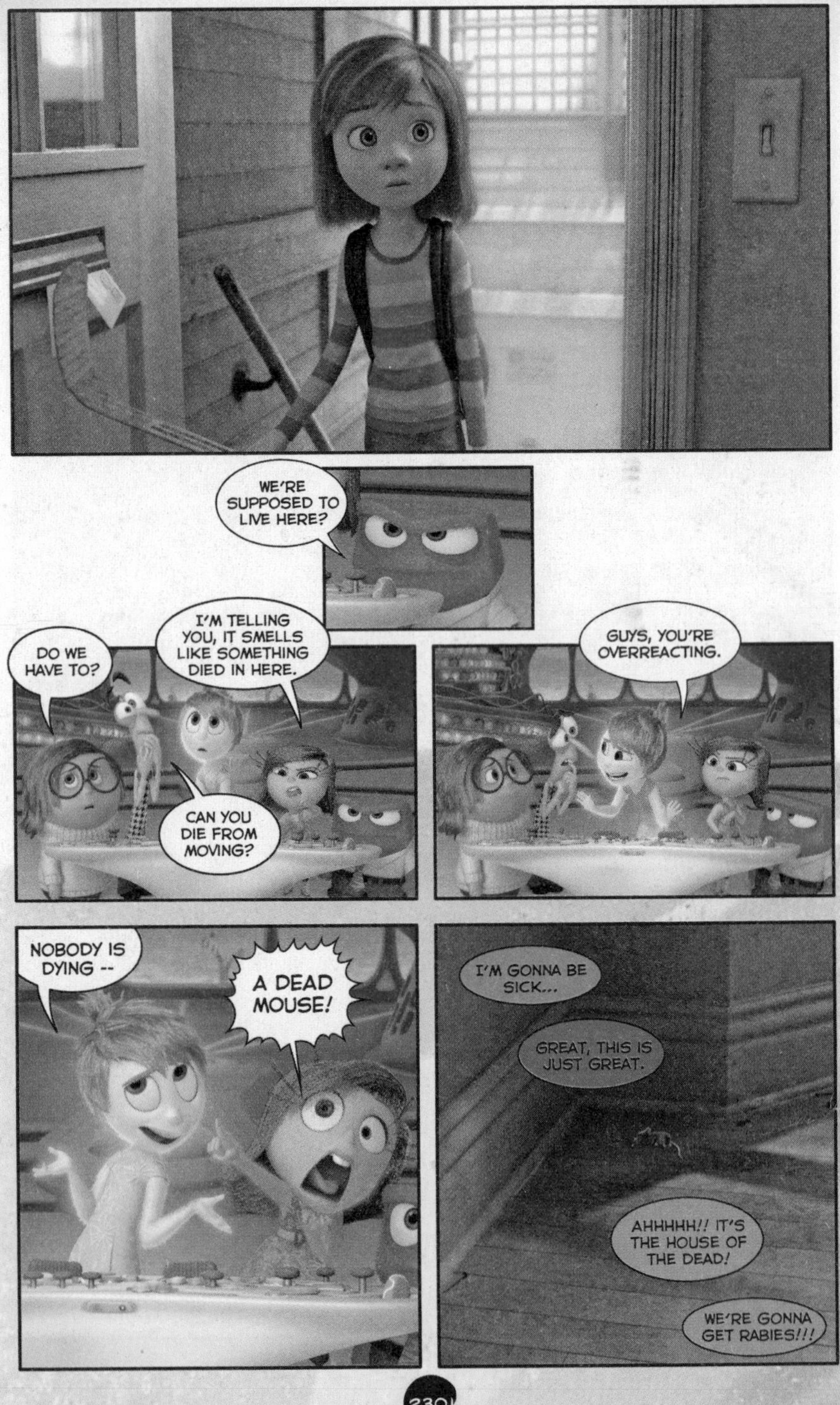
WE'RE SUPPOSED TO LIVE HERE?
DO WE HAVE TO?
I'M TELLING YOU, IT SMELLS LIKE SOMETHING DIED IN HERE.
CAN YOU DIE FROM MOVING?
GUYS, YOU'RE OVERREACTING.
NOBODY IS DYING --
A DEAD MOUSE!
I'M GONNA BE SICK...
GREAT, THIS IS JUST GREAT.
AHHHHH!! IT'S THE HOUSE OF THE DEAD!
WE'RE GONNA GET RABIES!!!